GLASS

and

BONE

CELAENA CUICO

Hardcover ISBN: 979-8-9887169-2-1

Paperback ISBN: 979-8-9887169-1-4

eBook ISBN: 979-8-9887169-0-7

Edited by: Vilandra Cuico

Cover by: Fantasy Cover Design

This book is dedicated to the person who pulled me out of the darkness and gave me a reason to live. Despite every reason I had to give up, you showed me just as many reasons to keep going.

RAKUSHIA

ROALLY

CENTER VALLEY

DELAQUAR LAKE

CHATIS

VANEAU

RAUNTIE LAKE

NOTERRA

CRA

BRAUNTFORD

PORT TOBEO

TELLAVID

Pronunciation Guide

Characters

Elaenor: EL-luh-nor
Evreux: EV-row
Sybil: si-BILL
Amaya: UH-my-uh
Thelonious: THUH-lone-ee-us
Kassius: CASS-ee-us
Nithe: NEE-th
Bijoy: Bee-joi

Demos: day-MOS
Delarus: dill-AR-us
Icana: ick-CAN-uh
Selkath: SELL-kath
Wyclif: WHY-cliff
Ela: EL-luh
Welan: way-LEN
Danieas: DANE-e-us

Places

Chatis: shuh-TEEZ
Noterra: NO-tare-ruh
Rakushia: RUH-koo-juh
Labisa: luh-BEES-uh
Khailes: KHAL-us
Delaquar Lake: DELLA-car
Brauntie Lake: BRON-tee
Colveil: coal-VEEL
Vaneau: VAN-oh

Tatus: tate-US
Ovobia: OH-vo-BEE-uh
Zivell: ZIV-elle
Aeqerian: ack-KEER-ee-un
Dorin: DOOR-in
Port Tobeo: toe-BAY-o
Senaya Sea: sin-NY-uh
Roally: ROW-uh-LEE

To those who have endured and survived.
To those who haven't yet gotten out.

I see you.

You are not alone.

Keep fighting.

Trigger Warnings

This book is a compilation of my thoughts and experiences. While princesses and magic are something from fairytales, the troubles of women in the modern world are very much real. Suicidal ideation, abusive relationships, sexual assault; those are all things I have experienced in my short life. In a way to prevent myself from succumbing to the ideations of death, I turned the horrors I have faced into a story of perseverance, strength, and the power of finding someone who makes you want to live. But I also threw in magic and fantasy because, why not? I only hope that as you immerse yourself into the world I have created, you find the strength to fight for yourself.

Glass and Bone includes triggering situations such as graphic violence, gore, murder, graphic language, suicidal ideation, depression, PTSD, anxiety, rape, psychological and physical abuse in relationships, kidnapping, torture, branding, decapitation, confinement, and the use of drugs for compliance.

Chapter One

Dark clouds loom overhead, threatening the prospect of rain and thunder. Fear courses through my veins like electricity as I stare up at the sky. My breathing erratic as terror sets in. The once deep blue and gray gradient that used to fill the open air above is replaced with dark purple and black. Electricity vibrates throughout the air, causing my skin to pimple and the hairs along my arms to stand up.

A storm is near, I can feel it. I can feel the lightning gearing up in the clouds, ready to wreak havoc.

I need to find shelter, find cover, before the rain and lightning start. The last time a storm broke out this severely, it knocked part of the wall down and almost damaged the palace. It left us open and unguarded, with anyone being able to enter the confines of the capital.

I will myself to move, but my body refuses. My muscles lock in place as I wait for it to start. I just stand and stare out at the hills and trees, watching the sky darken further as the seconds pass. The greens of the trees and bushes glow against *the blackening sky. Shining as if they were bioluminescent, as if they were their own light source.*

The feeling of something sharp pressing into my naked feet distracts me. I try to ignore it, but the pain is too maddening, too constant. I close my eyes and take a deep breath, softly shifting my feet, hoping to dislodge some of the pieces. My hands clench into fists and I dig my teeth into my bottom lip to keep from screaming. The jagged edges slice through my flesh, causing my blood to join theirs, creating a vibrant pool of crimson where there used to be grass. I squeeze my eyes shut, waiting for it to pass. Waiting for this to end. I can't move. I can't look. Terror prevents me from glancing down because I know.

I know the sharp edges cutting through my skin are that of glass and bone. And worse, that the bones in which I now stand on, belong to the ones I used to know.

My eyes flash open and I can feel my heart racing in my chest, my pulse echoing through my ears. My mouth tastes metallic, tangy, and a quick flick of my tongue against my lips lets me know that I drew blood. I take a slow, deep breath as I stare at the ornamental wall above, begging for the panic to subside. Begging for the pounding in my head to dissipate.

Gold and bronze filigree litter the ceiling in patterns of flowers and swirls, only meeting where multiple chandeliers of different sizes hang. The clear, quartz crystals dangling from the burnt-out candles reflect the small amount of light funneling in from outside into cascading rainbows across the rest of the walls, illuminating an otherwise dark and dreary room. A sight I used to disregard, purely out of contempt.

A sight I took for granted thinking this time would never come.

I have woken up to this ceiling every day for nearly 18 years, but now, as I know my impending travel is only one week away, I find myself wondering if I will miss it. If I will miss the dark palace nestled in the mountains.

I brush a loose tendril that escaped my braid from my forehead and notice the sheen of sweat that has accumulated there. My ragged breathing is lessening, calming, and I can finally take a slow, deep breath.

It was just a dream. I've been having nightmares every night for the last ten years, always the same exact thing.

Storms, blood, glass, rubble.

It's always exactly the same and never changes. Whether it is fear conjuring up the story that plays in my head every night, or a premonition I have so carelessly ignored, I am not sure.

I never believed in the power to see beyond what's there, but the palace prophet, Kassius, predicted my mother's death years before its arrival. I believed in him only for a moment, until that same prophet was beheaded for supposedly murdering her. Whether he truly committed the act, or my father was just afraid of the unknown, I'm not sure. The rumors that my father is the one who actually ended her life still haunt my brain.

I'll never know what truly happened to my mother that day, but part of me is convinced my father would do something so reckless if it benefitted him. He'd do anything if it somehow strengthened his own rule. The only thing my father loves more than himself is his country. I don't even think I make it into the top ten of things my father loves.

I inhale a slow and steady breath, grateful that my pulse has returned to normal, and allow myself to sit up fully, taking in the sight. My room usually remains tidy and clean due to the help of my ladies, but the luggage and clothing that will soon be confined to a single carriage litter every surface.

My sitting area with a plush, gray couch I have spent many nights falling asleep on, is covered in various gowns and tunics. The writing desk has been emptied, with only a single, small trunk sitting on top holding the art supplies I have never gotten around to using. I was convinced that I would use painting as an outlet for my emotions, but I could never bring myself to even try. Every time I picked up a brush or piece of charcoal, I got reminded of the life I would never have. The life others have and take for granted. An outlet one should use for the emotions that need to escape, just made mine worse.

I force my eyes to break away from the small chest of pain and glance towards the far wall. My dressing room door remains open, with most of the clothing and shoes on the floor in a large pile. An irritated groan escapes my lips as I realize I needed to actually sort through all of this and get it packed.

Heaviness settles deep in my belly, sparking the nausea that seems to be always present. Dread. That is the only word I can conjure to explain what I am feeling. It presses on my chest as if it's an unending presence sucking any bit of happiness out of me before it has a chance to manifest.

I denied the help of my three ladies in packing, knowing that this is something I needed to do alone. I am not sure if I will once again have ladies to attend to me in my new home, or if I will even have a say in anything regarding my clothing, or personal belongings. I don't know much about my destination, what protocol is like, what my life will be like when I get there.

But I do know one thing: I cannot allow myself to trust the people I will soon be surrounded by.

Royals are known for their games.

The knowledge of my supposed duty has been ingrained into me since the day I could speak: a princess must marry a prince. While my father's kingdom is one of the smallest, it still holds power and influence in the world of royalty and court. Everyone fears my father, as they should. He's an ambivalent, yet dangerous man who only cares for himself and the power he has.

However, he has always been an opportunist. Knowing that he will have gained additional lands and prestige when his daughter is wed to the Prince of Noterra, one of the largest kingdoms, he was quick to accept the proposal when I was nothing more than a babe. Quick to sign away any chance of freedom I may have had, and instead, handed my title of ownership to another country.

I was only 7 when we traveled to Noterra, and I met Tobias for the first and only time. He was tall then, as I'm sure he has remained so. He had thick, wavy hair in various shades of gold and copper, reminding me of the warm sun. He kept it pulled back with a leather strap as if it was unruly enough to warrant constraint. His skin was deep and golden, courtesy of the cloudless skies and summer sun that was visible all year round.

In contrast, his bright blue eyes looked like they held secrets and a history of pain and anger, as if he had never known a day of happiness and joy in his life. His hands were permanently clenched in fists, his jaw hardened as if he was biting back the urge to say something. I remember wondering how a boy that young could look so hurt, how the crown prince of the largest kingdom on the continent had anything to even be worried about.

That was before I felt pain and fear of my own.

His father looked similar to the one I was cursed with: towering height, muscular frame, and frightening. He had the same golden skin his son had, another perk of spending your entire life in a place where storms were rare. Frown lines and furrowed brows permanently etched into his perfectly shaven face, with only a small, pink scar above his right eye to remind you that he was once a warrior.

He wasn't born into power like my father and I, but fought a long and bloody war for his position. A throne everyone believes he stole from the rightful heir, but he had proven himself to the citizens of Noterra and the neighboring kingdoms.

The king is gentle and caring towards his people, providing the best of everything to all who reside inside the borders. Endless wealth and treasures, the best trade routes on the continent. He's beloved by everyone.

Despite his kindness towards his subjects, he is ruthless and abusive towards his child. I watched him hit his own son for not greeting me the way he believed a prince should greet his future wife. Tobias had kind and fearful eyes when they finally met mine. He was shaking, his cheek growing more purple as the moments passed. He seemed like he was trying to wordlessly warn me. His eyes were soft, pleading as if he was trying to convey a message to run before I could experience the pain he was in.

A message I couldn't consider.

We don't have a choice in this engagement.

I held onto those kind eyes all these years, hoping they remained so. If I were to marry a man like King Evreux, I don't feel my safety would be well kept. A man of his people, and only his people, just like my father.

I won't ignore the fact that I've heard the rumors that float through the kingdoms. How Tobias, who just had his 20th birthday, took after his father in all ways. How his playthings are usually found bloodied and bruised when he's finished with them. How he will be just as aggressive and abusive towards his future children as his father, maybe even worse than my own father. I can only hope that the rumors are false, and there isn't a monster waiting for me across the border.

I am worried about my future in Noterra, but it's not something I can control, at least not right now. I don't have any power here in Chatis as a princess, and I know I won't have any there. As a woman, I fear I don't have influence anywhere. Even as a future queen, my ability to have an opinion is limited to housekeeping duties. I only hope my future king values my happiness, as I plan to value his. Hopefully if Tobias is shown love and affection, he may be more willing to allow me to be his equal, be his partner, instead of just a body to warm his bed and bear him children.

However, I am too much of a realist to allow myself to hope.

I push the heavy covers off my body and stare down at my permanently pale legs exposed below the hem of my blush silk nightdress. My father's kingdom lies within mountains and doesn't see much sun. Chatis is a small country that usually experiences darkness and cloudy skies at all times of the year. The cloud cover never allows for many views of a bright blue sky, instead purple and black skies fill the air above my home nearly all year. Air that is thick with humidity, regardless of the season, makes everything look hazy. I don't think I can remember a time when I could actually see across our lands from my balcony.

While I try to spend as much time as possible walking the gardens or the grounds, my father doesn't allow me to leave the palace walls, sometimes not even my room. He claims it's for my safety, but I know it's for control.

He has many enemies, both at home and afar. I always wondered why, as he used to be a gentle ruler, used to be loved by his subjects. However, when my mother passed away, his kindness and devotion to his family and country took a turn and he became filled with hatred, destruction, and a thirst for power.

He focused his energy on conquering more land and starting wars instead of caring for his only child. Instead of caring for the lands he already had. Not to mention the wars he started did not go in his favor, and instead, his lands were reduced to just the northern plain next to the only body of water in the mountains, a small lake my mother called her own. Even with his failure to obtain the impossible, he still remained feared across the nation. He was still important enough to prevent any counterattacks on our own land, the other countries just fought him off and returned to normal life. It makes me wonder if they knew of his crazed tendencies and were just placating him instead of doing something about it.

I've heard my ladies speak about me with hushed voices. They believe I cannot hear them, but I do. They talk about how some citizens of Chatis don't even believe I exist. How I am a mere myth and that the king has no heirs or children, that all of his children died. That he is alone in his grief since my mother passed and that was the cause for his recklessness.

Any time I have made it into town, which isn't often, I am invisible. As far as they know, my face belongs to one of the many ladies of our small country, a Lord's daughter, nothing more. The only ones who truly know of my identity are a small handful of the kingsguard and my ladies. Everyone else believes I am his pet, someone he sought to control after his wife passed. I don't know why my father created this secret; I am sure it has something to do with politics.

Sometimes I wish it were true that I had a different father out there. One who would have loved me and cherished me, instead of abused and belittled me. One who would have allowed me to make my own choices instead of forcing me into a life with no chance at freedom.

I haven't traveled much throughout the nation, especially as I grew older. My last trip out of Chatis was near my 12th birthday, when I went to Rakushia with my father. The princess, Emery, is the same age as me, and I remember the feeling of relief I felt meeting someone my own age who was of the same status. But I also remember the jealousy I felt watching her interact with her father. The King of Rakushia was quiet, and soft with his daughter and his wife, showing them nothing but love. A gentleness I've never seen from my own father, even though the kings were cousins. Related by blood and name only, not by temperament. The traits of the Rakushian king weren't genetic it seems, unless my father was the outlier.

Sliding off my bed, I take a breath as my feet meet the cool, stone floors. A drastic difference to the pain I felt in my dreams, the pain that I can't seem to forget, no matter how many times I wish for new stories to come when I close my eyes. The same pain, the same shade of crimson running below my feet like a river, the same glass slicing down to the bone.

I have only mentioned my nightmares once, but the mender who I spoke to only said it was caused by the traumatic loss of my mother and would fade shortly. He gave me an elixir made out of wisteria to help me sleep, but I ended up sleeping for three days straight and it took weeks for me to recover. I refused to feel that way, that vulnerable, so I never took it again.

It's been years and a single night hasn't passed without the same dream replaying, but I stopped asking for help. To show a weakness would be to give my father ammo to further terrorize me, not that he needs it. If I told him I still dreamed of death and destruction, he would either ignore me or punish me for being weak and an irritation.

Walking to the balcony doors on the far side of my room, I pull them open. The clouds are dark, but a single stream of sunlight peeks between the gray.

Stepping out to the railing, I stare at the picturesque views that I can make out through the haze, stifling a chill from the brisk, humid air, but basking in what little sunlight touches my skin. Lush, green mountains and hills surround us on all sides, only breaking where the Delaquar Lake lies just beyond the walls. The lake that I used to swim in as a child when my mother was able to sneak us away from the confines of the palace.

I remember the smell of the salty water and the sight of the native fish that called that body of water their home. I haven't felt that sense of bliss in years, and I don't know if I ever will again.

I made myself a promise that I will feel the water in the Delaquar Lake one more time before I leave. That I will once again let the icy chill crawl up my spine, causing goosebumps across my pale skin. That I will use that time to say goodbye to my home, and the memories I have of my mother.

My eyes glance down to the palace grounds. I can barely see the only Chatisian town past the stone walls due to their height, even from the second story. Tips of beige and gray roofs and billows of smoke rising from the fireplaces peak out above the towering walls before mixing with the suffocating fog and clouds.

Inside the grounds, there's endless green grass and flowers, something my mother tended to, and thankfully the groundsmen kept up with after her death. People are bustling around, completing morning duties, all in sync with one another. Whether it's a guard, a council member, or a kitchenmaid, they all have a purpose. Or at least that's what my father says. He says they were born to serve and that's what they will do until the day they die.

I always said that wasn't a life worth living, but he never fails to remind me of the privilege I have. I won't ever forget, but I sometimes wish for an easier life. A life where I am nothing of importance.

But I'll never have that.

I have never been truly unhappy with my existence, but the thoughts of jumping off this balcony have entered my brain time and time again. Living a life in a home you feel more of a captive than a resident in isn't easy. Once my mother died, I thought about it. Running away, jumping off the balcony, or even eating the nightshade berries that litter the hills and letting the overgrown moss consume me. Anything that got me away from the loveless home I have been stuck in. Even now as I feel some sort of relief that I will be leaving these walls for good, I wonder if death would be an easier journey.

Easier than the unknown I will soon face.

Sighing, I turn back to my messy room knowing I will have to make an appearance at some point, but my actual motivation is the prospect of food. My stomach growls with hunger as I step down from the balcony, rivaling the nausea blooming. I search through the piles of clothes littering the floor for one of my favorite dresses, needing something to bring me comfort. Just when I spot the black lace peeking out from under a mound of gold and ivory, my door bursts open. I jump back in surprise, my heart rate skipping a beat, as the man forcing me to abandon my home, the man I hate calling my father, walks in.

His plain brown eyes are wide and glowing, a perfect contrast to his flushed cheeks and overly wide grin. His equally mundane chestnut hair is disheveled with an uneven crown resting on his head. Dark stubble covers his jaw and upper lip. His tunic and pants are wrinkled, messy. He looks as if he hasn't had much sleep, probably the result of another night filled with women and wine. He's pale, more so than usual, as if the years are finally catching up to him. Despite his disheveled state, he's excited, *elated*.

His shoulders are high, his spine straight and tall. A wild gleam sparks in his eyes as his lips part, revealing straight, white teeth. I can almost hear his pulse pounding throughout the room as adrenaline fueled excitement radiates from him almost as strongly as the stench of sex and alcohol.

"Elaenor, it's time. Get dressed." He barks as my ladies file in behind him, their faces filled with worry. They're refusing to make eye contact with me, a sign that something is wrong. They glance at each other, biting their lips and fidgeting. My father bends down and throws an ivory dress in my direction, nearly smacking me in the face.

"Father, time for what?" I glance around as my clothing and belongings are methodically making their way into the luggage, faster than if I were to do it. He means it's time to leave. My hand flies to my mouth as realization sets in, the dress dropping to the floor in slow, billowy movements. My chest tingles and it feels as if my stomach is filled with rocks. *No.* I nearly stumble, my legs threatening to give out. I had a week left. A whole week to either find my way out of this or come to terms with the idea of being someone's wife.

"King Evreux is sick; Tobias is set to be crowned the second he passes. You need to be wed before that happens if you wish to be their queen." He gives me a crooked smile, his white teeth peeking through his pale lips, his eyes widening into a look that does nothing but radiate superiority. His ruddy complexion deepens, and I swear he looks more like a mad king every single day. His plan is falling into place. I can see the impending power rushing to his thick head. The lands and fortune he is no doubt cataloging internally. The anticipation he feels is no match for the fear building inside me. One more week of freedom before I would be forced to marry a man I don't know, is just ripped away.

"Father, I am only 17. I have one more week," I try to plead, my voice wavering, but the warning in his eyes is enough to stop me in my tracks. I shut my mouth, clenching my teeth.

He takes two large strides towards me and his narrowed eyes trail down my body, making me shiver under his uncomfortable gaze as I'm reminded I am still in my nightgown. He almost looks proud of what he sees. His calloused hand grips my shoulder as he looks me up and down, his eyes snagging on the thin silk covering my breasts for just a moment before he meets my gaze. I force my racing pulse to steady as I suppress the urge to wrap my arms around myself. A flush creeps along my cheeks at his closeness and I try to keep myself from flinching from disgust.

"You have a duty, Elaenor. Your duty is to produce an heir as fast as possible. Let him have you before the wedding, it won't be a sin if he is to be your husband. It is your job to produce a son, one your mother failed to do." Disappointment pours from his eyes, his nose wrinkling and lips curling, as I let my own gaze fall. My arms protectively encircle around my stomach as his fingers dig into my flesh harder, no doubt causing more bruises to join the others he left on my body. I press my lips as tightly together as I can to keep myself from speaking my mind. That only ever ends in pain.

I remember the countless fights my parents had after my mother endured yet another miscarriage. Her pain and agony as she pushed the lifeless infants out of her body time and time again, only for them to be taken away before she could say goodbye. Their little bodies burned as the menders worried they were cursed. The continuous loss was causing her dark hair to pale earlier than it should have at the young age of twenty-seven, and by time she died it was nearly all white. She sought out the help of countless masters and menders, that's how she met the prophet who later became her closest confidant. My father never forgave her, blaming her as the sole reason he doesn't have a son. The sole reason his kingdom is at risk of falling under a new ruler.

"Don't fail me, Elaenor. You're not worth a penny of what I provided as a dowry unless you give Chatis an heir." The venom in his tone makes me flinch, but it shouldn't. That is the voice that I have come to know.

I shouldn't be surprised; I always knew I was nothing more than a tool to him. Women can't hold power here, can't hold a kingdom. If my father were to pass, the kingdom, my home, would go to whoever the court decides, or whoever fought for it and won. I would lose everything. The people of Chatis could possibly lose everything. This isn't about my happiness, it's about the lives of our people. They are the ones I need to consider when I contemplate running away, but my selfishness peeks through quite often.

I wonder why *I* have to endure so much for everyone else, why these choices are not my own, but fate is fickle.

"Yes, Your Grace." I whisper, my eyes still fixed onto the stone floor. Despite the lengthy monologue I wish to scream at him, nothing will make a difference. Any day now, I will wed Tobias and become a princess to Noterra. I inwardly sigh, letting my frustration and defeat be suppressed by the act of being the dutiful daughter.

His fingers release my shoulders as they slide down my arms slowly, sending a chill down my spine. I keep my eyes cast down, afraid to look him in the eyes and see what he's thinking. He has always looked at me like I was a piece of meat. It didn't help that everyone said I was identical to my mother and didn't resemble my father in any way, appearance, or personality. I guess I should be grateful for that.

With one last look of anticipation, he turns on his heels and walks out, his leather shoes loudly hitting the stone floor. "You leave by noon." He snaps as he crosses the threshold and disappears out of sight, no doubt off to find another courtesan to bed before he has to see me off. I only hope he does me the courtesy of foregoing that tradition. His face is not the last I wish to see before I depart.

A small shudder forces me to close my eyes and take a deep breath. My nails dig into my arms as I hold them tight against my body. There is no discussion to be had here and breaking down now won't change anything. The last week of freedom I had was ripped away by a foreign king's illness. Fear of what is coming fills my body. Fear of the man Tobias has become and what he will expect of me. Fear of the unknown world I will soon be entering. I'm not ready, but that little detail means nothing to the men who control my life.

I guess I should be grateful I am leaving. I should be happy that I will no longer be in the presence of the king, but I knew what to expect of him. What his favorite punishments were, his schedule, how to navigate this court without being seen. I won't have that in Noterra, and I doubt I will have much time to learn.

I won't be a secret there; I will be their queen.

Chapter Two

I leave the packing to my irritatingly silent ladies as I abandon my room. They refused to say anything and instead each kept a soft, sympathetic smile plastered to their face and their eyes averted, which is unlike them. At least out of the three of them, Scarlett is the least likely to keep her mouth shut. So I was surprised that she, too, shut me out.

I dressed quickly, throwing my unruly hair back into a braid before stepping into the hallway. While I feel like I should assist, they are usually more organized than I am. Admittedly, I also just don't want to do it. I don't have much time left here in Chatis, so I want to see it one last time. I made myself a promise that I would do this *one* thing before I leave.

I want to visit the Delaquar and see the trees all before I am ushered into a new kingdom.

I exit my room and the usual guards are patrolling the dim hallways. Their silver armor sparkling against their green tunics and pants. Swords of extreme length that have never seen battle are strapped to their sides, their hilts glowing a pale silver. They each have a deep, emerald cloak strapped to their chest plate, flowing behind them like a lush blanket of grass. They barely spare me a glance, but I give them a nod anyway and turn right, heading to the stairs.

There isn't much color in the Chatis palace as the walls and floors are made from dark gray sheetrock. The only color that seems to be present is the green of the moss, grass and trees and the golds and oranges of the torches lining the corridors, softly illuminating the area. The country's color is deep green, but they rarely decorate with it at the capital. I guess the grass and trees are enough greenery for everyone.

The grand staircase is an intricate combination of dark granite and stone with gold and bronze filigree, much like the ceilings. I always loved to stare at the tiny detailing of crowns and flowers pressed into the stone with thin metal wire. It took my ancestors years to complete all of the accents hidden in the stone. It was time well spent. I've lived here for almost 18 years, and I still find a new detail I missed every now and then. I faintly remember my mother yelling at me as I took a small blade to the stone, trying to see if the wire was able to come off. I had no reason other than a child's curiosity, but to my surprise, it didn't budge. It was as if they were fused together with time.

I rest my hand on the smooth railing as I slowly make my way down, my sandaled feet softly hitting the stairs. The foyer is empty, which is unusual. Usually a hoard of servants are bustling about this early in morning, but I do find myself welcoming the silence. The center stone table, made of the same material as the palace, lay empty in the center of the room. A single glass vase filled with water sits in the middle. Usually it is overflowing with the flowers growing in the gardens, but for once, it is empty, like me. My fingertips slide across the cold, glass rim, the water inside vibrating with the touch.

The palace was crafted out of thick, gray stone that absorbs any color and light. Half of the palace was constructed inside the mountain, making it partially hidden and windowless. It was done so the mountain itself wouldn't have to be altered, but instead of creating a fortress, it felt more like a dungeon. It didn't help that the only color the king kept was the metallic accents in the walls. Nothing else to create a homey, comfortable place to live. It was the perfect embodiment of the cold, callous heart made of stone living in my father's chest, and his father before him.

The only exception to the darkness of the palace is my room. My bedding is a pale white with beautiful beige furs. The curtains are a light blue, like the color I always imagined the sky to be. The floor is covered in plush rugs and carpets to stave off the chilly air that seems to always be present. I also try to avoid gray in my wardrobe, but the clothing that continuously appears in my dressing room is usually shades of black and ivory. Clothing is just another way for my father to control me.

I step around the table and through the open double doors. I shut my eyes and take a slow, deep inhale as I absorb all the scents I will miss. The thick humidity is the perfect breeding ground for moss and grass. The entire kingdom is covered in a lush green and a rich smell of foliage and flowers. My eyes open and I stare up at the sky. The ever-present blanket of clouds covers the sun, casting a dark shadow over the palace, but for once, I don't see rain threatening to ruin my day.

My *last* day.

I glance around before I make my way down the steps and to the path that leads to the wall. My father doesn't normally allow me to leave the palace, but just this once, I'm choosing to disobey him. In a matter of hours, I will be climbing into a carriage and starting a new life in a new home. With a betrothed and a family I do not know. With a new king to order me around. A whole new world I'll have to learn to navigate. He won't be able to control me then.

A chill runs down my spine as a sickening feeling creeps in. The idea of this arranged marriage has made me nauseous these last few days, something about it just doesn't feel right. My mouth has been dry, and I feel as if I have to constantly swallow back any bile that threatens to escape. I blame the flutters in my stomach on the nervousness and apprehension I feel. It's a new life, one I've dreamt of having, dreamt of living.

So why do I feel so sick about it?

I continue down the short path until I am across the small courtyard and near the palace gate. I can't exit through there as the guards will never allow it, so I take a quick left behind a row of trees before they can see me. During a large storm last winter, part of the stone wall came down under the weight of a fallen tree. It's been undergoing repairs, but its height is much lower than the rest of the towering stone barriers surrounding the palace. I found it one day when I was walking the grounds with Scarlett.

I have thought about jumping over it for quite awhile, but fear of what my father would do if he found out always prevented me. I have, however, spent a lot of time lounging and hiding under the tall trees that border the hills. The palace walls end when they reach the hillside, so I was always able to get lost in the trees without actually breaking any rules. It was the one place I could take a deep breath; however I always had an escort regardless. Thankfully Scarlett always volunteered, and she was skilled in keeping secrets. Usually I stay with Laenie and Rhea as well, but they tend to be a little bit more forthcoming when questioned by my father. Due to that, we all mutually decided that my escapades would be chaperoned by Scarlett. She has a mind of stone and has never let him break her; I can't say the same for myself.

I let my fingers brush the rough bark on one side and the damp stone on the other as I walk along the wall, hidden in the shade. I haven't been to Noterra since I was a child, but I do recall them having even more trees than Chatis. I can't imagine living in a place where forests take up the majority of the land.

More than enough places for me to hide.

Noterra also experiences seasons more accurately than our kingdom. With constant clouds, we mostly experience rain and snow, but Noterran summers have been a dream of mine to experience. To swim in the ocean, the water as blue as the cloudless sky, reflecting the sunlight as it filters down. To feel the warmth cascade over my skin as my porcelain flesh is tinted golden in the rays. It's a dream that will soon be a reality. That thought alone is enough to temporarily calm the uneasiness in my stomach.

I walk in silence for the better part of ten minutes, letting the noises from the courtyard dissipate as I follow the wall deeper and deeper into the mountain. The trees grow denser here as the path takes me around the side of the palace. No guards or workers venture over here, so the loneliness is welcomed. I find the damaged part of the wall and hoist myself up and over using what remains of the fallen trunk as leverage. I land on my feet on the other side, and I am met with a thick wall of trees.

This forest used to be my safe space. I would seek the trees every time my father and I fought, or when my mother died. There was something about the shade of green in these trees that pulled me in. The bright, almost bioluminescent colors that find a way to shine through the dark and dreary gray of everything else. These trees promise sanctuary and safety. They promise a sense of belonging and the wish to be anyone I desire. I don't have anyone to control me, disagree with my choices, or force me to marry here.

I am simply just Elaenor.

I step through the brush and smile as the tickle of foliage graces my legs, snagging on the billowy tulle of my dress. As I walk deeper, the bustling noises of Chatis disappear and are replaced with the singing of birds, the rustling of leaves as animals scurry about, the wind through the branches that send leaves raining down in slow motion. The feeling of complete and utter seclusion from reality is unattainable in a palace where you are the center of attention anytime you enter a room. I've never liked the attention being a princess, or as most believed a Lord's daughter, has brought. I wanted so badly to be a servant or kitchenmaid growing up. To be invisible. But I will never be invisible.

I continue through the trunks of varying sizes and only stop to lift my head up as a small ray of sunshine breaks through the clouds. I close my eyes as the sunlight beats down on my skin, warming me to my core. Utter peace. I could stay out here, and they would never find me. I wouldn't be forced to enter a marriage. I could find love, find somebody who makes me feel like this all the time. Someone who chooses to be with me instead of someone who bought me like a prized mare, because that's what Noterra did. I was sold for lands, protection, and allies. I am nothing but property.

I open my eyes as the sun disappears again. The brief warmth is replaced with a small chill as the clouds regain control. With a sigh, I continue the trek to the lake. It's fairly close to the wall and should only take a minute or two to get there, but I am in no rush. I want to enjoy this as much as possible.

The trees all look the same, the soft green leaves floating down around me. The forest floor is blanketed in grass and moss-covered boulders. Bushes of varying flower species hug the base of the tree trunks, displaying random colors of pink, purple, and blue to break up the green. Thickly curled birds' nests dot along the high limbs of the evergreen trees, housing the newest generation of sparrows and woodpeckers, birds who don't mind the northern cold and rain.

I'm not sure what the protocol is like for royals in Noterra and if I will be allowed to wander about, but I hope I will. I can't imagine jumping from one captor to another. I want nothing more than to be free to do as I please, but as a queen I may not have that luxury. Whether that will be due to the strict reign my future husband will impose, or just a fear of my safety, I don't know.

All I can think about is the beach, as the eastern edge of Noterra borders the sea, and the new forests that have yet to be explored. I dream about Port Tobeo, the largest trading port in the nation, and the merchants who no doubt have the best wares available. Scarlett has told me of the places she has visited with her family, of the delicious food, beautiful silks and cotton, and the different people she met. I want nothing more than to experience it myself.

My feet are silent on the forest floor, so a rustle to my right stops me in my tracks. It's louder than would be expected of the smaller animals in the forest. Chatis mostly experiences rabbits, mice, and a few felines, but nothing that can act as a true predator. There used to be bears and mountain lions, but they have long since migrated north to Rakushia after the Chatisian huntsmen nearly made them extinct. Rakushia has more caves in their hills, creating the perfect nests for predators to have a safe home. It also doesn't help that Chatis is the only country with persistent rain. Even the animals leave to experience the sun.

I squint my eyes and peer through the trunks and brush, but I see nothing but greenery. *You're imagining things.*

I take another slow, deep breath before continuing my journey.

I can finally see it just beyond the tree line, and I start to smile. The crystal blue waters are dark due to the cloudy sky, but still inviting, nonetheless. I take the last step out of the trees, and I am met with pure white sand. There isn't much, as it's mostly dirt and the forest floor, but the amount that is there always reminded me of the fine texture of the sugar I would stick my fingers in as a child. The kitchenmaids would always make me sweets and cover them in clouds of white powder. I called it snow as they very closely resemble each other.

I kick off my shoes and push my bare feet through the soft, white granules. It's cool and damp under my toes, but the relaxation that washes over me is invigorating. The soft lapping of the water as the small waves hit the shore make my smile grow wider. I can just barely make out some fishing boats farther out towards the center of the lake, their deep brown wood is a stark contrast to the blue waters. I can't tell who they belong to as the other side of the lake, that I couldn't see, belongs to Noterra, and the northern part belongs to Rakushia. All that separates our lands is a lake and trees.

Honestly, it's a wonder why King Evreux hasn't taken over Chatis. They have armies, and they could absorb this land within a day with minimal casualties.

With Noterra reigning over nearly half of the continent anyway, I don't see why they wouldn't make the move.

I kick my feet out from under the sand and run until my bare skin meets the icy water. The cold liquid causes my body to shiver, but I relish in it. The last time I was here was with my mother. This was one of our last outings before she died.

My father didn't like us out much, so she snuck me out one day during one of the only days we had sun. We dressed in common clothes, no sign of finery or wealth between the two of us. She took me out of the servants exit and the side gate in the wall that led to the market. We were out of the walls so quickly; my little brain couldn't comprehend it. No one paid us any mind as we walked through the cobblestone streets of the town. We were all smiles and laughs as we walked to the docks. She brought me along the edge of the lake to a small, secluded beach where we spent the next few hours swimming and sunbathing. It was the perfect day.

She died a week later.

I promised myself I would come back as much as possible, but I never did. I didn't dare exit through the servant's quarters with the increased guard patrol. I knew I could reach it through the woods, it was faster that way, but I never tried. I never allowed myself to go that far for fear of my father's hand, or his whip, until today.

When the wall came down during a storm, I thought it was my chance to finally go back, but I never had the courage to jump the wall. While I did venture into the woods and up the hills as much as possible, the tether that my father put around me was tight. I used to tell Scarlett how it felt more like a noose than a leash. She didn't find that amusing, but I wasn't trying to be funny.

I was trying to convey my pain.

Some say my mother killed herself, some blame the prophet who predicted her death, some even blame my father. I don't truly know what happened nor do I know what the official cause of her death was. I was too young so I was shielded from such things and now nobody will talk about her. Nobody answers questions about her, or even reminisces over her life. It's like she never existed, and that's how my father wants it. Maybe it's the only way he can live with himself. He is either struggling with the death of the love of his life, or the guilt over killing her has destroyed him. I wish so desperately for a prophet to share the details of that night, but I'm always told it's the future they predict, and they cannot see the past. I wish that weren't true.

I remember some things. I remember my mother saddened after each death. I remember my mother getting migraines and nosebleeds constantly and the many menders that frequented her room. I remember being curled up to my mother's side, half asleep, while she spoke to the prophet she befriended. He was always kind to me, gentle. I don't remember what he looked like, but I remember his eyes. They were such a bright yellow, I often thought he wasn't real. He always stayed by my mother's side, was always a shoulder for her to lean on as she wept for her dead children. Maybe the rumors are just different pieces of a bigger picture. Maybe he did kill her, or maybe it was my father. I don't think I'll ever know.

I return my attention back to the water. My eyes focus on the native fish swimming about in their home, no doubt in search of food. Their varying colors of oranges and reds shimmering under the water as they continue on with their journey. Their life seems so easy, so simple. Nothing to prove, no one to answer to. They just get to live and eat. Which reminds me that I failed to grab breakfast. My stomach rumbles in response to my thoughts and I groan.

I walk further until my dress is floating, and my knees are submerged. Goosebumps spread across my skin as the icy water tickles my thighs. My breathing catches against the cold, but I force slow deep breaths until I get used to the temperature.

I start to fully sink in when I get the feeling I am being watched, a sense of awareness washing over me. I still as I listen, waiting. Electricity hums across my skin in response to whatever it is I am feeling. My pulse quickens, pounding through my ears as I try to quiet my breath. The loud rustling returns, along with the snap of a twig and I flinch.

The silence that I usually crave is suddenly terrifying, as if I'm waiting for something to come out from beyond the trees and swallow me whole, but nothing does. I don't know how long I stand there, frozen in the icy water, my hands clenched into fists and my nails digging into my palms before I allow myself to release the breath trapped in my throat. My chest feels tight, my lungs burning as I wait out the silence.

"You are freaking out over nothing." I whisper to myself. I slowly turn around until I am facing the tree line and a gasp escapes my lips. I nearly slip on the mossy rocks and hold out my arms to steady myself.

Right behind a large trunk there is a tall man with dark hair. His broad shoulders are dressed in a tight black tunic, his feet are bare, his hands clenched into fists, mirroring mine. He's still, his bright green eyes that match the trees are fixated on me. They are so vibrant, so unnatural. His mouth is slightly parted open, revealing bright white teeth. His jaw is hardened and sharp, much like his high cheekbones. He has a light dusting of facial hair along his jaw and upper lip, darkening his already tan skin. Thick lashes flutter around the green, almost covering his eyes.

He's beautiful. He seems so familiar, something about his face, it's as if I had seen it before. He couldn't be any older than I was. His thick eyebrows slowly draw together in…confusion? No, not confusion. He looks like he's in pain, like he's concerned. He tilts his head to the side, his eyes softening. I blink and he's gone.

"Hello?" I call out as I try to get out of the water as fast as I can, slipping on the lake bottom underneath. My hands are shaking, but I bite back my fear. I rush into the trees, silently cursing at myself for running after the stranger, but the idea of anyone in these woods brings forth my curiosity, and my recklessness. "Who's out there?" I continue running, dodging branches and rocks along the way, but all signs of the man are gone.

There is no way I just imagined that.

He was there. He was standing right behind the trees. My heart is racing, and I stop to catch my breath, my hand flying to my chest as I swallow as much oxygen as I can. I can feel the sharp sensation of something stabbing into the bottom of my foot and I wince out loudly in pain, my nightmare briefly flashing through my mind. I lift my leg, using a nearby tree to steady myself, and see a small trail of blood dripping from my bare heel.

"What the…?" My eyes wander down to the forest floor, and through the leaves and debris, I see something reflecting what little sunlight there is. I bend down and let my fingers graze the cool glass. I grip the edges of the shard with my fingertips as I hold it out in front of me. The glass is clear with just a small drop of my blood staining part of it red. The piece is shaped into a perfect arrowhead, slightly bigger than the size of my hand. An arrowhead made of glass. I can't imagine anyone using such a delicate item for a weapon. It vibrates in my hand, as if it was responding to my racing pulse. I wonder if he dropped it.

Or if he was even here to begin with.

I grip the piece of glass tightly, but carefully, in my hand so I don't lose it, and rise to my feet, trying to ignore the sting of pain coming from my heel.

Looking up at the sky, I can see the sun is slowly getting higher behind the clouds and my time to leave is growing closer. I shake my head again to clear the engrossing cloud of panic. There was nobody there. I'm just seeing things. It's dark and cloudy and a tree could have easily been mistaken for a person. The glass is just a coincidence, and the shape was probably formed by the elements over years of wear. Nobody comes out here.

Nobody was there.

But I knew that was a lie.

Something about it, something about this random piece of glass, is pulling me. Calling to me. Begging me to not leave it behind. So I don't. I tuck it into the pocket of my dress and look around, my eyes desperately searching through the thick trunks and foliage for any sign that I'm not going mad.

As I am already halfway to the palace wall, I abandon my shoes and head back, ignoring the pain emanating from my heel with each step and the dirt that is no doubt lodging itself into the wound. I need to quickly change and clean myself up before it's time to leave, if I'm late, my father is sure to be angry. The last thing I need is to be sore upon my arrival in Noterra. As much as I want to hide in the trees forever, I need to face my fate and get on that carriage.

The sooner I am on my way to Noterra, the farther away from my father I'll be. This is a new beginning and I need to find a way to embrace it. The ever-present nausea settles deep in my stomach, and I inhale slowly, breathing through the wave, the tickle of tears pressing behind my eyes, but I blink them away.

As I trek back through the trees, the face of the strange man, that may or may not have been a figment of my imagination, is stuck in my mind. Haunting me. His face seems all too familiar, as if it's a face I've seen in my dreams. As if it's someone I know.

But I know for a fact I have never seen him before, especially out here. Who was he? Is this just a product of my imagination? Or was someone actually there, watching me?

The back of my neck tingles and I shiver. I could still feel as if someone was watching me, tracking me. I bite my lower lip and continue on through the forest.

I grip the glass through the fabric of my dress as I picture his green eyes that mimicked that of the trees. Bright, almost glowing, against his tan skin.

Glowing against the darkness of Chatis.

Chapter Three

The sun rises higher in the sky, barely peeking out behind the clouds, as I make my way out of the palace again and onto the grass. The courtyard is beautiful. With trees lining the walls and flowers filling every corner, the greenery flourishes in the humidity, that and mosquitos, but thankfully the cool air hasn't yet yielded to them. It won't be long before summer is at its highest, that is when the real humidity arrives. The rain never usually stops during the summer, well it never really stops any time of the year, but rain mixed with the heat tends to be so much worse.

I can never get through the summer without having received at least a hundred mosquito bites. Red bumps scattered across my body and the uncontrollable urge to scratch them until they are bleeding and raw. If it weren't for the tin of ointment I keep stowed away in my room, I probably would be peppered with scars by now, or at least scars caused by mosquitos.

I had to quickly bandage my heel on my own, if I asked for a mender, it would only raise questions that I didn't have the patience to answer. Thankfully the small tin of ointment I kept hidden works for more than mosquito bites and I was luckily prepared with some bandages. This wasn't the first time I had injured myself while exploring, so I knew how to take care of minor wounds. I quickly cleaned and wrapped it before stepping into my shoes.

I repocketed the glass arrowhead, keeping it close to me. It seemed to hum with electricity every time my skin brushed it. I knew it was nothing more than my imagination, but something about it made me question that. I did clean it though, ridding it of the small crimson stain caused by my blood. It was perfectly clear, and the light bounced off of it with a green hue, but maybe that was due to the reflection of the trees.

I take a deep, steadying breath and try to remember the sights as they surround me. While the thick, ever-present pressure of wet air reminds me of home, I can't wait to feel the clean, crisp air of Noterra. I can't wait to take a deep breath and not feel like the pressure from the humidity is causing me to choke. I can't wait to be able to walk around and not be drenched by the time I return, regardless of the season. I am sure Noterra experiences heat in the summer, but a dryer heat seems preferable to a wet, sticky heat.

As each person passes by me, a slight dip of the chin takes place. While I have been treated like porcelain my entire life, I have always hated the formalities that came with my position, or my *assumed* position. I was never allowed friends outside of my status or my ladies, nor able to acknowledge their existence. That was how my father willed it. To others who don't know, I imagine I seem as if I am a stuck-up lady who believes she is too good to converse with those below her. The king's pet who let power get to her head.

I smile at each person as they pass, wanting so badly to tell them I am not my father's daughter and that I am not a noble lady who finds their company an embarrassment. That I am kind and want so desperately to speak to those who reside in our country. If I ever return, I will be a queen. Maybe then I will be able to speak to whomever I please.

I am hopeful that life in Noterra will be different. That I will be allowed to have friends below my status, that I will be allowed to walk the grounds, or even explore the country, without fear of my father's hand, or my future husband's. I am hopeful that I will have a life worth living, because I fear I won't survive if I enter another world like the one I grew up in.

I refuse to bring a child into the world knowing they will have a similar childhood to my own, and as my father continuously says, my duty is to produce an heir. Tobias has to be a good man; I *need* him to be a good man and a good king. I just need him to be different from the men I have known in my life.

All I have ever seen is aggression or submission. Aggression from my father, and submission from every single other person I have ever encountered, even myself. I submitted to my father's lashings when he was angry. I submitted to the countless times he had me stripped bare in front of him and his friends so he could approve of how I was aging. I could still feel his poking and prodding as he deemed me too skinny or too fat in certain areas. As he deemed me unworthy. Those moments usually resulted in being withheld food for days on end or forced to eat more.

Whatever he wanted, happened.

I wasn't a willing participant, but I was a participant nonetheless.

My ladies are near the gate, speaking to the palace guards as they load my carriage. I stare at each of their faces, knowing this may be the last time I see them. I wanted so desperately to have them accompany me to this far away kingdom, but I knew that it was not their burden to bear. They shouldn't be ripped from their families and homes like me. They deserve happiness and the chance to find love, or just to find themselves as they would be without me tied to them.

I urged my father to pay their families well for the 14 years of service they provided. Thankfully, he listened. Their families will never want for anything and with substantial dowries, they will be able to marry for love and not for monetary gain. A life I would want for myself, for my children. I was surprised my father agreed to this, but he always did treat my ladies better than he treated his own daughter.

I take this time to absorb their appearances, fearing this will be the last time I can. All three of them sport chestnut hair, as do all of the citizens of Chatis besides my mother and I, that is, before her's began turning white. Scarlett and Laenie have long and wavy hair that's pulled back into bows, always looking silky and smooth. Rhea's hair is cropped short to her shoulders, straight and shiny, regardless of the humidity. I envied them. My hair was as dark as the night sky and had such tight, tangly curls, a brush couldn't tame them. I always wondered if it was the climate here in Chatis that caused the unruliness of my hair, but I am sure I will find out soon enough.

Dark, emerald, green eyes, pale alabaster skin, and light freckles. They are each truly beautiful and look more like triplets than friends. Half the time I think most people do mix them up. With their incredible kindness and infectious smiles, they will surely get any man they desire. I know for a fact that Laenie would no doubt be going after the Hand's son. Lord Hairy, as the rest of us call him. His real name is Perry or Jerry, or something, I honestly couldn't remember, but Laenie's attraction to him and his weirdly hairy arms were always something we joked about. Now she was able to pursue him, see if his desires were the same.

Scarlett could also find someone to love, but she's strong and stubborn. I know she's had many lovers, but she always loved herself the most. I don't think she will ever settle down, I don't think she'll ever allow herself to be shackled to someone, unless they are royalty. Rhea on the other hand, I always had an inkling she favored women over men. I often saw the longing glances she had towards Scarlett. She was the quietest out of three, not that I wasn't as close to her as the others, but she favored silence over chattiness. I find myself hating the envy I feel towards them. Towards their freedom. Towards the life that awaits them once I leave.

I sigh inwardly as I make my way to the carriage. The guards at the gate bow, as does my rider, Ser Danieas, and I give them a soft smile in return. Ser Danieas has been close to me for quite a few years, my sworn sword as my father calls it. He's one of the men who know of my true identity, and the only one I would have wanted to accompany me on this journey. I don't know if he will be staying in Noterra, but it is better than being alone. I turn towards my friends, the only ones I have ever had, and fight back the tears that threaten to escape, the lump rising in my throat preventing me from speaking. I would like nothing more than to shove them into that carriage with me, but it wouldn't be fair.

Giving each of them a bone-crushing hug and a hopeful smile, I climb into the cabin. Not wanting to endure long goodbyes for fear that I won't be able to do as I'm asked if I let my emotions win, I turn away from them, fighting the burning in my eyes and the trembling in my hands. As I take a seat, a calloused hand reaches in and grasps my wrist, ripping me off of the bench. I cry out in pain as my back slams against the outside wall of the cabin, the pain snaking down my spine and causing my breath to catch as adrenaline pumps through my body. I glance up and see the raw excitement and power brewing in my father's wild eyes, his mouth parted in a wide grin. A small gasp escapes my lips as I feel the rough wood pressing harder into my skin as he pushes into me.

"If you disappoint me, Elaenor, you will suffer a fate much worse than your mother's." His face leans in closer, his nose almost touching mine. His free hand is resting right next to my head on the carriage, but I can see his fingers flexing out of the corner of my eye. I smell the sweet wine on his breath as he exhales. A fate worse than my mother's. Is that a confession? His fingers around my wrist tighten as he stares down at me.

"I won't, father. I am doing as you asked." I whisper, my voice straining. He takes a moment before a sadistic smile replaces the one of excitement. I quickly glance around to see the concerned faces of my ladies. The guards and Ser Danieas are looking away, knowing by now that their king has a temper. This wouldn't be the first time they've witnessed his aggression towards me, but hopefully their last. My father enjoyed my suffering, enjoyed my pain. If sadism had a person of embodiment, it would be my father.

"I've heard the stories about this young man you are soon to marry," A low chuckle escapes his lips as he pushes into me, his chest brushing mine. I bite back my wince and turn my face away from his, shutting my eyes. "Do what he says and I'm sure he won't kill you, but I can't promise he won't have a little fun with you first. Once you produce an heir, you are nothing. To Chatis, to Noterra. You will be just a warm body for him to do with as he pleases. Your duty will be complete and there will be no need for your existence. So you better make him happy, in all ways, or he'll throw you away for a real woman." His voice is a little more than a snarl, his breath fanning over my ear, forcing a disgusting shiver to creep through my body. I knew he saw me as little more than a body to do his bidding, but his actual disgust for me is surprising. I always hoped he loved me deep down, as any child hopes. My stomach fills with rocks and I take a deep breath and open my eyes.

"Is that how you felt about my mother?" I spit. His eyes widen slightly, shocked at my question, as I turn my head to face him again, his nose almost brushing mine. "Was she just another warm body for you to do with as you pleased until she ceased being of use?" His muddy brown eyes narrow, mimicking mine, as his dark eyebrows furrow. "This is the life you want for your daughter?" My heart is pounding, electricity sparking through my limbs making them tingle.

I am almost afraid of his answer, afraid that the truth will come out. He doesn't care about me. He never has. I was a walking bag of gold that he couldn't wait to cash in.

"Don't attempt to wound me, Elaenor, and don't speak about your mother as if you had any idea what went on between us." His voice is low, warning, but his anger is temporarily hidden as he leans back slightly, releasing some of the pressure on my back. "She knew her duty, and she failed. If the Gods decided she was no longer fit to be a queen, they did what they had to do." My mouth falls open slightly. He truly believed her death was the gods' will.

"Is that what you believe of yourself? That you are just one of the Gods?" I snap, louder. He leans back in, his nose pushing against mine as he chuckles. I fight the gag crawling up my throat at his proximity, at his *touch*. My hands are sweating, and I wipe them on the skirt of my dress.

"Leave, and don't return, or I'll kill you myself." He whispers quietly. With a hard shove against me he steps back, flashing a wicked and dangerous smile. I can't help the tears that fall from my eyes now as I stare at the monster he has become. They burn, reminding me that everything that has to do with my father hurts. Everything that has ever had to do with my life has been painful.

How can a man be so cruel to his child, his *only* child? And how can he speak so ill of his deceased wife? His *queen*? This is not the man my mother married, but it is the man I have known for the last 10 years of my life. Aggressive, conniving, barbaric. He is the epitome of a mad king who cares for nothing besides himself.

I hate him. I hate him more than I hate the idea of marrying a stranger. I'd rather be married off to someone who is old and decrepit than stay here in his presence.

The anger and resentment I feel boils to the surface and, for once, I don't hold back. I *can't* hold back. Pounding in my ears drowns out our spectators, my eyes narrowed and focused on him. I will my voice to remain calm and steady as I finally say everything I have dreamt of saying for years.

"You are a *monster*." Fury flashes through his eyes as they meet mine, his brows pinching in disbelief. My father turns his body to face me again, his hands on his hips wondering if I'm going to continue. I let my hate fuel my words as I for once in my life say what I want. "It is your duty as a father to protect me, yet you throw me to another suspected monster for the sake of your own rise in status. I am a human being, not a pawn for you to play when it's advantageous." I can see his eyes frantically look around, seeing who is there to witness my admission to his parentage, the veins in his neck sticking out as he sucks on his teeth. I take a deep breath and a step away from the carriage, inwardly groaning as the wood releases my back. The pressure in my chest rises as the adrenaline courses through my veins like electricity, fueling me, strengthening me. "You are a coward. You are so fearful of a life beyond your kingly duties that you let your own daughter suffer through the loss of her mother alone. Even if Tobias is as much of a heartless savage as the rumors believe, I will have a much better fate in his hands than yours. I would rather *die* than be forced to live another day in your shadow." Stepping back, marking the end of my verbal attack, I exhale loudly, my heart beating rapidly in my chest. His face is frozen, his lips pursed as he stands silently, debating his response, I'm sure.

The corners of his lips twitch briefly before he reaches out and slaps me. My hand instinctively reaches up towards the stinging pain on my cheek, while his fingers find my throat, squeezing until the pressure causes my eyes to water. I can hear the quiet unsheathing of swords as our spectators are unsure of when to step in. He slams me against the cabin again, pulling my head forward enough so he can shove it harder against the wood. A sharp pain radiates from the back of my skull, my eyes threatening to succumb to the darkness that's creeping in the edges of my vision.

"Your Grace." I hear one of the others say, but he's ignored. My nails rip at my father's fingers as I try to remove the obstacle blocking my airway, drawing blood. Panic fuels my search, looking for a weakness. His touch cuts off my access to oxygen as he leans in close to my ear so that I don't miss a word of his torture, his chest pressing into mine.

"My duty is to my kingdom, not to you or your mother. You are a pawn in the game called court and you will do right by Chatis and marry that boy. You will do right by your kingdom and produce an heir that can inherit my legacy. That is all you are worth to me. If you don't, you will do well to remember I have friends in high places at Noterra. You are just one girl in a world of many. If you were to disappear, I would at *last* be free to take on a new wife and make a *true* heir." His breath hisses in my ear and I fight to inhale what little air he allows, only managing a small stream of oxygen.

"If you hate me this much, just kill me and be done with this." I croak out as his fingers twitch around my neck. His eyes meet mine, and a small glimpse of regret fills them before the amusement returns, I almost think I imagined it.

His hand releases from my neck and I take a deep, gasping breath, nearly falling to my knees. My tear-filled eyes find his again and I am disappointed that they are still filled with resentment. He has always hated me. He has always hated that his legacy is threatened due to the lack of a male heir, he's never even attempted to hide it. I don't know why I believed there was something deep down that fostered love for me. I don't know why I ever held out hope that he would be more than just a father in name, that he would love me.

"I am your daughter. I just don't understand why you care so little." I whisper and his eyes soften slightly, his arms hanging loosely on his sides.

"You are a royal woman, Elaenor. Your life will be filled with disappointments and men who will do anything possible to ruin you. The way I have treated you thus far is the same treatment you will get anywhere else. Do not think so highly of yourself that you think you deserve equality. You are a woman. The Gods have placed men on thrones since the beginning of time. Your existence and inability to understand that will not get you a throne of your own. It will get you killed." With one last look at me, he storms off, straightening the crown on his head as he retreats back to his impenetrable palace, almost as strong as the wall around his heart.

A flurry of hands come towards me as tears are wiped off my face, my dress fixed, and my hair pulled out of my eyes. "I can't tell if that was his attempt at conveying his regret for treating me so horribly, or if that was a warning?" I whisper, mostly to myself. I can't even spare a glance in the direction of my ladies as I slowly take my place in the carriage again, the soft cushion of the bench doing little to ease the pain in my back.

I needed my father to know how I felt before I departed. Not that it ever mattered to him in the slightest, he needed to know. *I* needed him to know. But his last statement has just filled my head with more questions. Is this the treatment I will truly experience for the rest of my existence, or is that just his excuse for his actions? I have seen firsthand how my mother was treated; she was beloved. Is that not the norm for royal women? What kind of world would that make if women were treated as nothing more than a body fit for breeding?

"I just don't understand how this life could be normal, that this is what I should expect for the rest of my existence. If my mother were here, she wouldn't have allowed this. She always told me I would be able to fall in love one day, but that day will never come." I glance down at my hands knotting in my lap.

"Do you want us to come with you?" Laenie's voice is soft, comforting. I offer her a sad smile and shake my head, her soft green eyes troubled.

"This is for the best, Elaenor. It's getting you out of Chatis and somewhere you can start over." Scarlett speaks. I meet her emerald eyes ringed in gold, they are full of worry and sorrow. She looks too wise beyond her age of 19.

"What if Tobias is a monster? What if he's just like my father?" Her eyes soften as she smiles. "I can't live like this anymore, I won't survive."

"You will find peace there. You just have to believe it. Believe in him. He may surprise you." She brushes my throbbing cheek with her cold fingers and steps back. I fight against my emotions and take a deep breath. "We will all come visit once you are settled, I promise!" She smiles and turns towards Ser Danieas. With a snap of her fingers, the carriage moves forward and through the open palace gates. Laenie and Rhea take their places next to Scarlett, waving me off with sad, but hopeful eyes.

As I head towards either my saving grace or impending doom, I take one last look at the palace nestled into the lush green hills knowing this would be the last time I see it. The stone fortress embedded in the mountain. The suffocating clouds and thick humid air. The green trees littering the hills I spent countless hours playing in. The courtyard gardens my mother tended. The place where she died. The place where I was treated like a hindrance to my father's legacy.

The place I wish would burn to the ground.

It will never be the same.

A single tear glides down my cheek as I pray to the gods I am not riding towards my death, but they can't help me now. They are the reason for all of my misfortune thus far.

Chapter Four

Green eyes that mimic the bioluminescence of the Chatisian hills framed with thick dark lashes stare down at me with a look of intensity. A look of panic. His dark hair tickles his forehead as his hand reaches out for me. His black silk tunic and trousers partially hide his body in the darkness, blending in like shadows. His bare feet are a stark contrast compared to the dark forest floor, his skin a golden shade of tan. I glance at his hand and take a tentative step forward, reaching for it, letting his presence draw me further into the woods.

Every step I make pushes him farther and farther into the darkness. Confusion and panic rise in my chest as I start to fight against the pressure on my lungs, gasping breaths leaving my parted lips. I run towards him, as fast as I can. His hand is within inches of mine every time I reach forward, but I never get close enough. I can never reach him.

He's always the same distance away.

The trees fly past me as I pick up speed, narrowly missing their low hanging branches. They move faster and faster as if I am flying through them. The darkness *grows along the edges of my vision, his eyes soften slightly as his furrowed brows relax. Pain, all I see is pain on his face. His hand falls through the empty air, resting by his side as he shakes his head. I stumble over something and land on my hands and knees.*

A small cry of pain escapes my lips as my bare skin is met with the sharp edges of glass, burrowing deep enough to slice bone. I reach for a piece coated in my blood and lift it up. The glass arrowhead reflects the moon's light, reflecting green. Smoke begins to fill the free air like fog, and I struggle to breathe. I glance up at the man who is still within arm's reach.

"What is this?" I call out to him, coughing against the smoke. My chest is pounding, my breathing erratic. What is going on? "I don't understand!" He shakes his head again before he opens his mouth to speak just as the thunder starts.

I expect the cold water of the Chatisian rain to drench me, but hard stones bounce off my shoulders and head. I cry out and cover my head with my arms. Pain shoots down my limbs as each drop of stone makes contact with my skin. I glance down at the growing pile of white surrounding me and lean forward, the glass digging deeper into my shins. My fingertips brush one of the stones and it moves as another one falls on top. I gasp and drop it, a scream lodged in my throat. I look around, panic and pain once again overtaking my senses.

It's not rain, it's not rocks, it's not even stones raining down on top of me. Bones.

It's raining bones.

The sound of the horses galloping over the cobblestone path pulls me out of my dreams, the carriage bumping up and down. My eyes are met with darkness, unable to make out any semblance of a shape. I must have fallen asleep at some point during the long journey to Noterra.

I push the wool blanket off my lap, and it falls to the carriage floor. The cool, brisk air causes me to shiver as soon as the blanket is gone. Reaching in the direction of the window, I grasp the curtain and pull it open. Moonlight fills the cabin and lightly illuminates the surroundings. All I can see beyond the window are trees and stars. A beautiful sight, one that I dreamt of seeing again since I was a child. The cloud coverage in Chatis never allowed for stars, but my mother told me about them every night.

"One day, my little love, when you are able to venture out on your own, you'll see skies as dark as your hair, filled with glitter." She whispered as she stroked my cheek. Her blue eyes are soft and full of love.

"Glitter in the sky, mama? Isn't that the wish of fairytales and magic?" I whisper back. She always said we needed to be quiet when we talk about places outside home. That my father won't like it. She smiles, revealing two dimples.

"You will experience so much magic when you are much older, my sweet Nora. The world is so much bigger than the tiny kingdom of Chatis."

Now, looking at the glitter in the sky, the starlight speckled in the black, I can almost feel the warmth of her touch. My hand finds my cheek, remembering the last time her fingers brushed my skin. A small smile curls at the edges of my lips as I faintly smell the lavender and vanilla scent of my mother. How I wish she was here now, to prevent this forced marriage. She wouldn't let me do it alone. She would have been enjoying this journey with me. A moment that should be filled with excitement and love is met with fear and loneliness.

The lonely king and his lonely daughter.

We were never destined to find happiness. I only hope that the rumors about Tobias's desires and shortcomings are only just that, petty gossip spreading throughout the kingdom about the Crown Prince. I wonder what he is truly like. Whether he inherited his father's muscular stature or his mother's soft features. Whether he was still brought down by pain and fear, or if he somehow found happiness in this world.

I won't have to wonder much longer.

Glancing back through the window, I feel the slight chill of the wind on my face. I lift my hand and peel the gauzy curtain back further. Just past the trees I can faintly make out the tips of the pearly white palace I vaguely remember from when I was a child.

The capital palace radiated warmth and clarity. The guards and staff smiling as they go about their day. The sunlight filtering through the many windows, illuminating the walls, reflecting off the white marble posts and floors. I don't remember much from my visit as a child, but I do remember how it felt like a refreshing place to be, like you could take a clean breath, nothing like the palace I called home. Everything was white and bright courtesy of the marble and glass that made up the entire palace.

This will be my home now. I will wake up to bright rooms and happy guards. I'll start each day smiling and end it the same. I have to believe that a better life is waiting for me at the end of this journey. A life where I fall in love with my betrothed. A life where I am crowned a queen. A life where I get to bring a child into the world. A child I will love and care for. A child that I will never allow to meet my father. A child who will never be given the chance to feel anything other than happiness. I have to believe it.

I have to.

I sigh as I lean back against the cushion, the curtain fluttering closed. As my thoughts wander, picturing what my life will be like in Noterra, the carriage comes to a hard stop. I brace myself against the window as my body is jerked to the side. I nearly fall off the cabin bench and have to grip the back cushion to steady myself. Pain radiates down my spine, where I am sure my father left a bruise.

Once I am certain we are staying still, I pull open the curtains and peer out. I see nothing but darkness where the road should be. Voices carry, but I can hardly make out the words or to whom they belong to. I can hear Ser Danieas speaking to someone, someone whose voice is low, their words hard to discern. I hear a loud shout and I jump, my heart races as if I was hit by electricity, my hands clammy. Taking shaky breaths, I stick my head further out of the window, looking for a familiar face.

"Hello? What is the meaning of this?" I call out into the night with as much strength as I can muster but get no reply. The silence is telling, and my heartbeat quickens. "Ser Danieas?" I call out again, my voice cracking as I feel sweat bead along my hairline.

I wonder if there was an animal or tree in the way? Surely, he wouldn't stop unless it was needed, but there was another voice, and a shout...

Without allowing myself time to think, I open the cabin door and step out onto the rocky floor below. Forgetting I had taken off my shoes, the frosted rocks come as a surprise. A chill runs through my spine as the eerily quiet darkness swallows my surroundings.

It's just a little darkness, Elaenor.

Taking a step towards the front of the carriage, I gather every ounce of bravery I have. One foot in front of the other, I have to keep reminding myself. I hold my breath as I step around the cabin. Nearing the front, where two delusional horses stand, I see no one.

"Hello? Ser Danieas?" I call out as I make my way up to the horses. I give the brown one a small pat as I walk towards the front of their large bodies. Glancing down the road, I can barely make out a dark lump in the center, just a few feet away. With only the moonlight to illuminate the object, I can't make out what it is. Maybe it's a boulder? I turn in a full circle, looking for any sign of the guard who was at my service, but come up empty. The chill returns and I rub my hands up and down my bare arms, hoping to generate enough warmth to keep the shivers at bay. I bite my bottom lip, attempting to curb the panic building in my chest.

I'm half tempted to climb back into the carriage and wait for someone to come or for Ser Danieas to return, but a part of me feels that no one will. Part of me knows that I am once again alone. *Maybe he saw something?* I think, knowing full well he would never leave his post unless he was unable to maintain it.

My eyes find the lump in the road again and I take a deep breath. Maybe whatever it is, prevented him from continuing on the journey, it does seem to be blocking the road. Slow, terrified steps bring me closer to the object of my confusion, the cold air causing me to shiver uncontrollably. It's nearly the middle of summer, but the air is still icy at night. As I near the dark lump, it starts to take shape. It could be a dead animal or possibly a tree trunk, but it doesn't seem large enough, and it's in the middle of the road.

When I am close enough to see what truly lies in front of me, a terrified scream escapes my mouth. My kingsguard lays wounded at my feet. Light green eyes wide open in fear, blood pooling beneath his chest where a deep gash sits, the warm liquid tickling the tips of my toes. Gurgling noises erupt from his mouth as he fights to breathe through the blood that is slowly suffocating him.

"Erik, oh my gods, what can I do?" I whisper as I kneel down next to him, my whole body shaking with tremors. I faintly feel the warm blood soaking into my skirt, plastering it to my skin, but I ignore it and focus on stopping his bleeding. He frantically pushes against me with what little strength he has, his face grimacing in pain. I press my hands against the wound on his chest, the blood slipping through my fingers. "Stay still." I beg, my breath coming in short rasps.

"Run." He spits out, fear lacing his strangled voice. With my senses heightened and the terror building within me, I glance around, looking for anything to protect me. I get tunnel vision, everything darkening along my peripherals. Everything in this light looks like a person, like a threat. What am I supposed to do? Grab a horse? I don't even know how to ride. Coming up with no plan and no weapon, I freeze, my hands still pressing on his wound. I don't know where I am or where to go. I don't know how many hours it has been since we left, or what time it was now.

"I don't know what to do." I whisper frantically, my lungs tightening as adrenaline courses through my veins. The snap of a branch to my left makes me flinch and I peer into the thick brush and trees, trying to see what is lurking behind them. "Please be an animal." I whisper, my teeth digging into my lip again.

"Run, *please*." He repeats, blood spilling out over his lips, as I stare into the darkness. A large movement on the tree line, resembling that of a person, was enough to know I needed to get up, which I did.

"I'm so sorry." I whisper. Abandoning Ser Danieas, my feet protest as they meet the forest floor. I try to ignore the shame, the sorrow, drowning me as I think about how I abandoned him. How he will die alone, terrified. I swallow it down, letting the panic and adrenaline fuel me.

The snapping of twigs and rustling of leaves fill my ears as I run at a speed I never knew possible. When the echo of footsteps starts behind me, I push faster knowing I don't have a destination in mind, but fear is pushing me forward. I don't know where I am or what direction Noterra is in, but I know I have to keep running. The faint memory of the tips of a pearly white palace beyond the tree line makes me relieved, knowing I should be going the right way.

The darkness envelops me, and I partially believe that hiding is the best option, but if my *kingsguard* is dying, someone who has been training for moments such as this his whole life, then I am no match to whomever is making me their prey. Whether they know who I am or not, they have to know that precious cargo was on the royal carriage.

As I dodge another tree, my foot gets stuck around a vine, and I fall. Rocks and other foreign matter dig into my shins and knees, slicing their way through my dress and skin. I suppress the cry of pain and quickly roll towards a bush, pressing my body against it. I clamp my hand over my mouth, hoping whoever it is can't hear me breathing as I try to ignore the strange sense of claustrophobia washing over me. It's as if everything, the darkness, the trees, the bushes, are all pushing in on me. Footsteps slow, but I can't make out anything through the trees. I stay still, willing my heart to stop pounding in my ears. When the footsteps dissipate, I release the breath I was holding. I could stay here, behind this bush, all night, or I can try and get to safety. Not that I even have experience regarding safety.

You can do this, Elaenor. I take another deep breath and slip out from behind the greenery. I throw myself back up and take a step just as a rough hand wraps around my arm, pulling me back against his chest. His grip is tight, commanding, and I freeze. *Damnit.* He's silent as we just stand in the darkness. I can hear the soft rustle of the wind in the trees. Feel the soft brush of the air against my skin. It's as if time stood still for a few seconds. Neither of us are moving. Neither of us are speaking. My throat dries, my pulse quickens, and I feel as if every breath passes through blades in my lungs.

"Who are you?" I whisper. He provides no answer. I feel a sharp kick to the back of my knee, and I crumble to the ground with a wince, landing on my hip. Slow, steady steps make their way around me. A predator circling his prey. His breathing is labored. Either from exhaustion or adrenaline, I can't tell. My eyes fixate on the dirty boots shining in the moonlight that are inches away from me. I fight against the tears burning behind my eyes and the urge to cry. I take a slow, calming breath before I allow my eyes to travel upwards in the darkness.

Hovering above me is the face of a man I do not know. His black cloak assists the darkness in covering the majority of his features, but his tan skin shines through revealing a pointed nose and dimpled chin. I search his cloak for an emblem, anything to provide insight into what kingdom he belongs to, but it is just as bare as my legs. I pull my dress down, from where it has gathered around my thighs as his sickening smile causes my heart to race. My mind wanders as I process the vile things I'm sure he has planned for me.

He kicks my legs apart and I struggle to scoot away from him. The rocks are digging into my palms and back as I try to pull my body out of his grasp. He kneels down in between my legs, and I feel a sharp pain in my thigh. I can't fight the scream forming on my lips as it echoes throughout the woods, tears instantly running down my cheeks. Glancing down I see the tip of a dagger pressing deep into my flesh, and I still. I watch as it slides further into my skin. I bite my lip to hold back the screams of pain. Blood falls down the side of my leg like a waterfall and I question whether or not he hit an artery.

"Please leave me be." I whisper, not wanting to raise my voice, as I was sure the lump in my throat would prevent it. A low growl escapes his lips as he leans down, his body weight pushing my back against the hard ground. One hand grips the earth right next to my face, the other slides the dagger up my body until it rests at the hollow of my neck. I swallow and feel the edge press ever so slightly, breaking through the delicate skin. The warmth of my blood dripping down the side of my thigh is a stark contrast to the icy air and I shudder, pain radiating down my leg.

"Where is the fun in that?" He chuckles. His voice is deep, and rough. His accent is thick, and not one I can place. Maybe a northerner? He smells of ash and brimstone. Like death and fire.

"Who are you?" I ask again, my eyes fixate on his, a deep brown that is almost black. His face is older, maybe the same age as my father. The lack of scars on his tan skin gives me an inkling that he may be of a noble line, one that hasn't required his services in war. His dirty and rumpled clothing is an indication that he hasn't showered in a few days. That and the slight musky scent filling my nose. Enough to make me want to gag.

"My identity is none of your concern, *princess*." His eyes focus on mine as I see the desire filling his brain. He searches my face, looking for a reaction as his teeth clamp down onto his bottom lip.

"You know who I am?" I croak in shock, again, my voice failing me. My breathing is ragged as I try to stay strong, trying to ignore the blinding pain coming from my thigh. Trying to ignore the feel of his legs against mine, the hollow pit in my stomach that is filling with bile and nausea. He nods as his eyes trail back down my chest, stomach, and then my bare thighs. I already know his plans. "Please don't do this. Just let me go." I plead, desperation fueling my emotion-choked voice. "I have money, I can pay you well. Just let me go."

My father warned me as a child of the predators in the forest who belong to no kingdom and answer to no man. I didn't believe him at first, I thought he was just trying to scare me into submission. That he was trying to prevent me from leaving the confines of the castle. But now I see that he may have been telling the truth. He must be one of them. He might have others coming to his aid, or hiding behind the trees where I can't see them. That thought only makes my heart race faster.

"Your money is not what I want." He whispers as I feel something hard pressing against my leg, something that feels *softer* than the blade. *Oh gods.* He shoves the dagger into his waistband, his fingers brush my neck and then follow the same course his eyes previously did, only stopping once it reached the spot between my abdomen and his goal. I shiver against his touch, against the feel of his fingers sliding in between my breasts down to my navel. His eyes fill with excitement as he licks his lips, a small groan rumbling in his throat. Gripping the edge of my dress with his hand, I can hear the sound of the fabric ripping as he sharply pulls it away from my body.

"Why are you doing this? Please." I cry out, attempting to stall him as much as possible while a plan forms inside my scattered brain. My hands are pushing against his chest in an attempt to get him off of me, but his weight is too much. Tears spring from my eyes, trailing down the sides of my face as I struggle to break free, my thigh cramping with every movement.

"I've never had a princess before." He whispers as his hand progresses down towards a place no man has ever been before. I freeze as his fingers touch me, torture me. His fingers find the place no one has ventured. The place I have been so careful to safeguard. I shut my eyes as I try to think of any way I can get out of this, any way I can end this before it has a chance to progress. *I'm going to have to fight.* I open my eyes again and quickly glance at the dagger in his waistband. I won't have the time to grab it, but I may not have any other options, not if I want to get out of this alive. His eyes watch mine, almost like he's daring me to move.

The second I do, his free hand reaches for my neck, gripping it with all his strength. Feeling the crush of my throat against his fingers, I struggle to breathe. I scratch at any part of his skin I come in contact with, looking for anything to make him stop, desperation and panic fueling my search. I feel my nails slicing through his hands, drawing blood. He shifts above me, the sound of his pants sliding down, and I fight to look away as I don't want to see what happens next. He holds my head in place with his grip on my neck, forcing me to look at him, my hands wrapped around his wrist. There is nothing I can do to stop him.

"Please don't do this." I cough out as the grip on my neck tightens, begging for him to spare me. Begging in a way that I always promised myself I wouldn't. "Please."

"Stay still. I'll make it quick." He groans as he rips what's left of my underwear off, the cotton disappearing on the dark forest floor.

This is it. This is the end. This is the easy way out. This is my chance to be free. If he just kills me–

"Jeremiah!" Another male voice breaks through the trees as the man above me stills and I jump from the volume.

"Please! Please help me!" I cry out, struggling against my captor who is effortlessly holding me to the ground. The man breaks through the trees and makes his way towards us. He's wearing the same cloak as the other man, with nothing identifying his house. They are working together, but maybe he has something against these actions, maybe he'll help. Or maybe he'll do worse, but I take my chances. Relief blossoms, breaking through the fear as I hope I am seconds away from being saved. "Please, Ser!" I cry out and kick at the frozen man on top of me. He stomps over, his face hidden in the darkness.

"Quiet!" The other man snaps in irritation as his foot slams into the side of my head. Darkness is all I see.

Chapter Five

I can feel my head rocking up and down as he carries me, each jostle sending shooting pain throughout my skull. My arms are dangling down his back, his hand firmly holding onto my thighs to balance me over his shoulder. My eyes open slightly, and I see the forest floor softly illuminated from the moonlight. I can feel the sharp, aching pain the boot left behind as it creeps up the side of my temple and behind my eyes. Small droplets of blood flinging from my face, disappearing into the black dirt below. My thigh is numb, as if it has been soaking in an ice bath. It makes me wonder if there is damage to a nerve, I can only hope that isn't the case. The overwhelming scent of ash and sweat fills my nose, making me want to gag, but I swallow it down.

The second man called my attacker Jeremiah. The only reason they let me know their true identity is probably because they are going to kill me, or make sure I never return to civilization. Either that, or they are stupid. I am desperately hoping for the latter. Fear that should be coursing through my veins is dormant, hiding. I feel numb, empty. I have no fight. I have no way to protect myself. I have a sour taste in my mouth, my pulse rivaling the lump for space in my throat. Is this what defeat feels like? Helplessness?

I've never learned to defend myself; I can't stand my own against one male, much less two. Being helpless has become a personality trait. I have never been given the chance to fight, against my father, against female oppression, and now against them. I used to watch the guardsmen train, their bodies slick with sweat as they clash swords and connect fists to skin. I could almost taste the adrenaline, the desire. Not for the men, but for the power that came with having the ability to defend oneself. I used to practice in my room, punching the air or pillows I strapped to the backs of chairs, but I knew I wasn't doing it right. I was weak, nothing more than an annoyance, rather than a threat. And these men know that. They know the only chance I have to defend myself is dependent on luck, and that isn't something that has ever been on my side.

They are both quiet as they move through the forest with ease, as if they could see through the suffocating darkness. I have no idea where they are taking me or what their plans are. Are they going to just outright kill me? Are they going to allow each other to have some fun prior? Am I going to be held for ransom? What is their end goal? While I may not be able to physically defend myself, I am not above testing my psychological skills. Maybe I can *convince* them to let me go. Convince them that I am better alive than dead. If they can get money and riches, or even some other political advantage with my release, it might be worth it for them. It *has* to be worth it.

I can't tell how long we've been walking, or in what direction, as they murmur to themselves. Time seems to be moving at an unnatural pace, with this night seemingly lasting forever. Their footsteps are even, but Jeremiah is clearly breathing heavy, straining against my weight. I only wish I had gained a few pounds prior, maybe then he wouldn't be able to traipse around with me on his shoulder. I force my breath to remain even, hoping my pulse quiets down enough so I can hear them over the pounding in my ears.

"It was too easy." Jeremiah chuckles. I can feel his laugh vibrate through my body as he adjusts me with a groan. I only hope he tires at some point, maybe then I'll have a better chance.

"Are you sure it's her? The king has brown hair, hers seems too dark." The other one speaks, his voice lacking the hint of exhaustion that Jeremiah has. They are silent for a moment; the only sounds are their footsteps on the forest floor and the pounding of my pulse. "Do you remember what her mother looked like?"

"No, I don't, but this girl had a carriage full of luggage and was arriving the same day they said she would. There is no way it couldn't be her." His fingers tighten on my thighs as he speaks, making me nauseous.

I bite the inside of my cheek. I want to rip every finger off his damn hands.

"She could be a diversion; she could be someone sent in her place." If I hadn't already confirmed my identity to Jeremiah, I might have had a chance at lying. I need to find something else I can barter, maybe I can convince them to take me to a different country, one I could start a new life in. I could disappear, I don't have to be the princess. Whatever they wanted of me I would do, just to get out of this. There has to be a reason why they chose me, other than my gender. They have to want *something*.

They both slow to a stop as an orangey haze spreads through the trees, slightly illuminating our surroundings. I can hear the soft chatter of other men in the distance, talking and laughing. We emerge through the treeline, and everything is bright, as if we are standing next to a firepit. They stand still for a moment, before Jeremiah's body turns and walks away from the direction of the light.

"Put her over there." The second man orders as he walks away from us. Jeremiah takes a couple more steps before sliding me down his body and onto the hard ground with a *thud*. I immediately shoot up, but his sharp hand across my cheek forces me back down where I land on my back with a wince. Black threatens the edges of my vision as I fight against the pain. I push myself up into a sitting position with trembling arms and try to shake my head to clear away the fuzziness.

Jeremiah's hood has fallen off his head, so I can see his shaggy hair and dull brown eyes perfectly with the light from the fire as he crouches down in front of me. His dark eyes are hardened, his skin clean and hairless. He looks ordinary, nothing setting him apart from the rest. I look around and similarly looking men all stand around, their eyes focused on me. Varying degrees of cleanliness spread around the camp, which makes me wonder if they have all come together under this one goal or if they were a group prior? I can feel the blood trickling down my cheek from my hairline as I look back at Jeremiah.

"Please, just let me go." I plead, attempting to keep my voice as even as possible.

"Shut up, princess." He snaps and rises out of his crouched position. I stay seated on the ground as I look around, the backs of my bare legs pressing into the cold mud. The only structure in the clearing is the fire pit, with the men all standing around, there has to be at least seven of them. No tents or horses, which makes me wonder if this is their actual camp or just a pitstop on the way. The ashy smell is emanating from the fire pit as I realize it isn't just wood they are burning. I can just make out something fleshy before I tear my gaze away, nausea pooling in my stomach.

My eyes blur as I fight back the tears and swallow against the lump forming in my throat. I try to pull my dress down to cover myself up, but the shreds remaining aren't enough and I am nearly completely exposed. I situate them to cover in between my legs, leaving my legs bare. Blood is steadily pouring out of the gash in my thigh, deep enough that I can see tendons and muscle through the blood. I place my hand on it and try to apply as much pressure as I can. I grit my teeth as I exhale against the pain. *Gods, that's deep.*

I take slow, calming breaths as I leave my fingers tightly pressed against the wound, fighting the screams lodging my throat. The sour taste in my mouth is replaced with a dry coppery tang that seems to coat my tongue like mud. I see the second man returning with ropes and I start to back away, my free arm straining against my weight as it digs into the mud, my breath nothing more than short gasps. The fire illuminates his figure, and he looks like he could be Jeremiah's twin. They have the same brown hair and dark eyes, same perfectly shaven face.

"Please, please don't do this." I cry out. He bends down and pulls my legs, sliding me closer to him. I fall onto my back and kick out, trying to get away, but he easily deflects my limbs. Rocks and dirt scrape up my back and legs as he situates me between his feet. He kneels down onto my shins, and I yell out as the compression makes it feel like my bones will snap in half. Starbursts explode behind my eyelids, and I bite my lip to keep the screams at bay. I try to move my legs to lessen the tension, but they are stuck. I can feel my thigh pulsing as the pressure on the wound is removed.

"Hold her down." He snaps as Jeremiah comes from behind and grabs my shoulders, pressing me into the wet dirt. The second man roughly wraps the ropes around my wrists, his eyes fixed on mine. I can feel the rough fibers slicing into my skin as he tightens them. He knots my hands together, leaving a bit of rope dangling out, probably to use as a leash.

"Please don't do this. I have money, I can pay you well." I beg again. He narrows his eyes as he finishes his knot, the movement causing me to wince.

"Your money means nothing to us, princess." The men around us all chuckle loudly as they nod towards me. No doubt amused by the sad little girl in front of them who is just moments from either being raped or murdered. I glare at them, but I'm sure I look just as menacing as a baby bird.

My captor rises and walks to the others, where they quickly become engrossed in a hushed conversation. Jeremiah stays crouched behind me, preventing me from making a run for it, not that I could get far. I can't hear what the other men are saying, but it looks as if they are planning something. Jeremiah is squinting in their direction, trying to hear just as much as I am.

"Why are you doing this?" I ask him, but he refuses to meet my eyes. "I'm a child. I am somebody's *child*. Please." I whisper. He clears his throat, but still doesn't look at me.

"That is exactly why we are doing this." His voice is rough, monotone. No hint of emotion or care.

"I don't have to be. Please, I'll disappear. I'll go anywhere. I don't want this life anyway." His eyes meet mine briefly, contemplating.

"You would give up a life of riches and royalty?" I nod. "That easy?" I nod again, and he just snorts.

"I don't want to be in Noterra. I don't want to marry the prince. I don't want any of this. I'll disappear, I promise. Just tell me what you want from me." I admit. His lips press into a thin line. It's the truth. This is the last thing I want.

The other man walks back over, the rest of them dispersing into the trees aside from Jeremiah. He bends down and grips the remaining rope, pulling me to my feet. I wince against the coarse threads cutting into my skin with the pressure as I stumble to regain balance, my leg almost giving out from my wound.

"Please." I cry as I lean to the left, alleviating the tension on my right leg.

"She said she would disappear, that she doesn't want to get married." Jeremiah interjects. His voice is softer than it has been, his eyebrows furrowed as if he's contemplating my words.

"And you believe her?" He pulls me against his chest, his arm wrapping around my stomach and his fingers splaying out over my mostly bare abdomen. He makes soft, slow circles against my hip with his other hand, and I fight against the desire to flinch. The feeling, it's intimate as if he's a lover touching his wife, not a savage holding a young girl captive. I dig my broken nails into my palms, not even registering as they slice through the delicate skin, joining the collection of half-moon scars.

"I do. We could use her to our advantage." I will my eyes to soften, false appreciation for the man who was seconds away from raping me. The man holding me against him just laughs, his body jostling. Fear finally shivers down my spine, breaking through the numb exterior of my mind. My pulse quickens and I can feel sweat beading on my hairline, either from the adrenaline making its way through my system or the pain that is constant.

"It's not worth the risk. She'll run the second she has a chance too."

"You don't know that." Jeremiah deflects, his hands moving to his hips.

"I won't, please. You can take me anywhere, I'll disappear, change my name. I'll never come back here." I will my voice to stay steady as I hold Jeremiah's gaze. His eyes soften slightly before he steps back and shakes his head, a deep chuckle erupting behind me, tickling the nape of my neck.

No.

"Watch the camp, Jeremiah. We won't be long." I glance around hoping one of the men will save me, prevent this, but I know that's unlikely. As my eyes drift over the clearing I see that they are all still gone. I can feel the bile rising in my throat as I try to think of anything that could get me out of this, but my mind is blank.

My father cursed me, doomed me, by not teaching me how to protect myself. He thought it was to protect himself without even thinking of the horrors that awaited me past our borders. He must have known enough to keep me hidden, but he is the reason this is happening. His selfishness, his greed, his inability to be a parent. He will be the cause of my death tonight, and I'll be damned if I don't come back and haunt him.

Without another word, he drags me past a silent Jeremiah and back into the trees, leaving the campsite behind. His hand is firm against my upper arm, his other hand holding the rope attached to my wrists, and I trip trying to match his quickened pace. The darkness envelopes us again as he pulls me deeper and deeper into the trees, the light from the fire all but gone.

"Are you going to kill me?" I whisper, tripping over invisible rocks, my feet slicing open against the rough ground. I wince with every forced step, my teeth digging into my bottom lip. He chuckles in response, sending a chill down my spine.

"Not yet." We walk for a few more moments, narrowly darting tree trunks. It's so dark I can barely make out the cloaked figure in front of me, much less any bushes or trees. He must spend a lot of time out here if he knows where we are going. He comes to a stop, and I glance around but see nothing besides the vague shapes of tree trunks.

The moon is bright, but it does little to illuminate the area after seeping through the canopy of the forest. He turns towards me, his eyes hungrily searching my body. He sucks on his teeth as his eyes trail down to my exposed legs. The tears return and I try to steady my breathing, blinking away the burn.

"Hm." He says, both as a laugh and contemplation. "So many options." He walks around me slowly, circling me like prey while fidgeting with his bottom lip. I take deep breaths to keep the nausea at bay, but I am so close to puking all over him. I lean to my left again, trying to alleviate pressure on my thigh.

"Please. I will do whatever you want." My voice cracks and I take another deep breath, trying to breathe around my heart as it seems to be lodged in my throat.

"I know you will." His voice grows deeper, huskier, as he comes back to stand in front of me, a satisfied grunt escaping his thin lips. I fight the urge to gag at the sound.

"I will disappear. I will go to any random country or continent. I never wanted this." I will my voice to stay even.

"I don't believe you." His eyes narrow, brows furrowing.

"My father has held me captive my entire life. I have never been free. All I *want* is freedom, and if I marry the prince I will only be shackled to another king. I just want to break out of this cycle." I admit. Honesty is the only thing I have to give. He doesn't speak, he just stares. "I will do anything you want. I will become whoever you want. I will completely disappear."

"And if I told you to become our spy? To marry the prince and do our bidding?"

GLASS AND BONE

"I don't want to marry him."

"You either die or become our spy. Pick one." His voice is little more than a snarl.

"Please, if I marry him, he'll be just as bad as you. Send me away. I don't know what you are trying to prevent or what you are trying to accomplish, but I won't be a party to it. I will disappear. *Please*." My throat cracks as I speak, and he just shakes his head.

He lunges down grabbing my injured leg and pulling it out from underneath me, knocking me to the ground. My back slams onto the hard dirt, knocking the breath out of my lungs, and he's on top of me before I can think of what to do next. My head is pounding, and I fight against the shadows creeping along the edges of my vision as my chest burns, and I take a ragged inhale.

"Stop!" I scream as I try to push him off me. Panic takes over, spreading through my veins like fire. His fist makes contact with my face and temporarily stuns me. I can taste the blood on my tongue as my teeth slice through my cheek.

"Don't resist." I can hear the clinking of his belt as he pulls down his pants. Evidence of his arousal is clear, and I force myself to look away. I push against his chest with my bound hands, clawing at any patch of skin I can find, but he's too strong and holds me down with just one of his arms against my neck. I thrash and push, bucking my hips in a desperate attempt to get free, but his strength doesn't falter. I become rabid, moving anyway I can to get away.

He's too strong, save your strength.

"Get off me! You don't know what this will do!" I cry out. He presses his chest against mine, his mouth right next to my ear. His hot breath tickles me as he inhales slowly, and I jerk my face away. His tongue flicks out and runs along the column of my neck and I try to squirm away from him but get nowhere.

"I know exactly what this will do." He whispers, his nose trailing across my cheek before he presses his rough lips against mine. A shiver runs through me, and I grit my teeth. He sharply bites my bottom lip, pulling it hard before he releases it. He sits back before getting up on his knees and grabbing my thighs, pulling them apart. He adjusts himself in between them before stilling. "Look at me." His eyes fix on mine, waiting until I focus. "Look at me!" It's hard to keep my eyes open. The pain from the bruises and cuts marring my body and the delirium from blood loss is clouding my vision. I kick out again, my legs going numb.

"Please." I whisper, weakening by the second. Begging one last time for him to release me. A smile spreads across his face as his eyes leave mine to look in between my legs.

With a single thrust, he buries himself inside me. I scream out as the blinding pain courses through me. I can feel my flesh ripping from his touch again and again. I kick out at anything, but there is nothing around besides dirt and rocks. My bound arms stretch and can feel the friction of dry skin against dry skin as his pelvis slams into me. It burns and I can't do anything to get it to stop.

"Stop!" I scream as his grip on my thighs tighten before he slips out of me. He flips me over so I am on my stomach. His hand finds the back of my neck as he bashes my head into the dirt, rocks grinding into my skin, before he thrusts himself inside me again. His pace quickens as I cry, his breathing becoming labored, *excited*. His fingers are tight against my neck, crushing my windpipe. I fight to inhale clean air but choke against the dust and debris entering my mouth instead.

Desperation and defeat fight for their place in my mind, coating my skin like grease. I try to crawl away, but his hold is unforgiving. He starts to groan, and I slam my eyes shut, digging my nails into the ground waiting for this to be over. I can feel them cracking against the rough forest floor, the mud and dirt caking beneath them. The fullness, the pain, it's too much. *It's too much.* I grit my teeth, willing myself to focus on anything else.

Focus on the stars, the sun, the future I'll never have. Focus on bioluminescent green eyes and the sound of Scarlett's laugh. Focus on my mother, her smile and gentle touch. I can almost hear her, telling me that everything will be okay, but I don't believe her. She isn't here to protect me.

His loud groaning fills my ears and I flinch against the sound. He thrusts one more time before he stills inside me as he finishes, as he *ruins* me. I can feel his seed emptying deep inside me, dripping out down my thighs. He pulls himself out, his hands leaving my neck. My hips and stomach fall to the ground and I kick out, trying to crawl away from him.

"Get away from me." I cry out through my sobs. I struggle to slide away as his hand grips my ankle, pulling me back towards him, my nails gouging lines in the dirt. He flips me onto my back again and leans over me. His eyes are filled with satisfaction, a lazy smile creeping over his face. He reaches between my legs, and I freeze, but he just unsheathes his dagger from his pants.

Sliding it up my body, much like Jeremiah did, he rests it on the hollow of my neck. The tears have stopped running down my cheeks and I feel numb. Everything is over. He's ruined me, and more than likely going to kill me. All I can feel is the pain his assault caused, both physical and emotional. My limbs burn, my vision hazy. I just want this to be over.

My life flashes before my eyes as if I am looking through a book of paintings. I see my mom's outstretched hand and her soft smile, beckoning me to join her. It would be easy to just let go. It would be easy to just let him kill me, but life has never been easy for me. I won't give him the satisfaction of being my end.

"Thank you for your sacrifice, princess." He smiles, if I didn't know any better his smile would seem inviting, genuine, but this man is a monster.

"Who are you?" I croak out, my eyes meeting his.

"Aleksander." His voice is curt, emotionless as he answers me, wetting his lips with a brief flick of his tongue.

"Why did you do this to me?" I ask, but I know the answer. *Because he can.*

"I wanted to. I also wanted to prevent *them* from attaining their desires." He winks at me, and I swallow the bile forming in my throat. He slides the cold blade across my neck, superficially slicing through my skin, leaving a line of burning flesh. But I ignore it. Just as I ignore everything else that is burning or throbbing. If I focus on it, if I let myself dwell, I won't make it. I won't get out of this.

"Who? Who were you preventing?" I demand, hoping he'll keep answering my questions. He removes the dagger from my neck and sits up with an irritated sigh. I stay still underneath him, my eyes refusing to leave his.

"Noterra. If they win, then we all die. They already took everything from us, we can't let them gain *you*. Gain an *heir* to continue their reign." He scoffs at the thought. From us? Who is he? If he's answering my questions that means he's not intending for me to leave. I swallow again.

"If I don't arrive, they'll find another to take my place." He shrugs.

"Then I'll find her too."

"Who do you and your men belong to, Aleksander?" He shakes his head. "Who are you fighting for?" I yell, but he just rolls his eyes, irritated.

"All in due time, princess." He rises to his feet and fixes his pants before bending down to grab my arms. He is holding the dagger in his right hand, and I realize this is my chance. I kick out at his wrist, and he drops the blade. I lunge forward and try to grab it, but he kicks me out of the way, and I land awkwardly on my shoulder, pain shooting down to my elbow. Abandoning it, he saunters over to me again, his eyes filled with fury.

"I wasn't going to kill you yet, but now you've pissed me off." I suppress the pain and roll onto my back, kicking out again, this time striking the apex of his thighs. He yelps loudly and drops to his knees, his face twisting in pain.

I twist out of the way, grabbing the dagger with my bound hands at the same time. I clamor to my feet and throw myself at him. I feel as the dagger pierces through the back of his neck with little resistance and I nearly faint at the sight of it. Surprise and disgust drying my mouth like chalk. I tighten my grip and still as I hear the gurgling fill his throat. His hands reach behind him, frantically searching for the dagger to hold onto, but he can't get to it. His fingers scratch at my arms, leaving lines of red on my flesh and I fight against the pain clouding my senses.

He starts to sag and lean back against me as he slowly suffocates on his own blood. The taste of copper invades my tongue as blood sprays my face, and I clamp my mouth shut. I push up against him, a scream of frustration letting loose from my lips, but I lose my balance and he lands on top of me. Hot, tangy blood pours out of his neck onto my chest, soaking me in his life's essence while he twitches. I gasp as I absorb his weight and try to get him off of me, but I can't. After a few seconds, he stills completely and the strained breathing stops.

I pull out the dagger and throw it to the side. Using my knees and hands to push him up, I struggle to slide myself out from underneath of him. It takes every bit of energy I have and elicits a loud cry out of my mouth. My heart is beating rapidly, my breathing ragged as I try to understand the last few hours. I scramble away from his body and grab the dagger. Gripping it in one hand and placing it against my wrist. I move the other hand up and down quickly, cutting the rope in between with my shaky hands. Panic bubbles through me, my heart lodged in my throat.

My limbs are vibrating as I absorb everything that has transpired. I can feel the dull ache inside me as the blood and *him* steadily drip down my thighs, an unnecessary reminder that this man just raped me. My head is throbbing, my knees on fire. Once my hands are cut free, I freeze. Before I can even prevent it, burning hot vomit explodes out of my mouth, mixing with the black blood on the forest floor. My tears join in as they stream down my face.

No prince will want me. I'm tarnished, my father will have me killed, if King Evreux doesn't kill me first. Where do I even go from here?

Oh gods.

Cupping my face with my bloody hands I let out a sob. I don't know what to do. I feel a strange sense of electricity coursing through my veins, but the only explanation I can find is adrenaline. Adrenaline because I just *killed* a man. I'll never get that noise, that sight out of my head.

You'll have time to grieve later, Elaenor, get up and run.

I jolt at the sound. The voice filling my head is not my own, but still feels familiar. As if it's a part of me. Taking two slow and steadying breaths, I push the panic down for later.

Just take deep breaths, Elaenor. In and out.

Glancing around frantically, I see the glass arrowhead poking out of Aleksander's pocket, slightly illuminated by the moon. The glass is completely stained crimson as I pull it out of his trousers. A sick combination of my blood and his. I shakily stand up and look down at the disgusting creature laying in a still lump on the forest floor as I shove the arrowhead into what's left of my dress pocket. I bend down and grab the silver dagger, gripping it tightly in my hand.

I can't let this break me. I can't let this be my story. What happens from here on out will either paint me a victim or paint me as someone who is strong and resilient. While I want the latter to be true, all I *feel* is victimized.

Broken.

I fearfully look around, hoping, for once, that I am alone. I listen, trying to hear any movement in the trees beyond this small clearing, but it's hard through the pounding in my ears. Once I am certain the other men aren't around or hadn't followed us, I turn the opposite direction of their camp and run.

The trees all look the same, making the world feel as if it is an endless circle that I am just running around. Nothing to guide me, besides the faint moonlight barely illuminating my path, I press on. I have been out of Chatis for less than a day and my rider was murdered, as I am sure he didn't survive, I was raped, and now I am out in the middle of the woods without the faintest idea of where I am, slowly bleeding out from the wound on my thigh, barely any clothing to cover me, and a hoard of savages hiding in the trees.

I murdered a man. He deserved it, but I figuratively and literally have his blood on my hands. How do you even move on from that?

The tears pour down my face as I try to ignore the pain I am in, mixing with the sticky blood that coats my skin. I can feel my thigh burning, the pain growing stronger with each step that turns into a limp.

"What did you get yourself into, Elaenor?" I whisper to myself, breathless.

Keep going.

The voice in my head doesn't startle me this time, it just propels me forward. Exhaustion creeps over me as the adrenaline starts to leave my body. I don't know how long I am running for. My head is throbbing, blood steadily dripping from my ear. I press on, wanting nothing more than to quit and then I see the light.

A break in trees just a few yards away with the sounds of voices and laughter filtering through, carrying me forward. I know I am nowhere near the palace grounds, but I hope the people on the other side are friendly and not an extension of the men I just met. I keep shuffling forward until I am inches from the light and see fire pits scattered right through the break in the trees along with white and silver tents.

White and silver.

Noterran colors.

My eyes begin to cloud over as I feel the blood loss and fading adrenaline weaken me. The desperation coming out of me in broken sobs. I push and push with every ounce of energy I have.

You are so close, just run, Elaenor.

I let the voice in my head fuel me, push me for the last few feet. Running straight through the treeline, my body slams directly into someone who was walking by. A man.

"Woah!" He yells out as he grabs my arms to steady me, holding me close to his chest. My eyes meet his. They resemble the lake I once frequented. A deep blue mirroring the sorrow I feel. They look fearful, confused, shocked.

"Help me." I whisper as I willingly let the blood loss and darkness take me.

Chapter Six

The thunderous clouds overhead threaten rain and lightning, but the sky always looks like this on Chatis. A chill runs down my spine as I embrace the cold air I grew up knowing. Looking around, all I see is rubble and smoke where buildings used to sit. My bare feet pressed to the hard ground, feeling the slicing of my naked skin in their presence. I know what it is I stand on, but I am too afraid to look. Glass and bone.

It's always glass and bone.

The faint roar of laughter and the smell of fire are quick to wake me up. Memories from the forest cause the nausea to creep in, but I swallow back against the lump in my throat. The pain between my legs along with the stab wound on my thigh are radiating throughout my body. My brain is throbbing from the boot that kicked the side of my head. All I feel is the growing wave of pain across my entire body, both physical and emotional, as I catalog the injuries I sustained. As I catalog what I have endured.

I open my eyes to darkness, and I glance around for anything that might give me an idea of where I am. I remember white and silver tents, which are the Noterran colors, but anyone could have these tents. I am just hoping they actually *do* belong to my future home. My back is stiff from the thin cot I was placed on, but I am sure the countless falls and scrapes aren't helping matters much either.

All I see is a small opening in the thick linen of the structure, slightly illuminating the inside of the tent with a golden hue from a fire pit. The voices outside are hushed as they have a quiet conversation. I steady my breathing and strain to make out the words they are speaking over the sound of my beating heart.

"Who is she?" A thick accent almost made the words impossible to understand, nothing giving me an inkling of who these men belong to.

Noterra holds people from across the world as it has the largest ports. It is the only kingdom with so much immigration that there is no native accent. Everyone who is able makes the journey to Noterra to enjoy the freedom, the perfect weather, the simple lifestyle. A lot of Chatisian citizens have found jobs and homes in Noterra as well, escaping the rule of my father. With Noterra's port, any supplies and goods that are headed for Chatis or Rakushia, or any of the kingdoms on this side of the sea, have to travel through Noterra first. That also usually means we got the goods that were left behind by those who picked through them first.

"She's dressed like a noblewoman, or what's left of one." A different man sneers, as the implications of their laughter fill my ears. Anger wells up in my chest and tears threaten to escape, but I blink them away. I can't break down now, I'm not safe yet.

I feel helpless. I don't know who these men are, but the fact that they are finding amusement with my misfortune, is disgusting. Maybe I don't have to tell them who I am, I could start over, I could be anyone. Lying about my identity might work in my favor, might make this group safer. I should have thought about that before I admitted my name to Jeremiah, but I'll just consider it a lesson learned.

"Maybe we'll get a taste for ourselves." They erupt into a chorus of laughter, sending a chill down my spine. I grit my teeth, my nails biting into my palms, as I blink back the angry tears forming behind my eyes.

"Enough." A loud, melodic voice laced with irritation commands as silence spreads. "What is wrong with you? Don't you all have something better to do than sit around and speak about a girl who has clearly been through a lot? Have you not considered that she can *hear* you?" His voice is muffled, farther than the others, but it's strong. He holds some sort of sway or influence over the other men, at least I hope that is the case. He could be their general, or commander.

Swinging my legs over the edge of the cot, I stand up and notice how my bare feet protest to the hard dirt. *Glass and bone.* I can feel every cut on the bottom of my feet as I press them into the ground. Even now, in the tent of an unknown group of men my dream still follows. It's always the same, and I always refuse to look.

I can't help the feeling that I one day won't have a choice.

Shaking my head, I quickly rub my face with my bloody hands, most of it dry and flaking off my skin from the friction. My head spins and I fight the dizziness as I glance down at my thigh to see a bloody bandage tightly wrapped around it. The bandage is soaked through and a steady drip trails down my thigh. It's throbbing against the pressure, and I wince slightly as I put my weight on my leg.

I slowly tiptoe over to the opening of the tent with a limp, trying to use my left leg as much as possible. I peer through the small slit and I can just barely make out the orange and red flames of fire. Every instinct is telling me not to, but I have never been one to follow instructions much less intuition. I take a deep breath before doing what I fear could possibly end badly.

I grip an edge of the canvas and pull the tent open to see at least ten men circling around the pit. All similar in age and size, all dirty and covered in a collection of fresh wounds and old scars. They wear mostly beige cotton clothes with muddy boots. No sigil, cloaks, or armor. Scouts, perhaps? *Or criminals.*

They turn to look at me simultaneously in silence, and I fight the urge to step back. I scan their faces, not a single one offering so much as a word or emotion to decipher. If their plans are to continue what the other men started, I need to know now so I can attempt to flee, or fight, not that I'd be very good at either in my current condition.

The crunch of boots meeting the ground to my left makes me jump as I whip my head over to see a young man not even two feet from me. He's tall enough to tower over me by at least a foot, and I am fairly tall for a woman. His pale golden hair falls in waves around his crystal blue eyes stopping right above his shoulders, with half of it tied up with leather to keep it out of his face. His soft, but angular features are beautiful. His broad shoulders straining against his white tunic and overcoat. He looks like a painting. This has to be the man I ran into when I crossed the tree line.

I meet his confused gaze as he stares at the condition of my clothing, anger causing his hands to ball up into fists and his nostrils to flare. Whether the anger is from my appearance, or he is just a naturally aggressive man, I do not know. I nervously attempt to tuck my unruly hair behind my ears as I take a small step back into the safety of the tent, my hand still clutching the fabric.

"Who did this to you?" He finally speaks, his voice even and loud, slicing through any other noise as he asks the question I'm sure is causing him confusion. I swallow as the uncomfortable gazes of the men linger. I look around at them before casting my gaze down to the ground. I drop the tent fabric and tighten my hands into a fist. My fingernails dig into my palms as I try to relax and breathe through the panic that seems to never dissipate, through the ever-present lump in my throat.

"I'm not sure, Ser. I only got their names. Aleksander and Jeremiah." I manage to whisper, my voice barely above a croak. It's mostly the truth, I really don't know anything else.

"Formalities are unnecessary." He responds, almost in amusement, his eyes lightening before flicking to my legs. "You're injured fairly badly." I instinctively wrap my hands around my stomach as the painful chill returns, causing me to shudder. Without asking, he shrugs off his brown overcoat and wraps it around me. I don't question it, mostly because I relish the idea of being covered, both for warmth and due to my indecency.

His hands linger on my shoulders, his face close enough to where I can feel his hot breath fan across my forehead. I shudder again, this time not from the cold, but from the proximity of him. His coat is warm and well kept, his face clean shaven and free of scars, the faint scent of spring air and sweet grass fills my nose. He looks familiar, but I can't place it. It's almost as if we've met before. I can tell he is of some stature due to his clothing and cleanliness, but there are many clans and noble houses between Chatis and Noterra, there is no way to know which one he and his men belong to, but it is plausible he is a nobleman or a Lord.

"You are safe now, none of these men will hurt you." He says softly as I gaze into his eyes, reminding me of the ocean I dream to visit with specs of black. So familiar yet new.

"Who are you?" I manage to whisper, a playful smile tugs at the corners of his mouth. He releases my shoulders and steps back, ignoring the crowd of men watching our every move.

"Theo." He answers and then gestures towards me, holding out his hand dramatically, asking for a handshake. "And you are?" I don't feel safe enough to let them know who I am. I am known across the kingdoms as the fictional princess, no one actually knowing of my existence, besides Tobias and his father. Being confined to palace walls didn't help that rumor much. That anonymity is helpful, as only a few know my name. The prospect of starting over brings the first bit of relief I've felt all night.

"Nora." I say hesitantly. Nora is the nickname my mother used to call me, adopting it as my persona now only feels right, but his questioning eyes implies he knows I am lying. I ignore his outstretched hand and he eventually drops it, crossing his arms in front of him. His skin twitches as the muscles on his forearms contract, briefly exposing thick veins that run along the side.

"Nora. What is it short for? I've heard that name before." His voice is emotionless, accusatory. I swallow and knot my hands together in front of me. He knows who I am without me even saying it. I can tell by his gaze. I contemplate using a different name, but something about him is telling me not to. He knows who I am, he just needs confirmation.

"Elaenor." I whisper. His eyes flash at the recognition of my name before he rolls his lips.

"You're the princess." He says flatly, which does nothing but make my skin crawl. I pull my bottom lip in between my teeth, biting down hard enough to make my eyes water. My pulse is beginning to quicken again as I look back towards the other men, the never-ending nausea blooming in my stomach.

"Holy shit." One of the men by the fire mutters as they all just sit there, eyes wide open, confused, and shocked. I barely manage a nod as I turn back to Theo and his eyes come to meet mine. Unsure of his motives, I tighten the coat around me. I'm assuming Theo can sense the fear on me as he quickly holds his hands up in reassurance. He takes a step towards me as I instinctively take a step back.

"You are safe here, princess, I assure you. These men," He motions to the men around the fire, who are still staring at me with open mouths. I want nothing more than to walk over and force their mouths shut, but fear has me frozen in place. His voice softens, speaking to me as if I was a wounded animal or a scared child. I guess I am both. "These men are the citywatch of Noterra. You have our protection."

He is not a threat to you.

The strange voice whispers into my head, followed by a short spark of electricity. I was *right* about the tents. Relief washes over me and I allow the tears that have been threatening to spill over to finally escape. My breathing is ragged as I feel the pain and emotion coursing through my body. I'm exhausted. I'm terrified.

But I am also safe, or as close to it as I can be.

"I don't know where I am. I don't know what to do." I sputter, letting the feelings take over me, finally letting my body have control. I bury my face in my hands as I try to steady my breathing.

"Go." Theo snaps. After a few brief seconds, the shuffle of boots and grumbles from the men fade into the distance as they make their way into the tents around us.

Warm arms wrap around my shoulders, and I flinch, but I let him guide me in front of the fire. I take a seat next to the flames and instantly embrace the heat they offer. The exhaustion is ravaging through my body as I shake uncontrollably. Theo's hands leave my shoulders as he takes a seat next to me, turning so he faces me directly. His soft, ocean eyes are filled with worry, his brows wrinkled, as he tries to reassure me.

"You have nothing to fear anymore, princess." He whispers as he pulls my hands away from my face. "I'll take you to the palace, they've been waiting for you." I stare into his eyes and watch as an emotion I can't quite place flashes across. Maybe relief?

"How did you know where I would be?" I whisper, distrust and hesitance filling my voice. How could they know I was missing so quickly?

"You were supposed to arrive a few hours ago." He answers. A few hours have passed already? "We were camped out here when a rider from court came and said you were late. We were set to head to Chatis and begin our search in the morning if you hadn't made it to the palace yet, but you found us first." He smiles and brushes a loose curl out of my face. I jerk away from the touch and his hand recedes. The idea of his fingers brushing my skin causes conflicting emotions. Panic and *desire*? Not desire like lust, but desire for comfort. Desire for a gentleness I've never known. He gives me a sad and knowing smile as he threads his fingers together, resting his forearms on his knees.

"Why are the citywatch camped out in the forest so far from court?" I ask, curious as to where these men are going. It's not normal for so many of them to be away from the palace, leaving it unguarded.

"There are some rumors floating around of another kingdom threatening to invade. Not that they'll survive against us. We were sent down to secure our borders and this was just a stop along the way. Half of these men are to be stationed on the border of Chatis and Noterra, not that there is any fear your father would attack us, however if he hears about this, he may feel differently." Leaning back on his stool, his eyes glance down at the blood staining my clothing and skin. I press my legs together, attempting to hide as much of myself as I can. He looks away awkwardly, his eyes briefly moving to the flames.

"I assure you; my father will have no remorse for the pain I have endured tonight. He doesn't care about my protection." I say softly, hearing his last words to me echoing in my head.

"Your life will be filled with disappointments and men who will do anything possible to ruin you. The way I have treated you thus far is the same treatment you will get anywhere else."

"That can't possibly be true, princess. He is your father. He is a king. It is his duty to protect his heirs." His voice is harsh, filled with disgust. I shake my head and look down at my hands. Dirt and scrapes have turned my once pale hands indistinguishable from that monster, the dried blood flaking off. I rub them on the shredded remains of my dress and fight against the lump in my throat. I take a deep, slow breath, trying to relax, but I fail.

"I am not the heir. He has never been a true father to me, just a symbol. As soon as my mother died, he stopped caring about my well-being and spent his free time bedding the maidens of Chatis." I blink away the tears as I rub at my hands even harder, scraping off any dried blood and scabs that have formed. My breathing is quick, ragged, my voice wavering. Theo's hands are soft and reassuring as he wraps them around my wrists, stopping me from picking at my skin. Fresh blood pools on my palms as he twists my wrists, so my hands are facing up. His brows pinch together as he looks at the wounds.

"It won't be that way in Noterra, I promise. You will be loved." He whispers and releases his grip, leaving my wrists cold. I quickly pull my arms against me, wrapping them around my stomach.

"I don't think they'll want me anymore." I whisper, gazing into his eyes and trying to convey my sorrow. He exhales as his jaw hardens and his eyebrows furrow. He looks down at his own hands, picking off any blood that got on him. He's quiet for a moment before he speaks again.

"It would be impossible for them to not want you." Admiration flickers across his eyes but is quickly replaced with resolve. He looks up at me, wiping his hands on his trousers. "Can you tell me what you went through? I can see some of the injuries, but without a proper mender there was no way for us to attend to them." I swallow, trying to suppress the lump that is threatening my voice as I prepare to share the torture I endured.

"I left Chatis when the sun was high with one of the palace guards–"

"Just one?" I nod, his lips pressing into a thin line. He tips his chin slightly, urging me to go on.

"I was in the carriage, and then it stopped. I got out to see–" My voice cracks and I try to fight against the memory of his bloody face. I look away from Theo and stare at the warm, comforting flames. "I got out to see and I found him badly injured on the road. He told me to run, and I saw a shadow along the tree line, so I did. I left him behind." I stop, not wanting to share anymore with this man, but the gentleness and patience he has provided so far is foreign and I find myself wanting to trust him.

Hoping that I can trust him.

But I feel as if my naivety is at play here, grasping for any semblance of decency in a person. Theo stays quiet, allowing me a second to breathe and to contemplate. I can't shake the feeling that we've met before, but I feel like I would have remembered him. I *know* I would have remembered him. But the familiarity of his presence is confusing.

"He caught up to me and knocked me down, but before he could do anything, another man appeared." He exhales quietly in relief, his shoulders dropping slightly from released tension, but I quickly look up at him to let him know that wasn't the end. "He kicked me in the head, and I fell unconscious.

When I awoke, we had arrived at a camp with other men. The first man, Jeremiah, put me down and then the other one took me into the woods and–" My voice catches and I bury my face back into my hands, my fingers slipping into my hair and pulling at the strands. Theo wraps me into his chest, and I push his arms away, leaning back. "Please don't touch me." I snap, harsher than I intended.

"Did he rape you, Nora?" I nod and maintain eye contact with him. I relish in the way he says Nora, no one has really called me that since my mother. I hate the comfort I find in it, find in him. He's soft, gentle, familiar, and I hate myself for how my heart is betraying me. "How did you get away?"

"There was a dagger," My voice trails off as I picture the blood pouring onto my chest, shuddering from the memory.

"Did you kill him?" He finally asks after a moment of silence. All I can manage is a weak nod. "Once we get you to the palace, the master there can check you for injuries. I don't know how much of that blood your wearing belongs to you, but he will still need to check you for–" He stops and slightly glances down at my bare legs. I press my thighs together and his eyes meet mine. He means they'll have to check to see if the monster finished his job.

No one wants a princess that can't guarantee the child they carry is theirs.

"They won't want me anymore, Theo. I already told you that." I rub at my shoulders, at my legs and arms. Anywhere those men have touched. I want the feeling of *his* touch, Aleksander's touch, to dissipate. I want the feeling of him inside me, taking everything away, to dissipate. I just want it all to fade away and be forgotten. I just want it to be over, but healing isn't that easy. I shake my head and stare at the dirt. "Not after what happened. I can't go to the palace."

"Listen to me, you can't make that choice alone. You have no idea what they will say once you arrive. If there is no evidence, if there is nothing there, you will be fine. Even if there is, there is always the tonic to terminate anything that may be present." I can't trust his reasoning; he doesn't know what I'm up against. What my father said he would do if I disappointed him. I can't rely on herbs to rid me of this. And if the herbs didn't work, what would I do pregnant in the capital with a murderer's child?

"I'm ruined. I'm set to be married, but who would marry an impure woman?" My voice is hoarse, exhaustion ravaging its way through my body. My choices are limited. "Who would take on the unknown that would come with any child I bear?"

"They don't have to know." His voice sounded less convincing and more questionable. He knows they'll be able to tell. My eyes meet his as I glare at him, my nails poking into my palms.

"There is no possible way for me to *hide* this. One check by the master and I'll be thrown out or beheaded for being a whore. You *know* that's true." I snap. The pain and frustration over this night is catching up with me and I just can't sit here and listen to him. I need to leave. I glance around, hoping a horse or something is tucked away that I can sneak on to. Anything I can use to escape, but there is nothing. At least not out in the open.

"Don't risk your life by walking away, either. The woods aren't safe, not if those men are still out there. You'll be safer once we get to the city. We aren't set to leave for another few hours, but when we do, you *will* be coming with us. I am not giving you an option on this. I am not letting you kill yourself out of fear of something that may not happen." He leans back and looks at me, really looks at me.

His eyes stare deep into mine and I find myself wanting to know more. There is something so recognizable and comforting about him, I can't place it. I don't know him, nor do I know if the words he speaks are true, yet here I am, wanting him to hold me as I cry. I need to go. This man can't possibly predict my fate, and if King Evreux is anything like my father, I will be either cast away or murdered upon my arrival.

"You don't understand. I'm risking my life either way." I shake my head, fighting against the tears.

"Fight for yourself, princess. You cannot predict the future." If only I was a prophet like the man who counseled my mother, then I could. Then I could see what going to the palace would entail, but I don't have that gift.

"No, but I have lived with a tyrant my whole life and if my soon-to-be husband is anything like the man I have heard about, he will surely kill me if he hears about this." I turn away from him and look at the bright flames that fill the pit.

"You do not know much about me, Nora, but I promise you that I won't let anything happen to you. You are safe now. I know of the man you are to marry, and he is not entirely like his father. You *will* be safe." His voice is reassuring, but I can't trust him. He is right. I don't know him. I don't know anyone. I barely even know myself.

"I don't know you, or your men, or the people I will soon be sharing a home with." My eyes find his. "How could you possibly ask me to risk my life by quite literally entering a lion's den? You don't know what it's like for women in general, much less one of royalty." My voice is strained, from emotion and exhaustion.

"I'm sorry that you went through this, princess, but I have orders. You cannot leave." He seems apologetic, hesitant, but that doesn't matter.

"You cannot tell a princess to do anything, Theo. You have no right." My voice is fueled by anger as I snap at him. I know he doesn't deserve it, but I can't help myself.

"Kings out rule princesses, and you are on Noterran soil." *Dammit.* Running is the only option I have here. If I get to the Noterran capital I will die. There is no doubt about it. I can't possibly risk my life for a marriage I didn't even want.

I don't see Theo allowing me to leave anytime soon, at least not on purpose. I need to find a way to sneak away, but I need to get away from *him* first.

"Fine. I will rest until we are ready to depart." I rise and he nods, accepting my excuse to part with a look of surprise. His eyebrows raise slightly in suspicion, before bending down and grabbing something.

"Here, drink some water." He hands me a waterskin and I gratefully take it from him. Gesturing towards the tent, he stands as I walk away, watching me. Keeping his overcoat on to keep the cold air at bay, I step in and close the drape behind me.

I drop down onto the cot and let the tears take over. My weakened body shakes with uncontrollable pain as I try to forget the last few hours of my life. Just yesterday I was waking up looking forward to my last week of freedom, now I am sitting in the tent of a stranger, broken and bloody and damaged.

Damaged.

That's what they'll see when I finally make it to the palace. A woman's virtue is a prized possession that men like to collect. A possession meant for my future husband, but instead, taken by a monster in the woods who knew exactly what he was doing. If my father finds out about this, he'll have me killed.

I can't stay here. If I make it to the palace, they'll turn me away. I have no choice. I'm dead either way, but at least if I run I have a chance.

Convincing my delirious self that this plan is the rational decision, I take a deep breath. I quickly drain the waterskin, the cool and slightly bitter liquid erasing any taste of blood from my mouth. I drop it on the cot when I'm done. I debate leaving the coat, but with the current state of my dress, I need it more than he does. I slip my arms through the sleeves and pull it tight around me.

Standing back up and wiping away the tears staining my cheeks, I make my way over the edge of the tent, silently cursing the persistent limp. I peer through the slit and see the fire abandoned, no one around. I slip through, keeping my back against the tent wall. Glancing around, making sure no one is there to see me, I slowly step towards the back of the tent, bordering the trees. Keeping my back to the woods and my face towards the camp, I continue until I am hidden by the brush.

Spinning around I begin to run. My leg retaliates, going stiff and numb as I try to pick up the pace. The pain between my legs spreads towards my core as I feel hot liquid running down my inner thighs, but I keep running as best as I can. Despite the pain and exhaustion, the weakening of my limbs, I have to keep going. I can't let them take me to the palace. If I'm pregnant or if they find out about this, I'll be dead.

I can't let them kill me.

I can't go back home.

I can't go anywhere.

The king will assume I never made it away from the monsters of the forest. They'll think I'm dead anyway and move on. My father will bear a new child with whatever mistress he has this week, and I'll be replaced.

Knowing none of this is true, the lies I tell myself are the only thing that keep me moving forward. And I have to keep moving.

I pick up my pace as my head throbs and the nausea overwhelms me, threatening to explode. I can't stop. I am running for my life.

Wait. That's it.

I come to a dead stop, my leg cramping, as I take in that last thought. I'm running for my life. A life I don't want. Maybe dying isn't a bad thing? Maybe I'll see my mother again, the only person who has ever made me feel like I'm loved. I never wanted any of this. King Evreux could consider that and let me live out my life as a citizen of Noterra. I could start a simple life. Make a life of my own creation.

But that won't happen.

Shaking my head in an attempt to get rid of the self-sacrificial thoughts, I begin my half-run half-shuffle again, breathing through the endless pain.

Everything is dark, the trees, the bushes, the forest floor. Sticks and rocks pierce through my feet as I continue, getting more and more breathless. My head is swimming, it's taking every ounce of strength to even keep my eyes open. I'm gasping for every bit of oxygen I can manage to suck in, narrowly dodging tree trunks hidden by the shadows.

I don't know how much longer I can run, the blood now steadily dripping out of every one of my fresh wounds, my feet going numb, the bile rising in my throat threatening to come out. Despite my mental protests and deep breathing, that's exactly what it did.

Falling to my knees, the vomit explodes out of my mouth for a second time and lands around me. Taking every ounce of energy and strength I have with it. My limbs burn, my head throbs, my mouth is unable to inhale an adequate amount of air, and my mind is spinning. My eyes cloud over as I fight to keep them open, my muscles shaking from exhaustion. I can't afford to stop. I can't afford to let the weaknesses inside me win.

You are stronger than this.

But this weakness is more than a symptom of my injuries. I feel as if my limbs aren't responding to my mental pleas, as if I have no control over my body. My heart is slowing, my lungs barely working. Something is wrong.

The waterskin.

He drugged me. He put something in the water, and I didn't even question it. He was prepared for me to run, and I didn't even realize it. I figured his attention was out of concern, but he only has one goal in mind.

His mission is to bring me back alive, and I walked right into it.

The crunching of twigs catches my attention as boots stop in front of me. I look up to see a cloaked man with no identifying sigil on the dark wool. He's not with the men I was just with, but one of the men who watched as Aleksander took me into the forest. He bends down and grips my arms, forcing me up to my feet and I wince. I try to pull my arms out of his grip, but I can't even get my feet to stay planted on the ground.

"Let's go." He snarls. The sound of cracking branches and the shouts of men echo through the trees behind me. He whips his head towards the noise, searching through the trees. I can just barely make out the sight of a torch in the distance. I look back at the man and let out the loudest scream I possibly can, but it's short lived.

A sword comes flying through the air, making contact with his head, slicing it in two, narrowly missing me. We both fall to the ground.

I try to stand, but my knees buckle around me, my body refusing to cooperate. I roll onto my back, staring up at the night sky. As black as my hair, sprinkled with glitter. A relaxed smile spreads across my face as I welcome the end.

Fairytales and magic.

Theo's face is the last I see before the darkness takes me again.

Chapter Seven

Glass and bone. Slicing its way through my naked flesh as I stand and watch the fire consuming the buildings. Consuming the bodies. The smoke filling my nose has a peculiar scent. What I expect to smell like burning meat and timber, a scent I can't figure out takes its place. A sweet and herby scent I've never smelled before. It doesn't quite fit into the scenery laid out in front of me.

What is it?

A hand reaches out and pulls me to him. I scream as my eyes land on him. His black hair and green eyes shining in the smoke. A single white strand of hair flowing in the wind, tickling his face.

"You need to run." He says, his eyes filled with fear. "You need to get out of there." His hands tighten on my shoulders as he shakes me. "Are you listening? You need to find me! Go!"

Cinnamon and herbs flood my senses, strong enough to burn the hairs in my nostrils. Fighting the urge to sneeze, I listen. The sound of someone moving around me, shuffling papers and bottles clinking, brings my body into awareness. I don't know where I am, or who it is that sits by my unconscious body, so I keep my eyes closed and focus on steadying my breath to appear like I am still asleep.

I use this time to take inventory of the physical pain I feel. My legs are stiff and sore, probably from the many falls I took. My skin feels tight, no doubt a result of caked on blood and dirt. A dull ache throbs on my forehead, the result of leather meeting skin. My throat feels tight, I can almost still feel his hands on me, squeezing my neck.

I take a second before I fully focus on the pain between my legs. It's a pain I have never felt before. It feels like I was stretched and ripped beyond reason, which I was, for the pleasure of a stranger. It hurts, but not as bad as it did at first. It's more of a dull ache that spreads to my core.

My virtue, the only thing that gives a woman value in this damned world, was taken from me. My hope is that I'm dead or at least not at the palace. They can't see me like this. I know that is unlikely, given that Theo's face was the last I saw, but I will it into existence with everything I have.

I am unsure if it was Theo who wielded the sword that beheaded my attacker, but it's a safe assumption. His head, sliced in two, sliding apart. It's an image I will never be rid of. The top of his head falling onto the ground, nearly landing on me. Blood pouring out of his body, covering me in yet another's life essence.

I find myself wondering what would have happened if Theo hadn't arrived. Do I even care what would have happened to me? I would like to think I would mind, but in that moment, and even now, my fear has been replaced with numbness.

Would the man have finished what Aleksander couldn't? Or would they spread me around like a bottle of cheap ale? The most likely answer is probably a mixture of both. I am grateful for Theo's rescue, but I am still worried about what my fate will be if I am indeed in the palace.

Will I be cast away like a common whore? Or will they accept my trauma and help me move past it? King Evreux isn't a kind man, but if Tobias is, my hope is that he will still agree to wed. I don't want to marry the prince, but if he is kind enough to take pity on me, maybe marriage is a better alternative to whatever else the king may think up. I internally sigh, with the fear of facing the unknown creeping up.

My muscles, tight and restless, make staying still a chore. Knowing that too much valuable time has passed while I lay here, pretending to sleep, I allow my eyes to open. I am immediately blinded by brightness causing my eyes to squint. Staring at the marble ceiling above me, I realize what I am seeing is sunlight reflecting off the bright, glossy stone. An interior I remember from my childhood. I made it to the palace.

Of course.

I quickly sit up until I am fully upright, throwing my legs over the side of the bed I am in. My breathing is labored as I immediately feel every bit of pain my mind was shielding me from, blood rushing from my head. Glancing down at the thin sheet wrapped around my legs, I rip it off, gasping as I take in the sight.

My pale legs are covered in bruises and cuts. There are swollen stitches on my thigh where the dagger had pierced my skin just below the hem of the pale nightdress I currently wear. The dirt has been washed off, which makes me wonder who it was that cleaned my unconscious, naked body.

Turning to face the person in the room, I see an elderly man with rosy cheeks and bright complexion, much like the sun filtering through the windows. He is sitting at a desk right behind the bed I was just asleep in. My eyes flick around the room and I see a row of empty cots line the wall behind him, with curtains in between. Only one curtain is closed, hiding whoever is injured or sick. The bed I am on seems to be in the middle of the room, right across from a large workbench. Windows line the back wall, illuminating the room through sheer, white curtains. Various shelves and drawers fill the empty spaces, with books and bottles crammed into the small nooks and crannies.

I turn back to the man next to me. He meets my eyes and gives me a look of relief and something else I can't quite pinpoint, maybe sorrow? His gray hair is pulled into a tight knot at the base of his neck. The wrinkles etched into his skin, along with his soft hazel eyes, make me feel at ease. He looks to be around fifty, old enough to be my grandfather. This man isn't a threat, at least I hope he isn't. His most noticeable feature is the thick red cloak flowing around him like a river of blood.

A river of blood that I saw pour out of a man not too long ago. Two men, actually, if I include the one Theo killed. I cringe at the thought.

Under his cloak, he is wearing a matching white and silver tunic and trousers, the silver threading catching on the sunlight and sparkling. Wealthy, from what I assume. Maybe he is the palace mender? A master by the looks of him, not a mender. Knowledge and authority come with age, and I am assuming he has spent nearly his entire life perfecting the art of healing, which gave him the title of master in the Noterran court. I let my eyes meet his again as I try to read him for some sort of inkling of what is to come, but he just looks at me with indifference. I figured he was expecting me to speak first, so it surprises me when he opens his mouth to talk.

"Hello, Your Grace. You have been out for some time." His voice is soft, barely above a whisper, but filled with wisdom, no doubt a product of the years he's lived.

"How long?" My voice cracks as I make an attempt at speaking, my breathing finally controlled. My throat feels dry, and stiff.

"Three days. We gave you the essence of wisteria to help you sleep and heal. We were worried about any residual swelling in your brain from your injuries, so we assumed it was best to let you heal as long as your body required. You were unconscious upon arrival, so you were brought here to the infirmary." He responds, watching my face for any sign of emotion. Three days I have been asleep. I stay stoic, unsure of how to react to anything somewhat surprising anymore. "It took some time to find all of your wounds and tend to them, thankfully they are healing rather quickly, with the worst being the stab wound on your thigh and the blunt force trauma to your head. There were also some bruises and cuts that didn't quite line up with the timeline of your attack, but I patched them up nonetheless." He stops, not entirely prying into the other wounds on my body but giving me the option should I wish to talk about them.

"Thank you." He nods, a small smile plastered to his face.

I sigh and dig my broken nails into the palms of my hands. I still feel light, delirious, as if someone else has control of my body. My muscles ache and are protesting against any movement I make.

"He drugged me." I remember. He nods. "It was in the water?"

"He had a feeling you weren't going to make the trip here easy, so he did what he thought was best." He smiles, failing to hide his approval of Theo's methods. "Do you know what happened to you?" I nod and he gives me a sad smile as he reaches towards a small glass and a decanter. He pours a thick, pinkish liquid into the glass and holds it out to me. I stare at it, hesitant, for a second before meeting his gaze. "It will not cause you to fall unconscious, Your Grace. I promise."

My hands close around the glass and I tentatively take a sip of whatever cool liquid he provided. It's sweet like nectar, or some kind of fruit with a hint of spice. Not realizing how thirsty I am, I finish the drink quickly. The thick tonic coating my throat easing the dry, scratchiness. I hand the glass back to him and he nods in approval before refilling it with a decanter sitting beside him.

"Well, you will be alright. You are not pregnant, we made sure of that, although you will have some herbs to drink today to ensure you stay that way for the time being. With the act you endured, we are going to try and force your monthly bleed earlier in order to rid you of any unwanted pregnancy. You will be physically fine in no time, dear." *Physically*. I nod again, not knowing what to say, so he continues speaking to fill the silence. "The guards combed the woods near where you appeared and found his body, the man you killed, and burned him. If he had help, they should take that as a warning to stay away. Although the king is not quite sure who he belonged to." I slightly lift my shoulders, shrugging to indicate my own confusion.

Whether it's fear or exhaustion at this point preventing a coherent response, I don't know. I can't possibly be exhausted if I've been asleep for three days, but I have no energy to engage in conversation, at least not one that forces me to relive that night.

"The other man, the one that was dealt with, was left in the woods as far as I am aware. No doubt acting as a secondary warning. I can never understand the reasoning behind half the things these men do." He chuckles but stops when he meets my gaze. His eyes hold mine and are full of wonder, probably contemplating what I am thinking. He hands me the glass back and I drink from it.

"What is this?" I swallow, my throat loosening. I can taste something floral and something super sweet, almost like peaches.

"It's poppy pollen and fruit nectar mixed with a mild pain reliever. It'll help your body heal as well as prevent any lingering pain from causing you discomfort."

"Poppies? Aren't they poisonous?" I freeze, the glass pausing in the air in front of my lips.

"Not in the dose you are taking, it is mixed with other herbs and fruits to dilute it. It'll just help you heal quickly with minimal scarring." I nod and drain the glass again, feeling the effects already.

"What's going to happen to me?" I whisper.

"I am not sure, Your Grace. That is not a decision I am a part of." He offers me a reassuring smile. I try to think of anything else to say, but my mind is blank. "What I can say is that the council has been deliberating your future the last few days. I feel as if they are taking into account everything you have experienced as well as the needs of the kingdom. I don't think any rash decisions will be made. As much as your situation may seem undesirable, Tobias is getting older and needs to wed. I also believe the prince has a soft spot for you already." He smiles, his cheeks reddening. How could Tobias already have feelings for me? We haven't even met, well we did once as children but that doesn't truly count.

"Has he been here?" I run my fingers along the edge of the glass, refusing to meet his gaze.

"Every chance he gets, Your Grace." I smile and try to hide my blushing cheeks. "He has been ensuring you are well taken care of. Despite the annoyance his presence sometimes brings, it is touching to see the prince act in a way he normally doesn't. He was quite fearful for you, scared that you'll have permanent scars to remind you of what you endured."

"That is unexpected." I whisper. "I wasn't sure what to expect of my arrival or his feelings about my presence." I admit. I know that I am unsure about our situation, but I never stopped to consider what *he* must be feeling.

"From what I have seen, the prince seems very fond of you. I think the king is taking that into account when discussing what to do about your situation." The sound of footsteps makes us both turn our attention to the ornate double doors framed in silver and dark wood, marking the entrance and exit of the room. Muffled voices try to make their way through but fail. It's quiet for a moment before I hear the doorknob turn. When the door finally opens, a man I instantly recognize, strides in.

Eyes the lightest shade of blue meet mine. Filled with strength, anger, and power, his nearly silver irises scan my body. Short, golden waves with hints of copper brush his forehead, just barely touching his eyebrows, shorter than the last time I saw him. His cheekbones are high and wide, giving him a perfect angular face. His lips are plump and rosy. He has a fine dusting of facial hair along his jaw, the makings of a small beard.

His black tunic and trousers complement his tan skin perfectly, hugging his body in a way that shows off his relentless training, that and his broad shoulders that seem to take up the entire room. He is the most gorgeous man I have ever seen. If I thought Theo looked like a painting, Tobias looks like a god. I curse my lack of practice with paint as I stare at him. No portrait would ever be able to capture him. With a strong stance and corded muscles tensing under his shirt, he looks as if he could take on the entire kingdom and walk away unscathed. However, I can see his pain. His sorrow, set deep in his eyes, is tenfold what I saw as a child.

I unabashedly stare at him, my breath exhaling in one long deep stream of air. I can feel goosebumps line my arms and adrenaline running down my spine, giving me a short burst of energy.

"Your Grace." The master acknowledges as he stands and bows slightly. *Tobias.*

As I sit here, frozen in this bed with nothing but a sheet and a nightdress that doesn't belong to me, I want to run and hide. His eyes devouring my body as he looks me up and down makes me feel slightly uncomfortable. I am the definition of vulnerability at the moment and cannot even begin to comprehend how ragged I must look. I hate how *this* version of myself is going to be his first impression of me.

"Elaenor, you are awake." His voice is smooth and strong. Deep, but lyrical and familiar, bearing no resemblance to the voice of the child I once met. I could listen to him speaking all day and never get tired of hearing the sound. Not that his statement required an answer, I nod, as that seems to be the only thing I am capable of at this moment. "How are you feeling?" He asks as he walks over to me. His rough fingers gently grip my chin and tilt my head up until I am looking at him. "Your face." He whispers as his eyes darken and his lips press into a thin line.

His free hand brushes what I am assuming is one of the many cuts on my forehead. Tobias's fingers lightly touch the bandage and I wince from the pain. A flash of empathy fills his eyes but is quickly replaced with anger. He smells like cedar and smoke, a lethal combination that makes me want to get lost in him. A smell that makes me want to lean against him and feel his warmth. A smell that reminds me of an afternoon in the woods, which is a strange smell coming from someone who's sparkling clean boots look as if they have never left these marble halls. His breath fans across my face before he clenches his jaw. He drops his hands and steps back, his arms crossing in front of his chest, and I already miss his touch.

His features are angry, hardened. Nothing like the 10-year-old boy I met so long ago. He looks like he's been through a lot, which he has.

The news that Queen Amaya passed not so long after my own mother spread through our kingdom quickly. She wasn't murdered like mine, but instead died during childbirth, much like many women before her. It was a little girl, who died during the birth as well. He lost a mother and a sister in one day.

When the news of the queen's death reached us, I remember the mourning that occurred. We had only just ended the period of mourning for my mother, when the black clothing made its way out of the wardrobes again. My father attended the funeral, leaving me in the care of the Hand and my ladies. The Noterran king didn't attend my mother's funeral, but it was expected that my father would extend that courtesy.

I remember Scarlett telling me about the small bundle wrapped in cloth sitting next to the queen on the pyre. She didn't attend, but she heard the kingsguard speaking about it upon their return. Her name was Thea. I remember how saddened I felt thinking about my own siblings who did not survive birth as well. I glance down, not wanting him to see the sorrow or pity in my eyes.

"Tobias. It's been 10 years." I finally speak, staring at the floor. My voice doesn't sound nearly as strained, and I silently thank the nectar I consumed. My fingers stop their nervous spinning of the glass and I set it on the bed next to me. With my luck, I would drop it and then have to deal with the shattered pieces.

"It has. You look the same. Even your unruly black hair you could never seem to tame." I look up and see the corner of his mouth twitch, hinting at a smile. I smile in return, not even wanting to know what I look like at the moment. While strangers, I feel as if I know him, as if my entire existence culminated for this very moment. The familiarity of his face is calming, slowly pushing out the fear I have. Maybe things are not as bad as they seem.

Maybe *he* isn't as bad as I have heard.

"You look different." I say, searching his face for any resemblance to his childlike self. The features of his younger self are there, but the hardening, maturing of his jaw line make him look completely different. I could just barely see stubble covering his jawline, shining like gold leaf in the sun.

"A decade of time has passed, Elaenor. The difference is to be expected." His voice is steady, emotionless as his eyes stare into mine, and I swallow against the lump that has formed in my throat. I have no idea how to speak to him, what to say, what to do. I was never taught how to speak to men, how to appeal to them. I was told to stay quiet, silent, unless spoken to. I was never really good at following instructions though.

"I was very sorry to hear about your mother and your sister." I whisper and offer a soft smile. "It was a tragedy felt across the kingdoms."

"As was I to hear about yours." He returns my smile, but it doesn't reach his eyes. We just stare in silence. It shouldn't be this hard, or awkward, to communicate. Yet, I find I don't have anything I wish to say to him. My heart skips and I bite my bottom lip.

The master is the first to speak as he stands and walks over to me, stepping in front of Tobias. His fingers lift the bandage on my forehead as he inspects one of my many wounds. No doubt uncomfortable by our awkward exchange. You could cut the tension in the air, its thickness suffocating any rational thoughts in my head.

"Your head wound seems to have finally closed." He murmurs to me as I silently wince from his touch, my lips pressing into a thin line.

"Will she heal quickly, Pakin? Will she scar?" Tobias asks as he peers over his shoulder, watching his movements carefully.

"She should be fully healed within a week or so. Some scarring is to be expected, but it will fade with time." Master Pakin murmurs as he smooths the bandage back over my forehead. His fingers move to the stitches on my thigh. I suck in a breath as pain races down my leg. "This wound is the worst of them, but even then, she was lucky."

"Lucky?" I snap and he flinches. I regret it immediately when I see the surprise in his eyes. He doesn't deserve my hostility.

"I apologize, Your Grace. That is not what I meant." I exhale quickly as I stare into his hazel eyes. He looks apologetic, and I know my irritation is not towards him. He has been kind, but I can't help the anger hiding inside of me. I softly smile as an apology, and he pats my leg.

"What did you mean, then? Hm?" Tobias's voice is hard, distant, sounding more like my father than anything as he presses Master Pakin to explain himself. "Did you mean she was lucky to have escaped? Lucky to have been kidnapped and beaten?" He gets close to the master, his chest almost brushing his back. Master Pakin freezes, his eyes focusing only on my stitches when he answers.

"Your Grace, I only meant that she was lucky that no muscles or tendons were severed. Painful as it may be, it is only a flesh wound." His voice is calm, even. If I were him, I would be shaking, in fact I am pretty sure I was. My eyes are focused on Tobias's, darkening by the second. Master Pakin steps away from me carefully, slipping back onto his stool and refilling the glass I had set beside me. Tobias just stares at him.

"Thank you, Master Pakin." I offer him an apologetic smile that I know doesn't reach my eyes, hoping to diffuse the anger pouring out of Tobias like the plague.

"You are very welcome, dear. I know you feel discomfort currently, but it should subside soon. You can have as much of this tonic as you'd like." He gestures towards the decanter of the cool, sweet drink I was consuming before, setting the refilled glass on the edge of the table. "There are no adverse side effects, and it should make you feel as normal as possible. You may get some bouts of tiredness, but that is just your body's way of telling you to relax if you push yourself." I nod and turn back towards Tobias.

He's staring down at my legs, the scrapes a bright red against my pale skin. He's close enough to reach down and brush my skin, which is what he does. Surprisingly, his warm, calloused fingers brush against a scar that's peeking through between the scratches, and not any of my fresh wounds.

"What is this?" I swallow loudly as I watch his fingers find another raised, flesh colored mark. He rubs his thumb over the healed scars, moving from one to another as he finds them all beneath the open wounds. Sparks of electricity tingle my skin each time he touches me. He's mouthing something and only when he moves to my other leg and does the same thing, do I realize he's counting them. He doesn't need to, I already know. There are one hundred and seventy-nine lashes on my skin.

"I was a clumsy child." I lie and swallow again, fighting against the lump in my throat.

While the scars are tiny, thin stripes covering my thighs and arms, the short whip my father used was anything but. I could still hear the snap in the air as the tip of the leather struck my skin, causing small, two-inch lines across my flesh. He was methodical, holding the whip in such a way that it only left short gashes, but that was before he really got angry.

If Tobias thought those were bad, he was in for a surprise should he ever see me without clothes. I used to be embarrassed about them, used to wear long sleeves and long dresses during all seasons to hide them, melting in the boiling hot summers. At some point, I stopped hiding. I stopped covering for my father and instead let his citizens see the wounds he's inflicted. I was saddened when I realized no one bat an eye, no one even looked.

No one cared.

"They don't look like normal wounds." He whispers. I instinctively reach forward and roughly push his hand away. He snaps his head up, his eyes meeting mine, surprised. I freeze as I realize what I just did, my heart pounding in my chest.

I am not sure what is allowed here in Noterra, but if I pushed my father's hand away like that, I would have much fresher wounds covering my body. I was property, and currently the holder of my title was Tobias. I was his to do with as he pleased. I swallow uncomfortably, searching his eyes for any hint of anger. He drops his arm and opens his mouth to speak, but then quickly shuts it. The sound of multiple footsteps and hushed whispers echo down the halls and we both turn to look at the door.

Chapter Eight

Tobias takes a small step to the left, leaving my side, to allow a hoard of people to file through the open door. All noblemen, from what I can tell by their clothing, and probably the men from his council. King Evreux is front and center, looking very much the same as before, with a thin scar above his right eye.

The only thing that is different is the grayish tint to his once tanned skin. His eyes deep into the hollows of his skull, causing noticeable dark circles. He looks ill, but ensures his stride remains strong as he makes his way over to me. He's wearing a matching crimson cloak to the master, with it flowing behind him. He's wearing a black tunic and dress pants made out of silk. The shiny fabric catches the light, drawing attention to him. He looks extremely kingly with his silver thorny crown resting upon his straight and short blonde hair, as if he just came from court. He looks me up and down, disdain causing his lips to thin.

"Princess Elaenor, you have awoken. Master Pakin has taken great care of you these last few days. How do you feel?" He looks at me with unfaltering strength, a hint of irritation behind his eyes, his voice strong and commanding.

No doubt he's unhappy with the terms of my arrival. For a man who is dying, as my father says, he does a good job at hiding it, but I can still tell.

The act of hardened strength is weak at best, I can hear the small tremor that vibrates through his voice at the end of his sentences. His throat protesting against the act of speaking, I can't imagine what it must feel like. It makes me wonder what it is that ails him. I know it's not something that has to do with age, but some other illness of the blood. To be able to feel your body weakening, failing, must be nothing short of terrifying.

The men behind him greedily search my body, no doubt taking in the scandal that is to be their queen. They are all older, ranging from mid-thirties to fifties. They seem to all be dressed similarly, silks and nice cotton. I assume they are all a part of his inner council as I doubt the king would be walking around with an entourage of low Lords. I slowly pull the thin sheet back over my bare legs, covering as much of myself as I can from their prying eyes.

"I am feeling okay, Your Grace." I respond with a respectful dip of my chin. I keep my eyes down, not wanting to meet his gaze, my bottom lip trapped between my teeth. My father was extremely strict with protocol, as I assume King Evreux is. The only king who seemed to disregard protocol was the King of Rakushia. Instead of curtsies and handshakes, King Thelonious favored hugs and tenderness.

"We were angered to see the way you arrived, to see what you had endured while traveling to us. You were lucky you found my son, or you may not have made it intact, or as intact as you can be given the *circumstances.*" I quickly glance at Tobias, knowing that it wasn't him who held me in his arms as I fled the forest. It wasn't him who drugged me and saved my life in the span of minutes.

He gives his head a slight shake and narrows his eyes. I wasn't aware there was another prince, but I see now that they have the same color eyes. However, Tobias's mirror that of someone who has been through hell, while Theo's eyes are bright and unbothered. They have the same melodic quality of their voice that commands attention, respect. Their is was different, with Tobias having hints of copper. Theo's looked like pale gold, at least in the little light a fire provided. They have the same sharpened jawline, but Tobias has a sprinkling of stubble while Theo has his face clean shaven. They could be identical, but it is obvious that Theo is happier than Tobias, freer.

"I understand your virtue has been taken by force." King Evreux states, not as a question, but a statement. My eyes flash towards him, filled with surprise and panic. His own eyes filled with disgust and contemplation.

"Your Grace–" My attempt at a defense is met with a raised hand, silencing me, and I flinch. His gold adorned fingers glowing in the sunlight, reflecting against the room in flashes of yellow. His eyes widen slightly, but I break his stare by looking back at the floor.

"Master Pakin has assured us that you cannot be pregnant, due to a combination of herbs and whatnot. While I would prefer you continue to take the tonic the next couple of days, it may affect your ability to conceive a real heir, and that is what you are here for." He scowls in irritation. Maybe he doesn't want me to marry his son? "Given that this is an unusual situation, we used the time you were unconscious to deliberate what your fate will be. Your father was summoned–"

"My father?" I blurt out, knowing full well he would give them permission to cast me aside, not wanting me to tarnish his name. My heart begins to race at the idea of his face, furious, sending me to the wolves.

Did he come here? Did he see me in my medically induced sleep? Did he see what happened to me? The irritation in the king's eyes cause me to lower mine again. Resisting the urge to cut him off again, my eyes find my bare feet, taking in the bruises and cuts that litter my flesh as I dig my nails into the palms of my hands to restrain another outburst.

"Your father and I came to an agreement. You will still marry my son, as there are no other valuable prospects of age, and this is an urgent matter. An heir for the realm is the only reason you are here, princess, otherwise we would find a new match. An heir was promised to me 10 years ago by your father," He steps closer, and his hand finds my chin, forcing it up to look at him. His eyes search mine while he catches his breath. The hot air fans over my face, laced with wine and an herb I can't place, no doubt some sort of tincture to keep the illness at bay. His strong fingers remind me of the man who held onto me in the forest, nothing but power and possession emanating from him, sending a shiver down my spine. "A promise you will deliver on. We will not have this conversation a second time. You will marry, *soon*. And as soon as you have had a successful bleed, your duties may begin."

"Yes, Your Grace." I whisper. His fingers remain on my chin, holding my head up, but he loosens his grip slightly. His eyes still stare into mine, but his anger is dissipating.

"You look much like your mother." He says with less malice fueling his words, being replaced with sorrow. "Her death was a tragedy to us all." I am surprised by his revelation, but I don't let it show.

"Thank you, Your Grace. I was saddened to hear about Queen Amaya and the princess as well." I respond. He stares at me with momentarily remorseful eyes, looking more like a man who is staring at his child, than the political headache I'm sure I have become. A look I have never seen from my father. Is this what it looks like to be on the receiving end of concern?

"Yes, it was tragic." He releases my face, but keeps his gaze fixed on me. "Your father, he has not taken your mother's passing well, I presume?" He speaks as if he knows the terror my father has caused me, which he might. There are scars littering my entire body, I am sure he's seen them.

"No, Your Grace." My voice saddens as I think about him, but I still remember the words he spoke when I left, his excuse.

If the Gods decided she was no longer fit to be queen, they did what they had to do.

"Tragedies have a way of separating the weak from the strong." He says softly. He could be implying my father is weak or advising me on what my next actions could be perceived as. I am not sure, but remaining strong is all I can do.

"Yes, they do." I straighten my back and raise my chin. A hint of amusement pulls at the edges of his lips.

"I will leave you to get settled." With one last look of curiosity and pursed lips, he turns on his heels and races out of the door with his noblemen close behind. Just as fast as he arrived, the king is gone. I let out a loud breath that I wasn't aware I was holding.

My eyes linger on the door, and I don't see Tobias walk back up to me. His demeanor is strong, like his father's, but his gentle touch reminds me that they could be different. Or maybe it's the hope inside of me that wills him to be that way. He rests his hand on my shoulder and looks down at me, his eyes filled with kindness.

"Once you are ready, one of the guards will show you to your chambers. We found your carriage and your belongings; they have been brought to the palace. I am sure you want nothing more than to change out of this nightdress and into something a little more comfortable. I will come find you, so we can discuss our situation. I am sure you have many questions, as do I." His soft smile gives me hope and I return it with a smile of my own.

"Thank you." He cocks a brow and tilts his head. "For taking care of me." He smiles, his face relaxing. "I'll admit I am not used to affection or someone caring for me. The last person who had any sort of concern over my wellbeing was my mother. It will take some time to get used to, and I hope you will be patient with me, but thank you nonetheless." My voice cracks and he squeezes my shoulder.

"It is my pleasure, Elaenor. Ensuring your safety and wellbeing is my responsibility now. I intend to take it seriously." I visibly relax. He cares. He *actually* cares about my wellbeing. I don't know why it is so much of a surprise, other than it being incredibly foreign. I believed I would be entering a marriage with a man sick with power and control, but this Tobias, this is the version of him I dreamed about. The version I had to believe would be the one I'd find upon my arrival, and it's real. He's real. His hand moves from my shoulder to cup my cheek.

"I don't know what sort of childhood you had, or life for that matter, but I promise that you will be happy here." He leans forward and I almost think he's going to kiss me, but he moves at the last moment to press his soft lips to my forehead. "Is there anything I can do for you before I leave?" He asks, pulling back to look into my eyes. I nod.

"Did you find my rider? Ser Danieas?" I ask, hoping he is somehow still alive. If they found him in time, maybe they were able to save him.

"Yes, he is still alive. He was gravely injured, so he is being tended to." He nods towards Master Pakin. I sigh with relief and smile softly.

"Please let me know once I can see him." He nods and then glances over at Master Pakin, giving him a nod as well.

"I will come find you." He kisses my forehead again before his hand leaves my face. He strolls out of the room, closing the doors behind him. My skin tingles where his touch has been, and I fight against the blush creeping along my cheeks.

"Your Grace, let's get you out of this room. I'm sure you are craving some sunlight and a change of clothes." Master Pakin says with a smile before holding out his hand to help me off the bed. I slide off the mattress and let my feet touch the cold marble. He releases my hand and opens a drawer in the desk, pulling out a pair of slippers. I give him a thankful smile before I bend over to put them on.

"May I ask you something?" I say as I straighten.

"Yes, Your Grace."

"The chances of pregnancy are slim, correct?" He nods as he bends over a set of notes and scribbles something on them. "How will we know for sure?" He continues writing.

"You will start your monthly bleed sometime within the next day or so. This will shed any unwanted growths in your womb and leave you ready to bear an heir for Noterra." I swallow, watching him scribble away on his notepad.

"Is it that easy?" I ask and he sighs, setting down his pen. He straightens and turns toward me, and I am surprised to see irritation in his eyes. "I am sorry, I just have so many questions."

"Did you not attend studies? Learn about science? About history and reading?" He asks, his voice stern.

"I did, but we did not learn about medicine. I was told I'd never have a need for it." I admit and he leans against the bed. "My studies were focused on reading, writing, and brief Chatisian history.

"Well if you are interested in learning more, I am sure the king can arrange a scholar to tutor you. It would do you some good to learn about the histories of all of the kingdoms and the basics of medicine." He doesn't sound condescending, but I can't help but feel like a child being told they are stupid.

"Okay."

"It is not a negative thing to strive to be more knowledgeable, Your Grace." He states, relieving some of the embarrassment I feel. "It is admirable to know where your weaknesses lie. As a queen, you will be expected to know the histories of our lands, of the continent. You'll have to be able to provide counsel to your subjects and speak intelligently about their woes, you'll need to comfort them. There is a lot you can learn." I was never taught court protocol or even proper princess etiquette. I was left to figure things out on my own after my mother died, but I don't have to do that here.

"I would like that very much."

Chapter Nine

As expected, the hallways and rooms are made of marble, floor to ceiling, only broken up by walls of glass windows. I knew Noterra was the largest and richest nation, but the sight of the grand palace has me in awe. When I was here as a child, I wasn't able to comprehend the grandeur this place holds. Marble such as this must cost an obscene amount. Our palace at home is grand as well, but this place makes Chatis look like a nobleman's house instead of a castle.

After a long and silent walk with a well-armed guard, I am led to a dark wooden door lined with silver detailing. There is a single guard standing in front of it. His body is covered in silver armor, a white cape hanging down his back. He doesn't look at me as the guard escorting me opens the door and guides me through with his hand on my upper back.

The room I will call my home for the foreseeable future is larger than I could have ever imagined. Giant pillows cover the large 4 poster bed, all lined with wool and silk. A roaring fire sits on the far wall with a white couch that beckons for me to fall into it. A sitting room and an office take up the middle of the grand room and a wall of windows sits to the right. Two double doors are open, leading out to a balcony. I can just barely make out the ocean behind the far away buildings. Much like the rest of the palace, the room is in varying shades of silver, white, and beige, making it feel clean and open. I take a deep breath and the scent of cedar and smoke fills my nose.

Tobias.

Glancing around I make note of smaller details I hadn't previously noticed. A half-finished letter lay on the writing desk, a gray overcoat draped over the side of the couch, a half empty glass of red wine sits on one of the nightstands. The bed made, but ruffled, as if someone was previously sitting on it. It is only then I realize this isn't just my room, it's Tobias's too.

I spin on my heels to face the guard, but just barely catch the glimpse of a smirk as he shuts the door, leaving me alone. I stare at the back of the dark wood, wondering what I should do. I can't request a separate room, nor can I make a big deal out of sharing quarters with the man who will soon be my husband.

King Evreux is clearly in a rush to get me to bed his son, but how could he possibly expect me to do so this soon after I have been assaulted? After I have been beaten and traumatized? I have only just met Tobias officially, as the one instance as a child doesn't truly count. I don't know him, or the king, yet here I am sharing a room with a foreign prince who has shared nothing but a few words with me.

I wonder what Tobias will ask of me. Will he force me into doing things with him, or will he be respectful of my injuries? What does he want from me right now? I need to speak to him, figure out our situation, yet I find myself nervous. I've never conversed with a man of this stature before. The only men I was allowed near in my home were those who swore to protect me.

With no other options available, I have to make it work, it's either this or my head. However, the latter is seeming more attractive as the minutes pass by.

My suicidal ideation has become more apparent since I left Chatis. I don't know if its fear driving these momentary desires, or an instinct that something is to come. I find myself wishing I had a friend here, or that I had requested the presence of my ladies, but I knew they would be happier staying in Chatis. It makes me wonder if I will be assigned ladies here. It is customary for royal women to have servants that tend to their needs, but I only crave their presence, so I feel less alone here.

My eyes scan the massive room in search of my belongings. In the far corner by the fireplace, a privacy screen sits in front of an open door, and I can just barely make out the edge of one of my suitcases, leading me to assume that is the dressing room.

As I take a step forward a loud *thud* causes me to jump, and a small squeal escapes my throat. My heart is racing, and I glance around for a weapon, panicked. Looking towards the source of the noise, I see a young man standing on the balcony. A man whose presence I strangely find myself craving now that I look at him. I visibly relax with a loud exhale, my shoulders dropping from where they seem to be permanently stationed by my ears from tension.

He must have jumped down from the floor above, his boots loudly slapping the stone. His messy blonde hair, thick and wavy, is framing his perfectly proportioned face. Half of it is tied up with a leather strap. His open white tunic, brown trousers, and dirty boots are a stark contrast to the all-black the man I am set to marry was wearing. His muscular chest peeks through the fabric and I find my cheeks heat. I quickly look down to mask my blush as I take a deep breath to calm my pulse.

"Hello." A simple phrase, but his melodic voice rings out crystal clear. Despite my earlier realization, it finally sets in.

Theo is the other prince.

"Hi." I manage to speak, my voice full of surprise and confusion.

"Theo, remember?" He gestures towards my body and gives me a sad smile. "A lot less blood than the last time I saw you. Have you decided on a different fashion statement? I heard nightgowns are all the rage down in Tatus." I blush and wrap my arms around my stomach instinctively, wishing I was given a dressing robe before being paraded around the palace.

Attempting to make light of the situation instantly provides relief to the otherwise awkward moment, but it doesn't help the incoherent thoughts that are threatening to spill out of my mouth like word vomit. He steps down from the balcony and makes his way closer.

"I see they moved you into Tobias's room. So it's true, they aren't even going to give you time to get to know one another?" I manage a shake of my head as I take note of the ease in which he speaks. He is strong, unwavering in his steps, sure of himself. He puts his hands on his hips and briefly bites his bottom lip. "Well, Nora, I'm glad you're safe." His voice is laced with sadness, which causes a frown to appear. I hate again how I find such comfort in his use of my nickname.

"Thank you for seeing me to the palace. I'm sure I wasn't the easiest travel companion." I finally speak with a smile, but he doesn't return it.

"I know why you ran, the fear of the unknown, it gets me sometimes too." He looks down, seeing something that's not there, no doubt thinking of his own troubles. Shaking his head, he gives me an exaggerated bow and a toothy smile. "Well, as always, it's a pleasure. I just wanted to ensure you were alright." He smiles and turns to leave the way he came.

"Wait!" I call out, taking a step towards him. I don't know what I wanted to say or what I wanted to tell him, but I knew I didn't want him to go.

"Yes, princess?" His voice is full of diplomacy, and I hate it, but I can see something else in his eyes. The way he looks at me makes my blood heat and my cheeks redden.

"Thank you, again." Is all I manage to say. "For helping me." I trail off and his sad smile returns.

"You were the one who fought the war, Nora, I just carried you to the finish line." He speaks with such poetic indifference, and I just want him to keep talking.

"I was unaware the king had another son." I state. He cocks an eyebrow, momentarily confused, but he lets it go with a smile.

"My father rarely speaks of me. He calls me his political headache as he has no use for me other than to gain land or power with a possible marriage alliance. It didn't help that I caused trouble and generally made his life hell. Second sons aren't worth much when you're talking about royalty." He grins mischievously, unashamed.

"I can say the same for my father. The only thing he requires of me is to produce an heir, one who could actually inherit a throne." My smile falls as I look around the room. He's getting his wish.

"You're his heir."

"Women cannot sit on a throne without a man by her side, Theo. You know that. Everyone knows that."

"Just because a tradition exists does not mean it has to continue." He responds. My eyes meet his and he starts to back up towards the open doors. I know he keeps trying to leave, but I selfishly want him to stay.

"I don't foresee a change in tradition in this lifetime, nor the next." I laugh softly. His eyes soften as he listens. "I know my place in this world, my father has made it very clear to me."

He surprisingly walks closer to me instead of leaving and lightly steps off the last step of the raised platform to the balcony. When he is only a foot away, he raises his hand. The back of his fingers lightly brush the bandages on my face. My breath gets caught in my throat in surprise and my eyes focus on his. He looks sad, hurt, as if he can feel my sorrow.

"Are you in pain?" He whispers, his soft breath cascading over me, bathing me in the scent of grass and spring air. My eyes flutter, wanting to close, but I keep them open.

"As much as to be expected." I respond with a voice that was mostly air and his eyes meet mine. Theo drops his warm fingers to my chin and slightly tilts my head up. I force my head to still instead of leaning into him like I really want to do.

"Your neck." His voice trails off as his free hand brushes the bruises I am sure are there and the cut that feels tight. I find my mind wanting to flinch, but my body disagrees. I fight against the urge to step into him. "It's like you can see his hand, gripping you." His voice catches in his throat and he takes a step back. His eyes meeting mine again before clearing his throat. "I apologize. I shouldn't be touching you like that." I shake my head, ignoring him, willing my racing pulse to slow.

"I will be alright, Theo." He nods, but I can tell it bothers him. "Your brother, is he kind?" I ask, hoping his answer is yes.

"My brother is much like our father, but he does care. He did inherit some of our mother's genes despite popular belief. He will treat you well, I presume, but," He stops, and I nod, urging him to go on. "Tobias has never been one to enjoy the company of just one woman. While I am not sure what his plans or feelings are when you are concerned, I wouldn't be surprised if he entertains others during your marriage. It is quite common for kings to have mistresses, even though I find the idea abhorrent." He frowns. "But I am not to be king, so my opinions are unrelated."

"Thank you for your honesty." I smile. "Finding someone who speaks the truth instead of lies to gain something is quite rare in court, so I appreciate your candor." He doesn't return my smile, he just nods.

"I have something for you." His eyes widen as he digs into his pocket, holding one hand out as a gesture to wait, and pulls out a black velvet bag.

He hands it over to me and I hesitantly take it. The velvet is soft, smooth, and tied together with a thin leather strip, much like the one he wears in his hair. The bag is weighted with something heavy. I glance at him nervously before untying the leather cord and dumping the contents onto my hand. Ice cold glass lands on my palm and I gasp.

The glass arrowhead lays against my skin, shining against the brightness. It's a little larger than my hand, and black leather has been tied around the base of it, providing a handle to hold. It is slipped into a sheath that looks like it belongs on my thigh. Theo took the piece of glass once stained with a mixture of mine and Aleksander's blood and turned it into a dagger. It's beautiful.

"Theo," I whisper as I stare at the weapon in my hand, the glass reflecting green in the sunlight. "Thank you." I smile up at him and his eyes relax. He must have been nervous, but he offers me a relieved smile. He turns back towards the balcony and walks to the edge, his hands resting on the marble railing. I take a step forward to follow him, but he turns and looks at me over his shoulder.

"I will see you later, princess." His voice is strained, saddened. He looks at me briefly before fully turning towards the courtyard and then he jumps off the balcony. Gasping in surprise, I race towards the railing to see where he landed. I don't know how far up we are, but as I reach the railing, I see him staring up from the grass below. He gives me a sad smile before walking into the palace and out of sight. My eyes linger for just a second before I allow them to wander, my fingers wrapped around the leather hilt of the dagger.

He's a very different man than I am used to. The only men I came in contact with at Chatis were guards who barely spoke. Tobias isn't even like his brother, at least from what I've gathered so far. He seems so sure of himself, so comfortable with everything, but I guess they are both similar in that aspect. One thing I do find curious is his revelation of his brother's inability for monogamy.

I shouldn't be surprised; he is right in stating it is quite common for kings to have mistresses. I just always wanted to marry someone who loves me, and *only* me. Maybe we could grow to love each other in the future, or maybe our marriage will be just that in name.

I find myself overwhelmed at the idea of being with a man, not in an intimate way, but being near one all the time. As a lonely princess, companionship is not something I am used to, and I am going to have to learn to navigate it.

Glancing out to take in the grounds, I strain to see the ocean. It's still hidden behind buildings and an endless forest of trees, but I can just barely see a sliver of waves. I've never been to the ocean before. The closest I have been to that expansive of a body of water is the lake back home. I am hoping I am not as captive here as I was in Chatis. Maybe I'll be able to visit the ocean, even swim in the salty water. I am not sure what Tobias has planned for us, or the king for that matter, but I am feeling more hopeful than I have in years.

This is a chance to start a new life, one I hopefully have a small amount of control over, especially if Tobias is distracted by other women, even if the thought of being in a loveless marriage makes me want to vomit.

I slip the dagger back into the velvet bag and hide it under one of the plush couch cushions. I am not sure if I am allowed to have such a weapon and I don't want it to be taken away. I have to admit, having one makes me feel a lot safer. While I know the palace is generally safe, especially with armed guards following me around, the uneasiness about this situation is still haunting me.

Chapter Ten

I change quickly, finding my comfort dress hung up in the dressing room. Long lace sleeves and a tight bodice that flares out loosely on the hips. It's black with a deep gray slip underneath, hugging my body like a warm embrace. I slip a pair of black sandals on and then step out of the dressing room. There is a large mirror leaning against the wall next to the partition and I hesitantly step up to it.

My hand instantly flies to my face as I take in my appearance. My skin is pale, almost as ashen as the king's. While the majority of my skin is covered, my neck and face are enough to make me want to cry. I have a clean bandage taped to my forehead, partially covering my hair line. There are dark circles under my eyes so purple I look as if I have been punched. My cheeks are red and not from blushing, but from the hands that have slapped me. I choke against a sob as tears well up in my eyes. My hair is a giant mass of unruly, tangled ringlets. I try to run my fingers through it, but they get caught. I turn away from the mirror and walk over to the vanity sitting next to it and sit down.

The beige wood has three drawers and an oval mirror attached to the back of it. I pull open the drawer on the left and find a bunch of cosmetics. Powders, creams, sticks of kohl, and colored lip paints fill the small drawer. I close it and open the one in the middle. I thankfully find a hairbrush, ribbons, and hair pins. I grab the brush and start hastily pulling it through my tangled hair. I can hear it ripping through the curls, probably causing more damage than it's worth, but I don't stop.

The tears pour freely down my cheeks as I stare at my reflection. Once my curls are detangled enough, I put it in a quick braid to get it out of my face. I take one of the thin strips of black ribbon and tie it around the end, securing it with a bow. I throw the braid over my shoulder and stare at my reflection again.

I have never looked as ragged as I do now. Even after my many lashes and whippings, I haven't looked as close to death. My tears are quick to dry up, but the stuffiness in my nose is here to stay. I hastily wipe away at my nose and cheeks, my heartbeat racing. I want nothing more than to scream and to break things. I rip the bandage off my forehead and throw it onto the table. The scab lifts slightly and blood begins to pool under it.

Get it together, Elaenor.

My head drops into my hands, and I let out a soft whimper. Too much has happened, too much has gone wrong the last few days. Would things have been different had I been traveling with more guards? What if I had been traveling with any of my ladies? Would we all have been killed? Would one of them have offered themselves in my place? No. I would never allow that. I would have done anything I could to protect them.

A soft brush on my shoulder makes me scream as I jump back and nearly fall out of the chair. My fingers tighten on the hairbrush in a death grip, ready to use it as a weapon.

"Shh, it's just me." I turn to face Tobias, where he is kneeling on the ground next to the chair. "Are you alright?" His icy eyes are saddened, his eyebrows bunched together. He drops his hand from my shoulder and reaches for my hand, loosening my grip on the brush. "I'm sorry I scared you." He softly pulls my hand into his.

"It's okay." I whisper, my breathing ragged. "I didn't hear you come in."

"I knocked, but I don't think you could hear me." I nodded and looked back in the mirror. A small drop of blood is trailing down from the wound on my forehead. I pull my hand out of Tobias's and grab a tissue from the tissue box.

"Sorry." I whisper as I press down on the wound.

"Why are you apologizing?" His confusion is apparent as he places his hand on my cheek, pulling my face towards his. He sits up a little and grabs the bandage off the vanity with his free hand. "Here." I drop my hand and he places the bandage tightly against the wound. It stings slightly, but I hold in my wince.

"Thank you." I whisper and look down at my hands.

"I brought you some of the tonic if you want to take some. I also brought the herbs for–" His voice trails off and I nod. I stand quickly, stepping around him to the coffee table where a glass and a vial sit. I drop down onto the couch and immediately want to curl up in a ball and fall asleep. The plush cushions cocoon around me, offering comfort. I sigh as I reach for the vial.

It smells like cinnamon, some sort of citrus, and mint. I quickly pour its contents in my mouth and almost gag as it burns its way down my throat. I set the vial down before grabbing the nectar and taking a sip of it. It's cold, despite the lack of ice, and slides down my throat, easing the pain.

"How are you feeling?" I almost forget Tobias is there as he speaks. I look over at him and set the glass down.

"I'm okay." His lips thin as he comes to sit down next to me.

"You don't have to lie to me, and you don't have to be okay. It's alright to need some time to wrap your head around everything." His voice is soft, gentle, and I can feel the prick of tears filling my eyes.

"I am just very overwhelmed." I spit out, fighting against the lump in my throat. His eyes soften even more, and he hesitantly opens his arms. He doesn't make a move to touch me, he just sits there offering his comfort if I want it. Without allowing myself to think about it, I fold myself into him. His arms wrap around me, holding me tightly against his chest. Cedar and smoke fill my nose as I inhale deeply. He's warm as if he had just been out in the sun. His lips press against the top of my head as he just holds me.

Affection isn't something I am used to. Touch has always been negative, painful. I barely remember the feeling of my mother's soft hands, her hugs, her love. I don't remember a lot of my childhood, especially what occurred before she died. I blocked out a lot of memories, as most kids do when they witness something traumatic.

I was told I witnessed her murder, but I don't remember it. I don't even remember waking up that day, just that I was all of a sudden hiding in the trees covered in my mother's blood and something else, but that's all. After that, the only memories I have were filled with pain. But now, as I let Tobias just hold me, I feel a warmth in my chest I have never felt before. I feel safe, protected, and it scares me. These feelings are fleeting, and safety can end in a matter of seconds. Scarlett always said to make the most out of every situation because you never know when the opportunity will be gone. His fingers run down my spine, and I sigh.

I shift slightly and his arms loosen enough for me to pull out of them. I reach up and cup my hand over his cheek. His golden stubble pokes my palm as he looks at me with surprise. I lean forward and softly press my lips to his. He doesn't move and doesn't attempt to deepen anything. I pull back and his hand catches mine before I drop it.

"What was that for?" His voice is husky, deep and breathless, as if that small kiss was enough to affect him. I smile softly, blood rushing to my cheeks.

"Master Pakin told me you stayed at my bedside these last few days, making sure I was taken care of." He relaxes and his lips twitch.

"I'm sure his exact words were that I was an annoyance." He jokes and I laugh.

"That is exactly what he said." He uses his free hand to brush a loose curl that somehow escaped my braid, away from my face before cupping my cheek the same way I was touching him.

"I know you are nervous and overwhelmed, but I want you to know that anything that happens between the two of us will be started by you. I am not going to push myself onto you, I am not going to do anything you don't want. While this is my room also, if it makes you more comfortable, I can sleep on the couch or find another chamber to rest in. I don't want you to feel any more forced in this situation than you already are." His voice is steady and soft, and I feel my heart breaking.

I have been so terrified of Tobias these last few years because of the rumors that had somehow made their way to Chatis, but this man is completely different. This man sitting in front of me is gentle, considerate, and is doing everything possible to make sure I am comfortable. I want to yell, to scream, to hurt anyone who has ever said anything unkind about him. This is the man I always dreamed of him being.

"Thank you. You have no idea what that means to me." I admit. He really doesn't. He leans forward and presses his lips to the tip of my nose before dropping his hand.

"Would you like a tour?" I nod enthusiastically and he rises, bringing me with him. I bend down quickly and drain the contents of the glass, before letting him take my hand and lead me out of the door.

My limbs burn with each step, my right leg limping slightly, but I force myself to keep up with his steady pace. My core is tight, aching, but I file it away in the back of my mind. I can't appear weak, or tired. I can't make it seem as if I am unworthy to be here, regardless of how I arrived. I just need them to see me as someone who is meant to be here, not the imposter I feel I am.

The hallways are identical, every time we turn it's the same: floor to ceiling marble, same dark doors. Nothing to set anything apart. I have no idea where we are headed, and if I didn't know we were in a different hallway, I would assume one of these doors was to our room.

"I could get lost here." I whisper and his fingers tighten around mine, causing my heart to race.

"You get used to it. You start to use the windows as landmarks until you eventually can walk around without even looking." He pulls me down another hallway and then into an archway. Marble stairs greet us, and he leads me down them. I bite my lip when a small wince bubbles up in my throat as my right leg hits the first step. When we reach the bottom, another identical hallway sits in front of us, and I silently catch my breath.

"Where are we going?" I ask as I let him lead me around the palace.

"I figured you were hungry." I blush and instinctively place my hand over my growling belly. He pulls me through open double doors into a room that holds enough seating for hundreds of people.

The dining hall is a big square with windows lining the back wall, illuminating the marble room. I'm starting to find a common theme with the windows, any wall bordering the outer portion of the palace is almost entirely made of glass. Deep, brown wood benches and tables fill the space. A few people, mostly nobles by their appearance, are scattered throughout reading and eating.

Along the left wall is a line of tables filled with food and drinks. I can smell the various scents of roasted meat and potatoes and my mouth starts to water. A few of the others look up at us, but Tobias pays them no mind.

He pulls me over to the buffet and hands me a plate before he starts filling his own. When he has ensured I have enough vegetables, meat, and bread to feed an army, he leads me to one of the tables in the corner. He helps me into my seat before disappearing. I look down at my overflowing plate and lift a warm roll up to my mouth. The flaky, buttery texture melts in my mouth and I groan.

I can hear Tobias's laugh as he comes back with two glasses of water and sits across from me. I smile nervously and take a sip of the water.

"When was the last time you ate?" He chuckles as he puts a forkful of beef into his mouth, his eyes lightening. A small dimple I never noticed before appears in his left cheek.

"Well considering I have been asleep for three days; I would say at least four." His eyes widen and I can tell he's about to apologize, but I smile and shake my head. "It's fine. I don't think it's the actual timeline of when I ate last that is affecting me as much as the quality of the food. This is the best bread I have ever eaten." I admit as I take another bite.

"Did you not have bread in Chatis? I would expect the royal family to be eating really well." He says around a bite of green beans.

"I'm sure my father ate decadent dishes, I, on the other hand, ate what was allowed." I say nonchalantly.

"What do you mean?" His confusion is apparent, and I set the roll down and reach for my water again, taking a large sip.

"Every week, like clockwork, my father would assess my maturation and then he would decide what I was to eat that week." I admit, regretting bringing this up already.

"What do you mean to *assess your maturation*?" He places his fork down on the table, his eyebrows pinching together and his eyes narrowing. I swallow quickly and look away. I didn't mean to mention it, but it just came out.

"He would just assess my body to ensure I wasn't gaining or losing too much weight." I murmur as I push food around on my plate. I can still feel him staring at me, so I look up again.

"How?"

"What?"

"How would he assess you?" His voice is clipped, monotone, and I can tell he is angry. His teeth are clenched, his jaw sharpened. I debate not answering, but he would find out the second he saw me naked. I swallow again and set my fork down.

"He would strip me down, bare, in front of his friends and they would comment on how I was aging. How certain parts of me were maturing." His eyes widen and his mouth opens slightly. "He would poke and prod to determine if I was too fat, or too skinny. He'd let his friends do the same, help him make a decision."

"Did they..." He stops and I shake my head.

"No, they didn't touch me like that. They looked at everything, but they never touched me like that. I guess it would have been preferable-"

"To what?" He snaps and I jump, my nails digging into my palms.

"It doesn't matter, and I don't want to talk about it." I whisper as I meet his eyes. He's furious, his eyes darkening by the second. He looks like he's ready to hit something. I stay still, letting him work through his emotions. He takes a slow steady breath and then exhales loudly.

"When you want to talk about it, I am here. Nothing and no one is going to touch you. I promise." I nod and go back to picking at my food, no longer hungry.

After a tour of the grounds and an introduction to the majority of the staff, I am filled with exhaustion and the ever-present ache in my limbs. I haven't seen Theo again, but I feel my heart quicken at the prospect of him joining us for dinner.

A page had stopped our tour earlier to let us know that King Evreux called for a royal dinner to mark the arrival of the new princess, my unfortunate entrance forgotten by everyone but me. Everyone here is so keen to move on as if nothing ever happened, and while I want that as well, I cannot so easily recover. My new life doesn't feel real, I feel as if I am dreaming and will soon wake up back in the trees. While I knew I would be living here eventually, it almost seems too good to be true.

Tobias holds my hand as he brings me into the royal dining hall, his fingers lace through mine. A large chandelier hangs from the center of the room, bouncing light off the walls. The ceiling has the same intricate symbols pressed into marble and silver that is present in our bedroom. The back wall is broken up into panels of floor to ceiling windows, exposing the city. Golden lights shine in the darkness marking fire pits and lanterns. The sky is a beautiful shade of purple fading into black as the sun leaves us.

The rest of the room is sparsely decorated, with torches and small tables lining the walls. The marble floor is bright, reflecting the lights, but interrupted by a large crimson rug that lay under the table. The table isn't huge, set for a small family, but a roast turkey and abundant sides fill the center. My mouth waters as I remember how little I ate earlier.

Tobias guides me to a seat in the middle and pulls the chair out. I smile at him and slide in. He takes a seat to the right of me before his hand finds mine again and gives it a reassuring squeeze.

As the day progresses, I find myself drawn to him. His charisma, the way he speaks to the palace employees. I see the way people look at him, in awe. The future king. My future husband. The rumors floating around home quickly escaped my mind as he catered to me and took time to show me my new home. His eyes lighting up when he spoke about the archery field and the beach, somewhere he said he would take me.

I find that I have never felt more relaxed, more...*happy*, than I do right now. I don't know if it's the distance from my father or the company of Tobias that brings that peace of mind forward, but I try not to question it. The pain is still present, but I am hopeful it will continue to fade so long as I drink more of the nectar.

Tobias straightens himself in his seat just as King Evreux and Theo walk in. The king takes the seat at the head of the table, and Theo sits opposite of me. I try to remain calm, but I can't help but feel my heart race when he's near. He reminds me of home, but I can't place why. He's warm, quiet, careful. He's the exact opposite of Tobias, but I hardly know either of them.

Maybe he isn't as wonderful as he seems.

As Theo relaxes in his chair, his eyes meet mine and he winks, sending a delightful chill down my spine. I can't ignore the flutters in my chest when he is near, pulling at me like a magnet. I stifle a smile and Tobias stills beside me, catching our exchange. Theo's eyes harden as he meets his brother's, but it doesn't last long as King Evreux stands.

He's wearing the same crimson cloak as before, but his tunic and trousers are now white. His crown is resting perfectly upon his blonde hair. He and Tobias look so similar, his parentage couldn't even be a question. The same high cheekbones and angular jaw. Broad shoulders and deep, intense eyes that hold secrets. I am not too familiar with politics, but I wonder what the king is truly like and how much of what I see is an act.

"To Princess Elaenor, and the *near* future her presence brings." He bellows out as he raises a glass. He sways slightly and uses his free hand to hold onto the table. His skin seems paler this evening, his scar looking more purple than before. We all reach for our own glasses and hold them up in acknowledgement. All eyes on me as I try to hide my discomfort.

King Evreux slowly drops into his chair and his eyes meet mine. Panic and shame are the emotions I would say are filling his face. I can't imagine how being ill must make him feel. Once a strong and powerful warrior who is now sick and dying. I find myself feeling bad for him. His eyes leave mine and look off at someone else, giving them a nod. A flurry of staff come in and begin piling our plates with food and topping off our wine. I take an eager sip and relish in the sweet liquid I'm not used to.

"Is the wine to your liking, Elaenor?" King Evreux asks with a hint of amusement in his tone as he sticks a forkful of potatoes in his mouth.

"I've never had wine, Your Grace. My father said it was reserved for–" I don't finish my sentence, so as not to talk down about my father in the presence of his friend, but I so desperately wanted to say *for the men*.

"Ah, your father, Viktor. An obnoxious, lonely man. Don't you think so?" I smile and my uneasiness edges off. "Here in Noterra, you will have access to the finest wine money can buy. Help yourself, I insist." I offer him a soft smile as I reach for the glass.

"Thank you, Your Grace." I take another few sips as my glass is refilled again.

And again.

And again.

Hours tick by and our conversation is minimal as everyone eats in mostly silence. The effects of more wine than I am used to is warming my body and causing a light flush to creep up on my face. My body almost feels numb besides the gentle thrum of electricity flowing through my veins. I can't help but notice Theo glancing over at me nervously every few minutes, the electricity sparking every time our eyes meet.

When conversations do begin, it's between sons and their father about what the future holds, something I am not used to hearing. I take this time to fully absorb everything around me, gathering as much information as I can. I was never privy to war or battle briefs in Chatis, so hearing it spoken about with such deference is surprising.

"Have they done anything that questions your reign, father?" Tobias asks, engrossed in the conversation.

I learn that another country, called Labisa, is angered by my arrival, as most thought our wedding would never come, nor did they believe I actually existed. They see this as a sign of increased strength as King Evreux basically gained control over Chatis, another kingdom under his belt, which I also learn makes five kingdoms King Evreux has control over. I am left wondering how the other three succumbed to his rule.

My first encounter with King Evreux was uncomfortable, but that seems to be a running theme here. Chalking that up to my own nerves and the horrors I faced the other night, I try to allow myself to relax.

"They are calling for a rebellion, they feel that their king is the one true king and should take the throne." He scoffs as he stuffs another bite in his mouth.

"Why would they think that?" I ask. Based on the look I receive from Tobias, I don't believe I should be speaking, but I ignore him.

"King Argent was Noterra's previous king's nephew. King Jahara bore no children, which is how his throne became *available* after his demise. After Argent suffered the same fate, the Labisian king was the closest kin to the Jahara line. They are distant cousins, not enough for it to matter." King Evreux responds.

"You became king because of the rebellion. Was it King Argent's men you were fighting?" I ask. Tobias shoots me a glance that tells me to shut my mouth, but I ignore him again. My father didn't believe it was important for a girl to learn the histories as they did not concern me, but I always wanted to know as much as possible. Not to mention, Master Pakin said it was important for me to learn about this.

"Yes, Elaenor. A war that I won. A war that directly benefits you. Your children will be on the throne someday. When you bear a son, he will be the heir of Noterra and Chatis, joining our kingdoms permanently." He smiles. I can't help but wonder if he will still be around when his grandchildren are born.

"What happens if I only birth daughters?" His smile falters and his eyes narrow. I feel this is a valid question, but it may not have been best directed towards the king. Maybe I should have asked Tobias when we are alone. I feel Tobias's hand grip my knee, telling me one more time to stop asking questions. This time I listen.

"That is not an option, Elaenor. A male child is what is needed, and it is what you will provide." His voice is cold, warning. I nod as he begins speaking about war and politics, but my head is still swimming with the idea that my children will be rulers someday. That is if I even have children. What happens if I am unable to conceive an heir like my mother? Will I end up like her? Tobias is staring at me, but I refuse to make eye contact with him.

"Nora, how are you feeling?" Theo's crisp voice cuts through the chatter in my brain and the king's speech about increasing his militia. I meet his concerned gaze and try not to let it affect me, but his eyes hold too much power over me.

"*Nora*?" Tobias questions, his voice fueled by anger and confusion as he so much as spits out my nickname.

"I am feeling a little off, but it's probably the wine." I smile, ignoring Tobias, and trying not to dwell on the dull pain between my legs and the cramping in my abdomen. I take another sip, knowing I should stop as my head is already spinning, but it seems to be a social response, not to mention it's helping to numb my persistently aching limbs.

"Perhaps you should retire to separate chambers tonight, so you can rest?" Theo's voice has a hint of fear mingled with concern. Concern for my safety? Is he afraid of what Tobias will do? He told me I would be safe here. Our gazes meet and I stare into his saddened blue eyes. I continuously find myself drawn to him, but I try to force myself to ignore the flutters in my chest when he looks at me.

"Why don't you leave my betrothed's comfort to me, *brother*." Tobias reaches for my hand possessively and brings it up to his lips. I hear Theo exhale loudly in irritation. I've never had a sibling, so I am not positive this isn't normal banter between brothers, but the tension in the air is thick enough to cut and it's making me uncomfortable.

"Theo, leave the princess alone. She is not your concern." King Evreux's voice is loud and demanding as he waves his hand at his children, but Theo's eyes refuse to leave mine. "Tobias, why don't you see to it her *needs* are met." Theo's jaw hardens as he searches my face for any sign of fear, but I keep it inside. I try to steady my breath as I break eye contact from him. Raising my face to Tobias, I give him a small smile. I knew royals were conniving, but I hadn't predicted that I would have to act so much. My feelings, my personality, I feel as if I'll become someone I'm not.

"I am rather tired; I think I should retire for the evening." I feign ignorant to the implication of what is to come, hoping Tobias is more kind than his father seems to be. He brushes my bruised cheek with his knuckles and then moves to stand, his chair sliding across the rug smoothly.

"We will be retiring to bed. Father," He turns towards King Evreux and gives him a nod of respect.

"Thank you for the lovely meal, Your Grace." I dip my chin at the king as a sign of respect.

"Please, Elaenor." He says, his voice filled with longing and something else I can't place, as his hand reaches for mine. "Call me Evreux. You and I will grow very close." I still as my eyes meet his and Tobias's hand tightens around mine. Glaring at Theo, Tobias pulls me up from my chair as Evreux releases my hand, and out of the room. I manage to meet Theo's eyes one last time before the door closes. His face was cold and mirrored that of his father's, but I assume their thoughts were much different.

Chapter Eleven

As the warm water envelopes me into a much-needed hug, I melt into the tub. Running my hands over my body, I remove the bandages covering my wounds and watch them float to the surface. I was introduced to one of my new ladies tonight, an older woman by the name of Lydia. She was quiet as she undressed me and prepared my bath, only making a noise when an uncontrollable gasp escaped her lips. Her eyes wide as she focused on the bandages and blood on my body for a mere second before turning away and rushing out the door, leaving me alone. I tried to give her a reassuring look, but she refused to make eye contact with me.

The room where the bath sits is small but has a few windows along the perimeter. One of which opens to the grounds, while the other opens to an inlet of the palace. A few candlesticks lit in the corners of the room cast a soft glow across the stone. My attention fixates on the window directly across from me where a candle was just lit. The room illuminates and I see a lone figure pacing behind the glass. I can't quite make out who the figure is, but the hostility of their pace clearly tells me that they are angry. The person stops and the window flies open.

To my surprise, Theo leans out of the window gasping for air. His hands run through his light hair, angrily ripping out the leather strap holding back his wavy strands and move down to his face. He seems distraught, I wonder why? As he lifts his head up, his eyes meet mine. He stills, as do I as our gazes hold. His hair falling softly to his shoulders, messy and unruly, much like mine. I shift in the water, a chill running down my spine.

Confusion and indifference fill his face as his eyes slide down to where my naked body meets the water. Thankfully, the water is high enough to where I am covered, but I find it strange how comfortable I am with him. More so than with his brother. His eyes are always filled with kindness and remorse, while his brother's express confidence and power. His mouth opens to speak, before he shuts it quickly and softly smiles. I offer him a small smile in return right before the door opens behind me. I break my glance to turn and see Tobias walk in, smiling at the sight of me. I hide my panic as I look towards Theo's window, but it is already shut.

Tobias's hands meet my shoulders as he rubs them slightly, his fingers pressing deep into my skin. I focus on stilling my breath in an attempt to hide the moment I just had with Theo. I don't even know what that moment was, or if it was even significant, but I know Tobias would be unhappy about it.

I lean my head back against the edge of the tub and gaze up at him, thankful the darkness and water are covering my body so only my shoulders and head show, but his proximity still makes me nervous. His breathtaking features are soft, and I find myself feeling guilty for the reservations I have towards him. I don't know this man and I shouldn't let the words of others alter my perception, especially with how sweet he was earlier today. His lips are pressed into a thin line, his face failing to hide his irritation.

"Nora?" He asks, his eyes searching mine. A hint of fury gleams in his ocean eyes as he lets the name roll off his tongue in disgust. His fingers press harder into my skin, and I swallow loudly.

"I introduced myself to him as Nora in the woods. I didn't want him to know who I was, just in case he was associated with the men who took me. It's nothing, I promise. I don't know why he still calls me that after learning my name." I explain softly, hoping it eases his anger. I can't help the mild panic brewing in my chest at the sight of his mood and the feel of his fingers digging into my flesh.

He's *not* like my father, he's just jealous, territorial.

That's it. *Right?*

"I don't like it, Elaenor. This relationship you seem to have with my brother." His eyes don't leave mine as the unspoken threat fills the room. How could he think I have a relationship with his brother? I've only known them for a conscious 24 hours.

"There is no relationship, Tobias. I promise you. I am sure he is just concerned about me due to the state I was in when he found me. There is absolutely nothing going on." I assure him, lying enough to cover whatever attraction I feel for him, because I do feel something.

It's different with Theo. My desire to be in his presence isn't forced, it's something I look forward to. I can't explain it. I know I shouldn't even think that way, but it's hard. Maybe it's just a trauma response and I don't actually feel anything towards Theo. Or maybe it is exactly what I'm feeling, safe when I am near him. I don't know. I don't have experience with any sort of feelings or attraction so I'm out of my depth.

"Good." His voice is clipped, strained. "I'll see you in our room."

Leaning down, he places a soft and sweet kiss on my forehead, and then he's gone, the door closing loudly behind him. I glance back towards Theo's window and the light is out. I'm not sure if that's his room or if it's another place in the palace, but I find myself wanting to find out.

I want to know more about him, about his wants and desires. I know I should be cautious of how I interact with Theo, but my brain and heart seem to be entering into an unwinnable battle. Tobias is to be my husband, and Theo will eventually be married to another. The thought of seeing him with someone else makes my heart race.

What are you doing, Elaenor?

I take a deep breath before dipping my head underwater. My eyes open as I stare up at the ceiling through the distortion of water, the oils and salts stinging my eyes. The ceiling is dark and never ending, as if it's a black hole coming to swallow me. My heartbeat slows and I relax into the warmth. Peace. This is what I imagine peace feels like. Just floating in the darkness, with nothing and no one around. I let my trapped breath out, the bubbles rising to the surface.

Come find me.

His voice echoes in my head as I see movement above the water. A dark figure leans over, his green eyes shining through his long black hair, but now, there is a thin streak of white blending in, getting brighter every time I see him. Slightly tucked behind his ear, the bright strands stand out. His hand reaches down, gripping my shoulder as he pulls me out of the water. I inhale sharply as my face breaks through.

"Your Grace!" A woman's voice shrieks as I blink away the water in my eyes. Lydia is holding onto my shoulders, panic filling her eyes. "Your Grace, are you alright?" She asks as she produces a small towel to dry my face. I take the towel from her and press it against my eyes, coughing the water out of my lungs.

"Yes, I am fine. I was just getting my hair wet." My voice is little more than a croak. She looks unconvinced as she wraps a larger towel around my shoulders, helping me out of the tub. I avoid eye contact as she guides me to a chair and starts brushing my hair.

As she helps me prepare for bed, I try to ignore the feeling of confusion and wonder that washes over me. I thought about the man, and he appeared to me. I may have possibly been dreaming, but I never fell asleep. He seems so real. I heard his voice; I saw his hair. Why was some of it turning white? He seems to be near my age, so it wasn't from aging.

What is causing it?

Why did he appear when it was actually Lydia staring down at me? Why do I keep seeing him? Master Pakin said I had potential brain damage from my injuries, maybe that's what is causing these delusions. He doesn't exist. Am I going crazy?

He isn't real.

After I am ready, I make my way back to the room I share with Tobias. I stand in front of the door, with the guards on either side. My heart is racing, and I want nothing more than to turn back and climb into the safe tub with the comforting warm water. Behind this door is a man who could possibly be expecting me to bed him so soon after the woods. A man who I do not know. I've never been near a man and now all of that is changing so quickly. I know I will have to come to terms with this arrangement sooner rather than later, but my head is still swimming. I am suddenly aware of the two men guarding the door staring at me. No doubt thinking about the crazy princess who stares at doors.

"Good evening." I whisper. They just stare, so I give them each a small, embarrassed nod and they reach for the door to open it.

When I enter, Tobias is sitting in bed with his back against the headboard, writing furiously in a journal. My interest peaks and I wonder what it is he is so passionately writing about. I make a mental note to check later, knowing I shouldn't read his private thoughts but the desire to know this man outweighs it. I need to know if he truly is the man everyone believes, or if there is something I should be wary about. Does he write about his thoughts and feelings, or is he writing down notes about the impending war? Regardless of the answer, I want to know.

I spent a lot of time sneaking into the council chamber back home to read the notes left after various meetings. It was the only way to get a general understanding of what was going on in the world, even if half the information was indecipherable. I want to learn as much as possible, and the thought of asking Tobias for a tutor is almost embarrassing.

His chest is bare, his sun-kissed skin providing contrast to the light bedding. His hair is floppy and messy, tickling his forehead. His eyebrows are furrowed as he focuses on his journal, his bottom lip jutting out a little in concentration. He barely notices me as I walk in and tentatively step towards the bed. My heart is racing at the thought of climbing under the covers with a stranger. Maybe I should take his offer regarding his sleeping arrangements. The couch does seem quite comfortable.

"Hi." I whisper and he quickly looks up. His face softens when he looks at me, setting his journal down on his nightstand next to the ever-present glass of wine. He climbs out of the bed and walks around it to me. Tobias's warm hands rest on my shoulders briefly before sliding the silk dressing gown off my shoulders without breaking eye contact.

I stand, frozen, as it falls to the ground, a chill running down my spine as my flesh is exposed to the cool air. The pale blue nightdress I am wearing is short, barely brushing the tops of my thighs, but I was grateful for the fairly conservative undergarments I was provided. Thin straps hold the nightdress onto my shoulders, and I feel as if they are going to break off in any second under Tobias's stare.

"I need to re-bandage your wounds." He says softly before stepping away from me and to the couch where a small basket sits. I exhale loudly, my heart pounding. He sits down, his shorts riding up his thighs, revealing a light dusting of golden hair. He motions for me to come over, so I slowly walk up to him with my nails biting into the flesh of my palms. He's digging in the basket, and I look up at the ceiling, taking deep breaths. He's just rebandaging your wounds.

Relax.

His fingers are warm when they brush my thigh, and I stifle a flinch. I look down as he's rubbing some sort of ointment over the stitches. It hurts, but not nearly as bad as it did this morning. The ointment is thick and white, the scent of mint and poppy tickling my nostrils.

"It's healing well, the stitches should be ready to come out soon." He says as he gently wipes off the excess ointment with a damp towel.

"That's good." I whisper. He's bent down, his head near my stomach as he leans forward on the couch. He takes gauze and some medical tape and begins wrapping it around my upper thigh. His fingers lightly graze my backside and I once again fight against the urge to flinch.

Every time his skin touches mine, electricity sparks through my veins as if he's shocking me. I look down at him and lift my hand, gently brushing it through his hair that's glowing in the candlelight. It looks more golden right now, soft and silky, flopping to the side. He stills after he finishes wrapping my leg and looks up at me. My hand drops back to my side, and he smiles. I bite my bottom lip in embarrassment that I just touched his hair, but his eyes aren't sending me the message that he didn't like it. They are narrowed slightly, but not in anger.

"Any others that need it?" He asks, his voice a little husky, and I shrug. I truly don't know. There were quite a few bandages that floated up to the surface of the bath, but the worst wounds were the one on my thigh and my forehead. He grabs either side of my waist, his fingers warming the silk between us, and leans forward to plant a gentle kiss on my stomach before standing.

I have to angle my head up to look at him, his blue eyes boring into mine. His lips part slightly, his breath gently fanning across my face. My eyes flit to his lips briefly before returning to his eyes. Part of me wants to kiss him, the other part wants to run as far and as fast I can. He slowly lifts his hand and I think he's going to cup my cheek, but he doesn't. He gently pulls away hair that is caught on the scab on my forehead before breaking eye contact and bending down, grabbing the ointment again.

"I hope this doesn't scar your pretty face." He whispers, as he rights himself again. I smile and close my eyes as he gently dabs the cream onto my skin. This one doesn't burn at all anymore, and I am feeling more than grateful that I am healing quickly.

"I don't mind." I reply honestly. I have enough scars on my body, another wouldn't be a big deal.

"I do." I open my eyes. He sets the ointment down and grabs a small bandage, placing it right over my wound. When he's done, he wipes his fingers on the towel and places everything back into the basket methodically. When Tobias straightens, he's holding another glass of nectar, this one smaller.

"Do I need it?" I ask as I take the cold glass from him. I wonder which part of it keeps it cold? Not that I'm complaining, it feels pretty good on my continuously scratchy throat.

"That's up to you, but if you are feeling any bit of discomfort, this might help." I nod and take a sip.

I still have cramping in my lower abdomen and a sharp pulsing between my legs slowly growing. As always, the nectar is syrupy and sweet, but delicious. I finish the glass and he takes it from me gently, his fingers brushing mine. I expect him to step away, but he maintains the mere inches between us. After he sets the glass on the coffee table, his hands come up to gently cup my face. He looks worried, his icy blues deepening into gray.

"What's wrong?" I ask, my hands lifting to gently wrap around his wrists. His wrists are a lot larger than I expect, my fingers aren't long enough to encircle them completely and I almost laugh at the thickness, but I don't. His grip is soft, but firm, commanding as his eyes search mine.

"I don't like seeing you hurt." His voice is strained, as if he is fighting some emotion, which fills my brain with a mixture of confusion and surprise. I smile and lean into his palms, relishing in the feel of his skin against mine.

"I'm okay, now. Really. I'm healing quickly and I already feel better, although that might be all the wine I drank." I laugh softly and his lips press into a thin line.

"Look, about Theo," He starts, but I open my mouth to cut him off.

"Don't think about that." I plead.

"I don't like it, Elaenor." He says through gritted teeth.

"What do you want me to do about it?" I ask. My hands fall from his wrists, and he drops his away from my face. "I told him my name was Nora, it only makes sense that is what he calls me. If it bothers you so much, tell him to stop. Or you can call me Nora, too." I offer with a shrug, and he rubs his face. "The only people who have ever called me Nora are my mother and *occasionally* my ladies back home. I was trying to hide my identity. I was worried about my safety." I knew that would reel him back in, or at least I hoped. He drops his hands from where they were tangling in his hair and lightly cups my face again.

"I don't want to call you Nora. You are Elaenor, and you are *mine.*" I nod, my breath quickening with the way he said mine. His eyes flick to my lips briefly and I quickly wet them. *He's going to kiss me.*

He brings his lips down to mine, demanding, wanting. I kiss him back, bringing my hands up to his chest and then to his face. Something delicious and warm fills my core and I find myself wanting more. Is this a genuine desire, or just a bodily reaction? I have no idea, but I don't care. I want this. I want him to keep kissing me. To make me feel wanted.

He pulls back, his breath fanning over my lips. I pout slightly, not wanting the kiss to end.

"I don't want you to talk to him or have anything to do with him."

"Tobias–"

"*Please*, I see the way he looks at you. Just don't talk to him, that's all I ask." And he can ask that. He owns me, he can make me do whatever he wants. I nod and his lips find mine again, forcing them open as his tongue curls around mine. We are all teeth and tongue and passion. He falls back onto the couch, pulling me on top of him. My thighs hug his hips as he pulls me closer. There isn't a single breath of space between us as he tightens his arms around me. The movement sends a jolt of pain through my abdomen, and I wince. I shake my head, willing the pain to dissipate. I tangle my fingers through his short strands pulling his lips harder against mine. I can feel his arousal growing, pressing against his sleep shorts, and rubbing against me. I shudder at the equal amount of pleasure and pain radiating from between my legs from the friction.

"What is it?" He whispers in between kisses.

"Nothing, just my stomach. It's nothing." I reply against his lips before pressing mine to his again.

That is all we are doing, just kissing. I can do this. As inexperienced as I am, I just need to follow his lead. I want this. I want to kiss him. It's nice to feel desired by someone who doesn't have an alternate agenda. Someone who just wants my company.

His hands tighten on my waist as he moves me against him, a slow rocking motion. I can feel my nightdress riding up, pooling around his hands as he holds me close. I roll my hips slightly without his assistance and he hisses, his teeth gently nipping my bottom lip. I do it again and press my thighs tighter against him as pressure builds.

A sharp stabbing pain hits my abdomen and I gasp against his lips. I pull back and rest my forehead on his shoulder. My breathing is labored, and I can't tell if it's from our kissing or the pain shooting through my core. I grit my teeth and shake my head, willing myself to focus on anything other than the discomfort. I let out a shaky breath and squeeze the back of his neck where my hands are resting.

"Tell me, what's wrong?" He whispers, just as breathless as me. He runs his lips up my jaw to that spot behind my ear where he places a soft kiss.

"I just have this weird pain in my stomach. I think I need more of that nectar." I admit, taking slow deep breaths. Tobias presses his lips to my shoulder before nodding and sitting up. He gently slides me off of him to the cushion beside us and freezes. "What?" I ask as I lean my forehead against the back cushion, breathing through the cramping. I turn slightly to see his eyes cast down. I almost ask him again, before looking at his lap.

He's covered in blood, and I look down to see my nightdress is also stained with it. His eyes widen as he looks at me and then down between my legs. I lean back to take in the actual pool of blood staining the white couch. Blood is smeared down my legs and across his lower stomach and I gasp.

"I'm going to get Master Pakin." He quickly sits up and goes to run out of the room before turning back towards me. "Are you okay? If I leave, will you be alright for a few moments?" His voice is clipped and panicky, his eyes wider than I have ever seen. I nod and he exhales loudly before leaving the room quickly in nothing but his sleep shorts and my blood.

I adjust myself on the couch, so I am leaning my back against the armrest, and wince as it sends a sharp pain straight to my core. Something about this pain feels so familiar, but incredibly sharp as if it's heightened. Maybe this is just my monthly bleed and it's just stronger due to the tonic? I hope that's the case. I take a slow deep breath, letting my body relax as much as possible.

I look down at my legs again and groan. I loudly curse the fact that I am on a white couch as I see my blood soaking more and more into the fabric. I slide off the edge of the cushion, slowly getting to my feet. My goal is the bathroom, but I stumble against the steps up from the living area. I trip and my knees slam into the stone.

"Ouch!" I yelp out. My head spins and I force a deep breath as I pull myself to my feet. I slowly make it to the door, pushing it open and leaving a bloody handprint. The two guards that seem to always be present turn towards me, their mouths opening in shock. I glance down at my short nightdress soaked in blood, the steady drips reaching my ankles. My feet go numb, and I can feel my knees wobble. I reach for the threshold but miss.

"Your Grace!" One of them calls out before my legs give out and I fall forward. Someone's arm catches me inches before my face hits the stone and I hiss as the movement jostles my abdomen. I can hear talking, but it's muffled. It sounds like it's far away. I can feel someone hoist me up into their arms, my head resting on someone's shoulder, my body shaking with every step. Did Tobias come back already? I try to whimper, but it comes out as a breathy groan.

Gods this hurts so bad.

"Tobias?" I whisper. I can feel my head fogging over, it's getting harder to focus on anything.

"Your Grace, you shouldn't be touching her. He will be back momentarily." Someone snaps and I open my eyes slightly, using every ounce of energy I have. Who's holding me? I can just barely make out unbound golden hair before my eyes close again.

Chapter Twelve

Eyes as green as the Chatisian trees filled with anger. The feeling of glass and bone slicing through my naked feet makes me cry out in pain. Or is it sadness? Sadness for the loss of the ones I used to love. Sadness for what my life has become. I drop to my knees, barely registering the pain I feel. Glass and bone burrowing through my flesh until my bones mix with theirs, knowing this is what I deserve.

I did this to them.

Their blood is on my hands.

It doesn't take long for me to wake, and I find that I am not surprised to see that I am in the infirmary again. The windows are dark, signaling that it is still nighttime, the room lightly illuminated by torches on the walls. I sit up and warm fingers gently push my shoulders back down to the bed.

"Don't move so fast." His voice is rich, like caramel as he whispers to me. I look over and see his messy golden hair glowing in the candlelight. He looks terrified, his eyes bloodshot.

"What happened?" I croak and force myself to swallow.

"It seems your monthly bleed has returned with a vengeance." Master Pakin says from my right, and I turn to look at him. He is wearing white night clothes and a thick dark robe. His hair is tied into a messy knot at the nape of his neck, and he looks exhausted.

"What?" I croak again and he pours what I know is a glass of tonic. I sit up again, and this time Tobias doesn't stop me but helps lift me up with his hand on my back. I take the glass and down it quickly, almost whimpering from the relief it provides as its syrupy texture coats my dry throat.

"You seem to be having a very aggressive cycle, Your Grace. It is most likely due to the tonics and probably the trauma you received. Your body has been through a lot, so it's not as strong as it should be." My face falls and I stare at him. "This is a good thing, my dear. It means you are not pregnant." I almost collapse with relief, and I would have if Tobias arms didn't wrap protectively around me, pulling me against his chest. I rest my head against him, fighting the yawn creeping up my throat and the tears forming in my eyes.

"Thank you, Pakin." Tobias whispers.

"Tonight should be the worst of it. I gave you a small injection that should finish up whatever is happening inside of you. It may be a rough night, so if you want the essence of wisteria–"

"No." I snap a little too harshly, my eyes widening. "I don't want to feel that way. It makes me feel vulnerable and I just can't feel like that again." I admit, my voice is softer. He nods, giving me a small smile as he stands.

"Alright, but please finish this decanter before you go to sleep." He gestures towards the metal pitcher sitting on the table. "It'll help with the pain and help relax you. Would you like to stay here in the infirmary tonight?" He asks.

"No, I'll watch over her in our room." Tobias responds for me, his hand rubbing up and down my bare shoulder. I am grateful for the warmth it provides, and I lean back into him. My eyes are heavy, and I just want to go to sleep. I can feel a sharp pricking sensation in my right arm, which must be where he gave me an injection. The throbbing in my core is still there, but it is duller, not as sharp and debilitating.

"Please call for me if anything happens, or should you be in too much pain." I nod with my eyes closed and hear as his slippered feet pad out of the room.

"Come on, I'll carry you." Tobias whispers as he bends down to scoop up my legs. The jostling of my limbs causes a deep cramp in my abdomen, and I hiss in pain. He pauses for a second, looking down at me, before I nod. He steps around the bed, and I catch the sight of the pitcher.

"Wait, the nectar!" I say, louder than I intended. I hate the dependency I have on it, but I know the herbs will help ease the discomfort I feel.

"Don't worry, Laris will bring it." I look over Tobias's shoulder and see one of the guards who stands outside our room walking in. He has dirty brown hair that is cropped close to his head and a little scruff on his jaw. His eyes are a piercing hazel, almost yellow. I recognize him as the one that walked me to my room yesterday. I close my eyes again and in what seems like seconds, we are back in our room.

"Can you stand for a second?" Tobias asks and I nod, opening my eyes halfway. He sets me down and holds out his arm to catch me if I lose balance. I shake my head and he turns around, heading for the dressing room. I walk slowly over to the bed, careful not to trip on my own feet, and lean against it while I wait for him to return. Gods I feel like I've been run over by a horse. When he reappears, he's holding one of his t-shirts and a pair of shorts. He bends down and holds the shorts open for me.

"Step into it." He commands and I grip his shoulder to steady me. He pulls them up and over my backside and up to my waist, electricity snapping at my skin wherever his fingers brush me. The cotton is soft, warm, as if Tobias himself is wrapped around me. "Hold your arms up." I pause and look up at him nervously. I wasn't entirely ready to be naked in front of him, something he was quick to pick up on, but it wasn't just the intimacy I was afraid of. "Turn around and I'll just see your back." I nod slowly with a long exhale and do as he asks, slowly turning my body. He pulls the bloody nightdress off of me and freezes. "What the *fuck*?" He mutters. His fingers brush my back and I stiffen. *Damnit.*

"Tobias," I whisper, frozen without a shirt on. "Tobias." I repeat.

"Elaenor, what is this?" His voice is strained, clipped. "Did your father do this to you?" His fingers are frantically running over the scars, and I shiver. I know what he's seeing.

He sees the twelve-inch puffy scars that line my back like stripes. Last time Scarlett had counted, there were 23 of them. All products of my father's whippings when I made him unhappy. The small ones on my arms and legs are nothing compared to these. These had me laid up in bed with infection for weeks, nearly costing me my life. Not once did he come see me as around the clock menders worked on debriding the dead flesh before it spread to my blood or bones. The only thing he asked was when I would be healed enough for another punishment. Scarlett convinced them I needed an extra week's rest, but my father wasn't quick to believe her lies. He added three more scars to my back before switching completely to the thinner whip on my thighs after the master said I wouldn't survive another beating like that.

"Yes." I whisper, my arms still up in the air. He slips the shirt over me and turns me around to face him, pulling my braid out front under the neckline. The soft cotton smells like him, cedar and smoke wafting around me. It's long, almost longer than the nightdress, covering the shorts completely.

"I am going to kill him." He whispers as he pulls me against his chest.

"Don't. It doesn't matter anymore." He kisses the top of my head. As much as I want to dwell on the horrors I endured in Chatis, if I don't let it go, I'll spend the rest of my days depressed and on edge. I don't like feeling vulnerable and if I was in a better mental state, I never would have let him see them. See my pain and my shame for allowing myself to be used as a whipping block.

"Yes, it does." He responds, and I can feel the fury roiling off him like a heat wave.

He tucks me into the bed after I finish the nectar and climbs in on the other side. He doesn't go under the covers, and instead, sits halfway up so he's looking down at me. He put a shirt on at some point and changed into clean shorts, which only makes me hyper aware that someone cleaned the blood off of me in the infirmary.

Who hasn't seen me naked at this point?

I am laying on my side, my hands tucked under my cheek as he settles himself against the headboard.

"Do you want to sleep?" He asks before reaching over and picking up the tail of my braid and twisting it between his fingers. I nod and he gently places it back down.

"Will you stay?" I ask, closing my eyes. I can feel him stiffen and then relax into the pillows.

"If that is what you wish." I nod again and take a slow, deep breath. I can feel him moving around in the bed, before stilling again. I open my eyes and his face is only a few inches from mine, his blue eyes glowing in the darkness.

"Can I ask you something?" I ask, breaking the silence. It is his turn to nod this time. "How did I get to the infirmary? I heard Laris telling someone to put me down, but I was borderline unconscious and couldn't make out who was carrying me." He swallows loudly and I try to ignore the annoying ache deep in my belly. I can feel the tonic spreading through my veins like ice, but it's not enough to get rid of every bit of discomfort. I know wisteria would have, and I probably should have let him give it to me, but being in a drug induced sleep scares me more than it would help.

"Theo. You wandered out into the hallway and nearly fell face first onto the marble. Laris was going to put you back in the room, but Theo came and took you." I can hear the frustration in his voice.

"I'm sorry." I know I shouldn't be apologizing, but I don't know what else to say. "I was trying to go to the bathroom to clean myself up. I was making a mess on the couch, so I was trying to fix it."

"I don't give a damn about the couch, I just wanted to make sure you were okay." He's rolling his lips and I can tell he's stressed. I place my hand on his cheek, his stubble lightly poking my palm.

"I *am* okay." I whisper and close my eyes again. His breath mixes with mine as we lay there in silence. My cramps are still present, but I can almost take a full deep breath now.

"Can I ask *you* something?" He says, copying me. I nod, my hand still on his cheek. "When you were taken, did you fight back?" My eyes open slightly, and I can just barely make out his in the darkness. Where did that come from?

"Yes, I did." I say slowly. He exhales through his nose. "I was never taught how to protect myself, so there wasn't much I could do. Despite how much I hate the word, I got lucky." I admit. I am lucky and I will thank whatever gods made that happen every day that I am alive.

"How so?" I sigh.

"The first guy, Jeremiah, was interrupted, and then Aleksander finished what he started. I knew I wasn't strong enough to prevent them from raping me, so I just bid my time. I tried to fight back initially, but I barely made him flinch, it wasn't worth my energy. I took my chance when it became available and kicked the dagger out of his hand. I didn't know what I was doing, it was as if instinct kicked in." I swallow and he places his hand over mine on his cheek, threading his fingers through mine. "When the dagger pierced his neck, he made these awful sounds. I know I didn't have a choice, but it was horrible." I shake my head, trying to get the sight out of my mind. I could still hear his gurgling and feel his body shaking as he took his last breath.

"Did they say anything?"

"He just kept saying that they couldn't let Noterra win and get what they wanted." He stays quiet. "I don't know how he knew who I was. They were clean, no scars. I feel like they may have been noblemen, but they knew what they were doing. This wasn't their first time attacking someone, that's for certain. I am not entirely convinced that they weren't going to kill me in the end, but I don't even know what they were trying to accomplish."

"It could have just been the carriage, an easy target."

"No, I heard them talking about it. They said that someone told them when I was coming. They knew where to wait." My voice gets quieter. "They planned this, Tobias."

"They failed. That's all you have to remember." I can hear the urging in his voice, his need for me to believe that everything will be fine, but I can feel the nausea creeping in. The same discomfort that has been there since I knew the time to head to Noterra was growing close. Ever since I started to question my safety.

"Am I safe here, Tobias?"

"Yes, Elaenor. I promise that I won't let anyone touch you." I nod and close my eyes again. His hand stays on mine as we lay in silence. "Are you in pain?" I nod and adjust so I am laying more comfortably on my back, my hand slipping out from under his.

"It's easy to ignore it with the nectar tonic thing. I just have to breathe through the waves of discomfort. It's not as scary knowing what it is."

"I thought you were dying." He exaggerates.

"It wasn't that bad."

"Well it was bad to me. Imagine looking down and seeing me pouring blood from my cock." He laughs as he says it and I giggle in response.

"Okay that would freak me out, too." I admit. He reaches over and places a hand on my abdomen, his thumb sliding up and down on my stomach, warming the cotton between us.

"I'm happy you are here, Elaenor. Despite this marriage being forced on us, I couldn't have picked a better bride." He sounds sincere, like he's telling the truth. I believe him. I smile softly before letting it fall from my face. My eyes are following the path of veins in the marble ceiling above, circling around the silver filigree, as I think of what to say.

"Did your father ever talk about me?" I ask.

"All the time. He used to get letters every few months discussing your age and personality. It was my favorite time and I looked forward to it." I envy him. I didn't have that luxury and if Evreux did send my father letters about Tobias, they were never shared with me. I close my eyes, taking a slow breath as I can feel the exhaustion setting in.

"My father used to talk about you. He used our engagement as a weapon. He said that if I didn't behave, he was going to teach you how to whip me. He said he would force me to marry you earlier so you could keep me locked up for breeding." I snort at the idea and his thumb stills on my stomach. I open my eyes and turn my head towards him. His face has hardened, from what I can see in the darkness, his eyes looking almost black.

"If I am ever given the chance, I will give him exactly what he gave you. I'll whip him until his flesh is just barely hanging onto his bones and only then, after he has suffered, will I slice his throat and watch him bleed out." My eyes widen and I swallow loudly.

The thought of my abuser getting the same treatment is fortifying, but the small part of me that still wishes my father loved me, feels saddened and horrified. Even if he wasn't my father, his words, his thoughts, they are surprising. The fact that someone can think of doing something like that isn't normal. At least I don't think it is. I stay silent, my pulse pounding through the air, and I am almost convinced he can hear it. His thumb continues its caress, and I can feel his eyes on me.

"You don't have to be scared of me." He whispers, answering my unspoken thoughts.

"Are the rumors true?" The question pops out of my mouth before I could stop myself. I'm hoping he knows what I am referring to. I have to know, especially after the threat he just made. He's silent for a second, his eyes unfocusing.

"I am not going to lie to you and say that I have stayed celibate waiting for you. I am also not going to deny preferring a rougher nature to the tenderness you are expecting, but I am not a monster. I have never done anything without consent and at any point those who have shared a bed with me were able to withdraw consent at any time." I feel a weight lift off my shoulders and I relax slightly, my tense muscles loosening.

"Can I tell you something without you getting angry with me?" My voice comes out as a breathy squeak, and I almost roll my eyes at my body's ability to make me appear weak.

"Depends." He responds with a smirk, his left dimple barely visible in the darkness.

"Theo told me you prefer to share your bed with multiple women and have never favored monogamy." He stills and then rolls on his back, his arm leaving my stomach and taking his warmth with him.

"First off, Theo needs to keep his *damn* mouth shut. This is why I didn't want you talking to him. Second, why in the worlds would I get into a monogamous relationship *knowing* that at any point I would be forced to marry someone. I would never risk my heart or that of another knowing that it was a doomed relationship from the start. Any relationship I have had has been purely physical. I have purposefully kept emotions out of it so they could be saved for you." Despite the irritation I'm sure he's feeling, his voice remains even, almost desperate for me to believe him.

I don't respond at first. He was saving any chance of love and emotions for *me*. That is why he slept around; it wasn't because he was a monster. What if I am not enough? What if he craves a variety of bodies and women? What if he still seeks another lover? I wouldn't be able to do anything about it.

"Will I be enough for you?" My voice comes out in a croak, my throat tight and my eyes burning with unshed tears as I look back at the ceiling. He rolls over quickly and puts his arm under me, pulling me to his chest, my back pressed up against his front.

"You already are, Elaenor." His arms tighten around me as he presses his lips to my hair. I breathe in the scent of cedar and smoke, relishing in the comfort and warmth. "Get some sleep."

It doesn't take long before I let sleep find me.

Fires. There are fires everywhere. Screaming. Children and adults running around, panicking.

"What is happening?" I scream as people run past me in all directions. I try to grab someone, to beg them to explain, but they shake my arm off and keep running. I spin around but all I can see are hordes of people streaming out of the palace gates, the walls crumbling around them, burying some of them alive.

"Run!" I hear someone scream as a loud boom echoes across the town. Rocks and debris explode in the air, throwing me to the ground. I hit the rubble hard, nearly knocking the wind out of me. I can tell I have broken a few ribs as I pull myself to my feet, wheezing. People fall to their knees with arrows sticking out of their chests and I have to scramble over their dead bodies to get away from their aim. I try to not look at their faces, but it's hard. Blood pooling beneath their bodies, eyes open and unseeing. It's too much. I scream in frustration as I make it out of the pile of rubble.

I run towards the palace, knowing there are underground bunkers. I just need to get as many people to them as possible. I push through the crowd but someone's hand wraps around my wrist and pulls me back.

"Hey!" I turn and come face to face with the man from my dreams. His black hair is filled with ash, a chunk of white tucked behind his ear. His nose is bleeding, a gaping wound on his shoulder.

"We have to run, Elaenor! We have to get out of here." He yells and tries to pull me deeper into the crowd.

"No! There are bunkers."

"Run, Elaenor. Run!*" Before I can respond, another bomb hits the square and everything disappears under a cloud of debris and ash.*

I sit up abruptly, gasping for as much air as I can get. Tobias is asleep beside me, softly snoring, with his arm draped over my stomach protectively. I look around the dimly lit room while my pulse relaxes. The sun is barely rising outside, casting an orange glow across the marble. I lay back down, forcing my breathing to slow.

In and out.
I am safe.
I am not in Chatis.
I am not being blown up.
People are not dying.
I repeat over and over until I fall back asleep.

Chapter Thirteen

These last few days have been a lot to handle, even with me being unconscious for the majority of it. I need to find some form of normalcy, or at least something to keep me preoccupied enough that the thoughts of that man and his warnings are kept at bay. Whether it is a hobby, or some other duty I can obtain, I need something of my own. But everything around me is tied to Tobias. My room, the guards, even my attire. I left Chatis after having everything monitored and controlled by my father, and now that seems to be the case here.

When will I truly be free?

Slipping into the crimson dress I found lying on the bed when I awoke a second time, I brush my hands over the silk. It truly is the most beautiful dress I've seen, but the color haunts me. The color of this nation is silver and white, yet Evreux is always in crimson, and now so am I one way or another. Whether it's blood or expensive silk, it seems I am destined to be wearing red, at least if Tobias has anything to say about it. As I step into my black shoes, I give myself a once over in the mirror by the privacy screen.

The dress features a lace corset in crimson with a beige slip, attached to a full skirt that brushes the floor at the perfect length. My black hair seemingly has been tamer since my arrival, which may have something to do with the soaps I have been given or the oil Lydia braided into my hair last night. Instead of frizzy untamable curls, my long black hair falls in soft waves down to the small of my back.

My pale skin has not yet had the pleasure of suntanning, so it stays a ghostly shade of white. Bruises around my neck and my cheek are bright against the shade of my skin, leaving purple and blue splotches. The cut on my forehead seems to be fully scabbed, enough where I was able to take the bandage off. My blue eyes are tired, as the bags around them reflect. Less like the ocean waves and more gray and dull than usual, surprisingly reminding me of the cloudy skies of Chatis.

My heart aches for home, but I know I am better off here, or at least I hope I am. Attributing the exhaustion and pale skin to the blood loss I have experienced, I take one last glance and freeze as my eyes catch on something. Sticking out of the top of my head is a single strand of white hair. I grasp it in between my fingers and pull on it. It breaks away from my scalp easily and I bring it to my face. I hold the single hair in front of my eyes and stare at the ghastly white color, spanning the entire length of the strand. It reminds me of the man I keep seeing, his black hair was turning white too. A knock on the door makes me jump and the strand of hair falls to the ground.

"May I enter, Your Grace?" I turn as one of the guards stands in the doorway. I remember him to be Laris. I wonder if he ever sleeps since he spends most of his time in front of my door.

"Yes." I respond.

"Prince Tobias is awaiting your presence." I nod and make my way over to the door that is being held open for me.

Tobias meets me in the hall, his eyes full of appreciation as he scans my new gown. He's wearing all black, like usual, with his tunic cut close to his body to show off his muscular frame. "You look beautiful, Elaenor." He smiles and bends down for a quick kiss. I allow it, before casting my gaze down to hide my reddening cheeks.

"Thank you." I smile.

He reaches towards me, and I take his outstretched hand. Walking down the grand hallways towards the dining hall, we walk in silence. I listen to the echoes of our footsteps, hear the birds singing just beyond the glass lining one side. I allow myself to relax. It has been a whirlwind of a few days and I'm having a hard time keeping up. While I didn't expect to assimilate into life here quickly, I didn't think it would be the way it is. I should have expected issues, nothing I ever do comes without problems.

Today is supposed to be my wedding day, however no one has mentioned it to me since yesterday morning. I expect that if I were truly marrying today, I'd be spending my morning getting ready instead of walking slowly and casually throughout the palace. As I am not ready to become someone's wife, I don't mention it now for the hopes it isn't a rushed affair and that they forgot, not that that's likely.

"How are you feeling?" Tobias's voice cuts through my thoughts. His fingers rubbing my knuckles as we walk.

"Better. My body is just trying to adjust to everything as is my mind." I admit, not lying. I awoke this morning in significantly less pain. I removed my bandages and was surprised to see scabs that have settled, and the swelling nearly gone. My stitches are still in, but I am hoping I can get them taken out soon. The cramping in my abdomen has subsided, and even the blood has cleared up. While I may not look it, I am feeling better than I have in a really long time.

"Elaenor." He stops, catching me by surprise, and looks at me. "I apologize for any pain I caused you. I don't know if us kissing or maybe the way we were sitting contributed to your pain, I just don't like seeing you hurt or bleeding." His eyes are lined with silver as he looks down at me and it nearly knocks my breath away. I have never seen anyone look at another this way, with such care and desire. I reach for his other hand and bring it to my face, wanting no distance between us.

"It wasn't you, Tobias. You weren't the one to hurt me. Th-" My voice cracks and I steady myself, not wanting to let the threatening tears spill. I never used to be sensitive, I had a pretty strong backbone, but everyone has their breaking point and I hit mine a few days ago. "Those men were monsters. He knew what he was doing, and he knew who I was. And the herbs that I was told to take were important to ensure that any child I carry belongs to you. That *we* have children, not me and some savage." Pulling me into his chest, he kisses the top of my head, his arms wrapped around me tightly. I inhale the intoxicating scent of cedar and smoke, wanting to just get lost in him, in this, in *us*.

"He's gone, Elaenor, they both are, along with anything they tried to create with you. You don't have to be scared here. This palace is safe from creatures like him. You have my protection, Noterra's protection, I promise." Relaxing into his touch, I take a deep breath and nod.

I barely know Tobias, yet I find myself believing him. Believing in him. That he can make me happy, that he'll treat me well. I feel nothing in this moment other than relief.

His fingers trace my spine as I lean back to look up at him. Hands on his chest, I stare into his eyes looking for any sort of hostility or danger that I keep fearing I'll see, but nothing. Nothing but warmth fills his blue eyes, and that's surprising. I don't know if I'll ever grow used to it.

I lean up onto my tip toes and press my lips to his. His hands tighten around me as he forces my lips to part, our tongues meeting. His breathing quickens as he intensifies the kiss, and I let him. I like how he feels against me, his strength, his protection. I want to be in his arms. This is what I have always wanted, what I have always dreamed of. I can feel that delicious heat pooling deep in my core, telling me that I want this more than anything.

Our embrace is short lived as a man, dressed much like Master Pakin but with a silver robe, walks up and whispers into Tobias's ear. I search his face for any sort of recognition, but all I see is irritation. He nods as the man stops speaking, too low for me to hear. With a last glance and a slight bow in my direction, he turns on his heels and walks back the way he came. Tobias's gaze meets mine and I stare up at him, concerned.

"Tobias, what is it?" I ask, my hands still on his chest, his around my waist.

"I have some urgent business to attend to. I'll find you later." He bends down and kisses me quickly before pulling my hands up to his lips and giving them a gentle brush of his lips. Walking in the direction of the other man, he disappears around a corner, leaving me standing in the hallway alone.

What am I supposed to do now?

I find myself wandering the halls in search of anything that I can remember. Every turn I make I am met with identical hallways. It seems the palace is much more like a circle than I previously realized. Without a guide to show me the way, I fear I'm lost. I had thought this was the way to the dining hall, but I seem to be getting deeper and deeper into the palace, areas I don't recognize, and I haven't yet found the staircase to lead me down a floor.

I pass two open double doors and to my surprise, it's the throne room. I was here once as a child, but it seems larger than I remember, emptier even. The two grand chairs up on the raised platform boast excellence and a deep coffer filled with riches. Steel and stone intertwined to look like thorns and vines. A single red rose made of stained glass sits at the top of each back, connected to the vines by a single silver branch. Matching red cushions are nestled into the seat for comfort and looks. The thrones are beautiful, and I can hardly comprehend how the one on the right will be mine someday.

I step into the round room and look up. Clear glass windows line the ceiling, shaping it into a dome. The bright blue skies and fluffy clouds sprinkled about feel foreign, like a painting. Every time I look outside, I expect the deep gray clouds, but a smile never ceases to pop up when I realize my new reality.

I look around at the walls, which are remarkably bare with the exception of a single tapestry boasting the kingdom's crest taking up the majority of the wall to the right. A diadem made out of thorns and vines, matching the thrones, covered in blood. It almost matches Evreux's crown, but this one looks delicate and sharp. No doubt an ode to the way Evreux claimed this land, but what should make me look away in fear has me wanting to step closer. My hand brushes the woven fabric, and I can see the sparkle of silver thread intermixed with white and red catching on the light.

The clearing of a throat causes me to yelp and spin around, where I am met with the sight of Evreux. He's wearing the same crimson cloak as before draped over a white tunic and matching trousers. His silver crown sitting atop his perfectly groomed blonde hair. His face cold, with the hint of a smile playing at the corner of his lips. His skin is looking gray, no sign of life, signaling that he's getting sicker. His stature is looking leaner, as if he is struggling to keep on weight. I have to force my face to stay neutral instead of allowing the look of pity to fill my eyes. I can't imagine how he feels every day when he looks in the mirror.

"Elaenor, do you like what you see?" He asks, his loud voice booming through the silence. Even as ill as he is, he still speaks with such power, but like before, I can hear the slight tremor at the end of his sentence. I swallow and do my best to hide my uneasiness as he steps closer, plastering a fake smile on my face.

"It's beautiful." I turn back towards the tapestry, letting my fingers linger over the woven blood as a distraction.

"I fought for this kingdom; it wasn't handed to me." His voice is close, his breath tickling my ear as I feel him barely brush my back. I stiffen slightly, regretting that I kept my defenses down. "That diadem," He grabs my hand and guides it up to the thorns and I fight the urge to pull it out of his cold and calloused grasp. "Represents strength and sacrifice. The rose is the native flower of Noterra, but rather than focusing on the petals, I built a kingdom out of thorns. They have the power to cut and wound while a flower is merely there for beauty and attention, much like a woman." His grip on my hand tightens as he holds it flat against the tapestry, his breath hot on my neck. I can smell a tincture, sweet and spicy.

"It's a beautiful way to incorporate every part of the flower." I sputter. He drops my hand and places his on my shoulder, spinning me around so I'm facing him, only inches between us. He leans down, looking into my eyes, his hands sliding to my waist. I freeze, unable to figure out what to do with my hands other than dig my nails into my palms. I can feel his fingers squeeze my sides, holding me in place.

"My late wife had a crown made to look just like this. Thorns and vines made out of silver with large diamonds pressed into it." His eyes are gleaming with mischief as he flicks his tongue out to lick his lips. "It will be yours someday soon." His hand reaches up and a knuckle grazes my bruised cheek. His gaze flits to my mouth before returning to my eyes. I steady my breath, trying to avoid the intensity of his stare as much as possible. Curious, dark eyes search my face as I stand there with my heart pounding furiously in my chest. I'm not entirely convinced he can't hear it. "You look just like her." He whispers, sorrow filling his fierce eyes.

"Queen Amaya?" I whisper. I remember her with golden hair, much like Tobias's, and gray eyes that nearly match the stone of the Chatisian palace.

"No, Sybil, your mother. She was so beautiful." His voice quiets as he gets lost in thought. His hand frozen on my face. I was unaware they had met; my mother didn't attend the trip to the palace when I was younger, my father made her stay behind. I remember them fighting about it before my father ultimately won. I wonder if it had something to do with Evreux? It's world knowledge that king's often take mistresses, but if a queen does it's a justifiable cause for a beheading. Why does he look so vulnerable when he mentions her? He looks hurt, broken.

"She was." I whisper. His eyes flash back to my lips, and I feel him take a small step forward, closing what little space there was between us. My breathing catches as I feel his chest press into mine and something else, something *harder* presses into my lower stomach. I swallow loudly. *Oh gods,* what am I supposed to do?

"It is no secret my illness has progressed, that's why you're here, Elaenor. However, an heir *for* the kingdom is what I need from you. I could care less about some silly little wedding." He chuckles darkly and a chill snakes down my spine causing me to shutter. His hand opens and grips my chin, jerking it roughly to the side. Leaning down, his nose rubs against my neck as he inhales. I squeeze my eyes shut, panic flooding my veins.

"So you want me to conceive an heir with Tobias prior to our wedding?" I ask, my voice cracking as I try not to move.

"Not entirely. You see, Elaenor, a child to continue the line is what a king requires, it secures their rule. Any bride can provide this, but I chose you a long, long time ago." His lips brush my throat as I swallow, hoping for anything to stop his touch. "Tobias needs a son, and he will get one, but given your father's inability to produce a boy, you seem to have an unfair advantage to only birth girls. You need someone who has a *history* of male children. As long as it's kept in the family, he'll never know that a child isn't his." He hisses, making the hair on my neck straighten. He presses a wet kiss to the inside of my throat, his arm further snaking around my waist, pulling me tightly against him. I swallow against his lips, sweat beading on my forehead.

I silently beg for anyone, someone, to walk by and get me out of this. He's the king. How am I supposed to defend myself?

"Your Grace." My voice croaks as I try to understand what it is he's implying. His teeth graze my skin and I squirm. The small moan that comes out of his mouth tells me he enjoyed the movement.

"There would be no way to tell who the father is. As long as the child carries the bloodline, I could care less. It's *my* blood that will flow through their veins regardless. I can make you happy in bed, my love. A *true* man." His nose trails up my jaw, he lips almost meeting mine. "Say yes." He hisses, his breath catching on the words.

"Tobias and I– we haven't done anything yet." I stammer.

"But you will, a few hours means nothing." His lips brush the edge of my mouth and I try to push against him. His breath is hot, fanning over my face.

"He's your *son*." My voice is loud and hoarse as I try to convey my discomfort.

"And you're *her* daughter." He growls before biting my bottom lip. I kick out, hitting him in the shin, but he isn't fazed. His hand starts to hike up my skirt.

"Stop, please!" I cry out and he pulls my lip into his mouth, sucking on it. He forces me back, the tapestry sliding over us as he shoves me against the wall. I resort to hitting and pushing, but he doesn't budge.

"We don't have much time." He mutters against my mouth, his tongue trying to force its way between my lips. How did he know I would be here without Tobias? How does he know when Tobias will return? Unless...

"You sent him away, didn't you?" I whisper into his mouth, fighting against his touch and nearly gagging at the taste of him. Whatever he is taking for the illness tastes like death, or maybe that's just him.

"You just needed to get away from him so you could find me, and you found me. I've been here waiting for you all along." His voice sounds pained as he pulls at the fabric between my legs. I scream loudly and he growls in anger. "You are making a scene." He whispers, his teeth biting down on my neck. I scream out in pain as his dull teeth pierce through my skin. He snarls before loosening his grip and stepping back. I nearly collapse onto the floor headfirst from the release of pressure, my hands barely catching me as my knees slam into the marble. "Very well, then." His face returns to its cold, empty nature, his eyes gaze hungrily down my body as he bites his lip. "Another time, perhaps?" He spins on his heels and walks out of the throne room as quickly as he came in. My eyes linger on the empty doorway.

I can feel the nausea creeping up on me and I frantically look around for something to vomit in. A small empty vase lies at the bottom of the dais waiting for flowers. I pull myself up and quickly run over to it, barely making it in time. My eyes water as burning liquid pours out of my throat. I shudder as the memory of his touch, his *taste* clouds my senses, sending another wave of vomit out of my mouth. Once I'm done, I sit back and try to steady my breathing. Tears stream down my face and I wipe them away with my cold, shaky fingertips.

His touch, his *possession* reminds me of those men. He owns me. The king. Tobias. My father. Everyone owns a part of me.

What is he hoping to accomplish? Is this normal? Was my father right all along? Am I truly destined for a life like this?

Once my breathing settles, I stand on unsteady legs. I need to tell Tobias, hope that he knows what to say or do. Maybe he'll just keep me away from the king. I'm sure he doesn't have much time left, not enough time to force me to be alone again.

Why does this keep happening to me?

Chapter Fourteen

I wait a few moments before I exit the throne room. I can hear his leather shoes slapping the marble floors to the right, so I quickly turn to the left, back the way I originally came. Tears are still pouring down my face, my nose dripping with snot. I turn the corner quickly and run face first into a hard chest. Sweet grass fills my nose as hands wrap around my shoulders to steady me and I get the strange sense of deja vu.

"Woah, Nora? Are you okay?" Theo dips his head slightly, so his face is level with mine. "What happened?" He demands as he wipes at the tears dripping down my face.

I can't fight the sobs that come out of my throat as he folds me against him. I know I shouldn't let him touch me, let him hold me when Tobias could walk by at any moment, but it feels good, and I hate it. My body fits perfectly against his, as if we were molded for each other. I can feel a spark everywhere his skin is touching mine. I can feel my heart begging and pleading to stay right here for the rest of time, and I hate myself for it.

"Talk to me?" He whispers against my hair, and I wipe my nose on my hand, trying to keep the snot off his tunic.

"The king." I choke out as I pull myself out of his grasp.

"What about him?" His voice is cold, stern. His eyes darken as I meet his gaze. "What did he do?"

"I was in the throne room, exploring, and he came up behind me." A small squeak escapes my lip as I fight against the chills running through my body. "He was touching me, trying to get under my dress. He was forcing himself on me, biting my neck and my lips." I nearly gag as I remember the smell of the tincture, the taste of his tongue. Warm fingers brush against my neck and he sighs loudly.

"There are *literal* teeth marks on your neck, Nora." Theo growls, his voice doing little to hide his anger. I start to shake harder, the sobs wreaking havoc on my body.

"Oh gods." I cry and he pulls me back into his chest.

"You *need* to stay away from him. Never walk around alone, always have Laris or Tano with you." Tano must be the other guard, the one with yellow hair. Theo's voice is hard, strained, as if it's taking everything in him to not go after his father and to just stay here with me.

"He said that he could get me pregnant. That he can guarantee I'll carry a boy, an heir, and that Tobias would never know." I mutter against his chest. The cotton tunic is partially open, his golden skin warm against my cheek.

"Gods. It has to be the sickness, or the medicine. It has to be making him act like this. This isn't him."

"He said he's been waiting for me for a very long time. When I said Tobias was his son, he said I was *her* daughter. He means my mother, right? Why would he be obsessed with me being her daughter?" He stills under me, and I pull out of his arms again. He refuses to make eye contact with me, so I step away from him. What is he hiding? "What do you know?" He sighs and runs a hand through his light hair.

"Your mother lived here at one time. I believe my father was in love with her." The way he speaks is so nonchalant, like it's common knowledge that my mother and his father had some sort of connection.

"Wait. What?" My eyes widen and my voice comes out louder than I expected, startling myself. "What about Queen Amaya?"

"Your mother was engaged to King Argent; did you know that?" I shake my head, my mind reeling. "She lived here with Argent for a couple of years. When he died, my father wanted to keep her as his queen, to rule over the kingdoms like she was meant to do with Argent. The problem was, he was already married to my mother, Tobias was a toddler, and my mother was pregnant with me. He couldn't leave her." This doesn't make sense. My mother lived *here*? How did she end up in Chatis?

"Wait, so how did she end up with my father?"

"As far as I know, my father gave her to him as a gift for helping him secure his throne. It's not a secret that he regrets it, hates himself for it. Even more so after she died." Despite it not being a secret, it's news to me.

"I don't understand. Why didn't I know this? Is this why I was engaged to Tobias so young? So your father could get close to me?" He shrugs and I look down at my hands.

"I don't think it was so my father could get close to you so much as getting close to your mother. You were here quite often as a child, too." My eyes snap back to his.

"*What?* When I came to meet Tobias at the age of seven, that was the first time." He shakes his head, his eyes soft.

"No it wasn't. You were here a lot. We grew up together, the three of us, how do you not remember this? I thought maybe you didn't recognize me when we met, and even when you said you didn't know the king had another son, but you don't remember me at all?" He's lying. He has to be. I shake my head, my eyes staring deeply into his. I don't remember him or his mother. None of this is true.

"That's impossible. I don't remember any of this." I step away and start to pace, wiping my sweaty palms on my dress.

"Maybe it was the trauma from your mother dying? I don't know, but I remember my mother telling me that you were going to be my sister someday. Even as toddlers they planned your marriage. I think it was something Sybil and my mother planned, spoke about." I walk back and forth, my shoes clicking on the floor with each step. His voice is so calm, so relaxed and nonchalant as if he didn't just drop a bomb of information on me.

"I don't understand." I don't remember much before my mother died. I don't remember ever leaving the palace, except for when I went to meet Tobias for what I thought was the first time. "My parents fought when my mother wanted to come with me to Noterra when I was seven. He didn't know she came here so often, did he?" Theo shrugs. I can't believe it. I *don't* believe any of this. I was here as a child? My mother lived here for a few years when she was engaged to a *different* king? None of this makes any sense. Why would this have been a secret?

"Nora, I know this is a lot." He sighs and steps towards me.

"Stop." I snap, holding out my hand. "Don't call me Nora and don't touch me. You need to stay away from me." His mouth opens slightly, his eyes hardening. I regret the words as soon as they come out. He's the one person my heart is telling me is safe, but my mind is begging and pleading for me to distance myself before I get hurt, or before I hurt him. He tries and fails to hide the surprise in his eyes before he clenches his hands into fists and sighs.

"Look, I don't know what he's been saying–"

"What is going on?" A sharp voice cuts Theo off and I jump. I turn towards the other end of the hallway where Tobias is standing. His arms are at his sides, his hands twitching. Tears pool in my eyes again as I quickly run over to him. He pulls me against his chest, his eyes not leaving Theo's. "What's wrong, Ela?" He whispers, using a new nickname. I almost melt into him. He's warm and smells like home, but it's not the same. I don't fit against him like I do with Theo.

"Your father, he attacked me." I croak into his chest, willing the tears to stop betraying me. He pulls back and looks at me while I quickly explain what Evreux said and did. His chin hardens as he clenches his teeth and his eyes narrow, absorbing everything I'm telling him in silence. When I finish, he lifts my chin slightly and runs his fingers along the bite marks on my neck.

"I'm going to kill him." He snaps.

"You can't kill everyone, Tobias." I mutter, surprising myself. He looks behind me and I turn to see Theo is still there.

"What are you doing here?" He asks, his voice clipped.

"She ran out of the throne room disheveled and in tears, I wasn't going to just ignore her." Theo retorts, his voice icy. His arms are crossed over his chest, and despite the wrinkle in between his brows, he looks more worried than angry.

"Don't come near her. Don't speak to her. She is not *yours*. If you see something wrong with her, find me or anyone other than yourself to deal with it.

Do you understand me?" His fingers dig into my shoulders pulling me back against him.

"Tobias," I plead, hoping he'll drop it. I try to shrug out of his grasp, but I can't. "He was telling me about my mother."

"What?" He looks down at me.

"Was she here a lot while you were children? Was I?" He tilts his head to the side, confused.

"Yes, you were here a lot. Our mothers used to tell us all the time we were engaged, don't you remember?" I shake my head, disbelief clouding my vision. "We played in the trees, we would take picnics down by the stables and watch the horses, my mother even put her crown on you one day so you could see what it looked like. She used to call you her little miracle." Her little miracle? I don't remember ever meeting Queen Amaya, I don't remember ever being in this palace besides the one time.

"I don't remember any of it. I only remember meeting you with my father when I was seven." My voice is quiet, my eyebrows pinched together as I dig through my memories.

"That was the first time your father was here, from what I remember, he acted like you and I had never met." His voice is distant as he thinks.

"I don't think he knew my mother was bringing me here."

"I told her about Sybil and how she was engaged to Argent." Tobias's head snaps up and glares at Theo.

"Why don't you stay out of this and stop filling her head with information that is only going to confuse her." He spits as I glance at Theo over my shoulder.

"I am here when you want to talk, Elaenor. I will always be here." Tobias growls in warning and Theo turns around to walk down the hallway. I want to call after him, apologize for my anger, but I don't. I need to stay away from him, not only to protect myself, but to protect him.

"Don't." Tobias warns as if reading my thoughts and I look back at him.

"Tobias. Stop being jealous of him for five seconds and look at me." He hesitates but eventually lets his eyes drift down to mine. "I ran out of that room trying to find you. I was looking for *you*, not your brother."

"I know, I just don't like how he looks at you." He mutters.

"Okay, and what about how I look at him? Or how I look at you? Am I also not a part of this?" I retort. He's silent for a second, his lips pressed into a thin line.

"You look at him with wonder, you look at me with duty." My mouth falls open, surprised.

"I do not." I respond, stepping back, his arms dropping from my shoulders. "I feel nothing for your brother except gratitude for him saving my life, for bringing me to *you*."

"And what do you feel for me, Ela?" *Ela*. My eyebrows pinch together as I tilt my head. What do I feel for him?

"I don't know how I feel about you, other than I want to be with you. I want *you* to hold me when I'm scared. I want *you* to lay next to me while I fall asleep. I want you, Tobias, not your brother." My voice is borderline begging and I almost hate myself for it, but I need him to believe me. I need *me* to believe me. He nods and steps forward to tuck a stray curl behind my ear.

"I'm sorry about my father. Are you okay?" I shake my head.

"He was so forceful. He was biting me like a rabid animal, he pushed me against the wall while he tried to lift my skirt up. I didn't know what to do. I was pushing him and hitting him, but he wasn't moving. He wanted to get me pregnant, he was so insistent on it, and then he just stepped back and walked away like nothing happened. It was so weird." He clenches his teeth, his thumb brushing my neck where I can still feel the sharp sting of Evreux's teeth.

"It could be a number of things; the illness may have spread to his brain. It could be the tincture, Pakin will know." I nod and we just stand there in silence. I can't think of anything else but my mother right now.

"What was the urgent business?" I ask and he rolls his eyes.

"I was told it was in regard to further developments in Labisa, but when I got to the council chamber the king had left. I waited around for a few moments before giving up and coming to find you." His voice is laced with irritation.

"It was a diversion." I mutter and he nods. "I would really like to talk about my mother, Tobias. I have a lot of questions." He opens his mouth to speak but closes it when he looks at something, or someone, behind me.

"Good morning, Your Graces." I turn around to see Master Pakin standing behind us. He bows slightly and I smile nonchalantly bringing my hair over my shoulder to cover my neck. He seems to be in a good mood, which may be due to my ability to conceive. He said it was *joyous* news, but it just makes me feel sick.

"Good Morning, Master Pakin." I respond.

"Please, my dear. You may call me Apollo." *Apollo* Pakin. I smile and nod. "I wanted you to know that Ser Danieas has awoken if you wish to speak to him." I exhale in relief at the knowledge that he is finally awake and step towards him.

"Yes, I would like that very much." I fail to hide the relief in my voice. I know Erik doesn't have information that I don't already have, but the idea of having another here from Chatis fills the emptiness inside me. I turn back to Tobias, and he holds out his hand, which I gladly take.

I follow Apollo through the marble hallways, down the stairs, and into the infirmary. He leads me to one of the closed off curtains and gestures for me to enter. I notice there are two other closed off curtains today, and it makes me wonder who has fallen ill or gotten hurt.

I grip the white cotton in front of me and move it to the side, Tobias staying close behind. Erik is lying in the bed, covered in a thick wool blanket. His skin isn't as pale as I expected, and instead slightly pink and healthy looking. His rust-colored hair is smooth against his head, short, as if it's recently been cut. His eyes are closed, but I can tell he isn't asleep. I step closer and take a seat at the edge of his bed, not wanting to disturb him, but wanting to see if he is truly alright.

"Erik, are you awake?" I whisper. His eyes flutter open, revealing his soft green irises. He smiles upon recognition, his face lighting up.

"Your Grace." He replies as he sits up. A small groan escapes his lips as he pulls himself up against the headboard. The blanket falls and exposes his muscular chest, which is covered in a thick bandage. His eyes follow mine before he quickly pulls the blanket up to cover himself.

"How are you feeling?" I ask, offering him a warm smile and pretending not to notice.

"I have been better, Your Grace." He smiles and I reach for his hand and squeeze it. "I am happy to see that you are alright." He looks relieved by my presence, but I can tell he's in pain. There is a slight sheen of sweat coating his forehead and his hand feels warm in my own. Erik's eyes drift behind me to where Tobias is standing and offers him a dip of the chin.

"Yes, well I'm alive." He frowns. "As are you." I smile, hoping to ease any of his worries. His eyebrows furrow as he notices the wounds on my face. I am thankful my dress covers the majority of my skin; I feel his reaction would be worse if he were to see the extent of everything I endured.

"The master told me little of what has happened these last few days." He states, probing for information. "How long has it been?" He pinches his eyebrows as he looks at me.

"I believe it has been four days since we last spoke. I was unconscious for most of it so I can't really say for sure." I frown and look down. "But we are both awake now, we are in Noterra, and there is to be a wedding today I think." I look up at Tobias behind me and he shrugs. I fake a smile and look back at Erik. His face is blotchy, his red stubble peeking through on his jawline. He isn't much older than me, nearing 24, but he looks as if he's just been to battle.

His father currently sits as Hand of the King for my father, brother to Lord Hairy, which is how he got the prestigious position of being my guard. He was only 16 and I was 10. I can still remember the crush Scarlett and I had on him. She used to joke saying that she was going to marry him someday, however guards aren't allowed families. If war were to strike, their only purpose was to keep royals alive, which wouldn't be possible if they had loved ones at home to worry about. He was the second son, meaning he couldn't be a Lord, so he devoted himself to the guard.

I grew up with Erik as a brother figure in my life. He was sworn to be my sword should I need it, but he also helped when it came time to defend me from my father. On several occasions he would intervene if he felt my safety was at risk. My father wasn't too happy with his interception, but the Hand always talked him down. He was the only one who could. Lord Danieas is one of the strongest men I ever met, and the only reason Chatis is still standing. Although my father wouldn't agree with that.

"Your Grace, if I may be blunt." I nod. "I can see you have sustained some injuries. I would like to know who the cause is so I can ensure you receive justice." His voice is filled with diplomacy, but he and I both know he isn't in a position to defend my honor.

"It is of no consequence, they are dead. The man who hurt you, and the men who hurt me." I shake my head and squeeze his hand, before releasing him and digging my nails into my palm. Jeremiah is still out there, but he can't touch me in the palace, at least that is what I hope.

"Tell me what happened." He demands. I sigh in response and look back at him. "I must know, princess." His voice is soft, filled with regret. He blames himself. Tobias places his hand on my shoulder, comforting me.

"I ran when you told me to, although I didn't like leaving you to die." He shakes his head. "They caught up to me. The first man, Jeremiah, tried to take my virtue, but he was stopped." He sits up higher, his face hardening. "A man named Aleksander intervened, but then he was the one who took it by force." I swallow, fighting against the ever-present lump in my throat, Tobias's fingers squeeze into my flesh, and I reach up to hold his hand.

"Elaenor." Erik whispers, using my first name. I glance up at him. His eyes are filled with sorrow, pain. I know he blames himself, but he nearly died trying to protect me.

"You'll be proud to hear that I killed him." I smile softly, reassuring him. "Afterwards I ran and ended up at a Noterran camp. They brought me here where I slept for three days, although that part is a little hard to remember."

"Did you see who they belonged to?" He asks. The same question that's haunting me.

"No, but they knew who I was. They knew where to wait when I was coming. They said they wouldn't let Noterra win. That they've taken too much already." He looks at me, his confusion mirroring mine. "King Evreux told me Labisa is angry with Noterra because of me, do you think those men may have belonged to them?" I ask. It's his job to know and understand the politics, but I don't know how much he is actually aware of.

"It's possible. I don't know how much they would be willing to do. I knew they were unhappy with King Evreux, but it's a war crime to harm a royal."

"Do war crimes truly matter if they are pardoned once the war is over? Royals lose their lives all the time regardless of the legality."

"No, they truly don't." He reaches for my free hand again. "I promise you; I will protect you here."

"I have nothing to be afraid of here." He knows I'm lying, but I can't express my fears to him. He would intervene like he always does, especially if he knew what the king attempted to do. "Can you tell me what happened to you? It all happened so fast."

"We were on the path, heading to Noterra. A man came out of the woods, acting as if he was injured. He approached, and I told him to stay back, but he wouldn't listen." His eyes darken as he relives the attack. "I got off to steer him away from the carriage, but that's when he produced a dagger, shoving it into my chest. He retreated back into the woods, so I thought he was going to leave, but then you," His eyes find mine, haunted. "You came out of the carriage. You were always so stubborn, never minding your business, it almost got you killed." He's angry that I put my life in danger, and he's right.

"I was worried about you." I admit.

"I thought he would leave, but then I saw him. I needed you to go."

"I did." I *did* but the threat still followed.

"I wasn't there very long before a rider from Noterra approached. He brought me here and assured me you would be found. That's the last thing I remember until I awoke this morning." I hear Apollo clear his throat behind me and I jump.

"Your Graces." He smiles at me and Tobias before fixing his attention on Ser Danieas. "I have spoken to King Evreux and when you are well enough to travel, Ser, your father has requested you return to Chatis." Apollo announces. I spin around to face him, shock filling my face. He is *not* leaving.

"No, he will not. I would like him to remain here and act as my sworn sword as he did in Chatis." I respond. He is the only piece of home I have, and the only person I trust with my safety. "He's been my guard for nearly 8 years, and I wish him to remain so."

"Your Grace, there are guards already here to take that role. Laris and Tano would be honored." I shake my head and stand, Tobias's hand softly sliding down my arm to my elbow. I can't trust any guards who aren't loyal to me, not until the king is dead.

"*No.* He will remain here." I turn to Tobias. "*Please.* You will see to it?" I ask, his face filled with pity as he squeezes my hand.

"Of course, Ela. I don't see why he couldn't stay." His voice is soft, as if he's speaking to a child.

"Your Grace, I don't deserve this position anymore. I failed you." Erik's voice is soft, tortured as I turn back to him.

"Erik, I will *not* allow you to leave." I can't let him go, regardless of his shame. "I am in a foreign land with no one here who is truly on my side. All they care about is an heir and a wedding, no one here truly cares about me. I need you." I reach for his hands again, pleading. "Please." Tobias's hand slips from my elbow as Erik's eyes quickly glance behind me.

"Yes, princess. As you wish." I smile as he lays his head back, relaxing into the pillow. I can tell he's exhausted.

"I will come visit you at a later time. Get some rest. I will see to it that chambers are prepared for you." He nods as he closes his eyes.

Chapter Fifteen

I stand and reach for Tobias's hand as we exit the infirmary. He's quiet as he pulls me down the hallway and I finally recognize the doors to the dining hall. I stop, pulling on his arm. He hesitantly looks at me and I fight the urge to flinch away from his gaze.

"I didn't mean what I said. I meant that your father and the council, they only see me as a prized mare fit to carry your children. I didn't mean you. You have been kind and caring and I know you would protect me. I just need him. He's all I have left of home." I explain as best as I can. He has to believe me. Tobias runs his free hand through his hair before nodding.

"I will see to it that he gets to stay." He says, his voice softer than I expected.

"Thank you." I whisper as I close the space between us and reach up to kiss him. His lips are soft, warm, gentle, but the delicious scents wafting out of the dining hall are more attractive to me at the moment. He smiles against my lips when he hears my stomach growl. Ending our embrace, he grabs my hand and pulls me into the dining hall.

It's still breakfast, so instead of roasted veggies and meat, the buffet table is filled with eggs, bacon, fruit, various pastries, and juices of every kind. I eagerly grab every flaky pastry covered in chocolate I can find and a huge bowl of fruit before I follow Tobias to a table. The hall is a lot busier today than it was yesterday, and most of them watch us like hungry vultures. I try to not meet their gaze, but it's hard. Everywhere I look there is a set of eyes critiquing me. I bring one of the warm pastries up to my mouth and take a bite. Flakes and crumbs fall everywhere, but the second it hits my tongue I almost pass out. A moan escapes my lips as the chocolatey filling hits my tongue.

"Oh my gods." I mutter as I chew.

"I'm guessing pastries also weren't very common in your diet?" He chuckles. I shake my head and pick up another pastry. "While I want you to enjoy every delicious thing you want, and I don't care about your weight or appearance, please try to eat some eggs and fruit. You are still healing from a very rough week, and you need fuel." I roll my eyes jokingly and plop a chunk of pineapple in my mouth. He smiles, a dimple appearing in his left cheek.

We are quiet for a few moments, the only sounds between us are chewing and swallowing. I think back to Tobias's response, or lack of response, in regard to the wedding.

"Are we getting married today?" I ask after I wash my mouth out with orange juice. It's sweet and pulpy and I try to keep my moans silent as I try each new thing. "You shrugged when I mentioned it."

"I honestly don't know. The reverend isn't even here, nor have any preparations begun to invite guests and prepare the palace. I figured you weren't in a rush, so I wasn't going to push." I nod and move fruit around on my plate.

"I'm not in a rush, but don't we have to be married before your father passes?" That's what my father said had to happen, but maybe he was wrong? I'm all for waiting, but it's just delaying the inevitable.

"Yes, but he seemed fine this morning, *besides* his delusions." He sips from a white mug, some hot bitter beverage. He told me it was called coffee and a sip nearly made me gag. "Do you want me to ask?"

"I don't know. I just don't want to skirt my responsibilities just because the king is too ill to realize." Tobias laughs softly.

"You are not skirting your responsibilities; I promise you that."

"So what are we going to do today?" I ask, wiping my sticky fingers off on a napkin.

"Well, I figured we could relax. We did the tour yesterday, so I was thinking of taking you out to one of my favorite lookouts where we can sunbathe and sleep and do whatever we want." I don't even attempt to fight the smile plastered to my face.

"We are going to leave the palace?"

"You aren't a prisoner, Elaenor. You can go wherever you want." Shivers of excitement trickle down my limbs and it's taking everything in me to not jump out of this seat.

We get to leave.

When we finish eating, Tobias takes us back to the room to change. He informed me that the dress I was wearing probably wasn't suitable for horseback riding, so he recommended I wear something else.

When we get to the room, he sits behind the writing desk, catching up on his correspondence, while I rummage through the dressing room. I find a pair of black riding leggings and slip them on, surprised that they are a perfect fit. They are made out of a thin cotton that hugs my legs like a second skin. I find a matching jacket that is tight fitting and pull that over a camisole. I was wearing head to toe black, and for once, I didn't mind that my clothes were picked out for me. I slip into a pair of beautiful leather riding boots before stepping out from behind the partition.

"Where did all these clothes come from?" I ask as I step towards the mirror. The black is slimming, not that the last few days of injuries and unconsciousness have made me in need of slimming down.

"They were made prior to your arrival. Your ladies sent your measurements over by rider." He says quietly, distracted.

Tobias is still at the desk, writing away, so I sit at the vanity and braid my hair into a single plait down my back. It feels silkier than usual, and it makes me smile. Despite the nature of my entrance to Noterra, it seems to be agreeing with me. My smile catches when I see the bite mark peaking over my collar. It's red and swollen, with just a couple small scabs where his teeth went through my skin. A chill running down my spine causes me to shudder as I tie off my braid and throw it over my shoulder.

I quickly look away from my reflection in the mirror and stride over to the balcony. The doors are open like they always seem to be, so I step out onto the marble and squint my eyes against the bright sunlight. It's brisk, the air slightly chilled, threatening an early end to summer. There are very few clouds in the sky, which leaves ample room for the bright blue skies to show. I take a deep breath and smile.

Right below the balcony is one of the courtyards with a huge fountain. There is no one down there, leaving the bright green grass vacant and glittering in the sunlight. I can picture myself lounging down there with a book and a blanket, sunbathing while reading. I want nothing more than to have my skin darken and the tiny freckles appear on my face that only show when I've been outside.

"Are you ready?" Tobias calls from the room and I turn around to see him standing up from the desk. I nod enthusiastically before bounding over to him.

We make our way through the palace with Laris and Tano following closely behind. We exit through a large double door that leads to the palace wall. People are walking around, Lords and Ladies, groundsmen and guards. They all smile and bow or curtsy as we walk past them hand in hand. I try to meet everyone's eyes and smile, acknowledge them like I wasn't allowed to do in Chatis.

My pulse quickens as we walk right up to the open metal gate and step past it. Trees as far as the eyes can see in all directions. Just bright green pines and evergreens forming a beautiful forest begging to be explored. I don't try to hide my awe as Tobias walks around me to a stone building on our right. In every direction I look, all I see is a thick tree line, with only a small path leading through them.

"Your Grace." Laris says as he gestures for me to follow them. I nod, tearing my eyes away from the trees. I step into the stone building and the scent of hay and manure assault my sinuses. I sneeze and hear Tano chuckle behind me.

Tobias is speaking to one of the stablemen, so I take this time to look around. Beautiful stalls carved out of sheetrock and dark wood line either side, hay covering every inch of the floor. My boots crunch as I walk over the golden strands up to the first stall.

A beautiful white horse munches on fresh feed, his brown eyes catching mine. His mane is long and wavy, shining in the sunlight filtering down through the windows on the ceiling. A golden placard above his stall displays his name as *Dawner*. I reach forward and run my fingers through his silky strands.

"Hi, Dawner." I say as he continues to munch on his feed. I slip my hand out of the stall and move to the next one.

A deep russet brown horse sticks his head out of the stall and swipes its nose across my face. I laugh as I nearly fall back. I rub his snout and glance up at the placard above his stall, *Wyclif*.

"Wyclif." I murmur as he sniffs my outstretched hand.

"This one is mine." Tobias says next to me as I let Wyclif lick my palm. "Don't ask me where the name came from. I was 15 and it was the first thing I thought." I chuckle as I pull my sticky palm away, rubbing my hand on my leggings.

"Who does Dawner belong to?" I ask as I look back over at the beautiful white horse still munching away.

"Theo, he named it after his favorite time of day." I smile and look back over at Tobias. "Your horse is over here." He puts his hand on my lower back and steers me away to a horse that one of the stablemen is saddling.

Silky black fur and mane sparkling in the sunlight. Bright hazel eyes that follow me as I approach. This horse is absolutely beautiful. He has a tall muscular body, taller than I could even imagine. It would take some very high steps to get onto his back. His head turns to face me as I walk forward, putting out my hand for him to smell. His breath tickles my palm before pressing his snout into it. I giggle as I step closer and run my hand across his soft cheek.

"He's beautiful." I whisper as I get close enough to press my forehead to his neck.

"*She* is." Tobias says from behind. "She used to belong to my father." I pull away and turn towards him. He's giving me his father's horse?

"Why are you giving me your father's horse?" I ask, my voice skeptical.

"Because she wasn't *actually* meant for my father. She was a gift for you, one my parents and your mother searched for. This coloring is rare, but it was important to your mother for you to have one that matched you. Her fur sparkles in the sun, just like yours."

"My mother?" My voice is soft, contemplative.

"Yes, but by the time they sourced a foal, you and your mother left and never came back, so my father took her." He pauses and lets his fingers run through her silky mane.

"Does she already have a name?" I ask as I resume my stroking. Her fur is so silky it slips in and out of my fingers like water.

"Sybil." I still as I turn and look at him. "My father named her Sybil." I can feel the tears welling up in my eyes as I look back at the horse that was supposed to be mine. The horse named after my mother and the starry night hair she gave to me.

"There is a lot I'm finding I don't know about my mother, about my childhood. Do you think she ever had any plans to let me stay in Chatis?" I ask as I stare into Tobias's blue eyes. They are soft, gentle. I can tell he is treading lightly, choosing how to phrase what he's telling me for fear of it being too much. "What is it?"

"I don't know much about anything, I was a child when all of this happened, but I heard some things. I heard my mother and yours speaking one day. You were maybe five or six, asleep with Theo on the bed. Our mothers were sitting by the fire, and I was pretending to be asleep on a settee next to them." He pauses and takes a deep breath. "I don't think Viktor is your father, Ela." My breath catches. *What?* "I think my mother knew who it was, but they didn't say. I heard them talking about how he treated you. How he abused you. She was crying, telling my mother that she didn't want to go back. My mother told her to stay, but they knew that if they harbored you and your mother, your father would be able to start a war. You were both his property."

"I-I don't understand." My breathing quickens and I stutter.

"I don't know any more than that. We were all so young, I didn't know what I was hearing." My hand slides off Sybil's neck, my arms dangling loosely by my sides. My father may not actually be my father? My mother was trying to get us out?

"Why don't I remember my childhood?" My voice seems weak, small. My pulse skips and I dig my nails into my palms, hoping it'll ease some of the panic rising up into my throat.

"I don't know. When news of your mother's death reached us, we were told you were killed too. It was weeks before my father received a letter in regard to your wellbeing. We thought it was a miracle."

"A miracle?" I whisper. "Your mother. You said she called me her little miracle?" He chews on his bottom lip as he stands there thinking.

"I don't think that has anything to do with it. Maybe it was because she always wanted a daughter?" He shrugs, but I file that information away. *Miracle.* Why would she say I was her miracle?

"Do you think that your father is my father?" I ask the question that has been floating through my mind since I found out Evreux loved my mother, begging to be asked. It can't be, though. Who would force their children to wed each other?

"Oh Gods, I doubt that. You think they would let us get married?" He smiles a little, but then lets it dissipate when he sees my frown.

"I want to speak to your father." I turn back to Sybil and press my forehead to hers. "I will be back for you, I promise." I whisper to her before I turn away.

"Ela, please. Do you really want to bring up the past?" He sounds irritated as he tries to catch up to me.

"Tobias, you know everything there is to know about your childhood and your life, but I know nothing. Everything I have been told has been a lie. I need answers and your father may be able to give them to me."

Chapter Sixteen

It doesn't take us long to track down Evreux in the council chamber. He's holding his head while he peers down at some sort of letter with squinting eyes. His hair is disheveled, and his crown lay haphazardly on the table next to an empty wine glass. He looks up when I stomp in uninvited, surprise flashing through his eyes.

"My sweet Elaenor, to what do I owe this pleasure?" He purrs, but his smirk falls when he sees Tobias walk in behind me. "What do *you* want?" His voice quickly drops his sultry purr as he lets his irritation show.

"Who is my father?" I blurt out. He flinches and lets his hands rest on the arms of his chair.

"King Viktor, I presume?" He says questioning, but I don't believe for one second that he doesn't know something. His tone is mocking, playful.

"How often was I here as a child?" I rest my hands on the back of one of the wooden chairs, facing Evreux head on.

"Oh Gods, nearly every other week for *years*. Your mother and Amaya were childhood best friends." He speaks with such disdain that I want to throw something at him.

"Why don't I remember?"

"You don't remember being here at all?" He cocks a brow as he stares at me, bewilderment flitting across his face, replacing the irritation.

"No. The first time I remember meeting any of you was when I came with my father at the age of seven to discuss my engagement." I admit, my voice cracks and I clear my throat, my fingers tightening on the wood.

"Well, that I do not have an answer for, Elaenor. Perhaps shock after the trauma you encountered." I clench my teeth as he rolls his eyes, clearly irritated from having to entertain this conversation.

"*What. Trauma?*" I snap. I am so sick of everyone giving me little pieces of information. Why can't somebody just tell me what occurred all those years ago? Spell it out for me if they have to. I need to know.

"Did you hit your head or something? How do you not know what you went through?" He stands and reaches for the decanter to refill his glass.

"Answer the question." Tobias's voice is sharp behind me, causing me to flinch as I forgot he was there. He steps around me, slightly blocking me from his father. I wouldn't put it past the king to do something, but I doubt he'd do it with witnesses. Evreux sighs as he drops back into his chair with a full wine glass.

"You were missing for weeks after your mother died. She was stabbed, repeatedly, in the chest while in bed." I can feel my face drain of color. No one told me how she died. No one ever spoke of it. She was stabbed. *Oh gods.* Did she suffer? "There was another pool of blood next to her, where tiny bloody handprints sat. *Your* hand prints." My legs shake and I lean heavily on the chair, nausea blooming deep in my belly. "Your mother was discovered by some man who claimed to be a prophet or something, Kassius. When he alerted the guards and informed them that you were missing, he was arrested and charged with her murder." He speaks as if he's telling a story, not the death of my mother.

"I remember him. I remember him keeping my mother company during her miscarriages and stillbirths. One of the last memories I have of him were my mother and I in her bed. He was sitting in a chair next to it, they were talking about something, but I was falling asleep." My voice is quiet, soft, as I recount small bits of my childhood. I remember my mother was playing with my hair.

"Yes, well, *anyway*." I scowl as he throws his hand up to get me to stop talking. "It was believed that he killed you and used your body in some sort of ritual or something. A few weeks later, a fisherman spotted you sitting on the shore of Delaquar Lake, on the Noterra side. Your nightdress was soaked in blood, and you had cuts and stab wounds partially healed all over you, but you were sitting there as if it didn't affect you. It was a miracle. You were gone for weeks, but you looked as if it had only been a few hours." *Miracle.* Everyone *keeps saying* I was a miracle.

"The secret princess." I murmur, my eyes widening. *That* is why he kept me a secret, because everyone thought I was dead.

"What?"

"My father kept my identity a secret. I thought it had always been that way, but it wasn't when my mother was alive. He told everyone I died, didn't he?" It wasn't for control.

"Yes. It was to protect you. He didn't know what Kassius had done to you, so he wanted to keep you away from the public eye. Hidden, just in case whatever he didn't accomplish would cause someone to come back for you."

"This doesn't make any sense." Tobias speaks. He steps back, putting his hand on my lower back. "How could she have been fine for weeks out there on her own?" Evreux shrugs, setting down his glass.

"No one knows. She was soaked, as if she had swam across the lake on her own, but other than that, she was perfectly fine and healed rather quickly, I heard, considering the extent of her injuries." How could I swim across a whole lake? I can't even swim.

"When I came here with my father, was that before or after my mother died?"

"After."

"That's impossible, I remember them yelling at each other about coming here. It happened before we came here?" My voice trails off. It can't be. Was that yelling before? When were they fighting? Why isn't the timeline adding up in my head? A deep throbbing ache spreads across my temples and I grimace.

"What was your father saying?" Tobias asks and I shake my head.

"I don't remember much, he said that he didn't want her coming here, but she said he couldn't stop her. That's all." I burrow as deep as I can into my memory. Why can't I remember anything? "What happened to me?"

"Elaenor." Tobias's voice startles me, and I look up at him. "Your nose is bleeding." He quickly wipes away at my nose, and I lift my hand to touch the wetness. My fingers come away red, and I wipe my jacket sleeve against my nose. The nausea hits me like a stone wall, and I back up.

"Excuse me." I whisper softly as I turn out of the room. I don't know where I am going, but I need to find something. I step into the hallway and look across at the wall of open windows. I run towards them and barely make it before I vomit over the ledge, and hopefully not on anyone walking below.

A warm hand gathers my braid up behind me, then another rubs my back up and down. I gasp in as much cool air as I can before straightening.

"Are you alright?" He says softly as he drops my braid back over my shoulder.

"Tobias, I am so confused. I have no idea what is true, what is real." I croak as he folds his arms around me. What did I go through? How did I get across the lake? How does no one know what happened that night?

"I know, Ela. I know." His hand rubs up and down my spine, warming me with its friction. I reach up and wipe at my nose, irritated that it comes back bloody. My head is pounding, pressure blooming behind my eyes.

"Come on, Ela." He whispers as he pulls me away from the window and down the hallway.

Tobias brings me to our chambers where I gladly change into a comfier outfit. He hands me a glass of sweet and syrupy pink wine that I am finding I love. I had a sweet wine at dinner and casually mentioned how much I loved it. Tobias said his mother had cases of an even sweeter wine and he had them pulled out for me as no one else likes it. I drain the glass quickly, wanting nothing more than to feel numb. He cleans up my face with a wet washcloth before helping me into bed. It's still early afternoon but being in this bed is all I wanted at the moment.

"Rest. I'll be back with some food." He bends down and kisses my forehead and then the tip of my nose. I inhale deeply, absorbing the scent of cedar as he sits up. "Laris and Tano are both outside the door, okay?" I nod and then curl up on my side. He pulls the wool blanket up and over my shoulders before he exits the room.

I was here, in this palace, almost every other week my whole childhood. I don't remember a single moment. I don't remember ever meeting Amaya.

No.

That's not true.

When Evreux had said I looked like her, I thought he meant the queen. I thought to myself, *no I remember her having blonde hair and gray eyes.* I remember her face, heart shaped and soft. High cheekbones that were always slightly pink. Thin eyebrows that angled around her eyes in a color slightly darker than her golden hair. She had dark lips that matched her deep, olive skin tone. I remember what she looked like and how her brows moved animatedly when she spoke.

So why don't I remember being here?

I didn't even know the king had two sons, but I apparently grew up with them. I shared beds with Theo because we were the same age. Children taking naps after playing too hard. Amaya called me her little miracle and we were apparently close. She loved me and I her, but I have no recollection of it. I don't remember the trips in the forest or the picnics we had by the horses. I don't remember playing in these halls, being near Tobias and Theo. Being close to them.

What happened the day my mother died?

Evreux said I was believed to be dead, my body used in some sort of sacrifice or ritual, but I remember Kassius. I remember his eyes being bright yellow and him being nice to me. I remember laying on my mother's lap, her fingers running through my hair while she and Kassius spoke. They were calm, friendly. There was never any animosity between them.

But my father.

He didn't want her going to Noterra with us. Did he know that she was always there? Did he know that she didn't want us to live in Chatis? I don't even know if that's true. I don't know if *any* of this is true. But their fight was *before* my father, and I came here. Before she even died. The timeline in my head, the one I remember, isn't real.

I remember my mother's blood. I remember running into the trees. Then he said they found me, weeks after her death. Weeks after I was supposedly murdered. I still had fresh wounds, with the only thing being different is the water, but I didn't know how to swim. I still don't. I was never taught. So how did I get across the lake? And why did Kassius murder my mother?

I flop onto my back, sighing. My eyes fixate on the ceiling, the marble shining in the sunlight casting the room in an orange glow.

I remember walking around. The guards, groundsmen, kitchenmaids. I remember them all being happy and smiling at me, but in Chatis they didn't know I was there.

I remember being in the kitchen with pastries and sugar that looked like snow, but that was *before* my mother died. That was before everything happened and I was restricted on my food. That was before everyone believed I died. Did they still think I was dead? Is that why my father is so insistent on a child being born? Why would he want to marry and have another child if he technically still has an heir? He wouldn't need to.

I am his heir. He is counting on me to have a child. But why didn't he marry so many years ago and conceive a son, especially if the world thought I was gone? That doesn't make sense. None of it does. I have no one I can ask. Evreux doesn't know much, or he isn't willing to share the information he does have.

What happened ten years ago? What happened to *me*?

I don't remember falling asleep, but as my eyes open to the darkness of the room, I realize I didn't dream. Not a single image played in my head while I slept for the first time in ten years. Not since before my mother died.

I stretch out, my legs finding the cool parts of the bed. A subtle ache throbs deep in my belly, but it's probably from hunger. I roll over onto my side and see Tobias's dark form huddled under the blankets. I reach out, letting my hand slip under the covers to softly brush his hair, but what I feel is wet. I pull my hand back, but I can't see what his hair is wet with. Maybe he took a bath before coming to bed?

"Tobias?" I whisper, but he doesn't move. I grip the edge of the blanket and pull it off of him. Where I expect to see golden waves, dark black curls greet me instead. Blood is pooling on the pillow, turning the beige linen a sickly shade of crimson. I gasp, my hand frozen in the air.

I get up on my knees and peer over the shoulder of the dark form and see pale skin shining in the moonlight. I let my fingers grab their shoulders softly, pulling them onto their back. A scream escapes my mouth as they turn and look at me.

Blue eyes look back, unseeing. *My* blue eyes. I'm wearing a pale pink nightdress, blood staining part of it red. My mouth parts slightly and water pours out of it. I scream again and back up, falling off the side of the bed. She, *I*, sits up and turns her head in my direction. Water continues to pour out of her mouth as she tries to speak, the covers slipping off of her bloody body as she gets up onto her knees.

"Elaenor." The me that isn't me croaks, but it's gargled, and I can just barely make out my name. I scream again and scramble to my feet, running to the door. I open it and see Laris and Tano staring back at me.

"Your Grace?" Laris says his hands out cautiously.

"Your Grace, are you alright?" Tano asks, turning to face me. I'm shaking as I quickly step into the hallway.

"Your Grace, please let us escort you back to bed." I ignore him as I turn to the right and start running.

My bare feet are slapping the marble as I run. The hallways are pitch black and silent, aside from the sounds of Laris and Tano running after me. I don't know where I am going, but I have to get out of here. I need to wake up. This is all just a dream. This isn't real. The hallway ends and I turn left, following another long, dark hallway.

Wake up, Elaenor. *Come on!*

"Princess!" I hear someone screaming behind me and I pick up the pace. My breathing is labored, my heart racing. I can't even think. I can't breathe. What the hell is happening?

I turn again and see an open balcony at the end of the hallway. It doesn't take long for me to reach it, and without thinking, I fling myself over and into the night.

Chapter Seventeen

I land hard onto the grass, and I cry out in pain as my legs collapse under me. I pull myself to my feet, my knees protesting, and run straight to the open palace gates. The courtyard is long, but I make quick work of the distance as I reach the stone wall. Men on either side holding torches look at me bewildered, their mouths open, questioning what to say.

"Your Grace?" One of them says as I fly right past them. I can feel their hands trying to grip my arms, but I slip between them, their leather gloves sliding over my flesh. My feet ache as they slap against the gravel, but I ignore it. I run straight into the stables, the hay crunching under my feet. I can hear people yelling, running towards me, but I can't let them get to me.

She's going to be there if I look back.

She'll be right there.

It doesn't take long for me to find Sybil in the back, her coat glowing in the moonlight. She has a bridle already on and I thank the gods. My hand grasps the latch to her stall and the door flies open. She steps out, whining. I grip onto her bridle and start to pull her out into the light as quickly as I can.

"Stop, princess!" Someone yells from behind me. I pick up the pace, dragging her along with me, and she doesn't protest. I run out of the stables and see a small stool to the right. I pull her over there and jump onto the stool.

Laris, Tano, and Tobias are running towards me, but I don't take a second to think about it as I see my bloody body running behind them, chasing me. Her entire dress is soaked in blood, dripping onto the ground. Every time her mouth opens, water pours out as if she is drowning. *As if I am drowning.*

I jump off the stool and onto Sybil's bareback. She grumbles at the feeling of my body slamming into her and takes off before I can react. I can feel the brush of someone's fingers as they rip part of my nightdress. I nearly slide off her slick fur, and I hold onto the leather reins as tight as I can. The cold air whips around me and I force myself to take a deep breath.

I can't tell which direction I am going, but when the road forks, I urge her to the left. I don't even have to push her, she just runs. I look back, my thighs gripping her back as tight as possible, causing them to cramp. Horses are starting to chase after me, but running right next to them is *me*. My dead face is grimacing at the pace, even though she is easily able to keep up with the guards' horses. Running as if she wasn't human. Running almost as fast as my midnight mare.

"Sybil, go!" I scream, urging her on.

"Elaenor!" I hear Tobias screaming, but I can't look back. If I do, she'll be there. Chasing me. Waiting for me to join her. "Elaenor, stop!" *Gods*, I'm going crazy. I am actually losing my mind.

We run as fast as we possibly can, and it is taking every ounce of strength I have to stay on Sybil's back. I don't know where we are going, but time passes at a pace that is unbelievable. I feel like we are flying through the woods and before long we'll end up at the edge of the continent.

"Gods dammit, Elaenor, wake up!" I scream at myself. This is a dream. This isn't real. I look back and they are farther behind, Sybil's long legs creating distance between us. I feel something fly past my leg and I look back again to see archers aiming at Sybil's legs. They are going to *kill* her. I tighten my hold on her back, and she responds, picking up her pace. She easily makes the turns to stay on the path as more and more space is put between us.

I can see the trees break up ahead and the bright orange glow of a line of torches. A stone wall that is open in the middle appears in front of us. Tents, bonfires, small buildings all litter either side of the path. People are looking up at us confused. *I'm* confused. This can't be one of the borders. They are all a few hours ride away, this is impossible. How long have I been running?

"Stop her!" Someone yells behind me, and the men reach for their swords. They don't have enough time to react as Sybil and I jump through the gap in the wall and land on the grassy plains behind it.

There is nothing but darkness and hilly land ahead of us as we continue on. I look back to see the horses stop at the edge of the wall. Tobias is in the middle. I can tell he is yelling for me, but I can't hear him. Her face, *my* face is right next to him. She gives me a bloody smile before dissipating into nothing, gone. I pull back on Sybil's bridle, and she slows before stopping.

I look towards the darkness, the grass that dips into pitch black. She led me here. She *wanted* me to come here. Why?

I look back at the wall and see Tobias, Laris, Tano, and Theo all off their horses standing on the border. Which country did I stumble into? When did Theo join them? I rack my brain trying to think of the map, but I come up empty. It's not Chatis, is it Rakushia?

Guards form a line behind them, waiting and ready with arrows nocked. I can go back right now, but would she just find me again? If I don't go back, are they going to just shoot me?

"Elaenor, please!" I can hear Tobias yelling, begging me to come back.

There is a reason I am here. There is a reason I was led here. *Right?* I can't go back. Not until I see this through. I look away from them and squeeze my thighs, Sybil takes off into the darkness, leaving Noterra behind.

We slow to a trot as the darkness envelopes us. Small hills line the grassy path, and we continue to follow it. The stars are bright against the night sky, and I shiver against the cold. I am still in my nightdress, a thin cotton in a light blue, but part of it is ripped, exposing nearly my entire right side. My bare feet are throbbing as they hang off either side of Sybil.

I don't know how long we are trotting forward, but I grow tired. I let go of her reins and lay flat, my stomach resting on Sybil's back and my arms wrapped around her neck. I can feel her slow down as I blink back at the sudden brightness.

A torch is being held up to my face and I flinch away from the heat. Dark eyes and black hoods surround me and Sybil. I sit up and tighten my hold on her reins.

"Who are you?" I ask as more and more of them appear from behind small hills. "Who are you?" I yell louder as they whisper amongst themselves. I look around to see them circling us, maybe seven or eight individuals wearing matching cloaks. One of them pulls on her bridle and she makes a shrieking noise. "Stop it!" I yell as a cold hand wraps around my ankle and yanks me off her back. I don't land on the ground and instead end up in someone's arms. "Put me down!" I scream and kick out. Someone restrains my legs and I fight against their grip.

"Knock her out." Someone says and I can feel something stabbing into my neck. I scream out in pain as fire spreads through my veins.

"Stop." I say. My blood starts to burn, and my breathing slows. Hooves from behind us start to fade in and the one holding my legs drops them. I am heaved over a shoulder, my head hanging across his back.

This position is familiar. The same position Jeremiah held me in. I can't let that happen again. I *can't*. I fight against the cloudiness in my head and slam my elbow into the space between his spine and neck. He yells out and drops me into the dirt. Hooves grow louder and I pull myself to my feet, but someone grabs my legs, slamming me face down into the ground. I wince as my nose hits the hard dirt.

I kick out again and hit his face, fighting against the weakness spreading through my veins with each breath. He lets go and I scramble to my knees, running towards the darkness. The hooves get louder, but I can't see. My eyes are clouding over, my limbs growing heavy, my blood burning with every heartbeat. It's too dark. I don't know where I am. I look back at Sybil being held back, whining, and trying to break free. *I can't leave her.*

I slow to a stop, begging my limbs to cooperate. The men aren't chasing me, they just stand there, frozen, watching.

"Who are you?" I call out. My pulse is pounding in my ears, drowning out any sounds from around me. An arm wraps around my waist from behind and pulls me against them. I scream and start digging my nails into their flesh, but another set of hands grabs my face, forcing me to look at him. Blue eyes.

"Nora, stop it." Theo yells and I drop my arms with a whimper. *He's here.*

"Theo." I cry as his fingers lightly brush my cheek before he lets go.

"You're okay, Ela." Tobias whispers behind me, his arms loosening around my waist.

"Tobias." I whisper as my legs grow too heavy to hold up. I relax into his chest, and he bends down to scoop up my legs. "Where am I?" I whisper. I rest my head on his shoulder and look at him. He has blood on his forehead, sweat dripping from his hairline. What happened? It feels like it's been five minutes, but something is telling me that isn't true.

"You are in Rakushia. I don't know how you got here so fast, it's like Sybil damn near teleported." His voice is clipped, angry.

"I don't understand." I barely have the energy to hold my head up against his shoulder. I relax it, and it falls back.

"Why did you run, Elaenor?" He's angry, but I am too tired. I can't listen to it. I can't deal with it right now. I just want to sleep.

"She was making me." I whisper, my eyes closing.

"Who? Who was making you?" He shakes me, trying to wake me up. Why can't he just let me sleep?

"Me." I feel my limbs tighten with some sort of spasm and then go numb. My arm slides off my stomach, dangling next to me.

"I think they drugged her." Theo's voice is so loud next to my ear I flinch. "She has a puncture wound on her neck." I can feel cold fingers prodding at the side of my throat.

"Grab the wisteria from the med kit." Tobias responds and I try to tell him no, I try to tell him I don't want it, but the words don't come out. Nothing comes out. It is almost as if my brain is no longer connected to my body. "Fill the syringe." He instructs. I groan, trying to tell them to stop, but they don't listen. "No, not that much, only a little. Good. Put it right where they stuck her the first time." Cold fingers return to my skin, but I can barely register it.

I can feel something stabbing into my neck and I want to scream as it pierces my skin, but nothing comes out, not even a whimper. Icy waves spread through my veins the same way the fire did before, but this time it takes the burning with it. I can feel it moving from limb to limb before settling in my brain, burning my eyes. I gasp as my legs tingle and my eyes open. I see stars and sparks in my vision before it fades into the night sky. My legs and arms twitch and Tobias struggles to hold me still.

"Stay still, Nora. Let it take effect." Theo whispers and then the iciness is gone. The cloudiness dissipates and I can feel my body waking up.

"Take a deep breath," Tobias's breath fans across my face as I inhale as deeply as I can. The air is thick and warm, and I almost choke on it. I test my voice with a whimper, and it comes out as a croak instead.

"Tobias. She was there." I whisper.

"Who, Ela?" He murmurs back.

"I saw *me*. I was dead. She was chasing me, water pouring from her mouth." I take another deep breath, trying to regain as much control over my body as I can. "She was covered in blood. And she only stopped chasing me after I crossed the border. I think she was leading me here." I look over at Theo whose lips are pressed into a thin line. My head painfully turns back to Tobias, and he is mimicking the same face. "It was real. I'm not crazy."

"Elaenor, I was the one in bed next to you." His eyes soften and his lips curl up slightly, almost in amusement.

"No." I snap before squirming in his arms. He sets me down and I only vaguely see Laris, Tano, and some other guards standing around dead bodies with black cloaks. They are all dead. Tobias spins me around to look at him, making me dizzy. I stumble a second before pushing his hands away.

"Elaenor, you woke me up by pulling the blanket off of me and pushing me. When I sat up, you screamed and fell off the bed. I tried to follow you, but that only made you run faster. Then you jumped off the balcony like a madwoman." He shakes his head. "I don't know how you didn't break your legs." He chuckles softly and I glare at him.

"It was real, Tobias." I turn towards Theo who is looking at me like I am crazy. "Theo?" Someone needs to believe me. I reach for him, and he opens his mouth to speak. "I'm not insane."

"Don't turn to him just because you are going crazy." Tobias grabs my arm and pulls me away before Theo can say anything.

"Let go of me." He brings me up to his horse, the russet brown stallion pulling at the grass.

"Elaenor, let's go home and then we can talk about this. I think you need to see the master." I rip my arm out of his grip and step back.

"I'm not crazy, Tobias. I need you to believe me." I plead and he tilts his head.

"I think you are under a great deal of stress, and you are not handling it well. Regardless, we need to get out of here *before* someone in Rakushia notices us. We are here illegally, Elaenor, and we just killed nine of their subjects." I look around at the guards mounted on their horses looking back and forth between the wall and the darkness. I reluctantly nod and he helps me onto Wyclif. He grabs Sybil's reins before jumping behind me in the saddle.

We make our way to the wall quickly, the horses galloping against the grassy floor. Tobias keeps one arm around my waist, his hand splayed possessively over my stomach. The other hand holds both Sybil and Wyclif's reins as he guides them through the open gate. I lean my head back against his chest as we slow, my eyes closing. I shiver and then feel Tobias move behind me. A second later a warm cloak is wrapped around me, fanning my face with the scent of cedar.

I'm not crazy. She was there. She was pushing me to Rakushia. She needed me to get here. *I'm not crazy.* Just because they couldn't see her, doesn't mean she wasn't real.

Chapter Eighteen

When we reach the palace, the sun is starting to peek its way over the mountains, turning the sky beautiful shades of pink and purple. Tobias leads me straight to our room where he cleans off my feet and forces me to change my ripped nightdress into a clean one. When we climb into bed the pinks in the sky are turning orange. He pulls me against his chest, one leg in between mine.

"Happy birthday, Ela." He whispers into my hair before kissing my neck. I smile slightly, my eyes fixed on the door. I keep expecting to turn around and see my dead body, but it's just him. Maybe I was hallucinating? My dreams are finally making their way into reality. I'm *not* crazy, I'm just tired and stressed. Overwhelmed.

That's all it is.

But it felt so real.

I touched her, me. I felt her bony shoulder and I could see her as clear as I can see Tobias. But she wasn't there. She was never there.

I don't understand.

I fall asleep quickly, and when I wake again, the sun is high in the sky. Tobias is still wrapped around me, and I try not to move and wake him up. I can feel him stir and then his warm lips are pressing right below my ear, I guess he was already awake.

"Good morning." He whispers before kissing my throat. I turn so I am on my back, and I look up at him. "Happy Birthday, again." He smiles, his dimple in his left cheek showing. His blonde hair is messy and more copper in the sunlight. His bare chest is sculpted, hard, as he leans over me. His breath fans over my face as he stares into my eyes. His ocean blues are the twins to mine. I reach up and cup his cheek with my hand. He turns his head and kisses the inside of my palm before adjusting so one of his hands rests next to my head on the pillow and the other brushes my hip.

"I'm sorry I ran." He shakes his head before lightly nipping the meaty part of my palm. I smile and use my free hand to pinch his stomach. He shrieks and collapses on top of me. "Tobias!" I yell in between laughs as he tickles my arms and stomach in retaliation. I'm breathless and laughing when he finally stops and rolls, pulling me down on top of him so I'm straddling him.

"Hmm, I like this." I laugh and smack his chest. He squeezes my thighs and then his smile fades. "Are you okay?" His voice is soft, hesitant, but I nod.

"I am. I just think this last week has been a lot and I'm grateful for you." He smiles, his perfectly white teeth shining in the sunlight. "Thank you for putting up with me." I look at my hands and pick at the dry skin on my palms. "I know I haven't been the easiest woman to be betrothed to, but I promise I am trying. I don't want to feel the things I do or see the things I see. I think I just need a break."

"A vacation?" I look up from my hands and he's smiling again.

"Can we do that?" He nods.

"We can do anything you'd like. Maybe a honeymoon somewhere tropical like Vodia." He chuckles before he pulls my face down to his. "Whatever you want, Ela." He whispers against my lips before pulling them to his, fierce and demanding. My hands rest on his bare chest, my fingers digging into his skin as he forces my lips to part. I can feel the intensity growing in another part of his body as my hips shift on their own and brush up against him, igniting a riot of wild and uncontrollable sensations inside me. Sensations I was quick to get lost into, *eager* to get lost into.

"Ela, don't move like that." He warns, his voice barely above a strained whisper. The mask of power, of indifference slips, and I can see the heat pooling in his eyes. I do it again just to spite him. "*Ela*." He says my name with little more than a growl as he flips us, so I am on my back, my legs still wrapped around his hips. He pulls at the hem of my nightdress, exposing my underwear. His hand finds my bare stomach and squeezes my side. My stomach flutters and I wrap my arms around his neck. He kisses me deeper, the type of kiss you could read about but never experience. The type of kiss that should be illegal. Cedar and smoke fill my nose and I get lost in the scent of him.

"Tell me when to stop." He whispers against my lips before putting more of his weight on me. I moan as his hand slides from my side to my knee, holding my leg against him. My stomach is doing flips internally and I can't get enough of him. A sense of anticipation and longing curls deep inside me, begging for more. His tongue is dancing with mine, his hands greedily pulling at me. I tangle my fingers in his hair and pull him closer to me, as close as I can. I can't get enough.

"I don't want you to stop." I whisper in response, and he whimpers in my mouth. His hand leaves my knee and sticks his fingers lightly under the waistband of my underwear. My body goes taut as he teases me. The tips of his fingers brush my skin, sending shivers down my spine. I arch my back, urging him to continue. His eyes meet mine and I see they have hardened. He looks hungry, *starved*, and it's a look that sends a shiver down my spine.

His thumb caresses my inner thigh before he slides his hand farther down, just barely brushing the little bundle of nerves down there. I jerk and he smiles against my lips. He presses down gently, and I move against his hand. He slides one finger down, past that little tight bundle until he is gently pushing inside me. I arch my back more, pressing harder against him.

"Gods, Elaenor. You're so wet." His lips catch mine, swallowing my breathy moan before I can release it. His breathing is just as ragged as mine as he slowly slips in and out, teasing me. He pauses for just a second before adding a second finger. I moan, breaking our kiss as he trails his lips down my neck. He nips lightly at my nipple pebbling against the thin cotton and I yelp. My fingers dig into his hair as my hips raise slightly, riding his fingers as they pierce my flesh. He picks up his pace, his fingers torturously pounding into me, and I can barely breathe. My abdomen is heating, pressure spreading straight down to my legs. I never knew this could feel so good.

"Don't stop." I whisper breathlessly as I feel the delicious curling grow more intense. Shivers run down my spine, and I slam my eyes shut as my back arches. I moan his name, or maybe I curse it, I can't remember. All I can feel is him. Everywhere.

"Fuck." He shudders as he slides farther down my stomach, his lips leaving little trails of kisses. He pulls his fingers out for just a second so he can pull down my underwear and before I can even react his tongue is sweeping over me and then into me. I cry out and tighten my grasp on his hair, pulling at the silky strands. He slides his tongue against me and starts to suck and lick up and up and up until he hits the right spot. I cry out again as his fingers slam into me over and over.

The pressure builds, I can barely take a deep breath before I explode. I see sparks and fireworks beneath my eyelids as he roughly slides his fingers in and out of me, riding the waves of my release. Spasms of pleasure flood every nerve, every vein, every limb as he guides me through my orgasm. I reach down and grip his wrist, urging him to stop as it's too much. I whimper as he pulls his fingers out and runs his tongue along my slit with a moan, savoring the taste.

My back relaxes against the mattress, and I shudder as he slides my underwear back up. When I open my eyes he's sticking his fingers in his mouth, sucking off every last drop of *me*. Gods, that shouldn't be as hot as it is.

"You taste so good, Ela. Like cream and vanilla." Tobias murmurs. He looks down at me with half opened eyes, a smirk plastered on his swollen lips. He presses his mouth to mine and I can taste *myself* on his tongue as it swirls around my mouth. Salty and sweet. I can feel a spike of pleasure creeping back into my weakened limbs, but he pulls back. Gods, if he asked me to, I would give him everything right now. Every part of me, even if he has already explored it all.

He collapses next to me, his hand going around my bare waist as I bite my lip and try to hide the blush creeping along my cheeks. I take a nice, long deep breath as the remnants of the pressure dissipates. I've never experienced anything like *that*. Scarlett used to talk about sex as if it was the most magical thing she'd ever experienced, but with Aleksander, it was pain and brute force. This was lust, need, affection, and I didn't want it to ever stop. I turn my face so I am looking up at him. He's already watching me, and I bite my lip harder to try and hide my smile, almost drawing blood. I can feel my cheeks heat even more and I slam my hands over my face, slapping myself.

"Ow." I mutter.

"Don't hide from me *now*." He chuckles as he pulls on my wrists. "Come on, let's change and get some breakfast." I didn't want to move.

"Can't we eat here?" I pout dramatically and he bends down to suck my bottom lip into his mouth, nipping it gently, the delicious scent of cedar and smoke wafting over me. I will never get over it, over *him*.

"If that is what the birthday girl wants." He presses a dramatic kiss to my lips before sliding out of bed. I roll over to my side to watch him make his way to the door. He's only wearing a pair of shorts and I can see the evidence that he also enjoyed our little morning activity. I smile and cover my face with the blanket. I hear the door open, and I peek over the edge, he's talking to Laris. I cover my face again with the blanket, but it gets pulled off of me.

"Hey!" I yell as he slips his arms under me, pulling me out of bed. "No, I want to stay in bed." He carries me down the steps to the sitting room all the way to the couch.

"They are bringing us food and coffee."

"I don't want coffee." I pout again as he sets me down on the couch. The blood stain is gone, and the couch is once again sparkling white. He collapses onto the couch next to me and I nuzzle up against his side. "I want pastries."

"I told them to bring one of every pastry the kitchen made today along with fruit and eggs."

"No, just pastries."

"You need fuel, Ela."

"Ela." I repeat. "I like it better than Nora."

"Good. I'm glad." He kisses the top of my head. There is a knock on the door and then it opens without us answering. Men carrying trays walk in and bring them over to the table in front of the couch. Plates and plates of various pastries cover the trays along with a fruit bowl, bacon, and eggs. The last tray has glasses of juice, mugs of steaming coffee and then tiny little pitchers of cream. They exit quickly without saying a word to us.

I excitedly slide off the couch to the floor and sit in front of the table. I grab a pastry that is dripping with some sort of jam and sugar. It melts in my mouth, and I groan. Tobias leans over and pours some of the cream into a mug of coffee. He uses a spoon to stir it before picking it up and handing it to me.

"Ew, no. I don't want that." I scrunch my nose and lean away from it.

"I promise you'll like it like this. It's how my mother used to drink it." I glance up at him with narrowed eyes and set down the sticky pastry. I grab the warm mug and smell it. It smells like coffee and dirt, but there is something else, something sweet. I take a small, hesitant sip and instead of the bitter liquid I tasted before, sweet, creamy coffee pours into my mouth. I can taste caramel and ice cream and it tastes rich and decadent.

"What did you do to it?" I ask as I take another large mouthful. He laughs as he picks up his own mug of black coffee and sips on it.

"I added sweetened cream. It makes it entirely unhealthy and more like a dessert, but if you like it that way then that's fine too." I swallow again, savoring the warm liquid cascading down my throat. "Don't drink it too fast, it has caffeine in it." I nod and set it down, picking up another pastry. This one has chocolate and almonds on it.

Tobias is quiet as he takes a few mouthfuls of eggs and some fruit. He eats very clean and healthy, unlike me and my sweets. I stare at him, his eyebrows bunched together while he chews. One hand loosely holding his mug and the other his fork. He's still shirtless, his fine chest hair glowing gold. His hair is messy, tickling the tips of his eyebrows. He keeps it short, only a couple inches long, still long enough for me to run my fingers through it. He looks over at me and freezes.

"What?" He asks and I just smile.

"I think I could love you." I admit and then my smile falls. "I mean, um." I bite my lip and look down, cursing the blood flowing to my cheeks.

"I think I could love you, too, Elaenor." He responds and I look back at him. I set my pastry down and grasp his face with my sticky hands, pulling his lips to mine. "You taste like chocolate." He murmurs into my mouth, and I giggle. He pulls back, taking a sip of his coffee. "Eat your breakfast so we can get back to relaxing."

I only managed to eat a couple pastries before my stomach protested against more food. Tobias leads me through the dressing room to a door I didn't even notice. He pushes it open, and we step into the bathroom. Why didn't I know there was a door to the room this whole time? There is already steaming water inside and candles glowing around the room. The windows are closed, keeping the room dim. He closes the door behind him and my feet step onto the cold marble.

He steps up behind me and runs his hands down my arms before grabbing the hem of my nightdress and pulling it up and over my head. I stand still as his hands return to my shoulders, his thumbs lightly brushing some of my scars. His hands trail down my back, stopping to touch some of the worst ones.

I almost stop him, but the room is dim enough to where I know he can't see much, but I still feel the urge to wrap myself up in a towel to hide my bare skin. He wraps his arms around me from behind, pressing his lips to my shoulder.

"Just a bath." I nod as his hands fall away. I can hear him taking his own shorts off as I step up to the tub and stick one of my feet into the steaming liquid. It's hot, milky with oils and I climb in. The scent of roses and cedar fill my nose. I inhale as I sit down, hugging my knees to my chest. This tub is almost deep enough to cover my shoulders and I enjoy its warm embrace. I keep my back to Tobias as he climbs in behind me, spilling water over the edges. I lean back against him, my back to his chest, his legs resting next to mine.

I can feel my muscles relaxing as I exhale. Tobias's arms wrap around me with one of his hands on my stomach and the other holding my arm. His lips press softly against my neck, and I close my eyes.

"Do you think I'm crazy?" I ask as his thumb starts to move up and down.

"Not at all. I just think you've been through a lot, and you have a unique trauma response." I stay quiet and he kisses my neck again. "I do think you should tell Pakin about your nightmares and your hallucinations. He might be able to help." I nod, my wet hair sticking to his chest.

"I spoke to one of the master's in Chatis and he said that it was just because of what I went through, but they never went away. Last night was different though. I was awake and it felt so real." I murmur.

"I know, and to you it *was* real. I only ask that next time something like that happens, don't cross a border. I don't care about the diplomacy bullshit, it's just dangerous. Your title doesn't protect you there, it just makes you a target." I nod and relax against him.

"Do we have to do anything today? Or can we just stay here all day?"

"I don't have anything that can't be done tomorrow. I'm yours today, Ela."

"Good." I turn my head so I can kiss him. His lips are cold in comparison to the bath. I lift one of my wet hands and wrap it around the back of his neck, holding him to me. My lips part as an invitation, and he takes it. His hands move down to my hips, lifting me slightly. He closes his legs under me, so I am sitting on his lap, and I turn sloshing water over the side of the tub. His eyes widen in surprise as I straddle him.

I can feel the length of him softly brushing the apex of my thighs as I settle down into his lap. I wrap my arms around his neck, and he uses his hands to slightly move my hips back and forth. I arch my back as his bare skin rubs up against me. He moans across my lips, and I push myself harder against him, searching for friction. It isn't sex, but it's the closest I've let him get. His fingers tighten on my hips as I take control, moving them back and forth against him. I can feel the hard length of him sliding through my slit, hitting that little bundle of nerves with the tip. I jerk as a spike of pleasure radiates through my core.

"Ela, if you keep moving like that I'm not going to last long." He says through panting breaths. I move faster, my lips forcing his to part. I feel needy, I feel desperate. I want it all and more.

"I don't care." I moan into his mouth. My core is heating, delicious pulsing pressure spreading straight down to my legs. I shift, wanting to keep the feeling, keep him, as close as possible.

"Fuck." He whispers as I feel him shudder. His lips press against mine, his tongue exploring every inch of my mouth as I open for him. I rub up against him, faster and *harder*. My breathing is coming in short pants as I tighten my legs, begging for more and more. The tip of him is pressing into my skin, into the right spot and I ride the waves of pleasure. I ride *him* and I don't care how selfish it makes me to not want to stop. I never want this to end. I can feel the pressure building and curling through my abdomen as I tighten my grip on his hair, forcing his lips back to mine. *Gods* I can't get enough. I want *more*. I whimper against him as he wraps his arms around me, holding me tight against his chest. "Ela." He warns, but I still find a way to wiggle.

"No." I whisper and push myself back against him.

"Ela, *fuck*." His lips leave mine as he bites into my shoulder. I explode around him with a cry, and I can feel his body shaking in response. His arms tighten around me, forcing me to still, but I still rock my hips, riding the wave of heat spreading throughout my body. I'm panting, trying to get as much air in as possible. His breathing is just as labored, but his arms are loosening. "This was just supposed to be a bath." He mutters breathlessly and I can't help but laugh.

Dinner is served in the room as well and is brought in while Tobias and I are still lounging in bed with towels. He told me about his first time on Wyclif, when he was still young. He has always been wild and hard to control, but for some reason he connected to Tobias. However, his first time trying to ride him, Wyclif tossed him in a trough and then ran away from him, leaving him soaked and dirty and over a mile away from the palace.

I told him about Scarlett, Rhea, and Laenie and how close we've been since we were children. I told him how Laenie is obsessed with Ser Danieas's brother, whom we call Lord Hairy. He thought that was funny, especially when I told him I didn't actually know his name. The sun sets, darkness filling the room and I fall asleep still wrapped in my towel, my head in Tobias's lap.

I knew without a doubt, this was the best birthday I'd had in ten years.

Chapter Nineteen

Tobias woke me up with kisses trailing down my arms, which led to another indescribable moment with his head between my legs. When he was done and we were tangled up together, a knock on the door ruins the moment and it takes everything in me not to throw something at the door.

"Come in." Tobias calls out after pulling the blanket up and around my naked body. A page opens the door, wearing a red coat and a black tunic. His hair is a dark brown, his eyes nearly the same color, his skin a beautiful shade of russet, reddish-brown. He looks young, maybe my age, and *very* uncomfortable. "What is it, Donovan?" Tobias's soft and playful voice is replaced with one that is deeper, commanding. I can hear Donovan clearing his throat uncomfortably.

"I was t-told to inform you that, uh, you and M-miss, uh, Princess Elaenor, are to b-be, uh, wed in a f-few hours." He stutters. Tobias doesn't say anything, he just waves his hand. I can hear Donovan quickly shuffling out of the room, the door closing behind him. I can't help but feel bad for him.

"Well, Ela, I believe it's time for Lydia to make you into as much of a bride as she can." He chuckles and I slap his chest before rolling on top of him and giving him a deep kiss. He groans against my lips, and I pull away, leaving him pouting.

Two ladies join Lydia in getting me ready. Her hands gently brushing oil into my hair and pinning braids in all directions. She's keeping the majority of it down, which for once I enjoy. With my hair less unruly, I am becoming quite fond of the raven strands waving down my back. One of the other ladies, who won't make eye contact with me, is adding color to my cheeks and lips. I am facing away from the mirror, so I am unsure of what the finished product will be, but I am trusting they won't make me look like a jester. I was never allowed makeup at home, so I am uneasy about what it will look like on me.

I stare at the dress hanging on the bedpost as I am readied. I was expecting a white gown, as is tradition, but I was surprised when I was shown another crimson gown, a request of Evreux's no doubt. This one littered with roses and crystals. A black lace train hooked around the waist and flowing behind. The sleeveless arms meeting a corset of my dreams. The silver detailing is gorgeous and reminds me of the imprints in the ceiling. I stare at this dress, one that is unlike anything I could have ever imagined, and it surprisingly looks familiar. I rack my brain trying to understand where I have seen it when I realize.

"It's Queen Amaya's wedding dress." I whisper.

"Yes, Your Grace." Lydia speaks as she gently lays a hand on my shoulder. Reaching up, I grasp her hand and squeeze, needing the support. With a final brush stroke on my lips, my hair and makeup are complete.

Guiding me out of my chair, I am assisted as I step into the blood tinted gown. *I will never be free from this color.* One of the ladies is slipping on my black heels as Lydia is tightening my corset with the help of the other. A soft knock on the door makes me look up as, to my surprise, Evreux walks in. His greedy gaze searches my body as he bites his bottom lip. I try to keep my expression stoic, but the way he looks at me, I know he senses my fear.

"Out." He bellows. All three ladies bow and scurry out behind him, and I almost want to beg them to stay. Lydia gives me one last glance before shutting the door. I feel a weird sense of deja vu, but instead of my father, it's Evreux. His eyes refuse to meet mine as he stares at the gown, his hands gripping a black, wooden box. His skin is getting paler by the day, and I can tell he's tired. He's wearing all black and a crimson cloak, matching me, as if we were the ones to be married. His eyes are hungry, his fingers flexing around the wood in his hands. "It fits you well."

"This was Queen Amaya's, wasn't it?" I reply, willing my voice to steady. He smiles.

"Yes, but it was *meant* for you." His eyes meet mine as he takes a step towards me. Trying to hide my discomfort, and confusion, I turn away from his gaze and walk towards the mirror.

My cheeks are a faint pink, my eyes lined with kohl. My lashes are long and dark, brushing my cheeks with each blink. My bruises are hidden by thick layers of creams and powders and my lips are the same shade as the borrowed dress I currently wear. My hair is mostly down with a few braids pinned back with thin, silver rope that catches in the light. I look like my mother. My complexion is rosy from the few minutes of sun I got the other day, my blue eyes shining with thick lashes. I don't feel like myself.

"Sit." Evreux says from behind, quickly reminding me he's here. I hesitantly do as he asks and sit in the chair in front of the mirror. He leans down, pressing his nose into my hair, inhaling. My breathing hitches as my body stills. "I have a present for you." He whispers into my scalp. Straightening his back, he lifts the lid off the black box. I realize what it is immediately.

The silver thorns and vines intertwined with diamonds of all sizes. The diadem is dainty and thin, but captivatingly beautiful. My mother never had a crown, as far as I know, but if she did, I feel it would be just as beautiful. He lifts it out of the box and gently rests it on the top of my head, twisting it slightly so the little teeth at the bottom catch on my hair to hold it in place. It's heavier than I expected, adding resistance to every move of my head. Its crystals sparkle against the light filtering through the windows. I am in awe. A princess's first diadem is a moment she will never forget, and I find myself hating that it was presented to me by Evreux.

"It's–" I stutter, my fingers reaching up to brush one of the silver thorns. His hand quickly clasps around mine and tightens. "Ow, Evreux–" I feel the cool metal pressing into the tips of my fingers and I wince.

"Don't disappoint me." Evreux whispers into my ear. Thorns piercing into my skin.

"You're hurting me." I whisper, tears welling up into my eyes. I can feel the blood trickling down my hand, and I can see a glimpse of the trail in the mirror in front of me, the blood staining the silver and ruining my ladies' work. His nose presses into my neck, followed by his lips. He presses a firm and commanding kiss into my skin as I shut my eyes, willing it to stop. His free hand snaking around my chest, pulling me back against the chair.

"You smell so good. Like roses." He whispers as he slowly releases me. Throwing myself out of the chair, clutching my bleeding hand to my chest, I turn back and look at him. His wicked smile causes a chill to run up my spine. My angry eyes bore into him, and he just looks amused. Unphased.

"I don't know what you think is going to happen between us, but you are mistaken." I snap, willing my voice to stay steady and clear. "I am to be wed to your *son* any minute and you think you own me? The only person who can touch me is my husband." His low chuckle mimics a growl more so than a laugh.

"That's not what I heard when tales of your adventures in the woods were brought to my attention." A shudder runs through my limbs, and I feel the adrenaline course through my veins like electricity. Throwing the chair to the side he saunters over to me. I step back until I am pressed against the mirror, cursing the fact that I let myself get cornered again. My heart is racing, and I feel like I can't breathe.

"Evreux, stop." I warn as his hand finds my waist, and the other my neck as he forces me to meet his gaze. My hands push on his chest, using every ounce of energy I have to shove him off. I struggle against his strength, but I am no match. Even in his ill state, I can't fight him off.

"You fail to forget. I am king. Everything in this kingdom belongs to me. That includes *you*." His face smashes into mine as he forces my lips to open, flooding my mouth with the taste of cinnamon and citrus. He groans as his hands explore my chest, pulling the corset down to reveal my naked skin. I push against him, trying to cover myself, which tightens his grip on me. His hands pull up the hem of my dress, ripping through the lace undergarments. His fingers torturously touch my inner thighs, possessively, as if I am his property.

"Please stop." I cry against his rough kisses and to my surprise, he pulls his face away from mine. His hand resting on my backside, his eyes meeting mine. Tears pour down my cheeks, no doubt ruining the work my ladies did. "Please leave me alone." I plead. He leans forward and bites my lip with a growl, slicing into it. He steps back pulling me off the mirror and throwing me onto the ground. I land on my side and cry out in pain as my hip slams into the marble. He quickly undoes his pants and drops on top of me, my hands fighting his, trying to get free from his touch. I kick out, trying to force him off of me, but he pins me down with his legs.

"Stop resisting." He barks as I try to push him off of me. "You wanted this. You *wanted* this!" He screams at me. I don't know if he's trying to convince himself or me.

"No!" I scream as loud as I possibly can. I know the guards outside belong to Evreux, but if I make enough noise, maybe they'll come in and he'll stop. Laris or Tano. One of them *has* to intervene. Before I can scream again, he slaps me, slamming my head into the stone floor. I taste the blood in my mouth, and I am temporarily stunned. My head is pounding, and I can feel the thorns stabbing into my skull. My eyes spin and I can barely make out the shapes of the chandelier above us.

"I'll make this quick." He grabs both of my wrists in one hand with ease before his weight presses against me.

"Stop it!" I scream as loud as I can as his mouth finds mine again, muffling my cries. He shifts above me, his hands pulling up my skirt again and I hear the door open. Footsteps running towards us, leather slamming onto the marble floors. It feels like it takes forever for whoever it is to reach us, as if everything is in slow motion, Evreux's tongue aggressively reaching for mine.

"Father!" Tobias yells in surprise as he pushes him off of me. He falls to the ground with a thud, his crown flinging off his head and hitting the mirror. It shatters and glass rains down on top of him. "What are you doing?" He snaps as he pulls me up onto my feet. I bury my face in his chest as he holds me. I pull up my corset to cover my exposed breasts as I try to steady my breath. I try to swallow the blood pooling in my mouth, but it makes me gag and I don't fight the tears pouring down my cheeks.

"What you failed to do!" Evreux screams as he slowly stands. "An heir. That is all I need. I need an heir! Don't you see. They have the power, if I don't have someone to continue my reign they'll win!" He yells as he places his hands on Tobias's shoulders and shakes him. His chest almost touching my shoulder as I hold onto Tobias. My body is shaking, tears flowing freely, and I whimper, fear coursing through my veins. I just want this to end. Tobias's protective arms are wrapped around me, letting me know I am safe.

"You have an heir, father." His voice is soft, reassuring. "Me. I'm your heir." He sounds scared, much like the little boy I used to know. They are both quiet for a second. I lift my head off his chest and look over my shoulder at Evreux. He looks confused and horrified as he releases Tobias and steps back. Blood is starting to drip down his nose and ear, along with the various cuts he received from the mirror.

"You don't understand. She needs a boy. She only has a girl. She needs a boy." He's shaking his head, staring at us distraught, pleading for us to listen.

"Father, what are you talking about?" Tobias's voice is quiet, concerned. "Mother had boys. Theo and I. She had us."

"He'll kill her if she doesn't have a boy. I can give her a boy." His eyes leave Tobias's, and he looks straight at me. "Please, my love, I can make this go away. Please." He grabs onto my shoulder and pleads with me as I tighten my arms around Tobias. His eyes are filled with utter sorrow as they search mine. My heart hurts as I stare into his frantic eyes. He's sick and he doesn't understand what he's doing. "Sybil, my love." He reaches for my face and Tobias slaps his hand away.

"Father, this isn't Sybil. This is Elaenor, her daughter." His voice is strained.

"My mother is dead." I whisper. His eyes fill with shock as he absorbs what I just said, his head shaking.

"No, no. You're wrong. He hasn't killed her, but he will." He mumbles to himself. "I can make this go away, just come with me. You can bring her, she'll be happy. My love, please." Tears are welling up in his eyes as he begs for me to come. He's talking about my mother. Is he talking about my father? Was he scared of him?

"Evreux, it's me, Elaenor. I'm not Sybil." His eyes search mine, panicked. "My mother died a while ago." I beg for him to hear me. The fear in his eyes mirrors the fear in my voice. Tobias is quiet, just holding me against him, keeping me at arm's length from his father.

"Yes, yes. You're right." He says softly. He picks up his crown and straightens it before making eye contact with me. "Excuse me." He pushes past us and out the door. We both stare at the open door for a few moments before I speak.

"Tobias–" He pulls back and places his hands on either side of my face. He leans down so that his eyes are level with mine. His thumb brushes the corner of my mouth, coming away red.

"It's alright, you're alright." He whispers. He kisses me softly on the lips before pulling me back into his chest.

"Why is he doing this?" I ask between sobs.

"I don't think he knows, Elaenor. He's confused." His voice is strained. "I'm sorry." He kisses the side of my head and squeezes me.

"I don't understand. He thought I was my mother. He called her his love. He said that someone was going to kill her. Do you think he means my father?" Panic fills my body as I start to shake. "What does he know about her death?"

"I don't know. He's just confused." He repeats. I need to know what he knows.

"I don't feel safe here, Tobias. I don't feel safe near him." I can feel him shake his head, his chin resting in my hair.

"It'll be okay. I'll make it okay. I promise." He tightens his arms around me. "Will you be alright?" I nod against his chest. He slides his arms down to my waist and then lifts my chin up, so I am facing him.

"Please don't leave me, Tobias." I whimper, my eyes finding his.

"I'll see you soon, okay?" He tries to reassure me, but I don't want to be alone. If he comes back, I don't know if I can stop him. Standing on my toes I kiss him fiercely, hoping that this will be enough to get him to stay. His tongue finding mine as he pulls me against him.

"Please." I whisper into his lips. I tangle my fingers into his hair and pull him as tight as I can against me, begging for him to stay.

"I have to go check on him, Elaenor." His voice is stern this time. When he finally pulls back, he looks conflicted. "I'm sorry." He gives me a sad smile, before pulling out of my embrace and leaving.

I stare after him for a moment, frozen and numb. I reach up to wipe my tears when cold, frail hands touch my face. Lydia is looking at me with pity as she wipes the makeup smudges away.

"Let's get you ready, Your Grace." I nod as she takes the diadem off my head and leads me to the chair.

Chapter Twenty

It didn't take long for Lydia to clean up the mess I was. With my dress straightened, and my makeup touched up, I am led down the hallway to the throne room. My head is throbbing, and I can still taste the blood in my mouth, no matter how many times I rinsed it out. My stomach is in knots about what has now been two encounters with Evreux this week. Tobias was keen on protecting me, but how far would he be willing to go?

I can't endanger him for my own selfish well-being. I can't do anything but wait. Evreux is sick. I just need to withstand his torture for a few more days, or until his sickness overpowers him. If I can just stay with Tobias, or anyone who would protect me while we wait out his sickness, maybe I'll be safe. But I know that I'll only be safe if he's gone. Tobias said he'll make this better, that he'll make this okay. I have to believe him.

Standing right outside the throne room with my ladies, I wait for my cue to enter. I allow myself to take a deep, steadying breath. This is it. After today, I will no longer belong to myself, not that I ever have. While I am the Princess of

Chatis, I will also be the Princess of Noterra. With that title, comes responsibility and a little bit of power. Power I will hopefully be able to utilize to gain protection if my husband isn't able, or willing, to provide it.

After today, I need to gain allies. That's my first job as princess, create a council of my own. I have no idea what Tobias has planned, but with Evreux's increasing need to torture me, the need for trusted friends grows. While a queen has a council and trusted advisors, I need to find a way to make that a possibility as a princess. I will not allow myself to be a prisoner here. I will not allow Evreux to win. I am grateful for Erik's presence at court. I know he is still recovering, but knowing I have someone who is faithful to me and not to Noterra makes me feel a little more at ease.

The music is still playing, but my cue to enter hasn't appeared. The guard standing at the door looks over at me, nervous. I look back at Lydia just as the music stops abruptly. My ladies, who are just as confused as I am, step aside as people begin quickly funneling out of the throne room. Temporary relief washes over my body, which leaves me confused. I step to the side as well, to allow everyone to exit as I look for Tobias. Master Pakin walks out with a nod and hurries off down the hallway. Tobias is next to exit, and I can see his panic as he looks around for me. Once his eyes meet mine, I push my bouquet of roses into Lydia's hands and rush over to him. He wraps his hand around my arm and starts to pull me down the hallway.

"Something has happened, Ela." His voice is strained, panicked.

"What is it, Tobias?" I whisper as I search his eyes for any clues. His face is stoic, but I can't tell if something is bothering him.

"It's my father, we have to go." He tightens his grip and pulls me down the hallway in the same direction as Master Pakin. I try to keep up with him, but the heels and dress weren't designed for fast paces.

"Tobias, slow down, *please*!" He stops abruptly and turns to face me, releasing his grip. His eyes are filled with fear, and I can tell he's terrified. "He was fine when he left us, what happened? I thought you went to check on him?"

"He was found at the bottom of the stairwell, Elaenor. He's dying." A single tear runs down his cheek. He's pale and his hands are shaking. I hate the sense of relief I feel for his death.

"You knew he was sick, Tobias. It's alright." I don't know what to say, how to reassure him. I never had anyone there for me when my mother died. I don't know what people usually say in these instances. I reach up and brush the tear from his cheek.

"I am not afraid of him dying because he's my father. I am afraid of what this means for me. I am to be king." His voice is soft, he once again sounds like the little boy I met 10 years ago. I wrap my arms around him and rub his back with my hand. This man, who has shown nothing but strength, is breaking down right in front of me. Terrified that he is just a few moments away from being crowned.

"I will be right there with you, Tobias." I pull back and give him a soft smile. "You are not alone in this. Despite feelings we may or may not have for each other yet, I am to be your wife, your queen. I will be by your side as you are crowned. I will be by your side while we rule over Noterra. Everything will be okay." He gives me a sad nod, but I can tell he isn't hearing anything I am saying. He takes my hand this time as he pulls me down the hallway again.

I don't know where this version of Tobias has come from, but he's different, less arrogant, and more human. He looks like he doesn't want to be king, or possibly he never imagined he would *be* king. He had to know this was coming. His father has been ill for some time, but maybe he was convinced this day would never come.

I allow him to pull me into a large room, almost triple the size of ours. The walls are lined with windows and crimson curtains. The largest bed I have ever seen sits in the center of the back wall. A seating area, couch, writing desk, and a large table with several chairs fill the empty space. The marble walls are bright but decorated with various shades of red and black. These are the king's quarters. A huge contrast to the room I have been sleeping in.

Laying in the bed is Evreux. His eyes are open as he listens to Master Pakin speaking softly to him. His skin is pale and gray, nothing like the man I saw a few short moments ago. He is tucked under several blankets and his hands rest on his stomach. Evreux's eyes glance in my direction before nodding. Master Pakin steps back and beckons for us to step forward.

"Father." Tobias whispers as he kneels next to him. I rest my hand on his shoulder and my eyes meet Evreux's. His face is soft, weak, a stark contrast compared to the man who was just forcing himself on me. I find myself wondering if this was a trick, if he is really feeling this ill, or if he is trying to garner sympathy. Or maybe the incident before truly was just a symptom of the illness he is suffering from. I find myself pitying him. This once strong, warrior king is now lying in a bed at such a young age, dying. I give him a genuine smile as I realize the fear that must be coursing through his veins.

"Son, do not destroy what I have built." Evreux whispers, his voice strained. "Rakushia is under attack, you need to send the militia. You need to regain power–" He coughs loudly, and my eyes widen as blood trickles down the corner of his mouth. Master Pakin returns to gently wipe it away with a cloth. I can see the ring of dried blood on his nostrils and the tiny cuts peppered over his face from the shattered mirror. "You are strong, you will be a good king." He coughs again and I look away.

Tobias's eyes are wide, and his face is proof that this is the first time Evreux has ever said anything that resembles kindness to him. Maybe Tobias's strong and arrogant demeanor is a mask as well, that he is truly a decent man who has been beaten down by his father over time, much like me.

I see movement in the corner of my eyes and catch Theo standing in the doorway. He doesn't look sad; he just looks angry. Instead of looking at his father, his eyes find mine. He looks at me, truly looks at me, and I can see sadness break through the cold exterior. My pulse skips and my lips part as I feel his eyes staring into my soul. "Elaenor, come here." Evreux's voice cuts through my thoughts and I tear my eyes away from Theo's to look at him. Sitting on the edge of the bed, I hesitantly grasp one of Evreux's cold hands as he reaches out for me. Despite the terror he has inflicted, no one should die alone.

"It'll be okay." I whisper reassuringly. He nods at Tobias who gives me a wary glance before standing and leaving us. He doesn't go far, he just stands off to the side, speaking with Master Pakin.

There is nothing he can do right now, Elaenor. Just breathe.

I force my pulse to steady.

"Elaenor. He is strong, but he is misguided. Don't let him make the same mistakes I did." My eyes leave Tobias's and find Evreux's.

"Mistakes? What do you mean?" His hand squeezes mine and he pulls me closer. I lean in slightly, not wanting to miss what it is he is going to say, but also worried about getting close to him. I can see Tobias watching us, worried. I hold my breath to avoid inhaling the scent of death and decay. He smells less like cinnamon and citrus and more like rot.

"Your mother was the love of my life." My eyes widen as they meet his. I try to pull back, but he keeps a firm grip on my hand. "Your father was never happy about you being their only child. He pushed her for an heir. So much. She was doing everything she could to conceive a boy, but they never made it to full term. Your father killed her when he found out she had been coming here. We promised her we would protect you, that is why you were engaged as children. She knew that you would never be safe with Viktor. She almost had your father convinced to send you here permanently as a child, to grow up here in court, but then she died." He pulls his hand away from mine to cough and I lean back, absorbing everything he has said.

"But my father said it was the prophet, that he murdered her." I whisper. My father murdered my mother? He murdered her because she fell in love with another?

"Love him, protect him. Do not let him allow anger to guide his actions." He reaches forward and his fingers gently brush my cheek. "You are so much like her. I only wish I would be here to watch you grow." Red tinged tears trickle down his face and onto the bed as he stares into my eyes. He looks so much like a father saying goodbye to his child, maybe he was kind once. Maybe my childhood self cared for him.

"I will take care of him." I whisper, fighting the tears that threaten to escape. This is a lot of information to absorb at once. My father murdered my mother, so he says. My mother was in love with Evreux, so he says. I am engaged to his son to protect me because Evreux made a promise to my mother, *so he says*. I don't know if I believe him, but I have no one else to provide insight into their lives. I don't think I'll ever know the truth.

"Both of them. Take care of both of them." He whispers.

"Can I ask you something, Evreux?" He nods weakly. "There is no chance you could be my father, right? If I am to marry Tobias–"

"No, not at all. I was never with your mother. When I laid eyes on your mother the first time, when she was engaged to Argent, my world shifted. It was as if everything suddenly made sense." He smiles softly as his eyes stare at something that isn't there.

"But Queen Amaya?" I stutter. Did he not love his wife? Will Tobias be the same?

"I loved Amaya, with everything in me, but we were not *in* love. We were only husband and wife in name. We were both happier that way." I nod, processing everything he's said. He coughs, blood pooling in his mouth. "I am so sorry for any pain I have inflicted. I never meant to cause you harm. I get confused, as if I am transported back in time for mere moments." Blood trickles out of his nose, and he inhales a weak breath.

"I forgive you." I smile and squeeze his hand before releasing it and sliding off the bed. I have nothing else to offer him, but forgiveness is something I can give a man on his deathbed.

Tobias senses the end of our conversation and returns, wrapping his arm around my waist. I rest my head against his chest as he stands and watches his father. It only took a few moments before he took his final breath, his eyes never leaving mine.

"Goodbye, Father." He whispers. I place a soft and gentle kiss on Tobias's cheek as he watches Master Pakin close the king's eyes. As he closes the eyes of one of the only people who could shed some light on my childhood.

"Long live the King." He chants as he drapes a clean cloth over his face, covering the once feared and beloved king. Someone who had unlimited power, riches, and support, reduced to a sickened man with no one on his deathbed.

Is this my future? Tobias's future?

What will my life be like when my time comes?

"Long live the King." I whisper.

Chapter Twenty-One

I glance back at the doorway, but Theo is gone. Tobias pulls out of my grip and walks over to Master Pakin, where they speak in hushed tones. I slowly sneak away until I am able to walk out of the room. Theo is leaning against the wall, his face is filled with anger, his hands balled up into fists. I almost don't want to approach him, but I feel as if he has no one. No one to check on him, no one to comfort him.

"Theo, I am so sorry about your father." I whisper, keeping my distance. He looks over at me and scoffs, running his hands through his hair and ripping out the leather cord tying half of it back.

"My father was a horrible parent; he will not be missed by me." His voice is sharp and cruel. His eyes fixate on mine, but they remain hardened. A once kind and playful man is replaced with hostility, hurt.

"It's alright to be angry, Theo. Any emotion you feel after you lose a parent is justified." I try to reassure him, but my words fail me. He ignores me and just stares deep into my eyes.

"You are going to be queen." He says flatly before turning away from me. His eyes flit up and down the hallway, looking for something.

"Yes, I am." I respond, not knowing where he is going with this. He sighs and throws his head back against the wall. We are quiet for a moment before he kicks off the stone and faces me.

"I am leaving. Without my father here I have no obligations and I sure as hell am not going to listen to my *brother*."

"Theo, you can't leave. This is your home." I shake my head.

"Walls do not make a home, Nora. You know that better than anyone." I hate the way his voice sounds when he says my name, as if it's a proclamation of love. His eyes find mine again and they soften when they see my sorrow. The blue is deepening, darkening, like the ocean during a thunderstorm. I can't shake the electricity that warms my blood as he stares at me. I dig my nails into my palms to keep from doing something stupid. I just want to touch his cheek, see if his skin is as soft as I imagine it is.

"Where are you going to go?" I ask, my voice quiet.

"I don't know. Maybe Tatus, somewhere far away. I can't stay here and watch you marry him. Watch you be with him." His voice cracks and he quickly clears his throat. He looks around the hallway again to see if there are any prying eyes before he fixates on mine.

"Theo, you can't feel that way." I whisper, breaking eye contact. I back away towards the door, trying to find a quick exit. "I should go."

"Are you saying you don't feel the same?" He reaches forward and gently cups my face in his hands, pulling me away from the door. "You can't tell me that this doesn't feel right." His hands are warm, the sweet scent of grass and spring air filling my nose as I inhale. It does feel right. It feels perfect. It feels like home. But my home is with Tobias.

"Theo, please, I barely know you." I whisper, refusing to make eye contact. I keep my gaze cast down onto his bare chest, his tunic open at the top like always. He can't act like this, so close to his brother, yet I'm not pushing him away either.

"I love you. I know it's absurd. I know we barely know each other." I try to turn away, but he holds my face still. "The moment you ran into me in the woods, I knew you would be my downfall. I knew I was going to love you one way or another. You were a fighter, covered in blood that wasn't yours. You were a complete surprise, a gift from the gods themselves."

"Theo, stop." I whisper, pleading. "I'm marrying Tobias." He shakes his head. My hands grip his wrists, trying to pull him off.

"No it doesn't have to be that way." His voice is panicked, like he's trying so desperately to hold onto everything he has.

"Yes, it does. I have to marry what fits my station. I'm sorry. This isn't my choice. I have to marry Tobias. Please let go of me." I beg, pulling at his hands. He has to let me go. I can't get in between them. I can't do this.

"Fuck Tobias. You should have always been mine." He growls before slamming his face into mine.

He forces my lips to part as he deepens the kiss. His hands holding my face in place, and I let him. I allow his lips to guide mine as I feel the raw, burning passion pouring from us both. This is the kiss of two people in love. No agenda. No pain. Just love and longing and desire. I can't feel this way, but I find myself melting into his chest. He's different from Tobias. He's hesitant, gentle, but Tobias is protective and sure of himself. He pulls back slightly, and his eyes meet mine. Pure adoration. He leans down again and presses a soft and gentle kiss on my lips.

"Don't tell me this isn't real." He pleads with me. "Come with me." My eyes fall. "Let's run away, Nora." I shake my head.

"It doesn't matter what I feel, Theo. I choose Tobias." I whisper, choking against a sob, before stepping out of his grasp and right into something hard.

A rough hand pushes me out of the way and into the wall before flying through the air and hitting Theo directly in the face.

"Tobias!" I scream as Theo collapses to the ground. Tobias jumps on top of him, holding him down before punching him straight in the nose again and again. Theo isn't fighting back; he's just taking it. Laughing as blood fills his mouth.

"Tobias, stop!" I scream as I grab at his arms, trying to pull him off. His arm swings out and smacks into my face. Sharp, burning pain replaces his hand as I fall to the ground. My eyes begin to water, and I reach up to wipe away the tears, only to see blood coming from my nose. I look over at Theo, his eyes watching me furiously. Tobias grabs him by the shoulders and slams him onto the ground again before standing.

"Don't you ever fucking touch her again!" He spits at his brother before walking over to me.

"Oh god, Ela. I'm so sorry." His face is filled with panic as he walks over to me.

"Tobias, please." I whimper as he leans down. He grabs my arms and pulls me to my feet and into his arms. "Tobias, please. It was nothing." I turn and look back at Theo, who is laying still on the ground, his eyes fixated on mine. Fear. All I see is fear, before we turn the corner, and my view is blocked.

Tobias's face is set in stone when we get to the room. He sets me down, but I slip in my heels and land hard on the marble floors. I look up at him as he paces around the room. I stay still as I watch, afraid to move. His eyebrows are furrowed and he's mumbling under his breath while quickly walking back and forth. He hit me. He actually hit me, *and* his brother. I don't blame his anger as he saw Theo and I kissing, but *he hit me.*

"Tobias?" I whisper. He stops abruptly before slowly turning towards me. His face softens as he walks over to me and kneels down. He reaches towards me, and I flinch. Hurt flashes across his face but is quickly replaced with anger. He brushes a finger under my nose, wiping the blood off my face. My heart is racing as my eyes fixate on his. What is he going to do with me? "Tobias?" I whisper again.

"I am so sorry, Ela. I'm so sorry." He pulls me up and onto his lap, his breathing labored as he sobs. The floodgates are open and he's letting everything out. I hesitate for only a moment before I wrap my arms around him. He's a sad and broken boy, just like me.

"It's alright, it was an accident." I whisper into his hair. It was just an accident.

"I didn't mean to hit you, you got in the way." He chokes. "It was an accident." He sits up and grabs my face. His cheeks are tear stained, his eyes red. "You have to believe me."

"I believe you, Tobias." I wipe away at the tears streaming down his face and his lips softly find mine.

It was an accident.

He didn't mean to hit me.

He apologized.

He needs you, Elaenor. Don't give up on him. I recite to myself. He pulls back and rests his forehead against mine.

"This has been an absolutely horrible day." He laughs softly before lifting his head back up. His saddened eyes stare at my nose and he lifts his hand to wipe away the blood again.

"It'll get better." I say with a soft smile that I know doesn't reach my eyes. It has to get better.

"Are you alright, please tell me you're alright?" His eyes search mine and I nod.

"I'll be okay, Tobias. You didn't mean to."

"I need to go check on Theo." He whispers before pressing his lips into a hard line. He doesn't move and instead stares at me, as if he's waiting for something.

"What is it?"

"Did you mean what you said? That you choose me?" He sounds hopeful, as if being chosen was new to him. I nod.

"Yes, Tobias. You are to be my husband, of course I choose you." I lean forward and kiss him. His whole body relaxes as he exhales into me. He stands quickly and helps me up before giving me one last look. He leaves the room, closing it softly behind him. I stare down at my hands, the tiny cuts on my fingertips, the blood smeared on the back of my hand. I barely have a second to breathe before Lydia comes in and rushes over to me. She always knows when I need her, without me asking.

She guides me over to the chair by the window with a saddened smile, and I stare blankly out onto the grounds. The sun is still shining, but it's starting to set. The once bright blue sky is replaced with pinks and purples. A whole day gone in the blink of an eye. A cool rag wipes away at my face as I stare.

My father used to hit me. He never hesitated and I grew up with the constant presence of bruises and scabs. Is this normal? He obviously also laid a hand on my mother if he murdered her. Was Evreux right? Did my father find out about them and kill her? Was my mother truly in love with Evreux, or was it one sided? And what about Tobias? What does this mean for our relationship?

Is this what I am to expect of our marriage? Fear? Abuse? Or was it an accident? He didn't know it was me. I was grabbing him; he was trying to get me off of him so he can–

No.

A deep and familiar voice echoes throughout my head. Is that the voice in my head? Is this my subconscious? Or is it *him*?

"Your Grace?" Lydia whispers, pulling me out of my thoughts.

"Yes?" I whisper back. Her soft, motherly eyes are welcoming. I want nothing more than my own mother right now, but I'm alone.

"You are finished." I nod, dismissing her. She gives me a slight curtsy before scurrying out of the room and disappearing from sight. I take a deep breath and walk towards the balcony. The doors are open, and a slight breeze comes through, ruffling my hair. I take slow, steady steps up to the landing, before stepping out into the open air. I look around the palace grounds. Torches are being lit, illuminating the already darkening sky. The grass is empty, everyone inside for dinner. How has it already been a full day since we awoke this morning? Since I was wrapped up in Tobias, his fingers softly running across my bare skin. Everything has changed.

I reach up and let my fingers grasp the crown that rests upon my head. With a slight tug, I pull it out of my hair and hold it out in front of me. The silver metal intertwining with the clear stones are beautiful. Staring at the thorns wrapping around the diamonds, I feel broken. I am a stone being suffocated by thorns, or by Noterran royalty.

Just a few hours ago, I was lying in bed with my future husband. Now, I am a bloodied, broken, shell of a girl who is to be queen. I can't let this break me. I can't let Tobias break me. He's just as broken as I am. We have to get through this together. That is what couples do. They get through the hard times.

Taking one last look at the crown, I return it to its rightful place on top of my head. Diadems are symbols of strength, power. That's what I need to be. Strong. Not just for Tobias, but for myself. After a deep breath, I stand up straight and turn back to the room.

I walk past the haunting furniture, the bed, the couch, the chair, and the newly replaced mirror. All possessions of Tobias's, as am I.

You can't think that way, Elaenor.

I look away and reach for the door handle but stop. I quickly turn back around and dig the glass dagger out of the couch cushion. I slip it into my garter under my dress before returning to the door. It's cold glass leaves goosebumps wherever it brushes my skin, electricity sparking against the flesh. Opening the dark wood, Laris and Tano are standing on either side. They give me a slight nod, and I return it before making my way down the hall. Their footsteps are nearly silent behind me.

I see a dark figure walking at the end of the hallway and exhale loudly as I recognize Erik. He smiles as he sees me, but his smile is quickly replaced with fury. I look down as I reach him, but he tilts my head up.

"Elaenor." His voice is quiet, warning. I pull my face out of his grasp.

"I'm alright, I promise. It was a misunderstanding. Tobias was aiming for his brother, and I got in the way." It wasn't a complete lie, but I don't know if it truly was an accident, even if Tobias says it was. I meet his eyes again, unconvinced. "Erik, I am fine. Please go get some rest."

"I'll be ready tomorrow to stand as your sworn sword." He responds, straightening his back, but I can see the pain in his eyes.

"Please don't push yourself, not for me."

"I would give my life for you, princess." He smiles and slightly bows before slowly walking away. I watch him disappear down the hall before turning back towards the dim hallway.

Chapter Twenty-Two

I find Tobias in the throne room. He's standing in the center of the circular room, his eyes fixed on two grand chairs on the platform. I walk up to his right, standing as straight and tall as possible. He doesn't acknowledge my arrival and just stands there, silent. His hands balled up in fists at his sides. His right fist is bloodied and bruised. From his assault on Theo, or myself, I'm not sure. Most likely a combination of them both. I lightly brush his arm and press my lips to it.

"We'll get through this, right?" His voice is soft, scared.

"Yes, we will." I reply, my voice muffled by his arm.

"Ah, there you two are!" A cheerful voice breaks the silence and I turn to see a priest in the doorway, holding a ribbon in one hand, and a scroll in the other. He gives me a smile and a slight bow of the head. "Your Grace, you look beautiful! Are you ready to be wed?" I give him a small smile and a nod. Tobias is still silent, facing away from us both.

"Will it be here, now?" I ask, gesturing towards the empty room, swallowing the lump in my throat.

"Yes, Your Grace. All of your guests already left the palace, so it will have to be a small affair." I nod as he walks over to us. He steps around Tobias until he is directly in front of us.

"Please hold out your hands." He says softly. I lift my left arm and Tobias places his right arm next to mine. The thin crimson ribbon is wrapped around our wrists, tying us together. He looks over at me with hopeful eyes. "We are gathered here today to bestow upon Tobias Rosenthal, Prince of Noterra, and Elaenor Pinewell, Princess of Chatis, a union." He stops and looks at both of us. "Did you write vows?" My eyes widen and I turn towards Tobias who shakes his head.

"We didn't have time." Tobias responds.

"Repeat after me, then, my dear." He looks at me and I give him a small nod. Fear courses through my veins as I am about to get married. Tobias is a confusing man. A man who makes me question everything about myself. A man who has hit me, whether accidentally or not, he laid a hand on me, and now in a few short moments, I will be his property by law. I am hopeful that his apology was sincere, but I can't even imagine what could happen in the future should I get in the way again.

"I, Elaenor, Princess of Chatis, pledge my life and loyalty to you."

"I, Elaenor, Princess of Chatis, pledge–" My voice catches and the priest's eyebrows raise. I swallow the lump forming in my throat as I try to will the tears away. Tobias looks over at me with fear. As if he's worried I'm going to back out. My heart skips a beat. I meet his eyes and continue. "Pledge my life and loyalty to you." I finish.

"This union is a promise to the gods and goddesses as well as the kingdoms in which we reside."

"This union is a promise to the gods and goddesses as well as the kingdoms in which we reside." I repeat while maintaining eye contact with Tobias.

"I will be yours and yours alone."

"I will be yours and yours alone." A single tear trickles down my face, and I turn away. His free hand finds my face as he forces me to look at him. His sorrow mirrors mine in a way I am only hoping is regret for what he's done.

"Wonderful, my dear." He turns his head to Tobias. "Do you know them, or would you like me to recite them?"

"I know them." The priest nods. "I, Tobias, King Regent of Noterra," Regent. *He's already been crowned regent?* "Pledge my life and loyalty to you. This union is a promise to the gods and goddesses as well as the kingdoms in which we reside. I will be yours," His hand finds my face again and his eyes bore into mine. "And yours alone." I smile, relieved that we for once seem to be on the same page.

"By the grace of the gods and goddesses, I now pronounce you husband and wife. A union formed by the will of the late King Evreux, and a promise for forever." *Forever.* He gestures towards Tobias, who turns to face me. Our arms are untied and Tobias leans into me, pressing a sweet and soft kiss on my mouth.

"Will we be undergoing the consummation ceremony?" The priest asks Tobias.

"No, Father Reynolds, we will not." He smiles at me.

"Then if I can just get you two love birds to sign here?" Father Reynolds holds out the scroll which is filled with neat handwriting and two lines down below with our names written beneath. Our marriage certificate. I take the quill from him and sign my name above the line on the right. Tobias does the same on the other, before nodding to dismiss Father Reynolds. This took less time than I expected, maybe because it was a short ceremony? I thought it would be a little more grand. I'm not disappointed, just confused.

"Was that it?" I ask, waiting for something else to happen.

"Yes." His voice is strained, filled with emotions hard to decipher.

"Tobias, about before–" He lifts his hand to silence me, but I reject it. "Tobias, don't dismiss me like that." His eyebrows furrow and he drops his hand. "Talk to me, say something." I beg.

"Whatever feelings you have for my brother will end. You are not to have contact with him. You two will never be alone." His voice is flat, monotone. As if he is giving me an order. "You will be accompanied by a guard at all times. A guard that answers to me, either Laris or Tano. You will do as I say, when I say it, or I will have you beheaded for adultery." I roll my eyes at his attempted threat.

"Tobias, for gods sake!" I snap. "Nothing happened between Theo and I. *He* kissed *me*. I will not allow you to treat me this way. I am your wife, and I will soon be a queen. I will not spend my life being threatened and fearful of you." I spit and rip my hand out of his.

"You don't have a choice." He exhales loudly. "Elaenor, we are wed. All I'm asking is for you to focus on me and not on my brother." His voice is soft, saddened.

"Tobias, I already told you that I choose you. I already told you that I had no feelings for your brother. Do you think I would marry you if my heart belongs to another?" I plead. I grab his hands and bring them up to my face. He leans down and rests his forehead against mine, our lips just barely touching.

"Say it." He begs against my lips. "Please." I pull back and look at him.

"What do you want me to say?" I ask, searching his eyes.

"Tell me you love me." I can see the moisture gather in his eyes and he frantically holds onto me. "Tell me you forgive me."

"I love you. I forgive you." I whisper. I don't know if it's the truth I speak, but in this moment, I needed to say it. He presses his lips back to mine. I am *his*. I let the tears fall freely as I kiss him back. He starts walking, pushing me with him until my back meets the wall. His hands leave my waist, and he starts to hike up my skirt.

"Is this alright?" He asks in between kisses, his hands pulling at the fabric. My pulse skips as I find that I was in a similar situation with Evreux the other day.

"Not here, Tobias, please." I push on his chest. I can't even bear the thought of someone walking in on us. He nods and kisses my cheek before pulling me out of the throne room, nausea blooming deep in my stomach.

The walk to our chambers seems like it takes forever. We've passed every person that seems to work here, they all bow and greet us. The regent and his bride. Hands shake mine; a few men clap Tobias on the back in congratulations. Subtle bows of condolences follow. The short trip takes an hour.

When we finally get to our room, Laris and Tano are standing at their post. With a quick nod from Tobias, the door opens, and he softly pushes me through the doorway. The room looks exactly the same as it has every other time I've entered it, but it feels different. Final. This is *our* room now. Not just a room we inhibited as individuals, but the room of a married couple. *Married.*

I turn back towards Tobias, and he opens his arms. I step into his embrace as he pulls me against him. His nose nuzzles into my hair as he tightens his grip, inhaling. We stand here for just a moment before he pulls back and looks at me.

"Tomorrow, after the ceremony, we'll move into the king's chambers." I nod, but don't return his gaze. "My father's things will be removed, and we can decorate it however you'd like. It'll be ours." I look up at him through my eyelashes and sigh. This has been one of the most overwhelming days of my life, and it's not even over yet.

"Tobias, I know consummation is required, but does it have to be tonight?" He brushes my cheek with his fingertips, and I feel the light sting where he hit me. "After your father, and everything that's happened, I don't want to rush into it if it doesn't feel right." I try to explain, but the look in his eyes lets me know he understands.

"No, it can be whenever you're ready. You can initiate it." I lean into his palm, and he pulls me back against him.

"Did you mean it, when you said you were mine and mine alone?" He doesn't answer right away.

"Ela, of course." He leans back and I look up at him. If I didn't know any better, I would say he was giving me a look filled with love, admiration. A look I've seen in Theo, in my mother. I find myself believing him. Believing that he wants to love me, and that's enough. That's enough for me. That's all I need. For right now. How pathetic. "I promise." I rise up on my toes and press my lips to his.

"Say it." I mimic as my lips brush against his chin.

"I promise." He whispers again and I wrap my arms around his neck. "I promise." He repeats as he lifts me up so that I wrap my legs around his waist. I can feel him walking me backwards and then slowly lower me onto the bed. His lips leave mine as they trail down my neck and my arms. "I promise. I am so sorry."

"Shh." I whisper and let my lips brush his while I speak. "It's okay." Those words were meant for him, but somehow also for me. This is okay. Having sex with my husband is okay. *This is okay.*

"Ela, you just said-"

"Don't." I whisper, a silent agreement to this. To us. His hands hungrily caress my body as his lips press against mine. He scoots me farther onto the bed, situating himself on top of me.

"I'll go slow." He pulls back and looks at me and I nod. His hands pull up my dress until I'm exposed. His eyes never leave mine as his pants slide down.

I reach up for his face and he brings it back down to me. He kneels in between my legs, softly sliding them apart with his own. His lips find mine again, but his eyes remain open. "This might hurt." He whispers and I close my eyes.

He shifts slightly and then I feel as he slowly enters me. The pain is dull, but present. I can feel myself stretching as he goes deeper and deeper. He stills once he's in all the way. He presses his lips to my temples, and he holds me as he begins to move. I tighten my arms around his neck as he picks up speed. I can feel the sweat beading on his back. I take short, deep inhales as I try to relax. As I try to tell myself this is okay. His breathing is getting ragged, but he doesn't stop. I feel a warmth spreading between my legs and I gasp.

"Are you okay?" He stops and pulls back, his face searching mine for any sense of pain.

"Yes." I respond with labored breathing. "I'm just adjusting." He nods and slowly moves again.

The warmth returns and I close my eyes, embracing it. It feels different. Stronger, more powerful than what we'd done so far. I arch my back, pressing myself against his chest, wanting to be as close to him as possible. He groans in my ear as he drops his head to my shoulder.

His arms slide underneath my back, pulling me tightly against him. I can feel his teeth as they lightly bite down on my shoulder. The warmth is turning into pressure and growing stronger every second, spreading throughout my core. I moan slightly and he responds with a faster pace. I can feel a release building within me, masking the pain and discomfort. My breathing is labored, erratic, as I try to relax into it. Into him.

"Elaenor." He moans as he thrust into me one last time and then stills. I freeze as I feel his muscles twitch on top of me. The sweat dripping down his collarbone onto my cheek. I keep my eyes closed as I feel the delicious warmth slipping away, taking the pressure with it. Taking my release.

When I open my eyes, he's leaning over me, his eyes open, waiting. "Hi." He smiles nervously, as my eyes meet his. I fight the urge to frown. The delicious heat is gone, leaving me cold and wanting.

"Hi." I whisper back. He pulls one of his arms out from underneath me so he can brush a loose curl off my face. His fingers are soft, light, as he traces my jaw.

"Was that okay?" I nod, worry fading from his eyes. I'm not about to tell him I didn't finish, not after this morning and everything that happened with Theo earlier. But that wasn't what I expected. I knew what happened in the woods was not how it should be, but this is still remarkably tame compared to what I always imagined. "I'm going to stay here for a few more moments, I just want to give us the best chance."

"At conceiving a child?" My voice is quiet, nothing more than a squeak. I knew a child was the ultimate goal, but the fact that I could be getting pregnant right now is surprising.

"Of course." I bite my lip and look away. "You said this was okay?" He's worried.

"Yes, it was fine. I didn't want to when we first came in here, but it felt right." I admit. I was scared, but after he promised. After he pledged himself to me. It felt right. It felt like it was the moment, but getting pregnant is not what I wanted out of this first night. "Tobias, about a child–"

"Hey, it's okay. If it doesn't happen now, it'll happen eventually." He leans down and kisses my nose, silencing me. "This will be good for us."

"Did you mean it?"

"Yes, every word."

"You didn't just say it to get me in bed?" He laughs.

"No, I did not lie to you to get you in bed. I'll save that for the whores." I scoff, but he just laughs even harder. "I'm kidding. I promised you I would be yours." I don't answer, so he bends down and kisses me again. When he sits up, he slowly lifts his legs so that he slides out of me. I moan slightly as the pressure leaves, and he smiles. "That's a nice sound." I close my eyes and attempt to laugh, but the exhaustion is creeping up on me. I feel his lips press to my shoulders as he lifts me up. "Roll over."

I roll over, onto my stomach, and I can feel his fingers untying my corset. When it's free he slides it off of me and throws it onto the floor. I feel his weight shift as he gets off the bed. He tugs on my skirt and slides it off of me.

"What is this?" His voice is stern, confused. I glance up, rolling onto my back, to see my dagger on my thigh. He raises an eyebrow before he slips it off of me. "What is this, Elaenor?"

"It's mine." I whisper. That's all I can think to say.

"I see that. Where did you get it?" He sounds angry, defensive, as his fingers brush the black leather wrapped around the hilt.

"Chatis. I got it in Chatis." That's technically not a lie, but I can't bring myself to tell him the truth. I bite my lip as I stare up at him. He stares at me for a second before putting the dagger on the bedside table. I exhale in relief, silently, before resting my head back on the bed. I hear him step away for a second and then his footsteps return.

"Sit up." He commands. "Elaenor, sit up." I groan and force myself to lift my limp body off the bed. With my eyes still closed, I feel him slip a shirt over my head and gently tug the crown out of my hair. "You're no help at all." He laughs before he kisses my nose. His fingers brush my shoulder and I wince. A perfect circular bite has left a welt on my skin. A brand. My face finds his as he effortlessly lifts me up and then plops me back down onto the bed, pulling the blanket over me. He leans down and kisses my temple before walking away.

"Where are you going?" I ask, sitting back up. *What could he possibly be doing right now?* He turns back towards me when he reaches the door.

"I have some business to attend to. Go to sleep." His voice is soft, sleepy.

"Tobias, it's the middle of the night."

"I'm going to check on Theo." He admits, his eyes refuse to meet mine and I know he's ashamed. He turns away again and leaves, closing the door behind him. I plop back down onto the pillow and exhale loudly. I know he's leaving to deal with his brother, but all I feel is abandoned. We just had sex for the first time, my first time, if I don't count Aleksander, and he leaves.

I can't possibly sleep now.

My eyes find the leather wrapped dagger on my bedside table. I quickly slip it under the mattress, hidden away for if I need it. I have a feeling Tobias would take it away if he knew I was fearful of him, of this place. I slide off the bed and walk towards the bathing room, grabbing a glass of that sweet pink wine on the way. Nothing sounds better than a hot bath right now.

Chapter Twenty-Three

I scream out in pain and fear. My blood joining theirs as the glass slices through my naked feet. The smoke fills my lungs, leaving me gasping for breath, suffocating. Everything is dark and gray. The thick clouds overhead threaten rain. The only color is that of flames and the bright bioluminescent green of the trees behind the palace, the only thing untouched from the destruction. I can't breathe, the pressure is too much. I scream and scream, hoping someone can help me, but no one comes. No one is going to save me.

I gasp as my face breaks through the water with the assistance of a strong grip.

"Elaenor! What are you doing?" Tobias yells as I force myself to cough to get the burning liquid out of my lungs. He pulls me further out of the water, and I drape myself over the edge of the tub as I try to inhale as much oxygen as I can.

My dreams have changed since I have come to Noterra. As if I am no longer replaying a small portion of the scene but seeing the rest of it. But it's not an *it*, it's Chatis.

The place in my dreams has always been Chatis.

I'm lifted out of the water and a warm towel is wrapped around me. My body is shaking, either from the cold or my dreams. My eyes are fixated on the tub as Tobias is speaking to me. I can't make out the words as my mind is stuck in Chatis. The burning buildings, the smell of blood and burnt flesh filling my nose. This dream used to be just that, a nightmare, but now I can't help but feel it is a premonition of something that is yet to come.

"Elaenor, are you listening to me?" A rough shake pulls my mind back into awareness and I turn my face towards his. He looks confused and scared.

"What?" I croak as my throat protests.

"What were you doing?"

"I fell asleep." I whisper, holding his gaze. His eyes look tired, hollow. I've never seen him as fearful as he is right now.

"How much of the wine did you drink before?" He's pointing at the empty wine glass sitting next to the tub.

"Just one." I shake my arms, forcing him to release his grip. "I'm alright." I say before walking out of the bathroom and down the hall to our bedroom in nothing but a towel, ignoring the door that leads straight to our room. A new set of guards stand outside the door, and they give me a quick nod before averting their gaze. Maybe Laris and Tano do sleep sometimes.

I loudly close the door behind me and make my way over to the privacy screen so I can change. I can hear the door open and close quickly as I slip on a fresh nightgown.

"Elaenor! You can't walk around dressed like that." He yells just as I step out from behind the screen. I walk right past him, headed for the bed, but his hand grabs ahold of my arm to stop me. I look down at his grip before slowly making my way up to meet his gaze, glaring.

"*Unhand* me, Tobias." I firmly say, not breaking eye contact. A flash of surprise crosses his face before he releases me. I walk over to the bed and slip under the covers, wanting this day to end, but also wanting to slip back into my dreams to learn more about what is happening.

"Elaenor, you could have died. What were you doing?" I sigh, loudly as my head hits the pillows, my sopping wet hair soaking into the linens.

"I fell asleep, Tobias. It's not a big deal." I say dismissively, knowing that isn't true.

"It is a big deal; do you need to be watched every second of the day? Should I be worried that you are acting recklessly?" He snaps, his controlling demeanor returns, and I close my eyes in an attempt to shut him out. I feel the bed dip down as he sits next to me. My eyes open and meet his.

"I am not suicidal, Tobias, despite every reason I may have to not want to exist." I say with the intention of malice, but all that comes out is a broken voice.

"Don't say that." I know I've hurt him; I don't even know why I am so upset. "Talk to me." He grabs my arms and pulls me up so I'm sitting. My wet hair plastered to my face, dripping onto the blankets. "Everything was fine when I left. Perfect, even. What's wrong?"

"Why did you leave? You were gone longer than if you were just visiting your brother." I ask, refusing to meet his eyes. "Was it me? Did I do something?" My voice cracks and I dig my nails into my palms.

"Elaenor, it had nothing to do with you." Still gripping my wrists, he pulls me into his lap so that I'm straddling him. I wrap my arms around his neck and let him slowly caress my back as I rest my forehead against his. His breath smells sweet, like wine. "Tomorrow you and I will be crowned. I had to ensure the proper preparations were in place, so we had nothing to worry about." I sit back and look in his eyes. He's telling the truth.

"I was worried you left to go–" I stop and look down as my voice cracks. To go be with another woman is what I wanted to say.

"My love, no." He presses his lips to mine and I relax. Both at his confirmation and that he called me his *love*. "I told you multiple times that I was yours and yours alone."

"I know, Tobias. You just left so fast, and it was my first time. I was just confused." My voice is rushed, frantic. I drop my hands into my lap, my nails dig into my skin, my eyes refusing to meet his. I know I should be embarrassed for being worried or jealous, but I *am* worried, and I *am* jealous, and I don't want to hide it.

"I know, I shouldn't have left you so soon. I wasn't thinking." He pulls my chin up. "Look at me. I'm sorry. It won't happen again." I nod and wrap my arms back around his neck, burrowing my head against his shoulder.

"I'm sorry." I whisper. He shakes his head.

"Please don't do that again. I can't lose you." His voice is strained, weak. Exhaustion creeps in on me as I let my thoughts wander. Chatis. Burning. Abandonment. "Let's go to sleep." He pulls me down onto the bed and I nestle against his side. I feel his lips press against my hair and I quickly fall back asleep to the sight of Chatis on fire with cedar and smoke filling my nose.

Green. Bright, bioluminescent green fills my vision. Trees, bushes, leaves, foliage, all the same shade. Untouched by the fires that rage on in front of me. I take a step forward and wince as the glass and bone dig deeper into my flesh. I try to take another step, but something is holding me back, someone is holding me back. I try to pull out of their grip, but it's too strong.

"Let go of me!" I snap as I struggle against them.

"Elaenor." A deep voice speaks. Its sound sends shivers down my spine. It's smooth and melodic and forces my breath to catch. I stop struggling and turn my head to see the man who is holding me captive. His eyes, dark hair, and white streak are familiar. His broad shoulders and tanned skin remind me of someone. Someone I feel like I know but is still a perfect stranger.

"Elaenor, wake up." He says, my body is tingling, burning. Like fire running through my veins.

"Who are you?" I ask, my head tilting. His green eyes match the color of the trees. Eyes I have only ever seen in one person. The man in the forest. The man who I didn't believe was actually there. "You were there that day, the day I was at the lake?" I ask. "And in the bathroom, that was you?"

"Yes," His voice is clipped, rushed.

"Please, tell me who you are! I feel like I'm going insane. I keep seeing you, please just tell me." I plead, begging him to just give me this one answer.

"Not yet, Nora. Now wake up." His other hand grips my shoulder, and he shakes me. Why is he calling me Nora? There is only one person that does that.

"Tell me!" I yell as I try to pull out of his grasp.

"Wake up!"

I inhale sharply and shoot out of bed. The room is dark, all of the candles have burned out. A soft wind flows through the open balcony doors and I stare out at the black sky. Why do I keep seeing him? Was he actually there in the bathroom, or is this all in my mind? *What is happening?*

I hear a soft snore and look over to my right where Tobias is peacefully sleeping. The blankets are only covering half of his naked body, exposing his tanned skin.

"*Nora.*" A whisper comes from the open doors. I jump and look to see the tiny flash of light hair. I slowly climb out of bed, so as to not wake Tobias up, and tiptoe over to the balcony. As I step onto the landing, a hand snakes out and pulls me into the corner. I try to scream, but his hand covers my mouth. I inhale the sweet scent of grass as he releases my face.

"Theo?" I whisper as he holds me against him.

"I just wanted to be sure you were alright." Even though he is whispering, I can hear the panic in his voice. "I wanted to see if he hurt you."

"I'm fine, Theo." I stammer as I pull out of his arms. "You shouldn't be here." I whisper, glancing back at Tobias's sleeping body.

"I know, I was just worried about you."

"Theo, I'm okay." I reassure him. He needs to leave before Tobias sees him.

"Is it true? Did you get married?" His blue eyes are saddened, one of them black and bruised. His nose is crooked and covered in stitches. Tobias really did a number on him. My heart aches as each movement of his face causes him to wince.

"Yes." I whisper. The moonlight is barely illuminating his face, but I can see the hint of silver in his eyes. "Theo, we knew this would happen. This is what I came here for." He shakes his head, reaching out to brush his thumb along my cheek where I am sure there is a bruise.

"I'm leaving, Nora." His voice is soft, clipped.

"Theo–"

"No, not because you're married. I am being sent to the borders, to help lead our men." I look at him confused.

"You're headed out to war?" I whisper.

"Yes, I–" We both freeze as I hear Tobias shift in bed.

"You need to go." I push against his chest, and he looks at me, hurt. His face fills with sorrow as he lets me guide him to the edge of the balcony. He looks back at me and I know he doesn't want to leave. I don't want him to leave, but I *need* him to. "Please." I beg as quietly as I can.

"I wish things were different, Nora." He turns away and gracefully climbs atop the posts and leaps to the other side. He makes it look so easy. Without looking back at me, he walks into his room and shuts the door.

"Me too, Theo." *Me too.* I want that more than anything.

"Ela?" A tired voice echoes behind me as I turn to face Tobias's naked body. His skin is shining in the moonlight as he leans against the door frame. I hate that this man is so gorgeous. His muscles lining his broad shoulders and his trimmed abs, his strong jaw, and mesmerizing blue eyes. Eyes that are watching me watch him. He smirks before walking over to me.

"I was just getting some air." I stutter as his hands wrap around me. He nuzzles my neck with his cold nose, and I jump.

"Come back to bed, it's late." He mutters before pulling me back into the bedroom. I briefly look over at Theo's balcony and see the flash of hair in the window before Tobias pulls me through the doors.

When I awake again, I am met with bright sunshine filtering through the open windows. The sounds of bird chirping and muffled voices come in with a slight breeze. I turn to the right and see the other side of the bed has been vacated. I sigh in relief that I am alone and stretch, my aching limbs protesting in response.

Climbing out of bed, I quickly slip on a robe before settling on the couch next to a tray of coffee and pastries. A single piece of folded parchment lies next to the tray along with a rose and I pick it up. It's crisp and smooth, but I can feel the indents caused by the pressure of a pen.

Today is the beginning. x

A single sentence and no sign off, but it doesn't need one. I pick up the single red rose that was lying next to it, its thorns piercing my skin. I let out a small wince as the blood wells up on my thumb and drips down my hand. The blood red color matches the rose perfectly. Crimson. The color I seem to never be able to get away from. I set it down and wipe my blood off on a black piece of linen under the tray.

Tobias and I are being crowned today. Before this day is over, I will be a queen. I sigh and ignore the pinprick of pain on my fingers as I reach out for one of the golden croissants. It's warm and buttery and makes my stomach growl as I fight to remember the last time I ate a full meal. I finish the pastry and reach for another coated in chocolate before I hear a soft knock on the door.

"Come in." I call out as I quickly take a sip of the warm, sweet coffee. It's so thick and decadent, it tastes just like ice cream. Syrupy and sweet, just how Tobias knows I like it. Lydia and my two other ladies, whom I still do not know their names, walk in with arms full of clothing. "Good morning." I say with a mouth full of food.

"Your Grace." Lydia says before the three of them bow. "We are here to get you ready for the crowning ceremony." I nod and they make their way in the room, closing the door behind them. I regretfully set my delicious coffee down and allow them to begin working.

I am gowned, my hair is done, and make up has been applied after a little over an hour of work. I let my fingers trail over the thin lace covering my chest and neck. While they had to apply quite a bit of cream to my face to cover the bruises, my gown features a black lace turtleneck, covering my fading wounds. The rest of my gown is a blend of crimson and white. I let my fingers slide through the perfect black waves framing my face as a thick cloak is tied around me. White fur gently caresses my back as I move, providing a soft brush against my bare skin. I stare at the woman in the reflection, astonished that it's me. I turn to dismiss my ladies and thank them for their assistance, but they have already gone.

My eyes look exhausted, dark and sunken in compared to my pale skin. Purple bruising under my eyes that Lydia covered in ivory creams just makes me look sick, dying. While I have a little bit of color on my face from the small amount of sun I've gotten, I am still pale. I can just faintly make out a small amount of swelling on my cheek from where Tobias struck me. My fingers lightly brush against my skin, grateful it doesn't hurt as much. My hair is long, falling in inky waves to the small of my back.

I lean forward and spot a single white strand of hair intertwined with the black. I grip it between my fingers and pull it out, just like I did last time. I stare at it for just a moment before throwing it on the floor. Stress can cause premature aging, that is the only logical explanation, but I know deep down that isn't true.

I shake my head to disrupt the thoughts and return my eyes to the mirror. A mix of braids and twists circle my head, but my head still seems bare. My crown was taken as it will be placed again during the ceremony, but I had grown quite used to its presence, even if it was only one day. I turn away from the mirror and make my way to the balcony.

The air is chilly, but the sun still provides warmth as does my fur cloak. The summer sun is leaving as autumn approaches. The sky isn't getting as bright, and the clouds are starting to make their place at home above Noterra. It reminds me a lot of home, but the air is thinner here, crisp.

There are people bustling about on the grounds, no doubt preparing for whatever festivities are to follow the crowning today. I remember there being festivals following my namedays, but I'm sure a coronation requires much grander activities. My eyes wander over to Theo's balcony as I remember last night.

His touch lingers as I feel his warm embrace. I feel safe with him, but my heart has to belong to his brother. I barely know either man, with only a few days of interaction between us.

Tobias can be a cruel man, as he displayed yesterday. The anger he felt was justified as his father just died and he caught his brother kissing the woman he was about to marry, but his need to lash out at me physically isn't something I can allow in the future. And then we had such a special moment before he *left*. He has made up for his aggression tenfold, but I still feel so hesitant in leaving my heart in his hands. I know he would protect me, regardless of the threat, but he also has a kingdom to manage now. If it came down to it, he would choose Noterra, but Theo, Theo would always choose me.

But Theo is leaving. He's leaving to help prepare the military for a war. I remember Evreux speaking about Labisa, but if Theo is riding to command the borders, does this mean more has happened? I want to ask Tobias about it, but I don't want to ruin this day for him.

I know I should feel elated being crowned a queen, but all I feel is fear. Fear towards my future. Fear towards the idea of carrying a child. Fear that I won't be able to live up to the expectations of my husband or the kingdom. I am not fully aware of what a queen's duties include, but I do know I will have to do more than follow Tobias around.

I can hear the door opening to the room, so I turn around and face the kingsguard. Laris and Tano enter the room with soft smiles. They have their hands on their swords as they stand in the doorway. While I should feel at ease with two guards by my side, I feel nauseated. Suffocated.

"Your Grace, we are here to escort you to the coronation."

"Have you seen my guard, Ser Danieas?" I ask, trying to peer around them as I walk down the steps from the balcony.

"No, Your Grace. We have not seen him." I nod and they step forward to take their places at my side. They not so subtly guide me through the door and down the hallway. Guards line either side as we make our way to the throne room. I have never seen this many guards in one place, so it calls to question what they are protecting,

"Is it normal for this many bodies to guide a princess to her coronation?" I ask as we walk.

"Yes, Your Grace." Laris, who's on my left, pauses before he continues to speak. "It is for your protection, should anyone wish to not see this ceremony take place." I force myself to swallow over the lump in my throat as we turn a corner. Who would be against this? I straighten myself, holding my head high, and keep my eyes forward as I glide down the long hallway.

I keep looking around for Erik, but he is nowhere to be seen. He said he would be ready to claim his post today, but maybe his injuries haven't healed as well as expected. I find myself worried about him, but maybe it's fueled with selfishness. While I have Tobias, I wanted another familiar face. After a few minutes of silence, we reach the entrance of the throne room, where Tobias stands.

He is wearing a white silk blouse with silver symbols intricately embroidered throughout. His matching white trousers are tucked into sparkling clean boots. His sword, that I've never seen him wear, is hanging off his hip and is partially hidden by an all-white cloak that matches mine. His golden hair is waved perfectly, falling in short tendrils to his eyebrows. His golden scruff lines his jaw, the makings of a small beard. I have to admit that I like it. His ocean eyes are watching me, his rosy lips pursed in amusement. I look away from him and bow my head slightly as an acknowledgement to the army of guards surrounding us.

"Elaenor." Tobias's voice is soft, gentle as he leans over and kisses my forehead, his hand gently cupping my face.

"Tobias." I respond, keeping my voice monotone. His eyes narrow slightly in confusion before he nods his head at the guards. I hear their footsteps dissipate, but not fully disappear. I am aware of their presence and their ability to still hear our conversation. His arms wrap around me, pulling me against his chest as he looks at me. I keep my face down.

"What is wrong?" He murmurs as he stares. I shake my head.

"I am just feeling overwhelmed." I admit. He's smiling when I finally look up at him. "What?" I ask.

"Everything will be okay. Today is the last day of events and then we'll have days to figure out a routine and our relationship before the carnival starts." His voice is positive, hopeful. Happy. I hope he's happy.

"Are you happy?" I slightly raise my eyebrows, waiting for his response. His smile falls a little as he looks away from me.

"Right at this moment?" I nod. "Yes, with you in my arms, I am very happy. But," He pauses. "I am also worried. Worried about taking my place on the throne. Worried about not doing a good job in leading and protecting our people. Worried that our duties will get in the way of us." He sighs. "I am going to be under a great deal of stress these next few days, as we assimilate into our new positions."

"I understand, Tobias. You will have a lot to navigate. I am here to ease as much of the burden as you allow." My hand finds his face and he leans into it.

"All I'm asking is that you be patient with me. I don't know what I am doing, nor what is truly expected of me." He sounds sad, lost, like the little boy I once knew.

"Okay." Is all I manage to say before his lips find mine. The kiss is soft, gentle, reassuring. With each passing moment in Tobias's arms I find that it would be easy to love him, but even easier to be broken by him.

"Are you ready?" I nod.

He turns to face the closed doors and I take my place beside him. No more words are shared between us as the doors open and we glide through the aisle.

Men and women of all status are standing in perfect lines as they watch us make our way to the front. Father Reynolds is standing in the front with an all-black cloak, his hands clasped in front of him. Men stand on either side holding beautiful silver crowns on plush crimson pillows. Music flows around the room as somewhere a harp is played. My eyes focus on Father Reynolds as I try to remain strong.

We reach the steps and we both drop to our knees, the cold marble making its way through the layers of my gown. His voice is loud and commanding as he recites the ancient script of crowning, but my ears refuse to listen. I hear my heart beating, roaring throughout my head. I try to steady my breath, but the adrenaline runs through me like electricity. Tobias stands next to me and bows his head. His crown is placed on his golden copper hair before he turns to face the crowd. Applause roars around us as he turns back around and makes his way to the king's throne. He stands in front of it, facing us.

I feel as if I might vomit.

Father Reynolds turns to me and gives me a soft smile. I slightly lift my head as he speaks.

"Elaenor, Princess of Noterra and Chatis, has been blessed by the Gods and Goddesses to reign as queen over this kingdom." He starts. Words of affirmation from the gods and goddesses echo around me as fate and prosperity are spoken about. "Her body will be the vessel for which our future kings will be grown. She has been given to us to create protection and spread light for generations to come. The face of acceptance and purity, a mother to us all." He looks down at me. "Do you, Elaenor, promise to uphold the legacy left behind by our late Queen Amaya?"

"I do." I respond, my voice clear and crisp as I look up at Father Reynolds.

"Do you promise to govern all subjects that reside under the territories of the Crown by the words of our ancestors and the laws they have laid forth?"

"I do."

"Gifted by the Gods, may I present for the first time, Queen Elaenor Rosenthal of Noterra." He gestures for me to stand as he places the thorny crown gently onto my head. Lifting my dress, I walk up the steps to the queen's throne and turn to face the room. Clapping and voices fill my ears as the pounding continues. My eyes are cloudy, unable to focus. Hungrily searching the crowd of unknown faces until I see it.

Until I see *him*.

His dark hair is flowing in messy waves around his face. Green eyes that seem to glow amongst the crowd. He's leaning against the farthest back wall with his arms crossed, watching me as I'm watching him. All of the cheering around is drowned out and all I can hear is the subtle buzz of electricity as it flows through my veins. He doesn't smile, but instead, he opens his mouth to speak, but Tobias's voice is what I hear.

"Elaenor." He whispers. I tear my eyes away and look at Tobias as the sounds of cheering and clapping returns. He's smiling at me, embracing the applause. Embracing the attention. I find myself uncomfortable, nervous, my nails digging into my palms. Tobias offers me a soft smile before sitting down. I follow suit and take my place on the throne. When I turn back to the crowd, he's gone. Unknown faces and voices fill my ears as I force myself to take slow and steady breaths.

"Long live the King. Long live the Queen." Father Reynolds starts as others chime in, chanting the phrase over and over again.

"Long live the King. Long live the Queen."

Chapter Twenty-Four

The grand room is filled with people I have never met. Every time a new person comes up to me, they bow and congratulate me. Congratulations seem absurd as my status was something I was born into, not something I worked for. Regardless, I thank them for the well wishes and they move along. Wine and food are passed around as laughter and talking buries me in an overwhelming pressure. My chest feels tight, and I can feel every single guest's eyes on me, watching me, judging me. Waiting for me to misstep or prove that I am not worthy of the crown sitting upon my head. Warm fingers grip my elbow, jolting me out of my thoughts and I turn to face Tobias.

"Congratulations, *Your Grace.*" He mocks. The scent of Tobias, cedar and smoke, fills my nose as I struggle to take a deep breath around the lump in my throat. The air is too thick, too many people. I keep my face forward, trying to seem as if I am watching the crowd of happy people, laughing, dancing, eating. All enjoying what should be a momentous day. While I am sitting here terrified and overwhelmed.

"Same to you, Your Grace." I reply, softly. I can feel the warmth of his body as it grows closer. His free hand finds my waist and pulls me against him. My breathing catches and I try to keep the glass in my hand steady as wine sloshes over the rim.

"Did I mention how much I enjoyed the way you look today?" His face is close to mine, his breath hissing in my ear sending a shiver down my spine. I manage a small shake of my head as his fingers tighten around me, my heart lodged in my throat. "I can't wait to take it off of you." I turn and finally offer him a smile. He's doing all he can to ease the tension, but I can't help the pit forming in my stomach. "What's wrong?" He asks, his playful demeanor slipping, revealing concern and something else I can quite place.

"I just feel *off*. Like something is going to happen." I admit, gripping the glass in my hands tightly. It's a different wine than I have been drinking, not as sweet, more bitter. It makes me crave the wine we keep in our room.

"You are safe. Nothing is going to happen to you here." His voice is reassuring, but I still feel tense. He kisses the side of my head as another guest walks up to us.

"Your Grace," I let out a silent sigh as a nobleman offers a bow to Tobias. "Jeremiah, Your Grace." He says as he turns his attention to me, holding out his hand. I tense up as I peer at this strange man's face. Clean, well-shaven, dressed noble, a man of status. But this man, this man is the one who took me into the woods. Who *gave* me to my rapist. Who now stands before me, in this palace, awaiting my response. My head spins and the glass of wine slips from my hand, shattering onto the floor.

"Elaenor!" Tobias says as wine sprays all over my gown.

"I am so sorry, it just slipped." I whisper as I look away from Jeremiah's smug eyes and down to the mess on the floor. I glance back up at Tobias, his jaw hardened as if he wants to be mad but can't.

"Elaenor, this is our Master of Coin. He sits on the council and manages the Crown's finances and estates." He finally says, ignoring the broken glass. He gestures for me to move aside slightly, and we all shift to the left as a servant appears out of nowhere, bending down to clean the mess.

Jeremiah smiles slyly, as if he's peering into my soul. He reaches his hand out again and I slowly place mine in his. He bends and places his icy lips onto my hand without breaking eye contact.

"It's a pleasure to meet you, my Lord." I whisper as I not-so-gently rip my hand from his.

His fingers are rough, calloused. I try to steady my breath as I remember how his hands felt on me. How it felt when he let his fingers trail over my stomach, touching me. I can hear the sound of my clothing being ripped away. The feel of the rocks digging into my skin as he held me onto the ground. The dagger he used to slice through my thigh, his attempt at keeping me still, at keeping me compliant. My heart is racing, it's becoming harder to breathe and I feel like I might faint. My head spins and I lean slightly into Tobias, using his body to steady me. His fingers catch my elbow, and he squeezes. I can't tell if it's to reassure me or to warn me to knock off whatever I am doing.

"The pleasure is all mine, Your Grace." His voice is sick, deep, fueled by unspoken words and Tobias is none the wiser. I pull my eyes from his and turn to my husband, who is oblivious to what is happening.

"My king, if you don't mind, I am going to see if I can find Lydia to help clean me up before the wine stains my beautiful coronation gown." I smile at him, pleading with my eyes to let me go, but I'm not sure if he understands. He doesn't even seem phased by the tension between Jeremiah and I.

"As you wish, my love." He places a soft kiss on my cheek and then turns towards Jeremiah, who bows slightly as I walk away. "Shall we talk about the carnival? I want grand, exotic, and lions. Do you think we could get lions?" Tobias's voice gets drowned out by the laughter around me as I push my way through the crowd. Every time I get past another person, one replaces them and offers a bow. I smile at everyone as I try to get out of the room, but it seems endless. I take slow deep breaths, trying not to panic, but I can feel it rising in my chest. My heart is pounding, my eyes are blurry. Oh Gods.

He's here in the palace.

Jeremiah is here and he is on the king's council. If I told Tobias that this is the man that hurt me, would he even care? Would he *believe* me? He has to. He promised we would work through everything together. He *promised*. I see the doors through the last group of people, and I quickly push past them. The guards on either side bow their heads slightly before opening the darkened wood.

As I reach the hallway I begin to run, my heels echoing across the vacant marble. I don't know where I am headed, but I need fresh air. I turn the corner and spot the balcony doors in front of the throne room open. I step out into the moonlight and take a deep breath. Leaning against the marble posts, I fight the panic coursing through my veins. I inhale deep and quick breaths, trying to clear the fogginess that fills my mind.

He's here and he's on the council. What am I supposed to do? He's infiltrated my new home, even though he's been here all along. *That's* how he knew I was coming. He knew when and where to be to ensure I never made it to the palace. But he *failed*. What if he tries again? Footsteps approach behind me and I freeze, sensing him before he even speaks.

"What a beautiful ceremony." He whispers. I slowly straighten myself before turning to face him. His dark eyes are filled with hunger as he takes me in. "I *much* preferred your other dress." He bites his lower lip as his eyes trail down my body.

"What are you doing here?" I lift my chin slightly as I clasp my hands together in front of me, my nails digging into my palms. As much as I want to scream, I have to appear strong. I can't let him know what his presence is doing to me. I can't let him even sense that I am screaming inside. He steps farther out onto the balcony and joins me next to the posts. His hands run across the smooth marble, and I angle my body to face him.

"Noterra truly is a beautiful place." He stares out onto the grounds, and I follow his gaze. The moon is illuminating the buildings past the palace walls. The sea is hidden behind trees, but you can almost smell the salty air.

"Did he send you?" I ask, breaking the silence. Does Tobias know? He scoffs.

"Tobias? No, he did not." He shakes his head and smiles at the thought. I find myself relieved. Tobias doesn't know, which means he isn't a part of whatever it is Jeremiah is doing. Was Evreux?

"What do you want, Jeremiah?" He turns towards me and lifts his hand. I flinch away from his touch as his fingers brush my cheek. "Don't touch me." I snap, stepping back, but he doesn't move.

"Was that him?" He asks, his eyes fixed on my cheek. "Or was that me?" He smiles again and I take another step back.

"What do you want from me?"

"I already told you; I can't let you continue their bloodline. It has to end with them." I steady myself as I try to hide the fear I feel. He's going to kill me *and* Tobias.

"Why, what have they done?" My voice raises an octave as it fights against the panicked lump forming in my throat.

"He isn't the true king." He rolls his eyes and I fight the urge to throw something at him. "We have been working for years to reinstate the one true ruler. The one to take control of us all." His voice sounds preachy, as if he's speaking to a crowd he has to influence. The only person I've heard call themselves the one true heir is King Davenport. Is he working for Labisa? He has to be.

"King Davenport? You are working on behalf of the King of Labisa?" I stutter as I express my revelation. He smiles, exhilarated by my knowledge, his eyes widening.

"See, you know it is true also! He *should* be king. You don't have to be harmed in the process. You can be safe, Elaenor." He reaches for me, grasping my shoulders with his strong fingers and shaking me. "Come with us, come to Rakushia. You can be wed to the true heir and help us fight against the rebellion that has taken over our land." If I didn't know any better, I would think he sounds frantic as he tries to get me to join his cause.

"I am already wed, Jeremiah! I cannot do as you ask. Nor do I want to." I shake my head and try to get out of his grasp, but his fingers tighten. I push at his chest, but he holds me at arm's length.

"You can get it annulled, Elaenor." He says with frustration, shaking me.

"No! I'm staying here!" My voice is louder now. His face drops, as do his arms. He sucks on his teeth and takes a step back from me, shaking his head slightly.

"If you don't, this will end badly for you. You don't have to be collateral damage. Think about it, before it's too late."

"As soon as I tell the king what you have done, you will be beheaded. I hope you take in the sights while you still have eyes." I expected a weak, terrified voice, but instead, a strong, commanding tone took its place. I'm not sure where it came from, but I am proud of it. Proud of my strength, even if it is a facade. I turn towards the hallway and make my way back inside the palace.

"Your boy king doesn't scare me, princess." His laughter echoes and I look at him over my shoulder.

"Queen." I correct him. He laughs in response, but I walk away before he can see the fear in my eyes.

I go the opposite way as the great room and quickly make my way down the hallway to our chambers. The many twists and turns make it difficult to ascertain where I am in the castle. I turn the corner once more and am met with a darkened hallway. None of the torches are lit along the walls, so the once white marble is nearly black. I stare into the darkness, weirdly finding it inviting. It's silent besides the distant roar of the party, yet I feel as if someone is there.

"Hello?" I call out, not truly knowing if I expect a response. Something shifts in the darkness, and I swallow against the sudden thickness of my throat. "Is someone there?" I call out again. The soft echo of steps in the darkness reach my ears as a body takes form. Dark hair mixed with green eyes peer at me from the darkness. He's tall, muscular, and *familiar*. The man from the lake. The man from my dreams. The man who seems to be everywhere and nowhere at the same time. "Who are you?" I whisper. I take a step forward as he silently stares. "Please, just tell me who you are!" I yell out. His mouth opens to speak, but just as before, another voice takes its place.

"Elaenor?" I turn my head to see Erik quickly walking down the hallway. I turn back to the darkness, but the hallway is lit. The torches lining the walls cast orange and yellow light across the marble. I take a step back, my hand flying to my mouth. *No.* He was there. He was right there. It was real. "Your Grace, are you alright?" He asks again as he reaches me. "What is it? I was with Master Pakin, getting my bandages changed, but when I joined the celebration, you were gone." His eyes are filled with confusion and fear, shining with the light from the fire. I turn towards him and step closer.

"One of the men, from the woods, he's here." I grab his arms, panicked, pleading with him to believe me. Someone has to believe me.

"What? Who?" His hand finds the sword strapped to his waist as he looks around, pulling out of my grasp.

"Jeremiah. The one who hurt you and took me." Fury fills his face as he steps closer to me. He looks around the hallway again, before pushing me towards the wall so he can stand in front of me. His hand presses to his chest and I hear him inhale a shaky breath. He's still hurting.

"Where is he? Did he hurt you?" I shake my head and place my hand on his arm.

"He's the Master of Coin, Erik. Tobias introduced us and then he followed me out of the great room. He works for King Davenport; he wants me to leave with him. He said that they can't let the bloodline continue, something about not letting them win. I think he's going to kill Tobias." My voice cracks as I hold onto his arm.

"We have to tell the king." His voice is loud, but I can hear it crack from whatever pain he is in. I look around expecting someone to walk up at any point, but we are alone.

"What if he doesn't believe me?" I shake my head and Erik resheaths his sword. I walk around him and stare down the once darkened hallway, the torches flickering.

"He would have no reason not to, Your Grace." He says from behind, his voice filled with worry. I know he wants to protect me, but he is still healing. I don't want him to get reinjured, or killed, and if he goes up against Jeremiah that might happen. "He's your husband, he'll want to make sure you're protected."

"By his own councilmen?" I turn back around to face him. "These are men his father trusted with his life. He wouldn't believe me if I told him his father was a bad judge of character." My voice is weak, soft. Tobias would believe me. He *has* to believe me.

"Your Grace." A deep voice bellows from the hallway and I jump as two kingsguard make their way over to us. "Your presence has been requested, Your Grace." I exhale and nod before taking a step towards them.

"By whom?" Erik's voice is commanding as he questions them, stepping forward to place himself in between us.

"The request came from the king, boy." One of the guards says with venom in his voice. My head whips in their direction and I glare at him.

"You will address Ser Danieas with the respect he deserves." I snap. "He is my sworn sword, and he will be treated as such." They hesitantly bow their heads.

"Yes, Your Grace. Our apologies." Their voices are snide, and they do little to hide it, but I follow them anyway. I can hear Erik's footsteps closely behind.

Chapter Twenty-Five

When I am led to Tobias, I find he's not in the great hall. He's frantically pacing in the king's chambers, where I notice a lot of our items have been moved. I see my small trunk of art supplies sitting beside the writing desk. Tobias's face is filled with rage, but I have no idea why. He places his hands on his hips and glares at me as I enter. He waves his hand, and the guards leave, closing the door behind me. I turn around just as Erik is being ushered out as well.

Tobias's hand returns to his hip as he stares at me, his eyes trailing up and down my body. He lets out a sigh before making his way towards me. I keep my eyes down, fixed on the ground, while he grows near. I feel like a child being scolded by their father with how he's looking at me.

His hand reaches forward and grabs one end of the rope affixed to my cloak. With a small pull, it unties and falls to the ground slowly. I stay still, frozen, unsure of what is going to happen. I can tell he's angry, but I haven't done anything to warrant this type of reaction.

"Where did you go, Elaenor?" He asks, his voice low as he walks around me, kicking the cloak out of the way. I feel his hand tangle itself in my hair and he sharply pulls it.

"Ow, Tobias!" I fall back into his chest, his mouth close to my ear.

"Where did you go?" He asks again, this time with more malice in his voice. His grip on my hair tightens and I wince.

"That hurts, Tobias." I whisper.

"*Where were you?*" He asks for a third time. "It wasn't with Lydia, because she came and asked me where *you* were."

"I went to get some air, that is it." I say through gritted teeth. His hand releases itself from my hair and he wraps his arm around my waist.

"Why are you lying to me?" He presses his nose into my neck and deeply inhales. I stare at the ceiling, wishing for my heart to stop pounding in fear. I can feel his teeth as they bite down on my shoulder, adding another welt. He's so angry. I've only seen him this way once before, and it was directed towards Theo.

"I promise, I am not lying to you. I went to the balcony near the throne room. I just wanted some air." I stammer. *What has gotten into him?*

"And Jeremiah? You were seen." He snaps. My mouth drops open.

"Seen doing what?" I retort in confusion.

"He was touching you." His grip around me tightens and I push against his arms. *He's jealous.* He releases me and I spin around stepping close so my face is mere inches from his.

"Jeremiah followed me. He wanted to make sure I knew who he was." I grab his arms and plead for him to believe me. "Tobias, he was the man who took me from my carriage the night I traveled here. He was the man who beat me and tried to rape me before his accomplice took his place. He wanted me to know he was here." His eyes are blank as he tries to make sense of what I said, his hot, wine-laced breath fanning over my face.

"You're lying. Jeremiah has been a trusted advisor of the Crown's for nearly a decade." His voice is stern, brewing with irritation. "You're just trying to cover your tracks."

"I am not lying, Tobias." I plead. I need him to know my fear in the hopes that he would act on it. I pull on his arms, begging for him to believe me. "Please, I need you to believe me. I'm scared."

"It was dark, you were clearly disorientated. You don't know what you saw." His voice is nonchalant, irritated, as he rolls his eyes.

"Then what of his confessions just now? Just a figment of my imagination?" I snap at his delusions.

"Just stop! You are making it worse. Why are you lying to me?" He pushes my arms away from him.

"Tobias, please." I reach for his face and his hand flies out, slapping me. I stumble into the writing desk, stunned.

"Enough!" He snaps. My hands find my cheek as I turn to stare up at him.

"*Tobias.*" I whisper as I watch the realization of what he's done come to light. His face softens and his mouth drops open.

"Elaenor, I'm sorry." He takes a step forward, but I retreat. "I didn't mean to." He's hurt, he didn't mean it, but I still find myself scared of him.

"Don't touch me." I whisper.

"Elaenor, please." His voice is strained. I know he's sorry, but I don't trust him. I can't trust him. He steps towards me again and I move around the desk.

"Tobias, don't." I warn. I can't be next to him when he's like this. He reminds me of my father in all the wrong ways.

"Come here." He begs, but I stand my ground. "Come *here*." He says again, this time with more persistence. When I don't move, I see the anger building inside of him. He tightens his jaw and squeezes his hands into fists. Reaching across the table, he grabs the crown from my head and tosses it to the floor before grabbing my neck and throwing me against the side of the couch.

"Tobias, please." I fall forward across the arm of the plush cushion, as he lifts my gown. "Please, Tobias. I am trying to talk to you about this." I cry out, trying to keep my voice strong. His hands find my hips, their fingers digging into my skin, pulling down my undergarments.

"You need to listen to me!" He snaps as he slams into me. I cry out loudly against the intensity, shoving me harder against the couch. "*Tobias.*" I plead as he pushes into me again and again. I hate how the momentary friction makes my core curl, wanting more. *Gods.* "Please don't do this to me." Tears stream down my cheeks as I grit my teeth, my hands fisting around a throw blanket. This can't be happening. *This isn't real.* He stills above me before pulling out.

"Gods, Elaenor. What are you doing to me?" He steps away as I slowly rise, turning to face him as my dress falls back into place, my core throbbing with both want and pain. He's pulling his pants up, sorrow filling his eyes as he looks at me.

"I am trying to have a conversation with you, Tobias. I'm trying to tell you that I'm scared. That someone here is threatening me. Threatening you! This is not how things are going to go." My voice stammers and I take a deep breath. "You don't get to do this with me." I step closer to him as he drops onto the oversized bed and throws his arm over his eyes.

"I'm the king, Elaenor. I can do what I please." He's trying to sound strong, but his voice is laced with regret. At least, that is what I am hoping it is I hear.

"Not to me, Tobias." My voice cracks, my throat tightening.

"*Especially* to you." He scoffs. I step closer until I can reach his arm. I rip it off his face, forcing him to look at me. His eyes snap to mine and narrow.

"Jeremiah is who I say he is. I may not be in danger, but he is still a threat." He sits up, his eyes parallel to mine.

"My father wouldn't have employed a man capable of what you say is true. You have to be mistaken, Elaenor." He's pleading with me. He doesn't want to admit that there is an enemy on his council, or that he and the enemy seem to have a lot in common.

"I'm not, Tobias. Please listen to me" I grab his face with my hands, willing him to understand, but I know it's useless. "Please believe me." I fight against the tears, but they break free.

"You are safe here, Elaenor. I will protect you." His hand finds my throbbing cheek and I press my forehead against his.

"How can you protect me when you are the one who's hurting me?" My voice is quiet, soft. "Do you see what just happened, Tobias? You hit me, *again*. After I was trying to tell you that someone is threatening me. And then, when I wouldn't come near you, you forced yourself on me. Do you understand that you are more of a threat to me right now, than anyone?" He's quiet, his lips almost touching mine.

"I will never hurt you, Elaenor." He whispers.

"You *just* did, Tobias." I step back, removing my hands from his cheeks. He looks confused, as if he doesn't understand. "What is so wrong with you that you can't see the harm you cause?" My voice is little more than a whisper, and his eyes find mine.

"I never meant to hurt you, I'm so sorry. Please forgive me." He's pleading, begging for me to say it's all okay, but it's not. This isn't okay. I can't let this be okay.

"Tobias, I can't forgive you. Not yet. Not until you prove to me that you mean it. That you won't do this again." He reaches for my face, but I turn away. I step around the couch and to the bar cart, pouring myself a glass of my favorite wine. He takes a slow, deep breath in an attempt to calm himself.

"We are done with this conversation for now. We have a room full of people who want to celebrate their new king and queen. We must return." He stands up and holds his hand out, reaching for me as I return to the side of the couch, but I shake my head.

"I'm staying here. Tell them I was tired or something, I don't know." He sighs again and turns towards the door.

"The guards are staying here. I don't want you wandering about just in case it's not safe."

"It isn't safe, Tobias. Not until you trust me." I sigh. What is even the point of trying? He doesn't believe me, and I don't trust him.

"I do trust you, Elaenor." He says, his eyes softening.

"Do you believe me?"

"I don't know, this is all too much. I don't know who to believe."

"Your wife, Tobias. Your *queen*." He's quiet, pondering what I said before he speaks again.

"Do you want me to grab anyone to stay with you?"

"I want Ser Danieas." I respond, staring at him.

"I will see to it that he is stationed by the door." He bends down and kisses the top of my head before walking away. I move to sit on the edge of the bed and watch as the door closes behind him. I wanted nothing more than to be free from the constraints of my father, but like I predicted, I was placed into a new prison. I quickly drain the glass of wine, the sugar coating my tongue, before setting the glass on the nightstand.

I fall back onto the bed, closing my eyes against the threatening tears. My face is throbbing, as is my core. I can still feel the pain as he slammed himself inside of me. Exerting his power, just because he can. This isn't him. This isn't the same man who lovingly held me last night. He did it without hesitation, like I was just a body for him to use as he pleased. Just like my father had said.

My gaze fixates on the ceiling. I am used to silver details pressed into the marble, but this room, our new chambers, has black and crimson flowers and swords pressed into slate gray stone. Three different chandeliers line the ceiling, illuminating it in a bright yellow glow. I sit up and look around. The red curtains have been taken down, so the entire back wall is just lined with open glass. The flooring is separated into three different raised landings and a drop down in front of the fireplace where the couch lies. A larger office space sits right by the door, and a huge privacy screen sits next to the windows.

I slide off the bed and walk over to it. A dark, wooden door is hidden behind the screen, nestled into the wall. I twist the handle and open it to reveal a huge bathing room. A claw-foot tub that could fit two or three people sits in the middle. Floor to ceiling mirrors sit behind it, reflecting the warm glow of candles. I turn back to the room, closing the door behind me and walking towards the bar cart again, draining another glass of wine.

At some point I end up in the bed, changed into a black, silk nightdress. I don't remember changing out of my coronation dress or climbing into bed, but here I lay with damp hair. It seems I may have taken a bath at some point, but even that isn't something I remember. I sigh as I blame the copious amount of wine I consumed earlier in the night.

I am unable to fall back asleep as I sit here in bed. It's far too large, and I can't get the thought of Evreux's dead body lying in it just a day prior. My thoughts wander as I think about Jeremiah and Tobias. I know I can make him believe me; I just need him to listen. I can't imagine what thoughts are flowing through his head right now. So much has happened in such little time.

I know he didn't mean to hurt me, or at least that he feels remorse that he did, but I can't help but hope that side of him fades. I sit up and reach for the wine glass I must have refilled on the side table, taking a sip of the warm, syrupy liquid. I hate that I find such comfort in alcohol, but this wine is all I crave when I want to relax. I stand and walk over to the fireplace. It's warmth cascading over me as I take a deep breath.

Green eyes infiltrate my thoughts as I remember that man. I have seen him multiple times, both in my dreams and in reality. He is familiar, comforting, but I don't know who he is. Maybe he is a figment of my imagination, and I am growing mad, or he is real and is stalking me. I need to know who he is, what he wants from me. His eyes remind me so much of Chatis, which makes me think of home. The trees and ever-present fog.

I wonder what my father is doing? If he even cares about my absence or what happened to me. Does he know the king is dead and I have been wed and crowned within the last day? Has he already found a new woman to marry and conceive a child with? Does he trust me to follow through with what I was born to do? I shake my head and step away from the fire.

The door opens and Tobias stumbles in with a glass in hand. He gives me a toothy grin as he falls against the wall. Erik is right outside the door, and he gives me a look of pity as he closes it.

"Hello, wife." Tobias murmurs as he tries to make his way towards me, amber liquid sloshing out of the glass and onto the floor. I set my glass down just as he stumbles into me. "You smell so good. Like roses and jasmine." He slurs, pressing his nose into my hair. He smells like alcohol and sweat mixed with his normal cedar and smoke, but there is something else there. Something metallic and tangy. I wrap my arm around his waist and guide him to the bed. "Where are we going?" He drops the cup, and it splashes onto the ground, bouncing off the rug.

"I'm taking you to bed." I grunt as I pull him towards the bed.

"Oh, okay." He smiles as I push him into the mattress. He wraps his arms around me, pulling me down with him.

"Tobias, let go." I snap and pull out of his embrace. He lets go with a sigh, his arms plopping down next to him.

"Lay with me." He whines and I roll my eyes. Who knew drunk kings could be such babies?

"Get some sleep, you have had far too much to drink."

"I'm so sorry, Ela." He slurs, his eyes saddened. "I am scared."

"What are you scared of Tobias?" I try to tone back the irritation, but my words come out in a breathy snarl.

"That you'll leave me."

"I'm not going anywhere that you aren't forcing me to go." He ponders what I said with his drunken brain.

"I think I love you." He whispers. My face falls and I sigh.

"Then love me. Stop hurting me. Believe *me*."

"I don't want to hurt you, my love." He reaches forward and lightly touches my cheek. "I'm sorry." I can see the tears welling up in his eyes and I feel pity.

"I know you don't."

"I believe you." His voice is quiet as if he's falling asleep saying the words. "I can't do anything without proof, Elaenor. I can't." I hold his hand against my cheek as his eyes close.

"We can talk about this tomorrow." He nods softly as he almost immediately starts snoring. His white shirt has small splatters of something dark along his chest, maybe red wine? His knuckles are bruised and scraped up, he must have tripped or fallen or gotten into a drunken brawl. I roll my eyes and turn away from him.

I step down from the bed and turn towards the room. My eyes fall onto the writing desk, and I once again think of my father. Sitting down, I grab a quill and paper and begin writing.

Father,

My time here in Noterra has been a whirlwind of events that have led me to be wed and crowned queen all within a day. Noterra is much different compared to Chatis, and I only hope I grow comfortable here. I am hopeful an heir will be provided soon so that our countries rest easy knowing there is a line of succession in place.

As King Evreux took his last breath, he spoke to me regarding my mother. You have never been forthcoming about her, nor did I seek out his words, but he told me some alarming details about his relationship with her. He informed me they were in love and that it was you who ended her life. I hope more than anything that is not true and just a delusion from a crazed man, but he spoke about her with such sorrow. Our relationship has always been undefined, and for my part in that I am sorry. I only hope you open up to me about my mother someday.

I also have many questions about the night of her death and the state in which I was found. Do you know why my memories have gone? Do you know what really happened to me that day?

My arrival to Noterra was anything but mundane, as I am sure you have heard. I am unsure if this is of any consequence to you, but I am alright. Despite every reason I have to be broken, I am strong. I believe that trait comes from you. I will make it here; I have to believe that.

Elaenor, Queen of Noterra

My hands shake as I fold the letter. The smell of burning wax fills my nose as I press the royal seal into the parchment. With a long sigh, I stand and open the door. There is a guard on either side and one on the other side of the hallway facing me, but Erik, Laris, and Tano are nowhere in sight. I hold out the parchment and wait until one of them takes it.

"Please have Ser Danieas take this to Chatis, to my father." My voice is calm and unwavering. I receive a nod from the guard across the way as he walks over and takes the parchment from my hands before turning and disappearing down the hallway. I turn to the other two and bow my head slightly. "Please send for Lydia, I would like her assistance in getting ready for bed."

"Yes, Your Grace." I turn around and quickly close the door behind me as his footsteps disappear.

The warm water feels like comfort and safety wrapping itself around me in an embrace. I know I must have already bathed in my drunken state, with my hair being damp, but I just needed this. I would spend all of my time in here if I could.

Lydia's fingers are soft as she brushes oils through the silky black tendrils. She's quiet as she works, which may be due to the late hour or discomfort. I close my eyes and try to relax as I soak. My mind wanders from Theo to Tobias to the mysterious man who appears randomly. My hands find my flat stomach underneath the water.

"Lydia, how long would it take for the signs of pregnancy to appear?" I ask, my eyes still closed.

"A few weeks, Your Grace." She whispers as she starts to braid my hair.

"Is there anything I can do, any herb or tincture, that would make conception guaranteed?"

"No, Your Grace." We sit in silence for a moment before she speaks again. "Do you feel you are pregnant, Your Grace?" I shake my head.

"I feel nothing but hope." I whisper, meaning more than just pregnancy.

"Then I shall hope as well." She squeezes my shoulder reassuringly before standing and exiting the room. My eyes wander out the window, focusing on the stars in the sky. They are bright and plentiful, just like glitter. Movement in the darkened corner of the room causes me to jump, splashing water over the edge of the tub. To my surprise, my mysterious gentleman has appeared. I freeze, as my eyes look him up and down, my mouth open in shock. He's wearing all black, as usual, and his face is filled with worry and pain.

"Elaenor." He whispers as his eyebrows furrow.

"Who are you?" I whisper back. He takes a step closer, and I sink deeper into the water for protection.

"You are not safe here, Elaenor." He whispers again. He kneels next to the bath, and I stare at him in disbelief. "You need to go. You need to leave before it's too late." His voice is rushed, panicked. His dark hair flops in front of his face, the thickening white streak tucked behind his ear.

"Who are you?" I ask again.

"Please, just listen to me." I shake my head and back away as much as I can in the porcelain cage.

"I don't know who you are, or what you want from me." I stutter, trying to control my breathing.

"It will all be explained in due time. We will meet sometime soon in the real world." He cocks his head to the side, as if he's listening for something.

"This *is* the real world. Who are you?" I ask again, my voice becoming more demanding. He smiles and reaches forward. I flinch, but his hand cups my face and I can feel the burning sensation of electricity spreading from his touch. It courses through my veins, setting my limbs on fire and I suck in a ragged breath.

"I am sorry I couldn't protect you. I tried, but I couldn't get through." He's sad, tears glistening in his eyes as he softly smiles.

"Please. Just tell me who you are."

"Listen to me, Elaenor. Don't take my warnings as satire. You need to protect yourself. You are not safe here. There are things happening that are out of your control, things you won't even remember. Sugar has a way of concealing even the most lethal of drugs." *Sugar?* I lean forward, my hands gripping the edge of the tub.

"Tell me who I should be afraid of. Is it Jeremiah?" He shakes his head. "Tobias? Theo?" He nods and his thumb traces my bottom lip. Which one? I freeze as I stare into his eyes. Bioluminescent green shining in the darkened room as if it were magic.

"They will be the cause of your death, Elaenor." His hand leaves my face, as does the electricity, causing my breath to catch in my throat. "I will see you soon, but for now, wake up."

"What?"

"*Wake up.*"

I gasp as my head breaks through the water. I cling to the side of the tub as I cough the liquid out of my lungs, splashing it across the marble floor. *What the hell?* I don't remember falling asleep.

It felt so real. It felt like he was really here. Every time I take a bath, he appears. Is that all it takes? To be close to death for him to show up?

He *feels* real. He was there and I could *feel* as he brushed my cheek. As he ran his finger across my lip. Is this the same as when I imagined my own dead body chasing me through the country? Is this the same as the dreams that plague me at night? Is this all in my head?

I'm not crazy.

I'm not Evreux.

What if he is real? What *if* the warnings are real? I would be stupid not to consider it. But am I stupid enough to even entertain it? Is this just another product of my imagination playing on my fears and concerns?

I stand and wrap the towel around me. It's warm and soft and I just enjoy it for a moment, standing still. I need to leave. He said they'll cause my death, but who is he to provide such a prediction? Unless he is also a prophet? Is this how they communicate?

He said sugar conceals even the most lethal of drugs. Is he saying I am going to be drugged? Should I avoid all sweets, or just ones given to me from someone I don't trust? What does this all mean?

When he touched me, it felt as if his skin was burning through mine, not in a painful way, but in a longing type of way. Like he was meant to be near me, meant to be touching me. I bury my face in the towel and let the tears of confusion soak into the material.

One week.

I have been away from home for one week, but it feels as if I've lived a lifetime.

Chapter Twenty-Six

I have received no response from my father, and it has been nearly 10 days since I sent the letter off with Erik. However, I am not 100% sure he even received it. The guards work for Tobias, not for me, and I haven't seen Erik since that night. I was careful not to write anything that may cause problems should it be intercepted, but I still don't know if he read it.

Theo hasn't been around since that night either. Tobias says he was sent off with the kingsguard the day of our coronation to prepare for any infiltration from Rakushia's borders. The last few nights have been uneventful. I seem to be consuming a rather large amount of sweet, pink wine as I don't remember how I end up in bed, bathed and changed, most nights. I know I should cut back, but it seems to be one of the only things that staves off the fear I have for Tobias. He has been ensuring there is a steady supply in our room at all times, which I am thankful for.

Surprisingly, Tobias has invited me to the council meeting this morning for the first time. He has meetings multiple times a day, and I have always wondered what is spoken about for hours on end. I have wanted to ask to attend, but we haven't been speaking much the last few days. I stand along with the other members in the hallway awaiting his arrival. I thankfully don't see Jeremiah anywhere, but three other men stand together, quietly speaking.

They are all fairly old compared to Tobias and I, probably closer in age to Evreux and my father. None of them have spoken to me besides the formal greetings. I don't attempt to speak to any of them, as my mind is elsewhere. I am unsure why Tobias chose today of all days to invite me to the council meeting; he has always excluded me.

We've barely spoken. He leaves before I awake in the morning, and at night we perform our duties without speaking much, then he leaves, and I drink more wine than I should and end up bathed and in bed. I will say I much prefer our relationship this way.

There is no anger, no physical abuse, just silence, wine, and dreamless sleep. I will gladly live out my days this way if this is what he also desires, but I also crave his soothing tone. His warm touch. He said he thinks he loves me, and I want him to. I want us to be swept up in each other, madly in love with one another, but that doesn't seem like it will happen any time soon, or at all.

I've spent the last few days learning about the housekeeping duties queens usually attend to. I have helped prepare the festival that will be taking place the next seven days. The entirety of Noterra is attending as well as the kings of the four other regions we rule over. That means my father may be in attendance. I don't know if I truly want to see him, but I am curious what he has to say about Evreux's confessions regarding my mother. On top of planning the festival, I have been tasked with managing other duties such as menus and staffing. I will say I don't truly enjoy planning menus or staffing, so I delegate most of it to whomever wants the job.

I have been given a page to serve me and assist with any need I have. His name is Donovan, and he spends most of the time looking at his feet. He's quite young, possibly the same age as I. His father serves on the council, who I assume is one of the men standing near me in the hallway right now. He's been quite helpful in acquiring any knowledge I seek pertaining to the crown. Tobias's schedule has been quietly monitored and it seems he spends most of his time in his study or out riding. I have to say, I am happy to hear he is taking his kingly duties seriously, but I do wish he would have a conversation with me. Especially one that isn't just basic formalities and niceties that one normally has with those they dislike.

My hands are clasped in front of me, my nails digging into my palms, as I await Tobias's arrival. The sun is filtering through the windows, making the marble walls sparkle in response. Footsteps approach from my left and I turn to see Tobias headed this way, guards following closely behind. His eyes are tired and bloodshot, his face pale. I don't imagine he has been getting much sleep as of late. At least, I rarely recall him being there when I awake in the middle of the night. I know it is my duty to care for him, but I don't want to step in unless he truly wants me to. The council members bow and engage in formalities while Tobias walks over to me.

"My queen." I offer him a small smile as he leans down and kisses my cheek.

"You are looking tired, husband. You need rest." I whisper so the others do not hear, but he shakes his head.

"I am fine, *wife*." I nod in defeat, my eyes drifting to the floor, and follow him into the council room. The three other men take their places in seats I presume they have always inhabited, and Tobias walks over to the head of the table. I place my hands on the back of a chair and look around. The room is large, rectangular. The walls aren't all marble here, as some dark gray sheetrock line the walls, much like our bed chambers. The table in the center is covered in papers and a map with small figurines placed around. The wood of the table is dark and tinted red with black veins running through. A fire is ablaze in the corner, making the room uncomfortably warm, even with the early autumn air. The men are all watching me, waiting, so I quickly pull out the chair and take a seat.

"Let's call this meeting to order." Tobias's voice is clear and commanding. He takes his seat and leans back, his elbow propped against his knee. "Jeremiah?" He questions as he looks around with a raised eyebrow.

"He had some duties to attend to, Your Grace." The man next to me responds. I haven't seen Jeremiah at all since the coronation, but Tobias also hasn't mentioned whether or not he has found proof of his treason.

"Very well, Cyrus, you may begin." Cyrus briefly glances in my direction before he nods and clears his throat.

"We have sent as many men as we can spare to secure the borders, but our militia is growing weak. Labisa can reach us from all angles, but if we send more men, we may risk our safety here, Your Grace." Tobias frowns and his eyes momentarily flit to me before returning to Cyrus.

"Labisa has set up the majority of their army in Rakushia. I don't fear our safety from Chatis so our troops can evacuate from their borders and join Theo and the kingsguard at the Rakushian border. Tatus is also under our banner, so their borders are secure as well. Send a rider to King Pax of Tatus and ask him to supply men to our cause. They don't need to leave Tatus but should be stationed on their eastern border that they share with Labisa. Tatus controls most of their trade, so I don't believe they are at risk of infiltrating their walls, however I want to be prepared." His voice is powerful, and I find myself in awe as he speaks to his men.

His tone is even, commanding. He listens to their thoughts and concerns and builds off of them instead of discrediting their beliefs. It's completely different from how my father rules, or how I've seen him rule. His word is law, he doesn't care about the opinions of others, but Tobias does. I can almost feel the iron chains I've been keeping around my heart loosen slightly.

He isn't my father. He isn't *his* father. He's his own version of a king, and I shouldn't judge him against the others.

"Yes, Your Grace. What of the beach towns that line the Great Sanaya Sea?" Cyrus pauses his writing to glance back up at his king.

"Close the smaller ports down and evacuate those who reside there to any of the larger towns inland. All trade will need to come through Port Tobeo for the time being. If we station our men there, it'll reduce the need to spread our army thin, and concentrating our population to areas we can manage will reduce the likelihood of any of our cities being seized." Cyrus nods. "You'll send word?"

Our cities being seized? Is he really discussing an actual war? I knew things with Labisa were strained, but I always thought it would pass or lessen in severity. But *this*, this is actual war. I can feel my palms dampening and I wipe them on the skirt of my gown. I take a quiet, deep breath, and try to focus.

"Yes, Your Grace."

"Does anyone else have anything to add?" He looks around, but the men shake their heads. "Welan, where are we on the situation with Rakushia?" Tobias turns towards the man to his right who boasts the pin of the hand.

"The reports have come back, Your Grace. He was beheaded in the town square of the capital a week ago." Tobias growls and stands, throwing his chair back behind him. I flinch, but everyone else remains unphased, as if this behavior is a normal occurrence. He places his hands on the table and peers down at the map. Small, carved stone figurines line the map marking the capital cities and locations of our armies. I focus on the border between Rakushia and Noterra and see a small, white rose figurine. Does that symbolize our armies? Or is it Theo's mark? The Noterra capital has a red crown and a silver crown. Is that supposed to be Tobias and I?

"Labisa has gained control over Rakushia." His voice is stern as his eyes fixate in front of him. I knew Labisa had infiltrated Rakushia, but I wasn't aware it was this bad, this *deadly*. His eyes find mine and he shakes his head in frustration. "If the king has been beheaded, Labisa now *owns* that territory according to the laws of succession." Tears well up in my eyes and I blink them away. I had met the Rakushian King many times as a child, he was a kind man with a daughter the same age as me. She was one of the only friends I was permitted to have. We were distant relatives, and I wish I had the chance to get to know them.

"What about Princess Emery, and the queen?" I ask, afraid his answer is that they joined the king in his journey to the other side. Everyone's eyes look up at me and I sink in my chair slightly. Was I not allowed to speak?

"Queen Arya died the first day they infiltrated, but Princess Emery is missing. They have not found her yet, at least as far as our intel knows. Our hope is that she somehow escaped. She has allies here in Noterra, as well as Chatis. She is surrounded by those who will help, she just needs to make it out of Rakushia to reach them." His voice is even, diplomatic.

"Will we look for her? If she's hurt or alone," My voice cracks as I fight against the lump in my throat. "It is not safe for her; we need to find her and bring her to court." I plead, hoping that he agrees.

"We can't cross the border right now, Your Grace. It will be seen as a sign of retaliation. Noterra is strong, but we don't want to engage in a war if it's not necessary." Cyrus responds gently, but I ignore him.

"But it is necessary. Tobias, they already declared war. They already stated they were going to fight Noterra as soon as they reached the borders of Rakushia, and probably have plans for Chatis as well. We have to be prepared. We have to help my father."

"Chatis has not been mentioned in any of our intel. Your father is feared, so I wouldn't be surprised if he leaves Chatis out of this." Welan responds this time.

"But why now? Why have they done this *now*? We have lived without wars for nearly twenty years. What has caused this sudden urge to enter a war?" The men around us mutter and I can hear them snicker in response to my questions.

"Because of you, Elaenor." Tobias says matter-of-factly. As if it is the most obvious answer. Quiet spreads, but Cyrus smiles smugly at Tobias's admission. I want to shove the pen he's writing with down his throat. I stand slowly, anger fueling my voice as I narrow my eyes at him and plant my hands flat on the table, copying his stance.

"How is this *possibly* my fault?"

"You exist, Elaenor. A princess that was presumed dead for ten years. You have aided Noterra in acquiring yet *another* country to control. It is no secret that my father wanted to be the one true king, and I am close. Out of 11 countries, Noterra controls 5 of them. Labisa knew Rakushia was next, we share a border, it only makes sense. With the help of Chatisian armies, we wouldn't have to lift a finger to gain access to another land." He runs his hands through his hair as he looks at me with irritation, as if my presence is an inconvenience to him.

"I had no choice in this marriage, Tobias. Neither did you. We were a political match." I say slowly, attempting to control my anger. The room is silent, everyone looking away from our exchange.

"It doesn't matter. You exist and you aided in strengthening Noterra. You are the reason, whether you want to be or not. If you never came here, they may have not raided Rakushia. Their king and queen may have still been alive, and our men wouldn't be risking their lives." The tears break through, and I shake my head, willing them to stop. I didn't choose this.

This wasn't my fault.

"This is as much your fault as it is mine, Tobias." I spit. He takes a slow, deep breath and waves his hand. The three men stand and bow before scurrying out the door, closing it behind them. "Is this why you asked for me today, to blame me for this war? For the death of a king and queen?" I snap.

"Elaenor." He reaches his hands towards me, and I flinch out of his reach, glaring at him with every ounce of anger I have. He straightens and steps out from behind the table over to the pitcher of deep red wine.

"Do you think I wanted this, Tobias? That I wanted to be sent to a foreign land, forced to marry a man I don't know. Do you think this is something I would have chosen for myself?" He doesn't respond. "Do you truly think this is the type of life I want for myself, for my future children? I never wanted to marry you and you know that. Can you honestly tell me you are happy with me as your wife?" I walk around the table and face him.

"Everyone has a choice in their fate, Elaenor. You could have said no." He sighs into his wine as he takes a mouthful.

"Agreeing to something means nothing if no was never an option. We do not have the luxury of choosing our partners. If you truly believe that we do, you are mistaken. I wanted to find love and marry for love and live a life full of *love*, but instead of that I got a stranger, who terrifies me to no end." Surprise flashes through his eyes as he takes in what I said. "After the pain you have caused me, both physically and emotionally, you know I am not safe with you. I don't want to be here. I don't want to be just another woman you destroy, so don't you dare say this war is because of me. I am merely a pawn on a chessboard filled with kings. I have no power here at all, or anywhere for that matter! This is *not* my fight." He slams the cup onto the table and reaches forward. His hand grips my cheeks tightly as he brings it close to his.

"You are more than a pawn, Elaenor. You are the queen that I will play when it is advantageous for the good of the realm." His face is close, and I can smell the wine on his hot breath as it fans across my face. His fingers dig into my skin as his nose almost brushes mine. His blue eyes are deep, swirling as if they were an ocean in a hurricane.

"You are just like my father." He laughs and releases his grip, picking his wine back up.

"Elaenor, I am a *king*, as is he. I will always do what is best for the country, your feelings are not relevant. This war was a direct consequence of our marriage. You may be correct in saying I had a part in this, but it is still your fault as well. We have to protect ourselves before they infiltrate our land. I asked you to come here today so you could hear what was going on. I figured as the queen you may want to know what was happening along your borders." His moods are quickly changing, and I find myself confused on how to respond.

"Thank you." I whisper. He turns to face me.

"What?" He's surprised.

"Thank you for including me in this. You didn't have to, and I appreciate that you did, but you don't have to be so cold towards me Tobias. I don't know if we will ever truly love each other, but we are married. We will be in each other's company for a long time, and we need to learn how to navigate this life together. I don't understand your need to demonize me and make me feel like a political headache you can't be rid of." His eyes have softened, but they still hold mine with anger.

"Were these last few days of peace not satisfactory enough for you?"

"It was. I appreciated the distance and the lack of anger you showed me. The truth is Tobias, I never know what you are going to do. Whether you'll hurt me or make me do things I do not want to do. I never know how to act around you in fear that you will lash out." He takes a deep breath and sets his wine on the table. Walking over to me, he places his hands on either side of my waist, looking into my eyes. I almost pull myself out of his grasp, but I hold steady.

"This marriage formed an alliance between our countries. Our duties are to ensure the line of succession is set. I will do what is necessary to make sure that happens, but I promise to do so without malice." I look away from him and step out of his embrace.

"Tobias, you have made this promise before. I cannot trust what I don't see."

"Elaenor, I do love you." I stop and hold onto one of the chairs to steady me. He's lying. He has to be.

"Tobias, stop. Don't say that if it is not true." I stammer as my heart beats erratically. This isn't love. How he treats me isn't love. So why do I feel as if I might faint at his confession?

"I know that I haven't shown it, I haven't acted like a man who loves his wife, but you are the most frustrating and difficult woman I have ever met. You believe so strongly in the good of others, even when you have no reason to. I am working towards finding the truth about Jeremiah, I promise you." I don't hear him walk up to me, but his arms snake around my waist again. I can feel his nose press into my hair.

"Thank you." I manage to whisper. "Thank you for looking, even if you have no reason to believe me." He spins me around and grabs my face gently.

"I have every reason to believe you, Elaenor. You are my wife. I have to think of Noterra, but you come first. *Always*. I promise." His lips find mine as he pulls me into a deep embrace. "I love you." He whispers against my lips. I hate my body and my mind for betraying me. For making me love this man despite the pain he's caused. I can't hate him, even if I wanted to. Even though I have every reason to. He's terrifying, confusing, malicious, and more, but here I am practically falling into his arms just because he said he loved me.

Who have I become?

"I love you, too." I whisper through my tears as I wrap my arms around his neck. He pulls me as tight as he possibly can against him as he kisses away all of my fears.

Chapter Twenty-Seven

I left the meeting room this morning feeling better than I have in a week. He believes me. He told me he loved me. We can get through all of this together. He said he's actively working to prove Jeremiah is a traitor, and I hope this marks a step forward, a step towards a better future. My hand rests on my stomach as I hope there is a little piece of him growing inside of me. Even with the threats that loom over us, a child is what this kingdom needs. It's what *we* need if we are to make it through this.

Tobias hasn't appeared by the time I am prepared for bed. I climb into the warm blankets and stare at the ceiling. Usually this time of night I am busy with Tobias, so I find myself unable to fall asleep. I just feel lonely. Theo is still gone assisting our armies. I don't know what his title is, but I did hear someone say he was the Lord Commander of the kingsguard, but I am unsure of the truth to that. Maybe it is a title Tobias provided to get him away from court, *and away from me*. Not that he needs to worry about my feelings for Theo as I don't think I have any. Not anymore. I can't.

I roll over onto my side and stare out the wall of windows. I chose to have them all open this evening so I could watch the stars. A light breeze is filtering through, marking the start of autumn. I didn't get to enjoy the Noterran summer this year, but instead I will be greeted with snow much like home. My eyes close and I enjoy the crisp air as I fall asleep with sweet wine flowing through my veins.

Burning flesh scorches my nose. I can feel the flames nipping at my bare skin as I stumble through the wreckage. Buildings and houses are collapsing all around me as I fight to make it to the woods in time. My feet are going numb from the debris slicing their way to the bone. Glass from the grand windows, bones from the villagers who used to walk about the grounds, rubble and brick. All of it piling up into a massive obstacle I can't seem to get around.

"Tobias!" I cry out. Spinning around, I search for any movement, any sign of life. "Hello!" I call out again, but nobody answers. I climb over a fallen pillar and stand, struggling to balance on the crumbling structure. The trees are just ahead, I just need to make it there. I bend down to slide off the side of a pile of stone, but something pulls me down. I collapse onto the hard ground and cry out. A hand is gripping onto my ankle pulling me further and further into the wreckage, my skin ripping open as I slide across the rubble.

"Stop!" I scream as I struggle to get away. The hand releases and I look back to see Tobias. Blood is dripping from his nose, splattering onto the ground as he drags himself out of the crevice.

"Where do you think you are going?" He asks as he stands. He bends down and grabs my arm, pulling me up to him.

"Tobias, please." I cry out as his hand finds my neck. "Tobias, I can't breathe." I spit out, struggling against his grip.

"This is your fault, Elaenor. You get to watch it all burn down." He spins me around, so my back is against his chest, but his arm replaces his hand, cutting off my oxygen as he forces me to look at my home burning to the ground.

"Ple–" I try to beg, but his arm tightens around my throat. I can't breathe. My eyes are clouding over, and I can feel my chest starting to burn. I hit his arm, but it's no use. My legs grow weak as I struggle to stand. He brings me down to the ground, holding me against him as I fight to take my last breath.

My eyes open to a man's face right above mine, his hands around my throat as I struggle to get him off of me. His face is red, as if he is straining to apply pressure to my neck. My nails scratch his face, leaving bloody gashes across his cheek. His dark eyes bore into mine as I try to scream, but nothing comes out.

"I gave you a choice. You should have listened." He snarls. I reach over the side of the bed, looking for my dagger, but it's not there. I look around, but all I see is the pitcher of wine on the table next to the bed. I reach for it with everything I have, fighting against the darkness that threatens to envelope me. My chest is burning, my pulse rapidly slowing with each failed breath. My hands are tingling, losing function. *Oh Gods.* Jeremiah grunts as he applies even more pressure. My hand finds the edge of the pitcher, but I knock it off the table instead of grabbing it. The metal crashes to the floor, echoing across the room.

"Your Grace?" There is a soft knock on the door before it opens. I push and push to get Jeremiah off of me, when finally his hands break free from my neck. I inhale in desperation and cough out the blood that has built in my throat. I vaguely hear screaming and struggling as he's being detained, but I can barely focus on it. I gasp for air at the same time as my body forces me to vomit. Blood and bile cover the wool blankets as an arm grabs my waist.

"Ela!" Tobias cries out as he pulls me onto his lap. His eyes are filled with panic as I stare up at him. I can feel the blood dripping out of the side of my mouth as I take slow, painfully deep breaths. My head spins and my limbs burn. His fingers gently brush my neck where I am sure there are growing bruises. "Ela, talk to me." He begs.

"Your Grace." Someone says from behind.

"Not now." He snaps back.

"We will take him to holding, Your Grace." Tobias nods and I can hear muffled yelling, probably coming from Jeremiah, as he's pulled out of the room.

"Talk to me, are you okay?" I nod slowly, still struggling to control my breathing and clear the fog that has formed over my eyes. I blink rapidly, trying to clear the cloudiness, but it's refusing to move. We are silent for a few moments, but it feels like forever has passed. My breaths come in short wheezes, and I resist the urge to fall asleep. It hurts. My neck feels as if I swallowed a thousand daggers. Tobias's arms are wrapped tightly around me, scared to let me go. I cough and see blood splatter across his chest.

"I'm here, Your Grace." I can hear Apollo entering the room and coming up to the bed. His white hair is in a low ponytail like always, and he is wearing a robe over his bed clothes. Tobias scoots me over to the side of the bed so he can take a look at me. Apollo's cold fingers press down on my neck, and I wince. He opens my mouth and looks inside before softly touching my cheek. "She will be alright; she will just be sore for a few days. There will be some swelling, but she will heal quickly." Tobias brushes the hair out of my face, and I close my eyes, exhaustion washing over me.

"Elaenor." Tobias shakes me and I open my eyes again.

"Keep her awake, Your Grace. Just for a few short hours to ensure there is no damage to her brain. Elaenor," He touches my face gently. "It will be painful to talk for a small while, drink this." He pours a cold liquid into my mouth, and I swallow with a wince. The sweet nectar coats my throat and I almost want to cry with relief. A deep cough escapes my throat as I feel blood pooling in my lungs. "This will reduce any pain you may feel, but please try to drink some water." I stare up at his concerned face, fuzzy and shaky.

"Thank you, Apollo." Tobias whispers as he turns his attention back to me. My eyes close again as he adjusts me, so I am sitting in his lap. I can hear the door shut as he holds me against his chest and rocks me. I'm exhausted, but restless all at the same time. I push at his arms and force myself up. His face is filled with worry as he watches me slowly slide to the end of the bed. I plant my feet on the ground and stand. I sway for a moment as my head spins and my eyes close. I don't dare to move until I feel balanced, using the bedpost to keep me steady. My breathing is ragged as I force myself to take a few shaky steps.

"What are you doing?" He asks, his voice is soft, concerned. I walk over to the vanity and fall against the table with a groan. I shakily lift my head to look at my appearance in the mirror and a wet gasp escapes my parted lips. My skin is pale and slightly gray. My eyes are red and swollen. A small trickle of blood is drying at the corner of my mouth. I try to avoid it, but my eyes fall to my neck. Two perfect handprints made of bruises sit on either side of my neck. My fingertips brush the skin and I flinch.

"I told you." I whisper, my voice is gone.

"What?"

"I told you who he was." I whisper again while turning to face him. "I told you, Tobias." My voice comes but it's weak and strained, little more than a croak. I swallow against the pain, but it just makes it worse. "You didn't believe me." He looks down as he gets off the bed and comes to me.

"I didn't believe you at first, I know." He runs his hand through his disheveled hair. "I'm sorry. I've been trying to find proof. I needed proof, Elaenor." I scoff and fall into the chair in front of the table, unable to hold myself up anymore.

"Was my word not enough? I told my husband that the man who helped his wife get raped has a spot on his council and he asked for proof. Here is your *proof*, Tobias." I close my eyes and rest my head in my hands. I'm too tired to fight with him, nor do I want to be in his presence. The dream was so real. It was him. It was Tobias who was strangling me, both in the dream and indirectly in reality. That man said Tobias would cause my death. What if he is the one who will actually do it? "Where were you, Tobias?" I croak, realizing that he never came to bed.

"I was tending to some matters." He responds, his voice a little higher than normal. He's lying.

"Tobias, where were you?" I ask again, lifting my head from my hands to look at him. He's chewing on his bottom lip, his hands on his hips, refusing to make eye contact with me. "You were with someone, weren't you?" He sighs in resignation and nods.

"Yes." I shake my head both at myself for trusting him and at him for breaking that trust again.

"*Damnit*, Tobias." I sob into my hands. He wasn't here to protect me; he was in the arms of another after we professed our love to one another. After he promised me he was in this. I take a painful swallow as I look up at him, my head spinning. "Who is she?"

"It does not matter; she is leaving court."

"Sending her away before she has the chance to out herself as your mistress?" I snap with whatever voice and energy I have left.

"No, Elaenor. She's leaving because she's pregnant." I freeze, my mouth slightly falling open. Oh my gods. He got another woman pregnant.

"Are you seriously telling me you conceived a bastard within two weeks of our union?" I try to remain strong, but my voice comes out in choked sobs.

"We had been seeing each other prior to your arrival, I have not been with anyone else since our wedding, Ela. I promise."

"Why didn't you marry her? You'd have an heir already and I wouldn't be here hurt yet again." I'm crying now, as much as I try to hold it back. I can't. Gods, I hate this. I hate *him*.

"Ela, I don't have feelings for her. She was just someone I went to for comfort before you. It means nothing. It *meant* nothing." He sounds sincere but all I can see is him with another woman. Holding another woman's child. Lying to me again.

"I don't believe you. If this is what you want in our marriage, then I have no desire to know how many women you stick yourself inside when you aren't in here bothering me." The lie comes easy, and I hate myself for it.

"No one, just you. I promise." He kneels down in front of me, his face begging me to listen.

"All I'm good for is an heir. That's all that matters." I push his arms off me and shakily stand. "Get out. Sleep somewhere else." I push past him and stumble, his arm catches me.

"No. This is my room as much as it is yours."

"Then I will leave."

"Where are you going to go?" His voice is soft as he holds me close to him.

"I don't know. I don't have anyone here."

"Elaenor, stop being dramatic." He sighs into my hair, and I relax against him, exhausted. "Gods, you terrify me." He whispers.

"What are you so afraid of?" I ask, blinking back the tears.

"Loving you, Elaenor. I'm scared of loving you." His voice cracks as he admits it.

"Why? I'm not going to hurt you. I'm here. I've *always* been here."

"Yes, you have, but I don't know how to treat you the way you deserve. I'm scared I'll hurt you." He tightens his arms around me.

"You've already hurt me, time and time again. And I'm still here. I don't know why. I don't know why I even try with you, but I am here. I am asking you to be better. I am asking you to be my husband. One minute you treat me as the reason for a war and the next you are professing your love to me. I'm getting whiplash." I look up at him with exhausted eyes. He bends down and kisses my forehead, lingering there for just a moment before pulling away, leaving me waiting for an answer. An acknowledgement. Anything.

"I'll have our bedding changed and then we will retire for the night."

"Is she actually leaving, or will she be raising your child in this palace?" I ask.

"I have no way to know that it is my child, Elaenor. I have to assume based on our history, but she is leaving. She is being well taken care of by some family friends on the other side of the port."

"What if it is your child, Tobias? You don't want to know him?" While the thought of him having a child with someone else makes me sick, it's not the child's fault.

"No, I don't. The only child that matters to me is one I make with you." He kisses my hair again walking towards the door.

"Tobias, what will happen to Jeremiah?" He sighs and turns back around.

"He will be questioned endlessly. He's working for someone; I just need to find out who."

"Will he go to trial?"

"No, there were more than enough witnesses to his attack. A trial isn't needed, but I am not going to execute him until we have learned all we can." I nod and he offers me a reassuring smile. "He will not harm you again, Elaenor." He exits the room, leaving the door open. Three different women come in immediately and begin changing our bedding while I sit on the couch, exhausted. Too much has happened. Too much information has been shared. I feel numb to everything. To Tobias, to my near-death experience, to life. Before long, I am yet again ignoring the advice of Apollo, and I fall asleep on the couch.

Chapter Twenty-Eight

When I awake, the sun is shining and filling the room with bright golden rays. I have a blanket draped over me that falls as I sit up. My fingers grasp the soft material and pull it up to my face. Cedar and smoke. I glance at the settee next to me and see Tobias fast asleep, blankets wrapped around him like a tourniquet. Today is the festival, and as much as I wish to stay hidden all day, I have much to prepare before our guests arrive. I stand and hesitantly check my wounds in the mirror. Surprisingly my face is less pale, and my eyes appear bright and awake. My neck is bruised, badly. I wince as I remember his hands on my throat.

My mind replays the whole thing. His soulless eyes as he strangles me. And Tobias. In my dream it was him, he was the one killing me, cutting off my oxygen. There is no way that is just a dream, it can't be. I've been having the same dream for years, but lately it's been changing, increasing in intensity. And the man. Who is he? Why does he always appear when I am close to death? Not just death, when I'm *underwater*.

It doesn't take me long to have the bath filled to the brim of hot soapy water. I climb in, feeling the burn as the water caresses away my trauma. I take a deep breath and before I know it, my head is underwater.

I stare up at the distorted ceiling as I wait. My chest is burning, my eyes stinging from the oily water. I want to breathe, I want to lift my head, but I force myself to wait. I can feel my ears pop as the water infiltrates every part of me. *Just hold on, Elaenor.* I hold onto the edges as my mouth opens. I exhale and watch as the air bubbles rise to the surface, breaking through just as my eyes close.

I know where I am the second my eyes open. The bright green trees surround me, the forest floor pressing into my naked flesh. I can smell the humid air that tells me I'm home. I turn and look around, waiting for him to appear, but he doesn't. I start walking through the trees, carefully stepping over branches and rocks. I can hear the soft lapping of the water that tells me I'm near the lake. I step through the tree line and feel the soft white granules of sand my feet sink into. The lake is calm, the sky clear for once. I walk forward until my toes meet the icy water. I smile and close my eyes as I remember how this feels. My eyes open again as I sense him appear, an awareness creeping over me. He's here. I don't hesitate to turn around and face him.

He's shirtless, his olive skin shining in the sunlight. His muscular stature is flexed as he watches me. His hands tightly in fists. He's wearing black trousers that loosely hang from his hips as he stares. His green eyes look like mirrors reflecting the trees behind him. His jaw is tense, his black hair tucked behind his ears with just a bit of the white streak peeking through. He looks angry.

"What are you doing, Elaenor?" His voice is deep, melodic, enchanting and familiar all at the same time.

"Will you please tell me who you are?" He sighs and thinks for a moment before he opens his mouth to speak.

"You know what I am." I shake my head.

"No I don't. You've never told me." I respond. I try to keep the irritation out of my voice, but it sneaks through. He runs his hand through his hair before taking a step towards me.

"If you haven't figured it out, then you aren't paying attention." He's sad as if me not knowing who he is upsets him.

"Please, enough with these riddles and the games. I need to know." I walk towards him, my wet feet sticking to the soft sand.

"I can't. I can't tell you." He reaches forward and brushes my cheek with his thumb, electricity buzzing between us.

"Why, why can't you just tell me?"

"You have to figure it out yourself. It is the way of the Gods. If I could tell you, I would." He sighs and drops his arms.

"Why can't I see you in person, and why do you only appear when I'm underwater?" He laughs, surprisingly.

"It's not the water, Elaenor. It's how you reach out to me that brings me to you." I stare at him, not truly understanding what he means. "I am with you. Every day. Every moment. I am there. I have been for years. I will always be there; you just need to ask for me and I'll come–"

"Come then. Come to me in person." I reach forward and grab his arms. I yelp as he shocks me. "What is that?" He smiles again but ignores me. His white teeth shining in the sun.

"I am not located in Noterra, but you and I will meet soon. I promise. I can't tell you anymore."

"My dream. Can you tell me if it's real?" He shakes his head. "Does that mean it's not real? Or that you can't tell me." He just smiles again. I throw my arms up and groan. "I can't get anything out of you!" His strong arms wrap around me. He smells like home. Like Chatis.

"I promise you that we will meet, but I need you to wake up."

"No, I'm not ready."

"It doesn't matter, you need to wake up now or we won't be able to meet." He squeezes his arms around me as if he's mimicking a heartbeat. Short, hard pulses. I close my eyes and take a deep breath.

"Please, my love. Not again." Crying. He's crying. I can't get my eyes to open, but I can feel the cold marble floors pressed into my back. Two hands rhythmically press on my chest, beating my heart for me.

"Your Grace." I hear Master Pakin, Apollo. He's trying to soothe Tobias. "It's been too long. It's been nearly thirty minutes, Your Grace." *Thirty minutes?*

"No!" He yells as he continues to press onto my chest. *Open your eyes!* I tell myself, over and over again, but they won't open. My throat is burning, my head spinning.

"Your Grace. I am sorry. There is nothing to be done." His voice is soft, but I can hear the pain in his words. Tobias's hands still and I can hear his heart wrenching broken sobs as he cries over my body. Am I dead?

Elaenor, breathe. His voice is in my head, pulling me back to reality even more. I try to inhale, but something is blocking my way. *Water.* I force myself to cough and feel the water bubble out of my mouth. I sit up as fast as I can as it cascades out of my lungs and onto the floor.

"Ela!" Tobias yells as his arms wrap around me. I frantically inhale, trying to get as much oxygen as possible. "*Breathe*, Ela." My eyes open and I'm blinded by the bright lights reflecting off the marble.

"Your Grace, can you look at me?" Apollo's hands are warm as they touch my face. "Can you speak?" I nod and he smiles. "Okay, then say something."

"I'm okay." My voice is hoarse, croaking. A combination of last night and this morning. Tobias rocks me against his chest while he frantically kisses the top of my head. My whole body feels as if it's been shocked, like I am being electrocuted.

"Why do you keep doing this?" He's crying as he speaks.

"I'm sorry." I whisper, my eyes closed.

"No more baths, not without me. *Please.*" He sounds terrified, and I don't really blame him.

"Okay, okay. I'm sorry." I reassure him as he holds my wet, naked body against his chest. I don't need them. Not anymore.

It's not the water, Elaenor. It's how you reach out to me that brings me to you.

Two days. Two days have passed since I last saw him. The festival has been going on for two days, with jousting and food filling our courts. Tobias hasn't left my side, fearing what I might do without him. I don't mind his attention; he's been kind and careful. A side of Tobias I've rarely seen the last two weeks. He makes sure my needs are met, in all ways. He's gentle and tells me he loves me every chance he gets, and I believe him.

I've asked him about Jeremiah. The only time he leaves me is when he's going to question him. He'll be gone for hours, leaving Donovan, Laris, and Tano to watch over me. As if three men truly need to be present to keep me safe. When he returns, he's tired and bloodied, but it's not his blood he wears. He won't tell me what is spoken between them, but I am hopeful that if it is important, he'll share.

Tobias has caught on to my nightly wine consumption and is convinced it's the cause for my drowning, so he has ordered it to be kept away from me, as if I am a child. All that's doing is forcing me deeper into my coffee and sweetened cream addiction, which he is more than happy to provide. He introduced me to something called decaf, which is coffee without caffeine. I can drink it at all times of the day and not have to worry about my sleep being affected. Not that I am worried about that. I seem to still fall asleep without remembering how or when I got into bed, but when I do awake, my body feels energized and healed from the inside out. Maybe deep, dreamless sleep has been the treatment I've needed all along.

I've asked around about Erik's absence, but all that's shared is that he is still in Chatis. I've asked if he will be returning, but no one seems to have an answer. I thought about writing to him, but I fear he is staying to nurse his wounds and I don't want to rush him back to court if he's not well. I don't believe he would abandon me, but if his father ordered it, he would have no choice as he is still a citizen of Chatis. Those thoughts bring me to my own father. Donovan confirmed that he received an acceptance letter in response to his invitation to the festival, but he has yet to appear, even though the week-long affair is almost half over.

I nervously await to hear his voice. Hear his commanding bellows ordering me about. He has no right to bark orders as our stations are more equal than before. Even then, I think my station is higher than his. Noterra is far too powerful for their queen to bow to a king of a smaller nation. Maybe that is why he is keeping his distance? He knows he no longer has control over me, and the idea is enough to keep him away. Or something has happened to him and Erik, and I haven't yet been informed. No matter how much I try to force it down, my paranoia still makes its appearance quite often.

I sigh as I lean my head back against the couch. Donovan is sitting at the writing desk keeping up with correspondence, or at least that's what he says he's doing. Instead, I catch him watching me every few moments as I sit here drinking my coffee. Lydia has already been in here to get me ready for the day, so now I just wait for someone to come get me to enjoy the festivities. While I know I am not locked in our room, I still hate that I feel as if I have to wait to be called upon before I can leave. Maybe that needs to be changed. I set my coffee down and rise. Donovan's eyes widen as he stands.

"Your Grace?" He asks, questioning my movements.

"I'm fine, Donny. I just don't want to be cooped up watching you pretend to catch up on my mail." He smiles, embarrassed. "Please, let us go for a walk. Do something other than wait around all day." I hold my hand out to him, but he doesn't take it. I roll my eyes as I head towards the door, his footsteps quickening behind me to catch up.

I push open the double doors and take a deep breath as I take in the moving bodies in the hallway. Too many people make me claustrophobic, but passing through the horde is the only way out.

"Your Grace?" Echoes behind me as the guards stationed to my room acknowledge me. I ignore them and keep walking, narrowly dodging staff as they prepare for the day's games. People I've never seen mixed with those I see daily, pass by. Donovan catches up to me, breathlessly.

"Your Grace, I was asked to keep an eye on you." His voice is strained, scared. Probably of Tobias, which he should be.

"Are you unable to use your eyes outside the confines of my room?" I question, my eyebrows raising. He smiles and relaxes.

"No, Your Grace. They work just fine." His voice is filled with amusement.

"Good, I want to go to the beach." I smile and begin walking again.

"Your Grace, that is an hour's ride away from here." I roll my eyes.

"Fine, fine. I just want out of this palace."

"Out of the palace?"

"Yes, take me to the stables." He stops and I look back at him.

"I'm not asking for a horse to run away on, I just want to be near a living creature other than you. It's been far too long since I have last seen Sybil, I don't want her to forget me." My tone is humorous, but my words sound angry. He nods and leads me to the stables.

The stables are technically outside the palace wall, but you don't always have to go through the main gate to reach them. When we finally arrive, twenty or so horses are lined up in their separate stalls. They are either eating, or staring, or doing whatever else horses do. I walk up to a black horse, her mane shining in the bright morning sun. She nudges my hand as I reach for her, letting her silky fur brush through my fingers and the smell of hay trickle in through my nose.

"That horse was the late king's, Your Grace." A thick accent and a booming voice behind me makes me jump. Donovan is staring up at whoever it is that has joined us, but I could recognize that voice anywhere. I drop my hand from Sybil and take a deep breath before turning around to face him.

"And now she's mine. Hello, father." I offer a smile as I clasp my hands in front of me.

"Elaenor." The way he says my name makes me nauseous. It rolls off his tongue with such disgust.

"She will be addressed by her proper name, *Your Grace*." Donovan stammers as he steps towards my father. I lift my hand and press it against his chest, pushing him back.

"It is alright, Donovan." I hold my head high as I speak, so as to not appear weak in the eyes of the man in front of me. The person who made me feel like a failure, and inconvenience, to him my entire life. "You came. I didn't think you would." I turn my attention back to my father, King Viktor of Chatis, and the one man who has the power to make me want to shrivel up into a ball and hide.

"Did I not send word? I could have sworn I did." He responds, his voice light, humorous.

"You did, but the festival started two days ago. It's rather rude to show up halfway through the events." I try to sound regal, diplomatic, but it sounds like I'm complaining. His eyes narrow as he looks at Donovan. I follow his gaze and tilt my head to the side, dismissing him. Donovan takes a few steps away, giving us privacy, but still near enough to be within earshot.

"I received your letter." That means Erik made it to Chatis. My eyes find him, and I hold his gaze.

"Is it true?" I ask. "Were Evreux and my mother in love?" He sighs before stepping around me, softly petting Sybil's mane.

"I believe so, yes." He was right? Does that mean he was also right about the nature of her death? "That is all I'm willing to share with you." He wipes his hand off on his trousers before turning to face me.

"Did you kill her?" My voice is barely above a whisper when I speak. "Was he telling me the truth?"

"No, Eleanor. I did not *murder* your mother." He shakes his head dismissively and I want nothing more than to ask him more questions, but he starts to walk away.

"That's all the information I get?" I snap. "After all this time, you won't tell me anything?"

"You have no right to any of this information!" His voice is loud, angry. "You do not know what it feels to watch your wife fall in love with another. You have no idea how it feels to hold her body while the masters are begging you to release them. You have no idea how it feels to see your only child's blood soaking into the sheets, but nowhere to be found! You have no idea what happened, and you never will. Be done with it." His voice cracks, but something feels off. His words feel forced, fake. I don't believe them. I don't believe him. Everyone has been lying to me, nearly my whole life. I knew not to trust royals, that their games are their way of life, but I never expected it would become mine.

"What about me? How did I cross the lake? How did I not die? I can't swim!" I raise the volume of my voice to match his. My father's jaw clenches as he bites back whatever it is he wants to say.

"My wife, there you are!" Tobias's voice is bright, cheerful, as he spots us. He steps around my father and embraces me in a warm hug, pressing his lips to my temple. "Viktor, it's so good of you to join in on the festivities, although a bit late are you not?" His voice is snide, knowing.

"Your Grace." My father's voice is laced with disdain as he bows his head slightly, but Tobias ignores him.

"Ela, your surprise has arrived." Tobias smiles mischievously and my father rolls his eyes. "Come on." He grabs my hand and pulls me away from my father and out of the stalls. I turn back to see Donovan and my father both following us as we make our way to the courtyard, with the former trying to get as far away from the latter as possible.

As we turn the corner and the stone wall disappears, I see it. Chestnut hair braided perfectly against her back, her dark blue dress flowing in the wind. Her hands animatedly talking as she faces someone. Someone with pale blonde hair tied up in a leather cord who's hanging on to every word she says. Theo. Scarlett.

Theo *with* Scarlett.

Chapter Twenty-Nine

"Elaenor!" Scarlett's shrill voice screams through the air as she bounds over to me. Her perfect braid bouncing with the movement, her arms circling around my neck, holding me tight. I don't even try to hide them as the tears start pouring out of my eyes and down my cheeks. Her shoulder is wet when she finally pulls back. "Oh, don't cry. It's okay." She whispers as she wipes my face.

"What are you doing here?" I ask, still holding on to her as tightly as she'll allow.

She's *actually* here.

"I rode in with the king! My parents received an invitation for the carnival as well as a request to move to court." She's smiling, her pearly teeth shining in the sunlight. I turn my head towards Tobias, who's grin is exposing his dimple.

"Is this true?" I ask him and he nods. I pull out of Scarlett's arms and throw mine around his neck. He wraps his arms around my waist, holding me tightly.

"I know things have been hard for you, and with Danieas still in Chatis, I figured you'd need someone here for you." He murmurs in my ear as I hold him closely.

"Thank you." I whimper before pulling out of his arms and turning back to Scarlett. "Are you staying? For good?" She nods and I squeal with excitement. "Are you to be my lady, or?" I ask, turning to look at Tobias behind me. He walks up and puts his hand on the small of my back.

"Actually, with the help of a substantial donation to her family in the form of land, Scarlett classifies as a Lady, so she will be here as such." My eyes widen and I smile again. "It is also my hope that Theo and Scarlett will announce their engagement this evening at the fireworks show." Tobias speaks calmly and slowly, judging my reaction. I don't let my smile falter as I look back at Scarlett who is beaming towards a silent Theo.

"We are going to be sisters!" She screams as she throws her arms around Theo. He laughs as he catches her, keeping her from falling over. His eyes meet mine and I can see the pain. I can see the sorrow pooling beneath the crystal blue. His gaze holds for just a moment before he whispers something in Scarlett's ear. I lean into Tobias and look up at him, a fake smile plastered on my lips.

"Was this a good surprise?" He asks and I nod. His lips brush mine softly before he looks up at something over my shoulder. I follow his gaze to where my father is standing, his arms crossed. "Viktor, I trust the journey went well?" He asks, his hand sliding from my back to my hip, holding me against him.

"Yes, Your Grace. The ride was lovely. We are not as fortunate with our weather this time of year, so the sunshine is welcomed." My father smiles slightly, but Tobias's face stays stoic, neutral.

"Ela, why don't you give Scarlett a tour of the palace?" I look between my father and Tobias before nodding. I lean up to press a kiss to his cheek before stepping away and linking my arm through Scarlett's. Theo gives me a small smile before joining Tobias in a staring standoff with my father. I tear my eyes away, pulling Scarlett along with me. The telltale sounds of rustling armor alert me that Tano and Laris are close behind. Scuffling shoes on the cobblestones also let me know that Donovan is following as well.

"I can't believe you're here!" I whisper as we start climbing the marble stairs to the entryway of the palace. Scarlett is here. Here and engaged to Theo. *Theo.* I am happy that Scarlett will be staying in court, and I am even happier that she has found someone who I know will treat her right, but seeing Theo with another causes my throat to tighten. I have no right to feel this way, but I do. Theo is to be *married* to my best friend.

I drag her through the many hallways, almost getting lost if it weren't for Donovan's gentle probing. We end the tour of the palace in the royal chambers, where she throws herself on top of the giant four-poster bed.

"Gods, I can't believe you live *here*. And are a queen!" She exclaims as she rolls around on the bed dramatically. I laugh and join her by sitting on the edge of the mattress.

"It has definitely been an adjustment." I admit as she relaxes into the furs with a sigh. "I am sure your chambers will be just as wonderful. I wonder where they'll put you. My old chambers were next to Theo's, so maybe there?" I wonder as she sighs again.

"He is so dreamy, Elaenor. His eyes and his hair. And he is *so* nice. How crazy is it that we will both be Rosenthal's?" She says with her sing-songy voice. I laugh and turn to look at her. I hardly ever hear Tobias's surname, or my surname now for that matter. Sometimes I still feel as if I am a Pinewell, just a princess of Chatis. She's lying on her back, wrapped up in furs as she stares up at the ceiling. "Is he as perfect as he seems?" She asks, her voice much quieter. *Yes. He is perfect in every way, and she has no idea.*

"Theo is the kindest man I have ever met. He saved my life twice in one night." I say as I collapse on the bed next to her.

"I heard snippets of what happened," She rolls onto her side, so she faces me. "Are you alright?" I stare up at the ceiling and nod.

"It was the worst night of my life, but also not the worst thing that has happened in the last few weeks." She stays quiet. "I was raped and beaten, strangled and slapped. The king, not Tobias, his father, was confused towards the end. He thought I was my mother, so he tried to impregnate me, claiming he could give me a son. Thankfully Tobias walked in at the right time, but I think that was almost more terrifying than the men in the woods." She reaches over and squeezes my hand.

"I'm sorry for what you went through. Is it better now? Is it everything we hoped?" I stay quiet for a moment, thinking. *Is it? Am I happy here?*

"I don't know how to answer that, Scarlett. I do think Tobias loves me, but it's different. We went through a rough patch, but I think it's getting better. At least I hope it is."

"I wish you could see the way *he* looks at you." She says quietly, with an emphasis on *he*. "He looks at you like you are the only person in the world." She sounds sad, so I turn and look at her. She's picking at a loose thread on the bedspread.

"That's good right?"

"I'm not talking about Tobias." She whispers before looking up at me. My pulse skips and my brows furrow slightly. "I am talking about Theo." I clamp my open mouth shut and sit up.

"I don't know what you are talking about." I slide off the end of the bed and walk over to the sitting area. A decanter of wine and some glasses sit off to the side and I pour myself a glass of the sweet, pink wine knowing Tobias would roll his eyes if he could see me.

"I'm not saying you do, but I am to be married to him, Elaenor." She joins me over by the fireplace before taking the glass out of my hand and stealing a sip. "Is there anything I should know?" I meet her gaze and tilt my head. I know I should be honest, but if I tell her my feelings, what would she do? Who would she tell?

"Theo kissed me the day his father died. I stopped it, but Tobias saw him. They got into a huge fight, but nothing ever happened. I love my husband." The last part was less than convincing, but I am still hopeful she bought it. She nods slightly, taking another sip of the wine.

"Should we go back to the party?" She asks and I offer her a smile.

"You have nothing to worry about with me and Theo. He is all yours." She returns the smile before setting the glass on the table. Her arms come around me again and I squeeze her back.

"I am so glad I came."

"I am too."

When we exit the room, Laris and Tano are on either side. I smile and give them a nod. Donovan is waiting against the opposite wall, his hands tightly around a small journal. He quickly joins me on the opposite side of Scarlett as we make our way down the hallway.

The halls are busy, packed with guests and staff. While I would have been fine weaving my way through them, they part like a great sea as I make my way through. I nod at as many as I can, noticing Scarlett staring at everyone with awe. When we finally break through the crowd, I exhale loudly. I don't think I'll ever get used to this many people.

Scarlett's arm is linked with mine as we cross the entryway and head back outside. I look around, trying to spot the silver crown in the masses, but I don't see him. I do catch a sight of my father standing next to a group of women who are all fawning over him. I roll my eyes and scan the crowd again. I can just barely make out a silver crown on a head of golden hair quickly making its way through the masses. I drop my gaze down to the woman walking next to Tobias.

Her auburn hair is down and wavy, shining like fire in the sunlight. She is wearing a tightly fit green dress that perfectly exposes her slightly swollen belly. Tobias's hand is clasped tightly around her upper arm, dragging her around the edge of the wall and out of sight. My pulse quickens and my mouth goes dry as I stare at the spot Tobias was in.

"Who is that with Tobias?" Scarlett asks and I tear my gaze away from the wall to her confused expression. Her face drains of color and she stumbled back a step.

"Are you okay?" I ask as I reach up to touch her forehead. It feels cold and clammy.

"Yeah, I just got dizzy for a second." She shakes her head and her brows furrow. I look back towards the portion of the wall Tobias disappeared through.

"Maybe it was the travel? You could be tired. Maybe you should sit down. I will be back in just a moment." I ask, pulling my arm out of hers. She tightens her grip on me and looks me square in the eyes.

"No, I am coming with you." Scarlett was always protective of me, and even now she can pick up on the emotions I have tried so hard to hide. I smile slightly and nod. I look back at Laris and Tano, who have kept a steady distance away from us.

"I will just be a moment."

"We are to stay by your side, Your Grace."

"I will just be a moment, please stay here." I say, sharper this time. They exchange looks before nodding in my direction. "Thank you." I say as I pull Scarlett into the crowd. She stumbles a couple more times, shaking her head to clear the dizziness. She probably just needs rest. It doesn't take us long to make our way to the palace gates, nodding at the men guarding either side.

We step through slowly and peer around. I don't see Tobias or the woman, so we head towards the stables. As we get closer, I can hear hushed tones. Scarlett looks over at me and we step quietly up to the doorway, staying hidden against the wall.

"Please, this is your *child*." The woman whimpers. I can hear Tobias scoff.

"I don't care, you need to leave. I *paid* you to leave Noterra." His voice is laced with venom, and I can almost picture his hardened jaw.

"I love you, Tobias. Let us be a family, appoint me as your mistress." She's pleading, begging. I glance over the edge of the wall and see her hands on his chest. His arms are dangling by his sides, his hands clenched into fists. "Please don't cast me away." She reaches up towards him, her hand cupping his cheek. His eyes close and he leans into her touch. I can feel the nausea blooming in my stomach as she touches his face. Her swollen belly lightly brushing his hips. She looks to be about three or four months pregnant. Which would put the conception well before my arrival.

Scarlett's elbow is digging into my back as she leans over me to look inside the stables with me. I shift slightly and Tobias's eyes flash open. I jerk back before his head turns. My eyes widen and I push Scarlett until we are quietly running around the side of the building. Calloused fingers grip my arm and jerk me out of Scarlett's grasp.

"Ela, what are you doing out here without Laris or Tano?" His voice is tight, as if he is struggling to get the words out. I spin around and his eyes are wide, scared.

"I was giving Scarlett a tour when I saw you go in there with that *woman*." I spit, ripping my arm out of his hand. I can see Scarlett biting her lip and looking down. "I thought she was leaving, Tobias?" I whisper, willing my pulse to relax and go back to normal.

"She did, but she came back. I'll make sure she stays away this time, Ela." He reaches for my face, and I flinch. His jaw hardens as he steps back.

"Get her out of here, Tobias." I snap and he closes his eyes.

"Lady Scarlett, would you please rejoin the festivities? The queen and I will join you shortly." He looks over my shoulder at her. She glances in my direction, and I give her a short nod, letting her know it's okay.

"Yes, Your Grace." She bows slightly before disappearing around the building. Tobias's hand grabs my upper arm, dragging me towards the tree line.

"Tobias, let go of me." He pulls me farther and farther from the wall, the sounds of the party disappearing as we cross into the woods. The sunlight is streaming through the upper canopy, casting golden threads of light onto the floor. "Tobias." I say again as we go deeper. He stops once we reach a small clearing, looking around before releasing my arm. The rich smell of foliage and dirt fills my nose and I almost dramatically inhale. It smells like home, but without the muskiness associated with the humidity.

"Elaenor, I don't want her here either, please trust me."

"You let her touch you. I saw your face; you were enjoying it." His lips pinch into a thin line as he crosses his arms.

"I'm not going to lie and say I didn't enjoy my time with her, but it doesn't matter. I am married to you."

"You don't want to take her as your mistress?"

"I thought about it–"

"You *thought* about it?" I yell, stepping back. "Are you serious?"

"If that is my child, Ela, part of me wants to know it."

"I can't believe this. What about what you said before? What if it's not your child?"

"There is no way to know until it's born."

"Is she going to stay until then?" My voice raises in octave, and I press a hand to my chest.

"I don't know!"

"Tobias, I am not blaming the child. That poor babe is not at fault for any of this, but I will not live in a castle that you have a mistress in." My threat falls short. He knows I don't have a choice.

"What are you saying?"

"I am saying you have to choose."

"Excuse me?" He scoffs.

"Choose who you are keeping here, because it won't be both of us." His eyes darken as he steps closer to me, the ocean iris turning into a stormy gray.

"Do you think you have choices here? That you have any ounce of freedom in this country? You cannot leave. I will not allow it. You are my wife." His hands are on his hips as he towers over me, but I'm not scared. Not anymore.

"Then act like it! Get rid of her, please, Tobias. I can't. I can't see her here, walking the halls, knowing you used to be with her. Knowing that your heir is growing inside her womb and not mine." His eyes soften as he reaches for me, but I step back again.

"Ela, I don't want to hurt you. I am trying so hard to be the person you want me to be. I want to make you happy, but I don't know how. You are always trying to leave."

"What are you talking about?" My brows pinch together. I have never tried to leave, not even once.

"The bath, that isn't the first time you've gone under for way too long."

"I'm not suicidal, Tobias. I fell asleep, I told you that." I whisper. He's both wrong and right. He pulls me into his chest, and I let him. My eyes glance around the trees, darkening in the fading sunlight.

"I'll make her go, just don't leave me." I shake my head and sigh.

"Fine." I pull out of his arms and walk back through the trees alone, rejoining the party.

Chapter Thirty

As the sky darkens and the sun sets, torches are lit nearly every few feet to illuminate the third day of the week-long carnival. Fire-wielders are making their way through the crowd, showing off their talents. Oil sprays from their mouth onto the lit torches, causing sparks to fly through the air. The collective gasps and clapping drown out my own thoughts as I walk through our guests. Laris is close by, following my every step. Tano has disappeared, no doubt following his king. I also have no idea where Donovan ran off to, but I silently hope he is enjoying himself.

My hands graze one of the many buffet tables, my fingers gently plucking a cube of chocolate into my mouth before taking the glass of red wine that is held out to me. It isn't nearly as delicious as the wine I have in my room, but it does enough to numb the emotions that are threatening to break free. I smile at the staff milling about, completing their duties as I continue to walk through the masses.

There are hundreds of guests here, and I am having a hard time placing all of them. I know there are the noblemen of our lands and their families, my father and some of his court, Scarlett and her family, the Noterran councilmen, and the staff and their families. Everyone is enjoying the food and drinks, the activities and games. The carnival is a big hit and while I worked on some of it, I am grateful I delegated some of the work to others. I don't think I could have done such a good job. Mostly because I didn't care. These types of events don't mean much to me, but I am glad to know it is appreciated by our citizens.

My chest is heavy, both with confusion and despair, as I continue to make my way to the outer edge of the crowd. I knew Tobias had a past, I knew there were others. Theo is the one who told me that. I also knew one of them was pregnant, but I hadn't been expecting to see her. To be *near* her. To see the effect she has on Tobias. To hear that she loves him. What is there not to love? I can see how he captivates the attention of nearly every woman he passes, even Scarlett isn't immune to his beauty.

I can't even lie to myself about her beauty, either. Her auburn hair was long and loose. It curled right near her backside in fiery waves. The green dress complimented her hair and her pale skin, perfectly. I couldn't see the color of her eyes, but her heart-shaped face and full lips tells me she'd be beautiful with any color. She is the kind of beauty that should be queen, I almost wish she had the job instead of me.

I can't help picturing what her and Tobias's child might look like. Would it have her red hair, or his golden-copper strands. Would they have his bright blue eyes and strong cheekbones? Would they be quick-tempered or soft and gentle? Would they be tall or short? Kind or conniving? What about our children? Will we even have them? It's been weeks and I still have not fallen pregnant, despite our attempts. Maybe there is something wrong with me.

I single tear forms in my eyes, and I blink it away. I can't change the situation, nothing I feel or say will get rid of their child. I can only hope that she leaves court, has the child somewhere else. It's not fair to Tobias to not be able to know his child, but I also feel like it's not fair to me. I can't help thinking about the child though. Will they grow up thinking their father abandoned them? Because that is what's happening, what I am forcing him to do. If we could keep the child without the woman, that would be fine, but then I could never forgive myself for forcing a mother to hand over her babe.

Nobody wins in this situation.

I finally reach the edge of the crowd and look over every single guest. Laughter fills the air, shouts of false fear when one of the flames gets too close. I can't make out anyone I know in the fading light. I, for once, enjoy the seclusion. Well, as secluded as I could be with Laris a few feet away. I enjoy being a spectator instead of a participant. I don't know where Scarlett ran off to, but I haven't seen her since earlier. I am sure she is familiarizing herself with everyone here, getting to know her new home as I had to.

I guess I should be grateful that Tobias offered to move Scarlett and her family here. I know he means well, and this surprise makes up for a lot of the tension between us. He knows I feel alone here, and he did what he could to remedy that.

A soft thud behind me makes me jump as I turn to face Theo. I glance at the palace wall behind him and realize he had to have jumped from there. I offer him a small smile as he steps over to me.

"Nora." He reaches out and I hesitantly place my hand in his as he brings it up to his lips. "Are you enjoying the party?" His hair is unbound, flopping in front of his eyes. He releases my hand to brush it back out of his face, his fingers catching on the pale strands. I can still see a shadow of a scar along his nose from where he had stitches.

"Yes, it is quite different from the parties in Chatis, though I was never invited to those." I turn back to face the crowd as he comes to stand next to me. I take a small sip of the wine, and it burns my throat as it goes down.

"Why are you not out there enjoying yourself?" He asks as he follows my gaze.

"I could ask the same of you." I murmur, staying quiet. Talking to Theo feels like a crime and I am worried if I raise my voice, it will reveal my pulsing heart rate and uneven breath in his presence.

"I'm sorry I never said goodbye." He says after a few moments of silence.

"I don't think you necessarily had a choice, Theo. You were shipped off." I take another sip of my mediocre wine, why couldn't it be the delicious pink one I like so much?

"Still. I didn't like leaving without an explanation." He responds. He keeps his voice quiet, probably to make sure Laris can't hear us. I glance at Theo out of the corner of my eye and see that he is staring at me.

"Tobias said you went to the border?"

"Yes, I just went to make sure our men were ready should a Labisian agent attempt to cross the border." I nod and take another sip of my wine. This wine doesn't quite numb me as quickly. Maybe the different colors affect the strength? I don't even know why I'm drinking it; it's disgusting.

"All is well?" I keep my voice even, emotionless.

"Yes, everyone is prepared." He mutters, uninterested. "Is this how it's going to be?" He asks, his voice louder than it has been.

"Excuse me?" I ask, turning my head towards him.

"Are you going to continue to be cold towards me? Despite any other feelings, we are still friends. Family even." My eyebrows pinch together as I turn my body to fully face him.

"I don't know what you want from me, Theo. I am married, you are engaged. There is nothing between us." Lying has become too easy here, especially when it comes to him.

"Nora–"

"Don't call me that." I say through gritted teeth.

"*Elaenor*, I don't believe you. There has always been something between us." I shake my head, squeezing my eyes shut. "I may marry Scarlett, but I will always love you." He admits and I feel my breath catch.

"Don't." I warn. I blink back the tears gathering in my eyes and turn away from him. *Damnit.*

"I love you. I will *always* love you. I will always want to be with you and only you." I glance nervously at Laris behind me, but he had stepped away at some point, leaving us alone, which makes me even more nervous. "I know that nothing can happen, but I will always want what is best for you, and that is *not* Tobias." He admits.

"You promised me he would be kind and treat me well." My voice is cracking from the stupid emotions filling my mind. Why does Theo have to make me feel so small, so in need of his presence to breathe?

"I know–"

"He loves me." Another lie.

"He loves no one but himself. You know that as well as I do." I do. I had suspicions that Tobias truly didn't love me, that he just loved his control over me. I've just been too afraid to admit it.

"Theo–"

"Has he hit you again?" I open my mouth to say something, but clamp it shut. "What else has he done?" I shake my head and look down at my feet. "What about Nylah?" I lift my head abruptly.

"Nylah?" I ask.

"The woman he got pregnant."

"How do you know about her?" My pulse quickens, my fingers tightening on the thin stem of the glass.

"I'm the one who escorted her out of the palace."

"Well you didn't do a good job, she's back." I mutter, draining what's left of my bitter red wine.

"She's going to stay. I know my brother. He wants to know if that child is his."

"I *know*, Theo. Don't you think I know that? That I know what he is going to choose in the long run?" I say with a sigh, my head buzzing. "It doesn't matter what I say, what I want, what I do. She's not going anywhere, and neither am I. He has made it very clear that I do not have a choice in this." I gather the skirts of my dress and start to walk towards the party, in search of more wine, *better* wine.

"Elaenor." I shake my head, but he grabs my arm anyway. "If I marry Scarlett, I will get to stay in court. I'll get to stay near you." My eyes meet his and I let the sorrow I feel peek through. He's close, close enough for me to feel his breath fanning across my face. Sweet grass and spring air. It's as if the first season of the year is embodied in him, that he himself is spring personified. It takes everything in me not to lean forward, feel his lips on mine.

"None of this matters. Nothing matters. Not to me. Not to Tobias. I feel nothing anymore." I admit before stepping away from his touch and back to the crowd. I don't look behind me as I push my way through the people. I hand the wineglass to a server before turning towards the palace. I quickly walk up the steps to the entryway, the double doors open to allow a steady stream of guests to enter and exit upon will. The hall is filled with more guests and more tables of food. It seems there is enough to feed a small country.

I turn down one of the hallways that I know holds a staircase, and gratefully find that it is empty. My footsteps echo across the room, the torches lighting everything up into an orange haze. It is only when I finally reach the royal chambers do I realize that Laris didn't follow me, and I am alone for the first time in a long time.

I sigh loudly before pushing open the double doors to my room and shutting them behind me. The room is dark besides the light from the fireplace, but I make my way to the bar cart by memory. I fill a glass to the brim with sweet, pink wine and drain it before stepping away. I walk up to the balcony and stifle a chill as the wind catches me off guard. I step back out into the night and glance down at the festivities below.

I can see smaller groups gathered around certain performers or tables of food. A group in the middle is dancing and spinning to the music. Violins and cellos are stuffed in the corner where a group of people play beautiful sounds that make you want to get lost in yourself. I yawn and rest my chin on the marble railing. My eyes shift to the night sky, focusing on the stars. Deep blue and black skies sparkling with thousands and thousands of stars. My mother used to say that each star was a soul, that when we pass, we return to our rightful place in the sky.

I hope that I end up there some day, but I also sometimes wish for the chance to disappear completely. Spending an eternity in the sky doesn't sound all that appealing. I just want to simply cease to exist.

I jump and a small squeal escapes my lips as the first firework goes off in the distance. The sky illuminates with red and purple sparks before fading. Another goes off and blue sparks explode in the sky this time. A bunch of them start to explode, filling the sky with a rainbow of colors and sparks.

I glance back down at the party and see the crowd illuminated in a bunch of different colors. The crowd parts and I see Tobias walk through it, his silver crown sparkling. He looks around frantically, and I feel like he might be looking for me. I don't move or even attempt to let him know I'm safe, I just watch.

He stops looking and motions towards someone. I just barely make out Theo getting down on one knee and proposing to Scarlett in front of the crowd, everyone cheering and clapping. She throws her arms around his neck, and he spins her around. I let a tear escape my eyes, trailing down my cheek, before I wipe it away and step back into the dark room.

Chapter Thirty-One

I ready myself for bed, taking a short bath and changing into a warmer nightdress. The temperatures have steadily decreased during the evening, requiring a new season of clothes. I sit up in the bed, hugging my knees to my chest. My hand leaves my knees and reaches in between the mattress, but my fingers come up empty. I still haven't been able to find my dagger, and a part of me knows it was Tobias who took it. I secretly hope he moved it somewhere safe, but I also know he is probably hiding it from me. I slide off the bed and go to the writing desk. Maybe it is in there?

There are stacks of parchment on top, some half-finished letters in Donovan's handwriting. I open one of the drawers and see the wax seal of our crest and some writing pens. I open the next drawer and see a small, black journal, reminding me of the one Tobias wrote in on my first night here. My fingers lightly brush the leather exterior before pulling it out. I glance around the room quickly before I step over to the lit fireplace and open the journal. A folded piece of parchment falls to the floor, and I bend down to pick it up.

The shipment is set to arrive prior to the princess's arrival. Master Pakin is under the assumption that it will be used for research and has agreed to boil it down into a syrup. Dosage should be increased as needed for desired effect.

Long live the King

What is he talking about? What shipment and what research? Is this about some kind of drug? Are they conducting research on some sort of medical warfare? I mean drugging your enemies could prove useful, maybe that is what it is for?

I shove the slip of parchment back into the journal and open it up on a random page. The page is filled with different numbers followed by either cc or kg, like he was testing the drug on different subjects.

Dose 1: Taken with food, no effect. 35cc's used on 55kg.
Dose 2: Taken with other liquids to dilute taste, no effect. 35cc's used on 55kg.

I turn a few pages past some scribbles and math equations.

Dose 17: Dosages have steadily increased, utilizing liquids to mask taste. Desired effect achieved, will continue usage as needed Current 60cc on 55kg used multiple times daily.

I wonder who he is drugging, someone who is 55kg. Maybe they are doing it to Jeremiah and that's why he's been keeping him alive. Are they using him as a test rat? I can hear the clanking of armor in the hall, and I quickly run to the writing desk, slipping the journal back where I found it. I get the drawer closed and collapse onto the couch before the door opens. I calm my breathing, attempting to look like I have been relaxing here the entire time.

"Ela, where have you been?" Tobias asks as he shuts the door behind him. "Laris and Tano have been scouring the grounds looking for you. We nearly sent the entire army out searching in case you were taken! Why did you slip away?" He's angry, his hands on his hips.

"I didn't slip away. I just walked in here, they didn't follow me." I shrug and stand from the couch, turning my back to him. I climb the two steps up the bed and climb onto my side.

"No, they said you slipped away." I take my place back at the top of the bed, hugging my knees to my chest.

"Then they must not have been paying attention." He scoffs and walks up to the bed. "Have you heard from Lord Danieas?" I ask, raising my head to look up at him. I can't make out his expression in the dark, but I could almost see his eyes narrowing.

"What do you mean?"

"When will Erik return?"

"He is a citizen of Chatis, Elaenor, we can't just force him to return. He will come back when it's allowed." I narrow my eyes this time as he sits on the edge of the bed. "You missed the engagement."

"I watched from the balcony." I respond, returning my cheek to my knees.

"What's wrong with you?"

"Where's my dagger?"

"Why are you asking so many questions tonight?"

"Where is it?" He stares at me in the darkness before standing and disappearing into the dressing room. I lift my head to try and peer into the darkened chamber, but I don't see him. He returns a few moments later and sets the dagger on my nightstand.

"Here."

"Why did you take it?"

"I was worried you were going to hurt yourself." I snatch it off the nightstand and clutch it to my chest. It vibrates in my hands, shooting electricity through my veins. It even looks as if it's glowing green in the dim light.

"I'm not going to hurt myself." I say softly as I slip it under my pillow. He sighs before bending down to press his lips to my forehead. I still and wait for him to pull back. "What is going on with Jeremiah?" Tobias groans and steps down from the bed and over to the wine on the table. He stills when he sees my empty glass and reaches for it but hesitates. I watch as he leaves the glass, walks over to the barcart and grabs a glass of bourbon instead.

"He's dead." My eyes widen and I drop my knees to the bed.

"What?" I say in disbelief. That fast? He's just dead?

"He wasn't giving us any information, so we dealt with him" My hands shake, and I don't know if it is relief or fear I am feeling. "Does that not bring you comfort?"

"No. What if there are more and he was the only chance we had of finding them? What if I could have spoken to him and gotten more out of him?" I counter.

"It doesn't matter. If there are more, they won't get to you. As *long* as you keep Laris and Tano with you." He takes a long sip of his bourbon and sighs. "Will you tell me what's wrong with you tonight?" I bite the inside of my cheek to keep from yelling about the journal and asking what drug he is researching.

"It was just a shock seeing my father." I lie. He walks up to the bed, placing the glass on the nightstand before sitting on the edge.

"My love, he can't hurt you either." I nod and he grabs my arms, pulling me onto his lap. "I promise that I am here to protect you. I love you." I nod against his chest as he wraps his arms around me. I don't know what I feel anymore or if what he feels is real. Theo says he's incapable of loving anyone other than himself, and I agreed with him.

"Do you?" I murmur against his chest. He rests his chin on the top of my head.

"I love you so much, Ela. I promise." I pull back and look into the little bit of blue visible in the dim light. I lean forward and gently press my lips to his. He relaxes as soon as our lips touch, his hands finding my face.

"Don't lie to me. Don't keep things from me. I deserve to know when it affects me." I whisper against his parted mouth. He nods.

"I promise. I won't keep things from you anymore." He whispers back before wrapping his arms around my waist. I kiss him again, letting my lips part, inviting his tongue. He twists until I am laying under him on the bed. My fingers tangle in his hair as he situates himself between my hips.

He is still clothed, but he pushes himself against me. He groans against my lips as I lift my hips to meet his. His hand slides down across my stomach, slipping under my underwear. His fingers don't hesitate before he shoves two inside me. I flinch, my legs twitching under him.

The delicious pleasure radiates through me as his fingers swirl around inside me, his thumb pressing firmly against the little bundle of nerves at the center of my core. Even if I am angry, confused, lost, this is always easy. Feeling this way, letting him touch me this way. I don't have to think about it, I just have to relax into it.

His fingers slip out of me as he pulls my underwear down. I lift my hips, helping him slide them over my backside. His lips tear from mine, trailing down my chest before softly biting onto one of my nipples through the thin silk. I yelp, my back arching. My fingers stay tangled in his hair as he moves farther down. His lips brushing the inside of my thigh before moving to the other side. He slides off the bed, taking my underwear with him. He kneels down and his tongue continues what his fingers started. I moan, my fingers gripping into his hair, tighter as I move my hips in tune with his tongue.

The pressure builds and builds, burning through every vein in my body. My legs begin to shake, and my breath quickens. His fingers slam into me while he sucks and licks my clit. I shake harder as I feel the pressure rising. He groans against my skin, a third finger slipping in. I scream out as I find release, shuddering against his lips.

He stands, bringing his fingers to his mouth to suck on them while he maintains eye contact with me. He quickly rips his shirt off and steps out of his pants. The evidence of his arousal is clear as he climbs over me, settling between my legs. I put my hand on his chest to stop him and he freezes, his brows pinching together in confusion.

I push on his chest until he is sitting up. I sit up on my knees and gently guide him down onto his back. My heart is still racing as I pull my nightdress over my head, my long hair falling in waves against my bare back. I don't know what I am doing, but I fake as much confidence as I can. I climb over him, straddling his thighs. His eyes don't leave mine as I lift my hips and gently lower myself onto him. His head falls back, his lips parting. My breath catches as I slide all the way down, reeling at the fullness of him. It's deeper this way, and I moan as I settle myself on top of him.

I move slowly and he groans. I pick up the pace slightly and his fingers dig into my hips. My hands rest against his chest as I ride him, letting my body move of its own accord. He sits up quickly, one of his arms snaking around my waist, the other holding himself up on the mattress. I press my lips to his and move faster. I can feel myself rubbing against his skin, friction causing the pressure to return.

His breathing quickens as does mine as we move as one. His eyes don't leave mine as we both shake. His fingers tighten on my back, his pulse racing. A ragged sound escapes his lips, his breath fanning across my face.

"Don't stop." He whispers as I move against him. A small whimper comes out of me as I feel my release coming.

I watch his face, his perfectly sculpted eyes and mouth, both open lazily with satisfaction. This man, this crazy unnerving man whom I can't help but love.

He's confusing. He's terrifying. But he can be gentle, and sweet and make me feel like the luckiest woman in the world. But he can also ruin me. He can break me and mold me into whomever he wants, and I would let him. I would let him change me, make me into the wife of his dreams, because I love him.

He grits his teeth as I explode around him, lights sparking behind my eyelids. I yell out as he finds his release at the same time. Our breath mixes as he falls back, taking me with him. I lay my head on his sweaty chest, his arms wrapped around me. We don't move for a few seconds, but when I can tell he thinks enough time has passed for conception, he rolls over on top of me. He slowly slides out and a breathy moan comes out at the feeling. He kisses the tip of my nose before sliding off the bed.

He disappears for a second before returning with a cold, wet cloth and wiping between my legs. I roll onto my side and force myself into a sitting position. He's still wiping himself down when it just comes out.

"Did you kill Erik?" I clamp my lips shut as he looks up at me. I have no idea why that question just escaped my lips, but I can't take it back now.

"What?" He asks, bewildered.

"Did you kill Ser Danieas?" He drops the cloth onto the floor and bites his lower lip. He sighs before walking over and leaning over me. His nose stops about an inch in front of mine.

"Why would you think I killed your guard?" He asks. I expect an attitude, but he's quiet, questioning.

"He's been gone for two weeks, and I haven't heard anything about his return. I would have heard something if he was forced to stay in Chatis." I mutter, rolling my lips.

"I did not kill Erik, but," He pauses and rests his forehead against mine. I don't move. "He is dead." I gasp and lean back, my eyes wide. He's dead. Erik is dead. After *everything*.

"Tobias." My voice cracks as I try to push past him to get to the floor. He puts his arm out, holding me to the bed.

"Ela, listen to me. I did not kill him. He died of infection." I shake my head, tears freely pouring down my face. "Master Pakin was doing everything he could to save him, but when he reached Chatis, he had a fever."

"No." I shake my head, closing my eyes. This can't be happening.

"The menders there tried everything they could, but he died that same day. I've been too worried to tell you. That's why I had Scarlett brought here, so you still had someone." He's soft, reassuring, but I just want to scream.

"No, he was fine!" I yell, collapsing back onto the bed. I can see his soft orange hair, his smile, his bright eyes that looked at me with such duty. I can hear his laugh as he catches my ladies and I calling his brother Lord Hairy. I can still remember the pure delight on his face during his swearing in ceremony. Day after day he found some excuse to keep my father away from me. He never failed to protect me, to put me first. But now he's gone.

"I am so sorry. I received word almost immediately, but I couldn't find the heart to tell you. You've lost so much already." I let the sobs wreak havoc through my body as I cry. He pulls me onto his lap, holding me close as I cry as hard as I possibly can.

He can't be gone.

He was fine.

He was healing so nicely, Master Pakin even told me that. Unless they were lying to me.

"I shouldn't have sent him. I shouldn't have sent him away." I stammer through the crying.

"It is not your fault. He wouldn't have made it anyway. There was nothing we could do, my love."

Chapter Thirty-Two

Morning comes and goes, and I refuse to leave the bed. Lydia tried twice to get me into a bath, but I refused to move. Scarlett came in and sat with me for a while, telling me about the arrangements being made for their wedding. She said she asked for an outdoor wedding, and they agreed, so they will be filling the courtyard with flowers and vines. She's trying everything to keep me distracted and I love her for it, but even thinking about my best friend's wedding isn't enough to break me out of this spell.

She tried to talk to me about Erik, but I couldn't hear her. Hear her say she was sorry and that she wishes she could do something to cheer me up. I wish there was something she could do too. She didn't know either and when I heard Tobias whispering to her about it before she came over to me, I could see the tears pooling in her eyes. He had been her friend, too. She was always with me, as was he. He was the big brother who annoyed us but always made us feel safe, untouchable. Especially when we were doing things we weren't supposed to.

She stayed as long as she could before someone named Malia came and collected her for bridal fittings. She told me she requested a pink dress. I thought she was kidding, but she wasn't. She figured that if I could get married in a red dress, one she is insanely jealous of, she could get married in pink. I can only assume Malia is one of Scarlett's ladies, as she will have some to attend to her once she becomes Noterra's only princess. I'm happy for her and her rise in status, but I can't bring myself to feel anything but sorrow, emptiness. I barely participated in any conversations, even when Theo and Scarlett came in before dinner to see if I wanted to join them outside. I don't answer, I just stare at the windows, watching the sun fade away and deepen the sky.

Food is brought and then removed as the day goes on, but I still lay here perfectly still, never moving. Tobias came in and tried to force me to eat a few times, but he knew it was pointless. Instead he pulled a nightdress over my head, so I wasn't naked under the blankets, and put thick socks on my feet to keep me warm since I had all of the windows open. He left me with a kiss on the forehead and a promise that everything will be okay.

Fireworks erupt outside as the sun fully disappears and I still don't move. I can't find it in myself to feel anything. If I let myself feel, it'll break me. Too much has happened. I have endured too much. I can't go through anything else. So if I don't allow myself to feel, to do anything, then I won't get hurt again.

At least that's what I tell myself.

Master Pakin comes in at some point and offers me a milky liquid in a small vial. I take it without fuss and relish in the deep sleep that comes quickly after.

Tobias is still in bed when I wake in the morning. The sun is shining, the birds chirping. It's cooler today than it has been, another sign that summer is ending. I slide off the mattress and nearly jump when my feet meet the icy marble, which leaves me questioning where my socks went. I step into the fur slippers by the nightstand and walk out to the balcony. My legs feel stiff, and I feel a little sore in my core, which is strange. It feels almost like it did when I lost my virginity, but not as bad. Maybe I am going to get my monthly bleed again. I hope not, that means I am not pregnant.

The festivities from last night are being cleaned up, with the great lawn being readied for today. People are running about cleaning up trash and dishes that litter nearly every surface. You would think some crazy party went on instead of a carnival, but I guess they are more or less the same thing. I feel horrible for those who have to clean up after these events, I only hope that they get to enjoy them too.

I stopped paying attention to what this week is supposed to entail. Each day something new happens, with the exception of the nightly fireworks. I am pretty sure the royal ball is today, which means we only have another two days of events. I have no desire to partake in the ball, but I know my presence isn't a request, it's a requirement. This entire week is put on to celebrate Tobias and I becoming king and queen, but it almost feels like we are bragging and pushing our ascension into everyone's face. Tobias told me that everyone loves welcoming a new king and queen and this is all for them as much as it is for us, but I still don't get it.

I look over to the left, thinking I'll see Theo's balcony, but I don't. I can't get his face out of my head, telling me loves me and that he doesn't want me with Tobias. What does he expect me to do? Run away from my husband and my kingdom? I have no choice; everyone has made that perfectly clear.

Even if I run, choose a life without any of them, what would it entail? I don't have Erik to keep me safe, Scarlett wouldn't leave now that she's engaged. I couldn't go back to Chatis and see my father, see the disappointment in his face. I don't have anyone on my side. Just like I told Erik when he was in the infirmary, everyone here sees me as a body for Tobias to utilize. He even said I was the queen he'd play when advantageous, whatever that means. I have no idea what I have gotten myself into. I never thought my adult life would be filled with even more hurt and despair than my childhood.

I return to the room and glance over at Tobias's sleeping body. He's snoring softly, his skin a deep tan from the sun exposure the last few days. I, too, have tanned a little. I have freckles appearing across my nose and cheekbones as my skin starts to deepen to a light olive. I always wondered if I would be the type of person who burns instead of tans, but I am glad to see that I have the ability to darken into a color other than red.

Tobias looks at peace the way he's laying. His face is soft, relaxed, and vulnerable. My feelings for my husband are confusing, fleeting, everchanging, but today. Today I feel nothing. Today I am numb, and I think I'd rather like to be numb forever. I turn away from him and enter the large bathing chamber. After a few moments, steaming water and bubbles caress my body as I slowly sink down.

The sweet smell of roses assaults my sinuses as I take a deep breath. I asked Lydia for something muskier, like vanilla and sugar, to scent my bath salts and oils, but it seems roses are the nation's flower in everything, including toiletry scents. The tub is deep enough to cover everything, leaving only my head poking out above the surface. I feel safe, protected, deep in the water like this. Like nothing could touch me.

I close my eyes and dig deep, looking for any tether to my green-eyed gentleman that seems to appear when he wants. I feel nothing, but emptiness. I don't want to go under the water, he said it wasn't necessary, but what if he's wrong? I push again at whatever mental shields I am able to picture, letting them open.

"Hello?" I call out to him in whatever mental chasm he is in but get no response. *"Please, speak to me."* I squeeze my eyes tighter, picturing him standing right next to the tub. I picture his green eyes glowing in the darkness, his inky hair with the white streak that is slowly growing. *Please.*

"Elaenor." His soft voice flits through my mind. I jump and open my eyes, but the bathing chamber is empty.

"Are you there?" I respond after my heart has had a chance to relax.

"I'm here." His voice is muffled, as if it's far away. Like our connection, whatever it is, isn't as strong.

"What is your name?" I don't waste any time as I close my eyes again. I can faintly see him in the darkness behind my lids, just a mere shadow. He's quiet for a moment and I thought he had left, but I can feel a small charge of electricity.

"You are quite persistent." I can hear him smiling and I can faintly make out his perfect white teeth and the twin dimples on his cheeks.

"Just tell me and stop speaking in riddles, you loon. And don't tell me you can't say. That's crap and you know it."

"As you wish, my queen. My name is Enzo." He replies eventually. I nearly yell out in accomplishment but stay silent.

"Is it short for anything?"

"Yes. It's short for Enzo." I mentally roll my eyes at him.

"Am I going crazy, Enzo?" He chuckles.

"No, Elaenor. You are not crazy. If you were, then that would mean I am and I think I am rather sane, in comparison to the rest of our cruel world."

"Why can I talk to you? Are you real? How is this possible?"

"Yes, I am very much a real person. The answers you seek I cannot provide, not yet. You'll know soon enough." His voice stays soft, inviting. Almost as if he can tell I am not okay mentally. *"Are you alright? It hasn't been as easy to feel you as of late."* I am not alright, but talking about it doesn't sound very cathartic. I ignore him.

"Please tell me something, anything." I beg, needing something to distract me. Something else to focus on besides my current life.

"Promise me something, Elaenor."

"Okay."

"Whatever happens, even if you think you are going to die, do not fight back. I know that is asking for a lot, but if you fight back, I won't see you. You won't find me. You need to survive. He won't kill you. You have to trust me." My eyes open and my pulse skips.

"What do you mean?" I shut my eyes again, but I can barely see him now.

"Promise me." I can tell he is yelling, but he's getting quieter. The image of him behind my eyes is fading, returning to black.

"I promise." It's silent in my mind and I push out again, searching.

"Enzo?" The gentle drum of electricity dissipates, and I am left alone.

A chill runs down my spine as the adrenaline filters out of my system. What was that? How was that even possible? I have to be crazy. Speaking to someone that isn't here should not be possible. And what about his promise? He won't kill me. Who does he mean? Tobias? He told me to not fight back, that I won't die, but that if I do fight back, I won't find him. Is he saying that if I fight back, I'll die?

What does he know that I don't?

I stay in the bath until the water turns cold, before getting out of it and wrapping myself in a large towel. My mind is still reeling as I step out of the bathing chamber. Tobias is drinking coffee and reading a letter on the couch. He looks up at me as I step into the room, dripping water everywhere.

"Hi." He says, startled. I walk up to the table and pop a grape into my mouth. I can feel my stomach devouring it instantly, starving after going a whole day without anything to fill the pit in my abdomen. "How are you today?" He asks as I pluck another grape off the vine and stick it in my mouth.

"Is the ball today?" I whisper as I pour sweetened cream into the other mug of coffee. He sets his letter down, watching me prepare my coffee silently. I don't look up at him, but I can tell he's confused. I don't blame him. I was silent and comatose yesterday, and now I'm acting like nothing has happened. Numb. I just want to be numb.

"Yes, this evening." I nod and walk around the table to sit next to him. My hair is dripping water everywhere, soaking the plush cushion and dripping down my bare back. I don't mind that I am still in a towel, the cold air is causing a chill to run down my spine. That's all I want to feel, physical sensations. My mind can't handle anything emotional. I lean my head onto his shoulder, and he presses his lips to my wet scalp. "Are you alright?" I nod and lift my head so I can take a sip of the rich coffee, the syrupy cream coating my tongue. He stays quiet and just watches me pick at the various pastries on the tray.

"When the carnival is over, can we go to the beach?" I ask.

"We can, but it'll be autumn. With the wind and the water, it'll be rather cold and unenjoyable."

"I don't care."

"Okay, then yes. We can go." I nod and tuck my legs under me, cradling my mug against my chest. "Ela, are you alright?"

"I will be." I say into my coffee before taking another sip. *I will be.*

"I wish you would talk to me." He reaches over and throws some of my wet strands over my shoulder, his fingers rubbing my neck softly. "I'll be here when you are ready."

"Has she left?" I ask without looking at him.

"Who?" His fingers freeze on my neck.

"Nylah?" He sighs, dropping his hand.

"Yes, I watched her get put in a carriage yesterday morning. She's leaving and heading for Tatus. As far away from us as possible."

"Good."

"I'm sorry." He sounds sorry, but it doesn't matter.

"I don't want to talk about it." I turn and look at him and his face falls, his lips pressing into a thin line. I take a slow, deep breath before setting my coffee down. "I believe you, Tobias. I know it was an accident and you are sorry. I'd like to just get past this." He nods and opens his mouth to speak, but someone knocks on the door.

"Enter." Tobias calls out before picking his mug back up. Donovan enters and seems relieved to see me out of bed.

"Good morning, Your Graces." He bows slightly and I offer him a smile. "Lady Scarlett is here with your ladies to assist in getting you ready for the ball, Your Grace."

"I will make myself scarce." Tobias says as he stands. He leans over and cups my cheek, tilting my head towards him. "I love you." I nod and he kisses my forehead before taking his coffee and exiting the room.

Chapter Thirty-Three

Scarlett lounges on the bed eating the leftover grapes from breakfast while I am readied. She is already dressed in a stunning blue gown that hugs her in all the right places before sweeping to the floor in silky waves. Her chestnut hair braided into a coronet on top of her head with a thin silver tiara stuck in. She was excited to show it to me this morning, saying that it was the original crown that was created for any future princesses, but Amaya never successfully bore a girl. It makes me wonder why it wasn't given to me, but I also know that Evreux was obsessed with seeing me in Amaya's crown.

Malia did her makeup as well and applied some kohl to her lids and a pinkish stain to her lips to match the rosy glow across her cheekbones. She looks effortlessly beautiful while Lydia has to put in actual work to make me presentable.

I opted for an all-black gown today, loathing the idea of stepping into another crimson dress. Much like Scarlett's, my dress features a tight, strapless bodice lined with lace and a silk skirt that flows down to the floor like water. I chose flats instead of heels due to the length of time I'll have to wear this gown. Lydia applied my usual red lip stain and darkened my lashes. Almost every bruise and wound has healed, leaving subtle scars that will fade with time. I am grateful for the fact that I no longer need layers of creams applied to hide them, it did nothing but make me feel dirty.

I ask Lydia to keep my hair down, enjoying the casual look of soft waves framing my face. I have seen a new white strand of hair every day this past week, and I have ripped them out each time. I'm going to eventually end up with half of my hair missing, but I just can't see what the stress of everything is doing to my body. Lydia obliges to my request and only adds my silver crown on top, twisting it slightly so the teeth on the bottom catch on my hair, holding it in place. She brushes oil that has a slight silver shimmer in it through the tresses, so it sparkles every time it catches the light.

It reminds me of my mother, and how my hair looks like the night sky filled with glitter. She was right.

Lydia offers me a smile and gentle touch of the cheek before she exits. I plop down on the bed next to Scarlett and pop a grape into my mouth. The sweet fruit explodes in my mouth, and it nearly leaves me drooling. I only ate a single croissant this morning with my coffee. I'm starving but eating right now feels more like a chore than a desirable act. I know it's not healthy, but all I want is wine.

"How was your evening?" I ask as I steal more grapes from the crystal bowl.

"It was dreamy." She swoons, rolling onto her back. "Theo took me out to the stables, and I met Dawner, then we had a picnic under the stars and watched the fireworks go off." She sighs and I almost mimic her. I, too, wish for a romantic, swoon-worthy evening, but Tobias's days of trying to woo me have passed and I honestly don't even know if I would want to participate in anything like that with Tobias. There is no point.

"I'm glad you are happy here." Is all I can muster as a response. She rolls back on her side and looks at me.

"I hate how sad you are, Elaenor." She pouts slightly, her bottom lip sticking out. I reach out and flick it, which results in us both laughing hysterically.

"I'll be fine, I've just gone through a lot, and I need time to process." I admit after the fit of laughter. I haven't told her about my mother's revelations yet, but once the carnival is over and things are more relaxed, I plan on talking it out with her. I just don't want to ruin her fun or put a damper on the ball.

"Once things are back to normal, we can just start fresh. Both of us." I nod and she offers me a smile before she slides off the bed, her heels clicking on the marble floors. "Alright, let's go." She grabs my wrist and yanks me off the bed and I yelp as her fingers pinch me. Looping my arm in hers, we walk out into the hallway. There are less people milling about today, and the emptiness is welcome. Tano is there to follow us around today, keeping a healthy distance.

"How are Laenie and Rhea? I miss them." I say as we turn the corner.

"Oh my gods! I forgot to tell you!" She exclaims, pinching my arm again.

"Scarlett!" I whine as I rub my welting skin.

"Rhea kissed me!" I freeze and my eyes widen.

"What?" I exclaim loudly as she turns to face me, forcing us to stop in the middle of the hallway.

"Yes, it was only days after you left. The three of us met up for lunch and to talk about everything. Laenie told me she was approached by Reggie-"

"Reggie?"

"Reginald, apparently that's Lord Hairy's real name." She stifles a laugh.

"What kind of a name is *Reginald*?" I snicker.

"Anyway, Laenie and him are dating, although I don't think they've done anything that *doesn't* involve a closed door." She laughs again and I join in. It feels nice to be able to laugh and joke around with my best friend as if nothing has changed. It feels good just to smile. "After lunch, Laenie left us to go find Reggie for another bedroom *dalliance*, and Rhea and I walked to the docks together, hoping to see some men with their shirts off of course. I told her I was just spending my days shopping and relaxing and that's when she told me she had something to tell me." Her eyes widen as she grins, a small squeal coming out of her mouth.

"*And?*" I push.

"She told me she likes me and she's hoping that since we don't have to marry for money or rise in station, that we could be together." She blurts it out in a rushed sentence before biting her lip.

"What did you say?" I grip her forearm impatiently.

"I told her I would think about it. And then she just grabbed my face and kissed me!" She covers her face with her hands, hiding her blushing cheeks.

"Did you kiss her back?"

"Well," She pauses and looks around the hallway. "I'll just say that we didn't leave the woods for a while." I scream and we both jump up and down dramatically. I look back at Tano, who is trying to look busy and *not* like he is snooping in on our conversation.

"I cannot believe that happened! What happened next?" She threads her arm through mine again and starts walking down the hallway again.

"Well, we stayed pretty much inseparable until your father showed up at my doorstep. He wanted my help in greeting some guests from Noterra. I obliged because I knew what he needed, a pretty face to impress the men." I roll my eyes. "When I reached the receiving room, Theo was there. He had just been talking to your father about the threats in Labisa, offering aid should they need it."

"I didn't know Theo went to Chatis." I mutter. Was this before or after he left for the border?

"Yeah, he stopped by on his way back to Noterra. Like I was saying, Theo was there, and well I fell in love instantly. He's so hot and kind and we hit it off." We turn another corner and head for the stairs leading down to the bottom floor. It seems Tobias was right, and I eventually did learn how to navigate the palace without paying attention. "He told me he was headed back to Noterra and had a letter from the king requesting my presence. I don't think your father knew; it was just by chance that he asked me to help out. In the letter, the king said he wanted to make the transition to your queenhood as easy as possible and asked if I would consider relocating to Noterra."

"I can't believe he did that." Tobias *could* be nice when he wanted. Why is that so hard for me to accept?

"I was excited and then I kept reading and it said if I accepted, the crown would donate enough money to classify my father as a Lord, making me fit to marry any station I please. I was excited, your father was not." She laughs, and I know she is picturing his face when it gets all red from frustration.

"That doesn't surprise me." I scoff as we start to descend.

"So I immediately sent a rider off to accept. By the time we got here, the king was waiting and mentioned that he would like to bestow his blessing for Theo and I to marry. We were both shocked, but at the end of the conversation we found ourselves agreeing. It's not a love match or a political match, but it gets me closer to you and out of Chatis, and Theo gets to marry someone he likes without being forced to marry elsewhere."

"It makes sense. I'm glad you said yes." Although it doesn't really make sense. I just think Tobias wanted to make Theo unavailable.

"Me too." She squeezes my arm as we reach the bottom floor.

"What about Rhea?" I ask, already forgetting about their time together. She sighs and drops my arm.

"I asked her to come to court and be one of our ladies." My eyes widen.

"What? What about Theo?" She looks around before pulling me to one of the benches lining the walls.

"I think I love her, and I am hoping that if I have them both, I'll be happy here."

"Scarlett, you can't have a mistress. It's not allowed."

"He'll never know. It'll be a secret, and even then, it's a woman not a man. It's not like I can fall pregnant. I'll still have Theo's children. I'm attracted to both sexes, Elaenor. Don't be a prude."

"I'm not a prude, I am just worried for your safety."

"You really think sweet Theo will send me off to be beheaded if I sleep, or not sleep, with another woman? I know men. I have been with *plenty* of them. He'll probably ask to join." A startled gasp leaves my lips, and we break out into another hysterical fit of laughter.

"Just be careful, please." She rolls her eyes and pulls me off the bench.

"I'll be careful, I promise." She squeezes my arm with hers as we walk to the large ballroom.

Candles are hanging on thin wire from the ceiling, lighting the room with a million little stars. Buffet tables line all of the walls, filled with trays and bowls ready for food and drinks. People are milling about trying to finish off all the preparations before it's too late. We look around the large room for a moment more before exiting into the hall. Tobias and my father are at the other end, engrossed in a heated conversation. Scarlett and I look at each other before slowly making our way over there.

"Husband." I say loudly and with a smile. His frown disappears as he looks over at me, taking me into his arms and kissing me gently.

"Your Grace." Scarlett says to Tobias and bows her head slightly. Tobias smiles at me before pulling back and I return it.

"Please, Scarlett, call me Tobias. We are going to be family soon." He smiles and then kisses her cheek. She blushes before turning to my father and narrowing her eyes. As a Lady, and soon to be princess, of Noterra, she no longer answers to the Chatisian King, and I can tell it pisses him off.

"Father." I say sternly, letting any anger I have fuel my words.

"Your Grace." He mutters before bowing deeply at the waist. I turn back to Tobias who is looking at my father with distaste.

"What is the matter?" I ask, looking up at Tobias. He looks down at me, his arm still around my waist. Cupping my cheek, he kisses my nose and then shakes his head. A silent command not to pry, but he knows I'll ask him later. I nod and pull out of his arms, looping mine through Scarlett's again. "We are going to go for a walk with Tano." I announce and we walk away.

"What was that?" Scarlett whispers as soon as we are out of earshot. I glance back at Tobias and my father, continuing their conversation animatedly and I shrug.

"I don't know, but I'll find out."

"You better share any juicy details." She whispers before pinching me for a third time.

Chapter Thirty-Four

The day goes by quickly as we walk the courtyard and explore. I introduced her to Sybil and Wyclif and then she proceeded to walk around the entire stable before pointing at a beautiful silver stallion claiming him as her own. He didn't have a name plate above his stall, so she yelled out until someone came running. She, very directly, instructed that a name plate be installed above the door stating that his name is Bijoy. We both laughed as he looked at Scarlett confused until I told him it was okay. He ran off so quickly that we both laughed even harder.

We ate lunch together by the stables and the grazing field, forcing Sybil and Bijoy to interact. They were both wary of each other but by the end of lunch, they were running across the grass side by side. We deemed it a success and then watched as the stablehands struggled to wrangle them back into their stalls. It seems Sybil and Bijoy only wanted to listen to us.

By the time we made our way back into the palace, the sun was setting, and we both smelled like hay. I found myself smiling the whole day, feeling more normal than I ever had. If this is a sign of how life will play out, maybe it won't nearly be as bad as I thought.

Despite the day, I still had Enzo in the back of my mind begging me to not fight back. He seems to think I'll be put in a position where I would want to fight, but I can't see that happening. After today, everything seems to be getting better. I asked for flowers to be sent to Chatis and placed on Erik's grave, which Donovan said he'd see to. While I miss my friend, I know that he had to have been hurting. He stood by my door for hours, protecting me all while he was suffering an infection. It still surprises me to think about it. To think he's gone that fast. I know Tobias meant well by keeping it from me, especially due to my assumed instability, but I still find a small piece of resentment towards him for it.

I take a deep breath as we enter the palace arm in arm. The music hits us quickly as the beautiful sounds of violin and pianoforte float through the halls. Laughter and voices slip through the music as we grow closer to the ballroom. Crowds of people are standing in the hall, all holding glasses of wine and champagne. They all turn towards me at the same time, making me freeze.

"Your Grace!" They all say seemingly as one. They bow and curtsy and I find my cheeks reddening.

"Hello." I say quietly and smile as they stand. They turn back towards their small groups and resume their talking.

"Was that just as weird to you as it was to me?" Scarlett whispers in my ear. My eyes widen and I nod in agreement, holding back laughter.

We enter the ballroom, and the smells of roasted meats, fruits, baked goods, and other culinary creations fill my nose as I take a deep breath. A hand yanks on my fingers pulling me away from Scarlett. I am spun twice before landing against a warm chest. My hands grip the black lapels of his jacket, and the scent of cedar overpowers the scent of food.

"My beautiful wife." Tobias whispers before dipping me and giving me a dramatic kiss. Clapping ensues around us, and I look around awkwardly as he stands me back up. "Did you have a good day? You caught some sun." His finger pokes my nose and I pretend to bite it.

"I did. Scarlett commandeered a horse and then we forced our horses to be friends." I giggle and his eyes brighten.

"You seem happier." I nod and lay my hands back on his chest.

"I feel happier." He leans down and brushes my cheek with his lips. Another hand grabs at my upper arm, but Tobias keeps me tightly against him. I look up to see Scarlett pouting.

"Dance with *me*." She says with a frown. I laugh again and lean up on my tiptoes to kiss Tobias before taking her outstretched hand.

We spin in circles and circles until we are dizzy and laughing. We drink glass after glass of wine and champagne and some other brown beverage that burns until we can barely stand. My crown slips off my head twice, with some random person catching it each time. After the second time, it ends up on Scarlett's head, in addition to her tiara, as she spins in place, her dress flowing around her like waves of water. I giggle and clap, encouraging her. She lifts her arms in the air and picks up her pace. People around us begin to clap and cheer.

She turns and lands right into someone's arms. Someone who is not Theo. He dips her and reaches for her face to kiss her before I pull her towards me. He looks at me with widened eyes before raising his hands apologetically. We both break out into laughter as we force our way through the crowd and towards more champagne.

I grab two glasses, handing her one, before downing mine. The champagne is cold and bubbly, gliding down my throat with a tickle. I set it down and grab another. I question whether or not I should, but I feel so good. My feet feel light, my head floating. The floor seems like it's spinning around me, and I close my eyes to relish in it. I can spin forever. When I open my eyes, Scarlett has disappeared. I frown and walk towards the open door.

I look up and down the hallway, but I don't see her. I take my glass and walk towards the open patio doors. The ballroom is on the bottom floor, but a fenced section off the ballroom creates a barrier between the courtyard and the hallway.

The air is crisp with a light wind. It's cold against my sweaty skin and I take a deep breath. I open my eyes to Theo standing a couple feet away from me, bathed in the moonlight. My heart skips a beat, and I can feel the blush reddening my cheeks. I lift the glass up to my lips and down it in a single gulp.

He's wearing a black jacket with matching trousers, casual but still put together. His hair is down, groomed so that it stays out of his face and tucked behind his ears. He's watching me as I watch him. I look around and set my empty glass on one of the tables off to the side.

"I've always wanted to fly." I stammer as I turn back to the railing. I kick off my flats and hoist one of my feet on top of the marble post. He cocks his head, watching me, a smirk forming. My other foot finds purchase and I shakily stand. A giggle escapes my lips as my feet feel numb.

"You're lucky you're on the bottom floor. I don't think you'll survive another jump off the second floor." His voice is quiet, floating through the air before gracing my ears with its melodious sound.

Gods, I could listen to him forever.

I smile and hiccup before jumping off the post onto the grass, attempting to be brave. At least I think I jump, but I not so gracefully fall face first towards the ground as my feet refuse to lift up. A scream lodges in my throat as the grass flies forward, but I never hit it. Theo catches me, his warm arms wrapping around my waist to hold me to his chest. He smells like grass, and I think I accidentally say that out loud because he raises an eyebrow.

"I've never heard someone refer to me as smelling like grass." He smirks before setting my feet onto the ground.

"It's better than smelling like dirt." I mutter, hiccupping from the champagne bubbles.

"Or like hay." I scoff and pull out of his arms.

"I do not smell like hay." He laughs, his hand finding my waist again. His hands are warm, and they fit against my sides as if they were made for me.

"You do smell like hay; you smell like you've been with the horses all day." His breath tickles my face and I smell whiskey. He's drunk. Just like me. His hand holds me against the small of my back, his other smoothing my hair away from my face.

"I *have* been with the horses all day." I say in between the hiccups that refuse to leave.

"Where is your crown? You look so pretty with your crown." He murmurs, his head leaning down slightly. I should push him away, run in the opposite direction, but I don't. My skin is heating everywhere he is touching, and I can't get enough. I don't know why, but I lift my head up nearly meeting his.

"Scarlett looks better in it." I whisper, his lips so close to mine.

"I don't think anyone could look better than you." His lips lightly brush mine.

"You smell like whiskey." I say, breathy.

"You smell like wine." He replies.

Before I can stop myself, I press into him. His free hand holds my face as my lips part, our tongues meeting. He pulls me tighter against him until there is no more space between us. We are all tongue and teeth, no grace or hesitance. Pure unrelenting desire urging us on. His hands hungrily search my body and I groan as he runs his hand along my backside. I can feel his desire growing, the hardened length pressing into my stomach.

"Theo." I whisper as I tangle my fingers in his hair, wanting him as close as possible. He bites my bottom lip before leaving a trail of kisses down my neck. My breathing grows ragged and then the nausea hits.

"Oh no." I whisper. I pull away and run towards a bush where I vomit away the gallons of wine I consumed. My throat is one fire, my lips swollen from his kiss.

"Your Grace." A deep voice causes me to look up and I jump. I sway slightly and see a very blurry Laris holding his hand out. He's handing me a handkerchief and I gladly take it, wiping at my mouth. I turn back around and see an empty courtyard. Theo is gone. My brows furrow as I turn back towards Laris. "Come on." He commands before gently guiding me back into the hall. "I didn't see anything." He whispers before his hand leaves my back. I glance up at him with a thankful smile before stepping through the open double doors.

Scarlett is first to find me, my crown still resting on her head. Her braids are half undone and she looks just as drunk as I feel. She grabs my arms and spins me and before long I am pulled back into the dancing, my kiss with Theo long forgotten. Tobias joins us at some point, his arms possessively wrapped around me as we dance until the early morning.

By the time we make it back to our room, I am still crownless and barefoot. Tobias and I are tripping over everything and at one point I end up sprawled out on the floor. He's laughing as he bends down to help me up, but I pull him down with me and he lands face first on the marble. I can't help but laugh in between my drunk hiccups as he pulls himself up. When I finally look at him through tears, his nose is bleeding.

"Oh gods, I am so sorry." I stammer and try to sit up. He wipes his nose with the back of his hand and stares at the red smudge before looking at me. His eyes darken and his jaw hardens as he stares at me. My smile falls and I think I knew what was coming before it happened.

His hand reaches out and grabs my hair, yanking me to my feet. I cry out in pain as he pulls me up the steps to the bed. I dig my nails into his arm as I slip on the marble steps. My knees hit the edge and I wince. I collapse on the ground by the bed when he lets go of me, a small tuft of hair hanging from his fingers. Tears well up in my eyes and I look up at him. He bends down, sitting on me, as he grabs my face with his hands.

"Tobias, please." I whine as I wrap my hands around his wrists, trying to pull him away from me.

"Do you think it's funny when you hurt me?" He leans down so his mouth is close to my ear. "Do you think it's funny to watch me bleed?" He growls, sending a chill down my spine.

"It was an accident." He leans back and slaps me. I can taste the blood in my mouth as my teeth cut the inside of my cheek.

"You're not laughing now, are you?" He hits me again and I grit my teeth. His hand finds my neck and squeezes until my oxygen is cut off. I kick out at nothing, my eyes widening. I try to force a breath, but nothing comes in. I can feel the fire spreading in my lungs from the lack of air and I try to claw at his face.

Don't fight back.

How am I supposed to not fight back? How am I supposed to sit here and let Tobias choke me? Tobias. My *husband*. Enzo's voice flows through my head over and over and I force myself to relax, despite the panic boiling in my chest. My legs drop, my arms fall away from his, and I just stare at him. My lungs are on fire, and I can feel my limbs growing numb. My eyes open, wide, ready. He flinches, his smirk wavering as surprise flashes through his eyes. I smile just before I close my eyes again, succumbing to the sleep pulling at the edge of my consciousness.

He needs you.

I have to trust Enzo, trust that he's right. Tobias needs me. He won't kill me. I *have* to trust him.

Don't fight back.

Chapter Thirty-Five

I am still sprawled out on the marble floor when I open my eyes again. There is light flooding the room, bouncing off the marble walls, blinding me. I am freezing, my thin dress doing little to stave off the chilly air. I swallow slowly and almost jump with surprise when my throat doesn't hurt, it feels fine. I sit up, my hands touching my neck. No pain. Nothing. I don't understand.

I look around and see Tobias passed out on the couch. He's still wearing his suit, his tunic unbuttoned and open. There is a small amount of blood on his nostril from where he hit it on the floor.

I stand and walk over to him. I see no other damage from what is visible, and it relaxes me for some reason. I am glad he isn't injured as badly as I expected, but his reaction was something else entirely. I don't even have words to describe it. But he didn't kill me. Enzo was right.

I walk around the couch to the dressing room and stare at my reflection. I am still wearing the black gown, but my hair is a mess and I have kohl running down my face and red lip stain smeared on my chin. I lift my head and there isn't a single bruise on my neck or cheeks. It was real. It had to be I remember everything. I walk back out into the main room and Tobias is up, stretching.

"Morning, wife." He smiles as he reaches for me. I stand my ground, refusing to grow closer, and he tilts his head. "What's wrong?" His arms drop.

"What happened last night?" He laughs and I raise my brows.

"We both had way too much wine, it's no wonder we slept half the day away." His voice is light, unbothered.

"No, what happened when we got back to the room?" I say, louder this time. He looks at me confused before plopping back down onto the cushions with a sigh.

"Well you fell and then brought me down with you, causing my nose to bleed." He smiles and rests his head on the back of the couch. "Then we tried going to bed and you fell *again* and then I woke up on the couch. So neither of us made it to bed before we drunkenly fell asleep."

"You hurt me." I say quietly.

"What?"

"You were choking me." He stands and whirls around towards me.

"What are you talking about? I didn't touch you." His eyes are wide, surprised and confused. My hand reaches up and lightly brushes my scalp where he had ripped out hair, but it feels fine.

"I don't understand." This can't be just in my head. My hand falls to my side and he steps around the couch towards me. I raise my hand and he stops.

"Ela, I think you had another bad dream."

"No, it was real."

"Just like the dead version of you was?" He says softly. He speaks to me as if he's consoling a child. I look up at him. His hands are raised, palm out, to show me he's no threat. My neck was fine, my head was fine, I could swallow just fine. But it was all so real. I drop my hand and he walks over to me again. He lifts my head and looks at my neck.

"What are you doing?"

"I am just making sure a dream demon didn't strangle you." He mutters trying to lighten the mood. When he's satisfied, he slides his hands down to my arms. "Are you okay?" I nod and he bends down, asking permission to kiss me. I lift my head and let his soft lips graze mine. "Coffee?" He asks as he turns towards the door, his black shirt wrinkled and open.

"And cream, please?"

"Always." He smiles and I force a smile in return. When he turns away, I drop to the couch, my hands finding my neck again. It had to be a dream. It couldn't have been real. I don't understand. How could it not have been real? I felt it. Every second that I went without oxygen, but there isn't a single wound on my body. There is no headache, not like when Jeremiah had strangled me.

Tobias is cheerful during breakfast, speaking about how today is a very relaxed carnival day. Apparently, the performers are back, and there will be jousting between some of our guests. I fake interest in the conversation, sipping on the delicious coffee. I pretend to feel ill, like I had too much alcohol the night before. He's sweet, attentive as he unlaces my corset so I can take a much-needed bath.

The water is boiling, and I nearly jump out of it. But I don't. I sink down wanting to feel it burn away everything from yesterday. The drinking, the dancing, the kiss. *Oh gods*, the kiss with Theo. We were both drunk, but we both wanted it. I wanted it. The taste of whiskey in my mouth, the smell of spring air and sweet grass. The feel of his calloused hands running down my back as he left kisses down the side of my throat. The feel of him pressing into my stomach, telling me he wants more.

I dunk my head in the steaming water and scream. Bubbles head up to the surface, and I follow, gasping as my head breaks through the surface.

"What is wrong with you, Elaenor?" I don't fight the tears that pool in my eyes, letting them join the bathwater as they drip off my jaw.

I have been attracted to Theo since the first night in the forest. He showed me care and concern, something I had rarely experienced. He drugged me, yes, but he did it to ensure my safety. And even the last few weeks here in the palace, he was there to make sure I felt safe. He protected me after Evreux and the throne room. He checked on me after Tobias hit me for the first time. He professed his love to me, saying that he would never find another.

He said I was always supposed to be his.

We spent our childhood together, granted I don't remember it, but we did. We shared a bed, toys, days and nights. But I was always promised to Tobias. I belong to Tobias, and no feelings I may have for Theo can change that.

I stay in bed the rest of the day, nursing the hangover I don't actually have. In reality, I feel perfectly fine. I feel energized, healthy, and strong.

Scarlett joins me in my room for dinner later that evening, and she looks just as bad as I feel like I should. She throws herself onto the bed and wraps up in one of the furs groaning. Her hair is disheveled, and she is still in her dressing robe.

"How do you look so awake and whole?" She mutters, her face pressed into the bed.

"Because I had a team of ladies to bathe and change me like an infant." I smirk and take a sip of hot tea. "What did you get into last night?" I ask as I dip a small biscuit in the steaming liquid and pop it in my mouth.

"Oh my gods, it was so perfect." She groans and sighs. "Oh I have your crown, or Malia does. She said she was going to give it to Lydia."

"Oh, thanks." I respond. I forgot she even had it.

"Theo walked me to my room, and we kissed. Gods it was so good. I invited him into my room, but he said no. I was disappointed, but I think he's under the impression that I am still a maiden." She snorts, rolling onto her back. "What about you guys? You left all wrapped up in each other." My face falls and I look into my mug, the boiling tea creating little billows of steam.

"We came back to our room, and then we both fell. His nose started bleeding and then I woke up still on the floor." I lie. Well it's not truly lying; I'm just omitting some of the events in between.

"What? No drunken sex?" She exclaims, feigning surprise.

"No, actually," I stop.

"What?"

"I had a dream that he hit me and choked me until I passed out." I admit, gnawing on my lower lip.

"Gods, Elaenor. What kind of fucked up mind do you have?"

"I thought it was real. It felt real, every part of it, but when I awoke this morning, I was perfectly fine. It just doesn't make sense." I shrug and set my mug on the nightstand next to my half-finished plate of roasted vegetables and chicken.

"You've always had nightmares, Elaenor." Her voice is soft, reassuring, but I still feel hesitant.

"Yes, but they were always the same thing, and they stopped."

"I don't know what to tell you." She groans as she rolls towards the end of the bed. "Maybe ask the master for something to help you sleep." Scarlett shrugs as she pads barefoot to the door.

"Where are you going?"

"Bath, sex, sleep. Not necessarily in that order."

"Good luck convincing Theo to take your virginity." I call after her. She blows me a kiss before opening the door and closing it softly behind her.

Tobias returns shortly after, kissing me on the forehead before going to the dressing room to change.

"Did you get enough rest?" He asks from inside the room.

"Yes." I respond just as loud.

"I wish I could have slept all day. I had to ensure Welan had everything under control with clean up and organizing the sendoff breakfast tomorrow. All of our guests should be leaving tomorrow afternoon." He comes out from the dressing room in loose pants that hang just below his hips.

"Okay." I murmur into my tea.

"Is that dream still bothering you?" I nod and he comes around to my side of the bed. He takes the tea out of my hand and scoops me up before plopping himself down onto the bed and me in his lap. He kisses my temple and folds his arms around me. I rest my head on his shoulder and inhale the deep smoky cedar that always seems to follow him.

"I just thought it was real." I admit and nuzzle into his neck.

"I wouldn't hurt you, Ela." He whispers. I nod as his fingers trail up and down my spine. "Do you want some wine?" He leans back, tucking my loose hair behind my ears. I nod and he kisses the tip of my nose before sliding out from under me.

I watch as he wanders over to the bar cart, pouring a large glass of my favorite pink wine and a smaller glass of whiskey for himself. He walks over, handing it to me and I take an eager sip. The syrupy sweetness is addicting, and I sigh as I feel it coat my throat.

He joins me on the bed, tucking me into the crook of his arm. We sit in silence for a second, waves of whiskey hitting my nose every time he lifts the glass to his mouth. My eyes are focused on the stars outside, the darkened night sky and the glittering lights. I am nothing but a speck of dust compared to the vast universe out there.

I used to wonder about how my life would have played out if I had been born someone who wasn't a princess. Would I have been happy? Would I have been in love?

"What are you thinking about?" Tobias cuts into my thoughts and I nearly flinch.

"I am just wondering what my life would have been like if I hadn't been born as Elaenor."

"Why?"

"Curiosity. Do you ever think of what your life would have been like had you not been born Tobias?" He shakes his head, and I take another mouthful of wine.

"I find thinking of such things a waste of time. There is no use wondering if you'll never know."

"Sometimes it's fun to imagine." I admit, my voice is no more than a whisper as I take the last sip of wine in the glass.

"I would like you to speak to Pakin tomorrow." I pull out of his arms and look down at him.

"What?"

"You never saw him after your nightmare that sent you running for the literal hills. And after last night, I am worried about you." He sets his whiskey down on the nightstand and cups my cheeks. "I want to make sure everything is okay. You've been under a great deal of stress and now you are imagining me hurting you. Ela, I would never hurt you."

"He would and he will, and he did."

Enzo's voice is loud, crisp, and I almost jump out of my skin.

"Enzo?" I call out, but the telltale sign of electricity isn't there.

"Ela, are you hearing me?" I look back at him and he's sitting up, nearly towering over me. I nod and he cocks a brow. "I am saying that if you are pregnant, this could be a symptom."

"What?" I sputter. Pregnant?

"Hallucinations. My mother had them with Thea." I reach behind and set the wine glass on the table.

"I don't think I'm pregnant."

"Why?"

"I awoke with a weird cramping in my core yesterday. It felt almost like when Master Pakin used that tincture to force my monthly bleed. I felt *raw*." I admit. I see his eyes widen slightly, but they return to normal so quick I almost think I was imagining it.

"Well, I guess we'll have to wait and see." He mutters. I fall back against the pillow, my head spinning. I ate a normal amount of food today, but the small amount of wine I had is making me groggy, tired. I sigh, burrowing deeper into the bed.

I open my eyes a second later and the room is pitch black. All of the torches have been extinguished and the moon is high in the sky. Tobias is asleep next to me, snoring softly. I'm cold, shivering. I look down and see that I am naked, my nightdress gone. I look around and see it thrown on the floor, along with Tobias's cotton pants. My brows furrow and my lips part as I stare at our discarded clothing.

What is going on?

Chapter Thirty-Six

Two weeks pass and I find that I have now been out of Chatis for a month. A lot has happened in the last 5 weeks and there is a lot I still don't have an answer for. Donovan still follows me around per Tobias's orders. He is still attached to me when he doesn't have other duties to attend to. Scarlett has traveled back to Chatis for a while to get everything taken care of back home before she moves here permanently. I haven't seen Theo since the night of the ball, but I can still barely look at Laris out of embarrassment. He hasn't said anything, but I feel like if he does, he'll wait until the moment is advantageous for him.

Scarlett is expected back today and, while I am sure it will cause more problems than we already have, I am hoping she has Rhea with her. I know Laenie wouldn't leave Reggie, but I am hoping to have another friend in Noterra. At least one that originated from home, and not from Noterra. Maybe we can convince Laenie and Reggie to move here also. They don't have to stay in the palace but having them close would be nice.

I haven't had any other dreams, not even the nightmares from before since that night. I am sleeping better than I ever had, and I think it might be due to my nightly glass of wine. Maybe the alcohol is enough to keep me asleep. Despite Tobias's protests, he eventually concedes and lets me have a single glass nightly, just because he thinks it's helping me. Tobias is insistent on producing an heir as soon as we can, which results in us having sex multiple times a day, whenever he feels like it. I can't say I'm complaining as it is quite enjoyable for me too. He's been sweet, gentle, and I have nothing to complain about.

My fingers run up and down his chest as I am tucked into the crook of his arm. He's doing the same thing to my arm as we lay in silence. The sun has already risen, but neither of us has made an effort to move out of the comfort. I lay my hand flat on his chest and look up at him. He's staring up at the ceiling, but he feels my movement and looks down.

"You okay, Ela?" I nod and smile at him. He brings his free hand over to grasp my chin, pulling my face up towards his. His lips find mine, immediately forcing them to part as he maneuvers so that he's leaning over me. I wrap my legs around his waist just as he angles his hips towards mine. I inhale sharply as he quickly fills me, stretches me. My fingers tangle in his hair as he starts to move, meeting my hips thrust for thrust.

He's quicker this time, experienced. The delicious heat spreads to my core as his pelvis rubs against my clit, creating enough friction to make me squirm. He knows what I like and what helps me finish and so, within minutes, we are both sweating and panting. He stays leaning over me, still inside me to try to ensure our chances of conception are optimal. His arms rest right next to the side of my head, caging me in. And I map his face with my eyes, picking up on every subtle mark, every pore and freckle.

He's letting his facial hair grow a little, so the golden strands are short and pokey. I run my fingers along his jaw, and he bends down to nip at my fingertips.

"If we haven't conceived a child by now, I'm going to start thinking you're incapable." He mutters, leaning down to press his lips back to mine. I playfully slap him, and he pulls back. His hair has gotten longer too, as it now flops right in front of his eyes. I brush the golden copper strands away from his face as he slides out of me. "Come on, out of bed." I groan as he throws off the blanket, revealing me to the icy air.

It looks like it's going to snow today, which is strange considering it was just the end of summer a couple weeks ago. I wrap a fur blanket around me as I pad over to the dressing room. I have taken a liking to riding leathers and jackets as opposed to dresses the last few weeks, which no one has complained about, not that they should. I also haven't worn my crown since the ball, so it stays tucked away in a chest for safe keeping.

I slip into the tight leather pants and camisole, but I opt for a warmer fur lined jacket today. I've been walking Sybil nearly every day and riding her when I can. She's my safe space, my escape. Laris or Tano, whoever is stalking me that day, usually sits by the stables and watches me ride in the fields, letting me be alone. It's nice and quiet and one of the only times some noble isn't trying to garner my attention.

When I make it to the stables today, I notice Bijoy is looking lonely. I slip his reins on and walk him out to the pasture, his silvery fur glinting in the sunlight. Sybil whinnies behind me and I glance over my shoulder and laugh.

"Don't be impatient, I'm coming back." I reassure her as I take Bijoy through the gates and let him loose. He turns and waits as I go back for Sybil. Once they are both locked behind the gate, they take off to the other end of the field. I rest my arms on the wooden posts and watch them. The wind is picking up and I pull my jacket tighter around me. My braid whips in front of me and I struggle to restrain it. I glance behind me where Tano is sitting, looking bored. His eyes are frozen, unseeing, as he looks out into the woods.

"Do you ever get tired of following me around?" I ask as I turn back to the horses.

"It is an honor, Your Grace." He replies. I scoff.

"Be honest, Tano. You don't have to lie to me." He chuckles as I turn around to face him, his arm laying casually on the back of the bench.

"Honestly?" I nod and he smiles. "I don't think you need a someone to watch over you. While it is my job to ensure your safety, I don't think you have anything to fear here on the grounds and you won't start feeling safe if you don't trust your home. If *we* don't act like we believe you are safe, *you'll* never believe it." He leans forward, resting his forearms on his knees.

While it's comforting that he feels I am more than safe here, I don't feel like I am. Nothing has happened since Jeremiah, but with the rising war in Rakushia, there is a bounty on my head. What's going to stop another from finishing what he started? What's going to stop someone sneaking in and killing me in the middle of the night? They wouldn't even need to sneak into the palace. I spend nearly all day right here outside the walls. Someone would just have to wait and watch. I feel a little safer since Tobias gave me my dagger back. I keep it tucked into a sheath on my thigh, ready for if I need it. However, I still haven't received proper training. I thought about asking Theo, but Tobias wouldn't like that.

"I appreciate your candor, Tano." He nods and I turn back around to watch the horses. They are both drinking out of one of the troughs, looking more like friends than before. Before she left, Scarlett joked that she wished they would have babies so we could have little foals to play with. I wish that too. "Is there any word on Scarlett's return?" I ask with my back to him.

"No, Your Grace. We have not received confirmation that she is on the way." I stay quiet. I know there is a small army of men with her, but the road from Chatis to Noterra is where I was attacked. It's not safe and I'll feel much better when she returns to the palace.

"Your Grace?" I turn as Donovan appears, bowing deeply at the waist.

"Hello, Donny." He blushes at my pet name and walks over to where I am standing.

"If we could, can I speak to you alone for a moment?" I nod and look over at Tano who stands and disappears around the edge of the stables with a curt nod.

"What is it?"

"I overheard something. I don't want to cause any problems, but I thought you'd want to know." I nod, urging him on. "A small group of our armed soldiers have been sent to Chatis, instructed to not let anyone in or out." My eyes widen and I drop my arms from where they were resting on the posts.

"What?"

"I heard Lord Cyrus talking to the Hand. They said they were warned that your father had plans to cross into Noterra and try to take you back." His voice is quiet, hesitant.

"That can't be true. Why would he even want me back? I'm no longer a citizen of Chatis."

"It is only what I heard, Your Grace." I stomp away from him, and I can tell he's struggling to keep pace with me. "Where are we going?"

"I'm going to ask Tobias. Have him explain." My voice is short, strained as I quickly make my way to the palace gate. *The horses*. Tano is close behind, so when I stop, he nearly runs into me. "Donovan, can you have the stable hands put the horses back in their stalls?"

"Of course." He bows and hurries off as I pass through the stone gate. I quickly make my way back into the palace, my riding boots clicking against the marble. I find Tobias alone in the council chamber pouring over maps and documents. Tano walks in with me, but I hold my hand up. He steps out and closes the door behind him. Tobias looks up at me, a smile spreading as he steps around the table and reaches for my waist.

"This is a surprise." He leans down and kisses my cheek and I fight the urge to melt against him.

"We need to talk." His lips trail from my cheek to my jaw.

"We can talk later." I lightly lift my chin, exposing my neck and his nose gently runs across. I shudder against him, closing my eyes. I take a deep breath as his teeth find my shoulder and push him away.

"No, now." He drops his hands and turns back to the chair he vacated.

"What is it?" He asks as he drops down into the cushioned seat.

"Are you sending our military to the border of Chatis and Noterra?"

"Yes."

"Why?"

"To keep us safe."

"You have nothing to fear from my father." I snap.

"I have *everything* to fear, Ela!" He runs his fingers through his golden strands.

"What are you talking about?"

"At the carnival your father told me he wanted you to come back home for a while, to visit. When I told him no, he started to push harder, saying you needed to be with your friends and family after everything you've been through." He starts to explain, his hand running through his hair.

"Okay? And that justifies starting a war?" I raise my eyebrows and his lips press into a thin line.

"I told him no, *again*, and he said that if I didn't let you go, he would come and take you himself." I snort. Like my father would even make it into the palace before he was apprehended.

GLASS AND BONE

"Why does he want me to return?" His face softens as he rises from the chair. "He's never cared about me before."

"He claimed a prophet came to him, claiming to know information about your mother." I swallow as he steps closer. "That prophet told him you were not his daughter and that he knew who your father was."

"What?" I spit out. My heart starts to race, and I lift my hands so Tobias doesn't step closer. We had our suspicions, but if it's been confirmed...

"Your father, Viktor, seems to think that because you are not his blood, he has a claim to you."

"As what?" I spit.

"His wife." The nausea explodes deep in my belly and my hand flies to my mouth.

"Are you serious?" I barely choke out. Tobias just nods. "This has to be a joke. I am his daughter, and I am already wed."

"He says Sybil owes him, since he now has no heirs. He said you are not a princess; therefore you have no claim to either throne and shouldn't be the queen. He was trying to get me to annul our wedding, saying that you were married above your station." My eyes widen as I meet his gaze.

"What are you saying? That I can't be a queen?" My hand flies to my throat and I try to steady my breathing.

"No, not at all, Ela. That doesn't matter to me. You were Sybil's daughter, and she was a queen, that is *all* that matters." I shake my head and walk over to the bar, pouring a glass of amber liquid.

"I don't understand." I take a sip and nearly cough as it burns its way down my throat.

"I don't either."

"So you are preventing anyone from entering or leaving Chatis?" He nods. "What about Scarlett and Rhea?"

"They are with our men and will be free to cross when they are ready." I nod as I take another sip. It's both delicious and disgusting at the same time.

"Who is my father, Tobias?" The prophet must have told him who it was if he were to be believed.

"I don't know, Ela. I don't think it matters." Images flash through my mind of a handsome dark-haired prophet who kept my mother company.

"Kassius." I whisper.

314

"What?"

"The prophet who counseled my mother, Kassius. He had dark hair like my mother and I. Could he be my father?"

"I don't know. Based on the timeline, she would have to have been sleeping with him either right before marrying Viktor or at least right after." I set the glass down and walk to the doors. "Where are you going?"

"I need to breathe." I choke out.

"Ela." He calls after me, but I ignore him. I don't say anything else as I walk out of the council room. Tano starts to follow but I spin on my heel and face him.

"Can I be alone for once? *Please*?" I hate the venom that laces my words as I clench my fists and look up at him. He looks skeptical but eventually nods and steps back.

I don't waste any time heading down the hallway to one of the side exits of the palace. Within minutes I am through the gate and in the stables. One of the stablehands is brushing Sybil's inky black mane when I walk up.

"Your Grace." He bows deeply and I can see the faint reddish tint to his cheeks when he stands. "I was just attending to our Sybil here." He smiles and resumes brushing her.

"Hello." I offer him a smile. "I know you just moved her, but I think I would like to ride her around the pasture if that is alright?" I run my fingers along her nose.

"Of course, Your Grace! I will ready her at once." He steps away to the storage room, grabbing her saddle and bridle. I reach for an apple out of the bucket on the wall, letting Sybil eat it out of my hand. Apple juice and saliva drip from her mouth onto my palm as she takes it from me. I smile as I wipe my sticky hand on my leggings.

Within a few moments, I am pulling myself into Sybil's saddle and guiding her to the pasture. The gates are already open for the field, but that isn't my destination.

I look around and find that the stablehand stayed inside the barn. No other guards are around, besides the ones stationed next to the gate. Sybil trots over to the fence lining the field out of habit, but I force her left before she can step through. She starts down the cobblestone path without guidance. A few minutes later I urge her into a run as we make our way out of the Noterran capital.

"What are you doing, Elaenor?" I whisper as the palace is hidden from sight, being replaced by an endless wall of trees.

Chapter Thirty-Seven

I am grateful it is still early morning when I leave the palace behind. I push Sybil to run faster as we reach the fork that takes us either to Port Tobeo or Chatis. I take the left towards Chatis, and we break through the trees. Birds are chirping, the sun is beating down, but a brisk autumnal wind whips my braid around. I grit my teeth against the chill and tighten my thighs on the saddle.

I know Chatis is only a half a day away by carriage, but I am hoping it isn't nearly as long on horseback, especially as Sybil can outrun any normal horse. She continues steadily and I let my mind wander.

Who is the prophet that came to my father, and why did he wait until now to do so? And how does he know who my father is? Prophets can't see the past, which means he either learned it, or something is going to happen in the future that brings that information to light.

And what about Viktor? He thinks he has a claim to me because I am not his blood? Does he think that I would marry him, let him touch me like that? Regardless of blood, he is my father, and the idea of being anything more is revolting.

Unless he's lying. He saw me happy, even if it was an act. He saw me happy, powerful, married to a doting husband. He's jealous, or angry that I am having a life he didn't deem me worthy of having. So what? He's going to kill me? Hold me captive?

Am I just walking into a trap?

The sun has nearly reached the center of the sky by time I see the horde of Noterran soldiers making camp a few feet from the border. The bridge across the Delaquar is empty, with a few Chatisian men standing on the other side. I slow as I reach my men. Their hands reach for the swords almost instantly, but they quickly drop as they recognize me.

"Your Grace." One of them approaches Sybil as I slow to a stop. He's wearing silver armor and red cotton underneath. His blonde hair is partially hidden by his helmet, but his piercing green eyes are uncovered.

"Good afternoon. I am here to visit my father." I will my voice to sound even, diplomatic. He nods and reaches for Sybil's reins. I don't need their permission. I have to keep remembering that. *I* am in charge here.

"Of course, Your Grace." He looks behind me at the lack of an escort and his fingers tighten on the leather. "Where are your guards, Your Grace?" I glance around at the crowd of men and swallow.

"I didn't need any for such a short trip, Ser." I respond, my eyes meeting the gaze of others. He doesn't make a move to release her reins and I quickly start plotting an escape plan. I shouldn't have to escape. I can visit whomever I like.

"I am sorry, Your Grace. We cannot allow you to go any farther without an escort." His voice is strained, as if he's uncomfortable. I hope he is if he thinks he can order me around.

"I don't need an escort; I am the queen, and you will release my horse and let me through." I snap, my brows furrowing.

"I am sorry, Your Grace. We cannot." He looks apologetic as he starts to lead Sybil away from the road. I quickly dismount before he can drag me away, landing hard on the cobblestone road.

"Fine then." I mutter as I start walking towards the border. A hand not-so-gently reaches out and restrains my upper arm.

"Your Grace, we must request that you stop." I try to yank my arm out of his grip, but he remains firm.

"Unhand me or this will be the last time you have hands!" I hiss through gritted teeth.

"Enough." I glance up at Theo who is making his way over to us. I visibly relax and the hand on my arm disappears.

"Theo." I whisper, relieved to see a friendly face.

"What are you doing here, Nora?" He whispers as he gets closer to me.

"I am here to speak to my father." His lips press into a thin line. "Tobias told you?" I nod. "Then you know why I can't let you go in there." I roll my eyes. I am so sick of these *damn* men thinking they can tell me what to do.

"You can't stop me, Theo. I have to know what my father knows. What he learned. Who he learned it from. I don't believe it. I have to know." I plead, beg. I aim straight for his heart, hoping it's weak enough to let me in.

"It's not safe, Nora."

"Then come with me." I whisper, softening my gaze and biting my lip. He glances around at his men before reluctantly nodding. I push past him quickly, before he can change his mind, and he follows closely behind.

"Just don't run off, Tobias will have my head."

"He'll already have mine. He doesn't know I'm here." He groans and I can hear his knuckles popping as he nervously clenches his fists.

"Elaenor, you need to stop running from the safety of the palace." I scoff and turn to face him.

"I run one time and you hold it against me?" He fights a smile before he chuckles softly. We walk in silence for a few moments before we reach the gate at the other end of the bridge. I nod at the kingsguard stationed and they motion for us to enter.

"We need to talk at some point." Theo says quietly behind me.

"About what?" I play ignorant as we cross through the stone wall.

"That night." I stop walking once we are far enough away from the men at the gate. I nervously look around the small town before turning to face him.

"We were both drunk, Theo."

"Yes, and people who are drunk do things they wouldn't normally do that they actually really *want* to do." He explains and I nearly roll my eyes.

"That's confusing."

"Nora."

"Stop calling me that." I snap.

"I love you."

"You've known me for two months; you can't possibly love me."

"Do you love Tobias?" I bite at my lower lip again.

"I think I do." I admit.

"What about when he hurts you?" My brows furrow.

"He hasn't hurt me in a long time, Theo." I shake my head and start walking again. "Even then, it was an accident."

"Are you sure about that?" I stop, spinning around.

"What are you talking about?" I snap.

"It seems your husband has ordered a large shipment of hemlock root and poppy." He says nonchalantly and I cock a brow.

"Okay, and?" I push.

"Do you not know what that is?"

"I mean I know there is poppy in the nectar Master Pakin gave me."

"So you know that poppy helps speed up healing and provides pain relief?" I nod. "Well in its purest form, it can speed up healing incredibly fast. In large doses, you would just get tired, but within hours any pain or injuries would be long gone, as long as they didn't break the skin. Scabs take longer to heal, but bruises can dissipate within hours. But hemlock, hemlock causes extreme memory loss for periods in which the herb is the most potent."

"I don't understand." I shake my head. There is absolutely no way Tobias had been drugging me. Hurting me without me knowing it. But the notebook, he was using something and testing it.

"When you fall asleep, have you been having nightmares?"

"No, I haven't." I shake my head.

"But you used to. Every night?" I nod. "And when did they stop?" I pause and think back.

"I can't remember, but it's been awhile."

"Has any part of your routine changed?" I go to shake my head, but that isn't true. I've been having coffee with sweetened cream and a nightly glass of wine. Sugar. Enzo said sugar could be used to hide even the most lethal of drugs.

"Coffee. I've been drinking a few mugs of coffee with sweetened cream every morning. It tastes like ice cream, super rich. And wine. I have a sweet pink wine every night. Tobias found it and said it used to be your mother's favorite. So he ordered a bunch of it for me."

"I would guess that is where he's been putting it." He mutters.

"No, Theo. You are wrong." I shake my head again. There is no way he's been drugging me. I walk away from him, but he pulls me back. His skin touching mine sends electricity through my veins. I look down expecting to see sparks, but they don't appear.

"Is there anything that has been happening you can't explain?"

"I mean I wake up sometimes not remembering going to bed, but it's the alcohol." I explain. It has to be.

"I am scared for you, Elaenor. I am terrified he is going to go too far." His voice is soft, panicked.

"I don't remember any of it. Any of the supposed abuse you think he's doling out." He's wrong. He has to be. Things with Tobias have been good, really good. He would have no need to drug me.

"I can't explain it, I just have a feeling." He reaches up and lightly brushes the hair from my face. "We can still run."

"Theo, you need to stop with this. You need to stop trying to get me to run from him. I am married. He owns me. I can't do anything about it. What I can do is stop drinking the coffee and wine and speak to Viktor who may have information about my heritage that I don't. So please," I pull on my arm. "Let me go. You can either come with me or not, but I am going into that palace." He slowly releases my arm and I push past him, crossing the town square.

My senses are assaulted with the thick humidity and lush smell of foliage. It's not as cold as I expected it'd be in the autumn, but I am happy about it. I didn't plan ahead and bring anything other than the fur lined leather jacket I currently have on. The town seems nearly empty, with everyone inside for lunch. It's small, so it doesn't take me long to reach the palace gates and walk through them. The courtyard is filled with the usual servants and guards, and I pass by all of them without a smile.

I climb the few steps to the entryway and nod at all of the guards stationed around. I quickly make my way to the council chamber, hoping he's there, which he thankfully is. He's speaking with his Hand, Lord Danieas, and a few other council members. I step into the room and all eyes turn towards me. My father's eyes widen as he stands.

"Elaenor?" He looks clean, in shape. His hair isn't as messy, his face is shaved, and for once he's wearing clothes that aren't wrinkled from the night before.

"Father." I respond, nodding my greeting to the others.

"Leave us." He says as everyone quickly rises and pushes out of the room. Lord Danieas offers me a soft smile and a pat on the shoulder as he walks by. "You too." My father snaps at Theo.

"No, he stays." I respond. He grits his teeth, but eventually nods.

"To what do I owe the pleasure of having Noterra's queen grace our small country?" He sneers with disgust. It takes everything in me not to roll my eyes.

"Who told you I wasn't your daughter?" I blurt out. He doesn't even flinch.

"Did you know?" He asks as he lifts a glass of clear liquid to his mouth. Based on his history, I am almost certain it is not water.

"I had my suspicion after I learned my mother and I were frequent visitors of Noterra when I was a child." He smiles and leans back.

"Do you remember?" I shake my head. "Anything from before that night?" I stay quiet and he snorts. "Figures she'd do something to prevent that."

"Prevent what?" I snap.

"Prevent you from remembering."

"How could she possibly do that?" He sets his glass down and looks up at me, irritated.

"Your mother was a witch, Elaenor." I scoff as an uncontrollable giggle escapes my mouth. I turn towards Theo who has a brow raised. "This is not a joke, Elaenor."

"Yeah, okay. A witch? Are you serious?" I spit. He has to be joking.

"Yes. I am."

"There is no such thing."

"Yes, there is, and your mother was one. She was born in Zivell and was only brought over to the country when she was betrothed to King Argent."

"Zivell?" I ask. My knowledge on the histories of our land is scarce as my father wasn't keen on geography lessons.

"It's north of Tatus, its own country. But your mother was born there. I never met your grandmother, but I knew of her heritage. I only guessed her power when she seemed to disappear into thin air and reappear elsewhere."

"She could *teleport*?" I was aware my mouth was open in disbelief. This couldn't be true. I rest my hands on the back of a chair and try not to laugh at the absurdity.

"Yes, other small magics too, such as memory suppression. She used it to get people to forget they saw her quite often." I shake my head and pull out the chair in front of me, plopping down into its plush cushion.

"Witches are nothing but folklore." Theo says loudly from behind.

"Don't raise your voice at me, boy. You are lucky I am even allowing you to be here since you seem to be preparing for war at my border."

"None of this explains who told you I wasn't your daughter." Viktor sighs before taking another sip of his drink and tearing his eyes away from Theo.

"A young man, around your age, appeared here. He seemed to have a lot of information about Noterra, Labisa, Rakushia, and some other countries. He said that you were not my daughter, but that you were descended from someone else. He also said you were in danger in Noterra and that I needed to help him get you out. He offered me quite a large sum of money to ensure your safety out of the country."

"What did he look like?" I ask warily. It couldn't be...

"Dark hair, green eyes, tall. Why does this matter?"

"Enzo." I whisper.

"What? Speak up." He asks, irritated.

"Was his name Enzo?"

"Yes, why?"

"Oh my gods." I stand quickly, the chair almost falling back. Enzo was trying to get me out of Noterra, and he succeeded. He's been trying to get me out of there this whole time, telling me I'll meet him eventually. That I just need to be patient and bide my time.

"What is it, Nora?" Theo whispers from behind me.

"We need to go." He's been trying to get me to leave. He pushed me towards Rakushia. He wanted to get me alone. What if he's not the good guy here? What if he is working for *Labisa*? "I don't know why, but I need to go back."

"What?"

"I have a weird feeling that Tobias is in danger." His eyes widen slightly, and he nods before turning to the door. He grabs the handle, but it doesn't turn. He shakes it and I hear a deep chuckle.

"I'm not letting you leave, Elaenor." My father says from behind.

"Father, we have to go." I plead. I hate begging, especially to my father, but I can't stay here.

"No. You can't go back there. It isn't safe."

"Since when do you care about my safety?" I spit. "You used to whip me, beat me, let your friends touch me. You treated me like I was nothing but a body for you to use and abuse. You don't get a say in anything that happens to me anymore." Theo's hand rests on the small of my back.

"Does your husband know his brother is in love with you?" Viktor laughs, sending a chill down my spine.

"Stop. Let me leave, please father." I plead.

"I am not your father."

"But I am your daughter. *You* raised me. Not some other person. And what about what you told Tobias? That you deserve me and that I am not fit to be queen?"

"You're not, but I want nothing to do with you. Someone will come to collect you soon." He claps his hands together once and the doors open. My arms are wrenched behind my back as something cold snaps over my wrists.

"Father, please!" I cry out as they tighten to the point of pain.

"Don't struggle, Nora. Just relax." Theo says calmly next to me as he is cuffed. They pull us out of the room and down the hall to a set of stairs I'd never seen before, leading us down into darkness.

Chapter Thirty-Eight

They stupidly throw us in a cell together and as soon as they depart, we work on trying to get the cuffs off. We tried to use my dagger that is still sheathed to my thigh, but I was worried it would break. The cuffs are made out of silver and seem to be impenetrable. We have our backs together as Theo tries to pull mine off. I wince and hiss between my teeth every time he forces them to get tighter.

"It's not working." He snaps, frustrated. He lets go of my hands and turns around.

"Do you think he's telling the truth?" I whisper as I look around. There are seven other cells that we can see, all empty aside from chamber pots and small beds of dirty hay. Small windows at the top of each cell lightly illuminate the dungeon, but they are too high to reach and too small to fit through.

"About which part? That you aren't his daughter, or that your mother was a witch?" He nearly laughs at the second part, and I don't blame him. The idea is ridiculous.

"All of it." I say with a loud exhale. This past month has been nothing short of confusing and painful.

"I find it hard to believe there are witches in the world and no one knows about them. I think your father is an alcoholic and may be going insane." He lets his laugh out this time and I look up at him. His light hair wrestled itself free from the constraints of the leather cord and was now dangling in front of his face.

"We need to get out of here." I start to pace nervously. Tight spaces were never an issue before, but I can't just sit down and wait. I *need* to get out.

"Who is Enzo?" He asks after a few seconds of my pacing. I bite my lip and look everywhere but at him. "Nora."

"I'm not a hundred percent sure." I admit. "I started having dreams about Chatis being bombed and burnt down, and he was there. I saw him once in the woods outside Chatis and again in the bathing room at the palace. He keeps telling me I am not safe, that I'll be with him soon and he'll protect me. He told me not to fight back if Tobias ever hurts me, that if I do, I won't live to see the day that we unite." He exhales, his mouth hanging open in disbelief and also worry. He probably thinks I am just as crazy as my father.

"Okay...but who is he?" I shrug. "Are you sure he's real?"

"Clearly he is if my father saw him." I snap. "He's the reason I almost drowned in the tub. I thought I could only see him if I was in water, but then he told me that wasn't true. He said I could call him to me at any time, I just needed to focus."

"Nora, I know we don't believe in witches, but if what you are saying is true, then you might also be a witch."

"That is ridiculous, Theo." I roll my eyes and groan, resuming my pacing.

"Can you at least try to call him? Maybe he can help us?" He looks skeptical, but he's right. It may be our only option. I sigh and walk to the corner of the cell, dropping down onto the cold stone.

"Fine. But don't watch me." I mutter and he turns to face the other way. I rest my head on the cell and close my eyes.

"*Enzo?*" I call out. "*Enzo, can you hear me?*" I push against anything in my mind that can be construed as a shield and search for him in the darkness.

"Elaenor." I jump and a small squeak comes out of my mouth as my eyes open. Theo turns and looks at me. I shake my head and close my eyes again. A subtle buzzing noise hums through my ears, sending chills down my spine.

"I'm trapped. I need help."

"You can't go back to Noterra."

"I need to. I think Tobias is in danger."

"Why would you think that?"

"You keep trying to get me to leave Noterra. The body chasing me in the woods?"

"I'm trying to keep you out of danger, Elaenor. I don't know what you are talking about in regard to the body."

"That wasn't you?"

"What did you see?"

"I saw a dead version of myself. Every time she, I, opened my mouth water came out. She was covered in blood and started chasing me. She only stopped when I crossed the border."

"The border where?"

"Rakushia. I made it pretty far in, but there were these men in cloaks who tried to take me. Tobias and Theo got there in time and rescued me. This was a while ago."

"You were in Rakushia?"

"Yes."

"Elaenor, you need to go back."

"To Noterra?"

"No, to Rakushia. I am in Rakushia."

"How can I trust you?"

"I just need you to believe me. Come to Rakushia." His voice is begging, pleading, but I don't trust him.

"I can't really go anywhere right now, Enzo. Even if I could, I don't trust you. I don't know who to believe or what to think. My father said someone is coming to collect me soon. Do you know who that is?"

"Yes, my men. They are coming. Help is coming, Elaenor, just be patient, please." The dim buzzing in my ears dissipates before I can answer, letting me know he is gone.

"He said help is on the way."

"Seriously?" His brows are furrowed, skeptical. I just shrug. I can barely believe that I can speak to Enzo, much less that my mother was a witch. I close my eyes again, exhaustion washing over me in waves.

"He said I need to go to Rakushia."

"No, Nora! Are you crazy?"

"What?"

"We are in the middle of a war, and you want to march right into their lands? Do you not remember the men who tried to take you?"

"Of course I remember, Theo, but Enzo is in Rakushia."

"You don't even know who this guy is, Elaenor."

"He's never lied to me."

"He may not even exist!" He snaps and I clench my teeth together. I open my mouth to speak when the door to the dungeon opens. To my surprise, Scarlett and Rhea run in. She's holding keys and shakily tries to find the one that goes into the lock.

"Stay quiet." She snaps. I ungracefully rise to my feet and run up to the door. Tears pool in my eyes as she finds the one that fits. The metal door groans as she pulls it open. I throw myself at her, my hands still cuffed behind my back. "Are you okay?" She whispers and I nod. I throw myself at Rhea next who is sobbing. She brushes the hair from my face when she pulls back.

"It has been too long." She whispers.

"I missed you too." I whisper back. Scarlett's cold fingers clasp onto the cuffs and within seconds they fall off. I nearly moan with the release of pressure on my shoulders. She gets Theo's off, and he brushes her cheek softly. She smiles before turning back to me.

"We need to go." I nod as she grabs Rhea's hand and Theo grabs mine. We quietly climb the stairs back to the ground level. She goes out first and reappears seconds later to let us know the coast is clear. Within minutes we are exiting out of the servant's door and into the woods.

"Is everyone okay?" Theo asks. His fingers gently rub my wrists and I offer him a smile.

"I think so."

"We need horses." Scarlett says as she looks around uncomfortably. Her hand is still tightly clasped in Rhea's.

"Sybil is with Noterra's guards." Theo nods and grabs my hand again before pulling us deeper in the woods. I can hear Scarlett tripping over every rock and root and squealing when she sees a bug. It's hard to keep a smile off my face as we all silently laugh, even though we are on the run from both my father and Enzo's men. I can't wait for them to come get me. Theo is right, I don't know who Enzo is. I have to go home.

The trees break and I can see some of our guards milling about in their camp. Theo pulls me faster and we step into the clearing.

Everyone's heads whip towards us as we stumble out between the trees. Sybil is tied up on one of the posts next to a beautiful white horse. *Wyclif.*

"Tobias?" I say out loud, knowing he is here somewhere. He steps out from under a tent, and I move to run towards him, but Theo's hand tightens on mine, yanking me back. "Theo, let go." I say as I pull on my arm.

"No, he's been hurting you, Nora." I shake my head as Tobias saunters over to us. His gait is slow, measured, as he assesses the situation.

"Theo, stop." I whisper. Now is not the time or place for this discussion. Tobias reaches us, his fingers threading into my hair and yanking back, forcing me to look at him. Theo's hand is still holding mine captive.

"When are you going to stop *fucking* running?" His voice is laced with venom as he forces my head to tilt up. My eyes widen in surprise, and I gasp.

"Let go of her." Theo snaps, stepping closer. Tobias's fingers tighten, pulling my hair and I wince. My other hand reaches up to grip his wrist, hoping to ease some of the pressure.

"Ow, Tobias. Stop, please." I cry out. Tobias looks at Theo's hand wrapped around mine.

"Let go of my wife, Theo." Neither of them moves and I can hear Scarlett and Rhea breathing heavily behind me. "I won't ask you again."

"Fuck off." Theo growls as his jaw clenches. Tobias's hand releases my head and I stagger back from the release of pressure, nearly falling on my back. He unsheathes his sword, the metal ringing through the air.

"No!" I heard Scarlett scream as the sword is brought down in an arc. I feel pressure pulling my arm down and then I am falling backwards. I land on my butt and look up. A scream pierces the air as Rhea's limp body falls to the ground, Tobias's sword still stuck in her skull. Scarlett falls to her knees, and I look up at Tobias, his eyes wide with fear.

"Oh my gods. Help her. Please! Somebody help her!" She cries as she pulls Rhea's bloody body towards her.

"What did you do?" I croak out as I turn back to Tobias.

"I was going for Theo's hand, she got in the way." He's shaking, surprised and scared. He's actually scared.

"What did you do?" I scream as I scramble to my feet, throwing myself at Tobias. We both fall to the ground, and I reach out and slap him as hard as I can. He restrains my wrists and flips us, so I am on my back. I kick out, but he doesn't move.

"Stop, Elaenor."

"What the fuck is wrong with you!" I scream as I struggle against him. Oh gods. What did he do? This can't be happening. He killed her. He *killed* Rhea. Tobias reaches out and slaps me, momentarily stunning me.

"Calm down!" He yells and I just scream. I keep screaming, rage fueling every ounce of my strength as I kick him off of me. Theo's arm goes around Tobias's neck, pulling him backwards. They fall to the ground, struggling against each other in the dirt. I reach for Tobias's sword, ignoring the sound of it coming free from Rhea's head. I stand on shaky legs, the long blade heavier than I expected. Theo has Tobias in a chokehold and he's sputtering. Blood is steadily dripping from both of their noses.

I turn and see Rhea's eyes open, blood pouring out of her head where it was cleaved in two. Scarlett is shaking and screaming, trying to push the halves of her skull back together.

I don't even think. Rage consumes me, electricity flowing through my veins. My hands burn and I can almost see sparks along the edges of my vision.

I raise the sword above my head, ready to strike. I can barely hear Scarlett screaming before I am thrown to the ground, an arrow narrowly missing my chest.

I glance up at Scarlett crouched over me, her dress covered in Rhea's blood. Her mouth is open, as if she froze while in the middle of speaking. It's only when the first drop of blood drips from her mouth that I see the arrow protruding out of her back.

"*No.*" I cry out as she tries to sit up. I drop the sword and grab her shoulders, steadying her.

"He was aiming for you." She whispers as her eyes lock on mine. I look behind her to see one of the guards holding a bow, his mouth open in shock.

"Scarlett, no." I whimper as she falls against me. I hold her against my chest, tears pouring down my cheeks, mixing with her blood. "I am so sorry."

"He was aiming for you." She says through the blood in her throat.

"You shouldn't have done that. My life is not worth yours." I can barely get the words out between the sobs.

"I love you, Elaenor."

"I love you too, Scarlett." A choked sob escapes my throat. "Please don't die on me." I cry out, my hands shaking as I press on the wound in her chest.

"I'll see her again." I look down at her, tears dripping steadily off her cheeks. She takes a deep breath before relaxing. "I see her." She whispers, her eyes staring at nothing as she smiles.

Chapter Thirty-Nine

I barely notice being placed on Sybil's back, blood soaking my black leggings. Someone gets on behind me, holding me tight against them. I stare at the trees, unseeing. Scarlett's body is still lying on the cobblestones next to Rhea's. Men standing over them, someone is pressing on Scarlett's stomach when we move between the trees and out of sight.

Numbness spreads across my body as we quickly trot back to Noterra. I don't notice the time pass, I don't notice getting off the horse, or being placed inside a soapy bath. My eyes don't move, they freeze in one direction. My body is cold, vibrating with each slow and steady breath. My head is pushed beneath the water and then immediately lifted up. I am hoisted out of the bath and wrapped in a thick warm towel. Seconds later a shirt is pulled over me and I am tucked into a warm bed. I hardly even register the thin silver cuff attached to my wrist as I am hooked onto the bed. A prisoner.

The bed dips down next to me as Tobias climbs in. He pulls me against his chest, careful not to pull on the arm attached to the bed. His hand caresses my hair as he speaks. I don't hear what he says. I don't register anything that's happening. I don't protest when a glass of wine is handed to me, and I drain it quickly. Letting the thick, syrupy texture coat my throat. The syrupy drug he had been giving me all along. I eventually fall asleep.

So much screaming. So much pain. Blood is pooling under my feet. My wrists are tightly clasped into chains that are attached to a horse, dragging me through the wreckage. Smoke fills the air, choking me as I try to breathe,

I look up at the person riding the horse I am attached to. His silver crown is sparkling in the flames, reflecting into his golden copper hair. He has a smirk plastered on his face as he looks down at me.

"Welcome home, Elaenor."

My eyes open to darkness, a soft snore coming from my left. I slowly move my head to see Tobias sleeping soundly next to me. I shift slightly, pulling on my arm. The metal clinks together when I lift my hand, preventing too much movement. I sit up and look down. I am wearing one of Tobias's cotton shirts. The only blood that remains is the dried blood under my nails. I fight back the tears begging to escape as I lift my head to look around the room.

The room is dark, but it isn't hard to see the armed guards standing by the door, their gazes fixed on me. The men staring at me aren't Laris or Tano but guards I haven't seen before. I meet their stare and they shift on their feet uncomfortably.

"Don't mind them." Tobias says from my left, almost making me jump. "They are here to protect you."

"Protect me from you?" He sits up and forces my face to his.

"I would never hurt you." I clench my teeth together.

"You have been, haven't you?" He doesn't flinch. "Is that what you've been putting in my coffee and my wine? Hemlock and poppy root?"

"How many times have I told you not to talk to Theo? He just fills your head with lies." He shakes his head and releases my chin.

"How long? How long have you been drugging me so you can beat me to where I don't remember."

"I don't know what you are talking about."

"The night of the ball. You strangled me. I remember it, but when I woke up, I was fine, and you told me it was just a bad dream. The number of times I have awoken, bathed and naked, or sore." He sighs and leans back against the headboard. "How long, Tobias?"

"I told you I liked things a little rough. You got hurt and if I didn't do something you would have died."

"What are you talking about?"

"We were having sex and my hands held your throat for too long, you passed out. Apollo recommended poppy root to help you heal. I was so scared, but when you woke up the next morning, you didn't remember."

"That's a lie. You planned this." The note said he ordered the hemlock and poppy before my arrival. He was *planning* for this in advance.

"You woke up the next morning so refreshed, and you told me it was the first time you hadn't had a nightmare in ten years." He speaks as if he did me a favor, as if he hasn't been abusing me.

"Oh my gods, Tobias. You used the hemlock and poppy root so you could do whatever you wanted to me, and I wouldn't remember it?" He nods and I force myself to swallow back the bile in my throat. "What the hell is wrong with you?"

"Would you rather I fuck other women?"

"If that's what you are doing, then yes!" I snap before trying to slide off the bed. I can't go far as the chain pulls me back, but I scoot as far as I can from him. He gets out of the bed and comes around to my side before I have the chance to back away. He has a vial in his hand, and I flinch away from him.

"Take it."

"No." I slam my lips shut and shake my head.

"Take it willingly or I will forcibly pour it down your fucking throat." I shake my head again and scoot back on the bed. He reaches for my face and clenches my cheeks. "Open your mouth." I pinch my lips tighter together. "Open your fucking mouth, Elaenor." I spit at him, and he takes it as his opportunity to shove his fingers inside. I try to bite down, but he has my jaw clenched between his fingers. He sticks one end of the vial in his mouth, pulling out the tiny cork before tipping it into my throat. The liquid is sweet and oily as it slides down my throat. It tastes like pure sugar with a floral hint. He releases my face and I try to spit it out, but it's already gone.

"What is it?" I ask as he sets the vial down on the nightstand.

"You know what it is." He reaches into the nightstand and pulls out my glass dagger.

"Why are you doing this to me?"

"You've been lying to me." He says softly as he holds the blade between his fingers. I glance between the shiny glass and his eyes. "I knew the second I saw this dagger, who made it. This leather," He pulls at one of the leather cords tied around it. "This is Theo's leather. He uses a special kind on the hilts of his weapons, dyed with dragonink to make it stand out." He spins the blade in his hand, so the tip is pointed at me. I freeze, my eyes on his. "How long have you been fucking my brother?"

"I'm not!"

"You're lying." He says through clenched teeth. He climbs onto the bed and pushes me onto my back. I try to pull away, but the tether holding me to the bed is too short.

"Tobias, I'm not. It's only been you. I promise." My voice is shaking. He has to believe me. He pushes my thighs apart and leans over me. I keep my gaze fixed on his as he slides the tip of the dagger down my arm. A scream escapes my lips as I arch my back, trying to get away from the pain. He drags it down the entire length of my arm, shoulder to wrist. I can feel it slicing through my skin to the bone. I can feel it cutting through muscle and tendon. I scream so loud my ears are ringing.

"You're a liar and a whore." His free hand slaps me as the hand holding the dagger moves to my abdomen. He lifts my shirt up, revealing my bare stomach. I'm shaking from pain and fear. I'm crying so loud I can barely hear him. I can't see what he's doing but I feel as soon as the dagger slices into the skin. He does one horizontal and one vertical line, unbothered by the blood curdling screams coming out of my mouth over and over again.

"Tobias, please." I whimper, my throat hoarse. He throws my dagger to the side, and I can hear it slip off the bed and land on the floor, glass shattering. Breaking just like my soul. He grabs my face with his hands, forcing me to look at him.

"You're going to watch while I fuck you and when you wake up tomorrow, you aren't going to remember. But don't worry, I'm leaving a reminder." He pulls me up into a sitting position, with his hand in my hair, forcing me to look at my stomach. Tobias carved a capital T into my bare stomach with the dagger. *Oh gods.* The blood is pouring out of the wounds as he flips me onto my stomach. I cry out in pain as my sensitive skin touches the fur blankets, my wrist twisting around the chain.

"Tobias, please." I cry into the furs, begging. "Please don't do this."

He has been lying this entire time. He has been pretending to be sweet and caring, but he's been torturing me and drugging me to forget. Theo was right. My *father* was right. I wanted to believe the best in him. I wanted to believe that he loved me, no matter what the others said. I wanted to believe that once we got past everything, we would be happy, but it was all a lie. We were never going to be happy.

One of his hands hoists my hips up as he slams into me over and over again. I bite the inside of my cheek to keep from screaming. He's rough, rougher than I could have ever imagined. Worse than Aleksander. Worse than any of the whippings my father doled out. This is about more than power and control; this is about enjoying the act of causing pain. All the times I woke up sore and raw, thinking it was normal. All the times I woke up in the bed, forgetting when I bathed. Or the times I woke up naked when I went to bed with clothes on. He was cleaning me, changing me, so I wouldn't see the evidence in the morning.

His free hand snakes around my waist, digging into the sliced-up flesh on my stomach. I scream again as I feel his finger ripping through the skin, making the cuts deeper. He's groaning, *enjoying* my screams and the metallic scent of my blood in the air.

"Keep screaming, my love. It only makes this better." I clench my fists, biting my lip to keep from screaming so hard it tears through the flesh and I can taste the blood in my mouth.

He stops and slows as he empties himself inside me with a moan. He stills, leaving himself inside me as he controls his breathing. I open my eyes to see the two guards still standing, staring. Watching me get sliced open and raped. I'm shaking, the pain is too much but also fading. As if it's going numb. Numb. I wish I was still numb.

Tobias flips me over, his hand finding my neck again. My stomach protests at the movement and I whimper. The chain is twisted, wrenching my wrist in the wrong direction, but I barely feel it. He has blood around his mouth as if he licks his fingers.

"Did you like that, *Ela*?" He whispers, his lips close to mine. His teeth are tinted red as he smiles. A small sob comes out of my mouth as he squeezes the sides of my throat. "Who do you prefer inside you, whore? Me or my brother?" I don't fight the quiver of my lips or the tears escaping my eyes.

"Please, just kill me." My voice comes out broken, weak. My head is spinning, and I have the weird sensation of falling.

"I'm not going to kill you Ela; I'm just getting started." He releases my neck and I take a deep breath. I try to sit up and push him away, but my limbs fail to respond. *No*, the drugs. They are already taking effect.

I lift my neck as best I can to look at my stomach and see that the wound has almost closed. Blood is spread across my abdomen, but the slices aren't as wide. I can't believe it. It actually heals that quickly. I glance at my arm and see the same thing. I drop my head back against the bed, weakness over taking me.

"Please." I whisper. Tobias curls up next to me, pulling my head to his chest and kissing my temple.

"Sleep well, my love." He whispers. I fight to keep my eyes open, but they have a mind of their own.

Chapter Forty

I open my eyes in my bed, back in Noterra. I have the weird sensation that time has passed, but I just remember seeing Tobias in Chatis. And Scarlett. *Scarlett.*

I gasp as I sit up, but something is holding me back. I look at my wrist and see a metal cuff tightened around it. The skin underneath is raw and swollen. I follow the chain with my eyes to where it connects to the bedpost. I grab it with both of my hands and pull as hard as I can, but it doesn't come off, a frustrated groan coming out of my mouth. I stop and look around, breathless, to see two guards standing by the door, their hands on their swords as they stare at me.

"What day is it?" My throat feels raw as if I had been crying. I have been. I was screaming over Scarlett's body. They don't respond, their eyes just staring at me, unseeing. I look over to Tobias's side of the bed, but it has been vacated. The pale linens are covered in a black, fur blanket I haven't seen before, and I pull it towards me. A pool of blood lay underneath the blanket, dried to a dull brown.

I drop the blanket and reach over to it. It's slightly damp, but mostly dried. I glance down and see dried blood smeared all over my thighs and my stomach.

"What the fuck?" I whisper. I get up onto my knees and lift the hem of my black shirt. A startled cry escapes my throat as I see two fresh scars on my stomach forming a perfect T in the center of my flesh. "What is this?" I scream at the guards, but they still ignore me.

When did this happen? When did I get here, to this room? What the hell is happening?

"Please, please get me out of here." I beg anyone who might be listening. "Laris! Tano!" I scream over and over again, hoping they are within earshot. My throat is rough, my body weak, as I exert all the energy I have. "Please." I cry before dropping onto my side. I lay in my dried blood, tears steadily dripping off my nose, for what seems like hours.

The door eventually opens, and Tobias walks in with a tray of food. He's wearing his normal black tunic and trousers, his sparkling clean boots slapping loudly on the marble floor. I don't bother sitting up, I just track him with my eyes.

"Good afternoon, my love!" He exclaims as he sets the tray down on the nightstand. I instantly smell the coffee with sweetened cream and my stomach rumbles. I sit up and reach for it, but my hand falls short.

There was something about coffee that I wanted to remember. Something telling me not to drink it. I drop my hand back on the bed and lay down, ignoring the pastries piled on the silver plate. Tobias frowns and puts his hands on his hips. "I brought you your favorite, are you not hungry?" I shake my head. "What's wrong, Ela?" His voice is soft, worried. He sounds so much like the man I married, but he's not.

"What happened last night?" I murmur, my throat rough.

"What do you mean?"

"I don't remember consenting to being branded." He chuckles darkly and I take a slow deep breath to keep from freaking out.

"You must have had way too much to drink, Elaenor. You kept telling me how much you loved me and wanted a part of me to be with you forever. Before I could stop you, you carved a T into your stomach. I could hardly believe it!" He throws his hands up in the air with bewilderment. "I had to rush and get you some salve, so you didn't bleed out.

"I don't remember anything." I don't. I can't even remember how I got into bed, much less what happened.

"If it makes you feel better, it was after a very *very* good fucking." He purrs as he climbs onto the bed. I roll away from him, but he grabs my arm to hold me still. "Look at me, Ela. What can I do to make this better?"

"Where is Scarlett?"

"She's gone, my love. You know that. We talked about it yesterday." I shake my head.

"You killed her."

"No, one of the guards did. He was aiming for you, so her death is actually your fault."

"Why?" I look up at him with tears pooling in my eyes.

"You wanted to kill me, they were protecting their king." I close my eyes and shake my head again. "Once you get better, we can talk about letting you go. A lot of people are calling for your head, but I told them you were unwell. Apollo has given me some medicine that will make you feel better, help clear you of whatever mind sickness you have. Then you'll be my Ela again."

"No, please." I whimper as I try to pull away from him.

"Oh, Ela, this is for your own good." I don't even see someone walk up to us before a needle is jabbed into my thigh. I cry out in pain as fire spreads through my veins. "Hold still, Ela, if you fight it will hurt more." Don't fight back. That's what Enzo had said.

But where is Enzo now?

I grow weak and before I can fight it, I fall back asleep.

I feel my body jostling, but my mind won't awaken enough to open my eyes. Something is hitting me. Not hitting me, pounding into me. I can hear his grunting, his ragged breathing before he stills. Cold hands wipe hair from my face before lips take their place.

"Good girl."

My skin is burning, my blood is boiling. Everything hurts and then it doesn't. Ice spreads through my veins, getting rid of any residual flames taking my sanity with it. The pounding happens again. I don't even try to listen. My body moves with his and then I am asleep again.

I'm screaming, my throat raw as I feel the dagger slicing through my skin over and over again. I can feel him inside of me, grunting as he thrusts over and over, digging the dagger in deeper each time.

"Fuck yes." He mutters. He's touching me, that little bundle of nerves he knows I love so much. I hate it. I hate the way my body is responding to it. I can feel the fire, but it's spreading throughout my whole body.

"Yes, Ela. *Oh gods.*" He yells as I erupt. I scream and scream and scream as I come undone. And then I am falling back into the pit of darkness.

I feel less drowsy this time, and I can almost open my eyes. I beg and push and finally they give way. I squint against the bright light. My body feels clean, awake, as if I had the best nap of my life. I look around and see that I am tucked into bed, furs wrapped around me. It's snowing outside. I can see it through the open patio doors. Laris is by the door and offers me a sad smile.

"Hello, Laris." I say, my throat surprisingly clear.

"Good Morning, Your Grace." He bows his head slightly and I reach up to wipe the hair from my face. A faint red welt wraps around my right wrist, burning in the cold air. I lightly brush it with my fingers and wince.

"What is this from?" I ask, my eyes still searching my pale skin.

"I am not sure, Your Grace. If I may be blunt?" I lift my head and look at him, nodding. "You and the king seem to favor a rather rough pairing, so I am assuming it is from that." My brows furrow and I look down at it again. A rough pairing? Tobias has always been gentle with me.

"What day is it?"

"It is the day before Winter Solstice, Your Grace." I freeze, my eyes meeting his.

"What?" I stammer before climbing out of bed. My legs feel weak and almost buckle underneath me. "No, it was just the beginning of Autumn."

"Are you feeling well, Your Grace?" I stop when I reach the sitting area, my hand resting on the back of the couch.

"I don't know." I admit. "Where is Tobias?" I ask, looking around the room.

"He is with the council this morning."

"I would like to see him." I head towards the door, but Laris sticks his arm out, blocking me.

"I have been told you are not to leave your chambers, Your Grace." I glare up at him.

"Excuse me?"

"You have been ill, Your Grace. It is for your own good. We don't know what ails you and we wouldn't want you to spread anything." He drops his arm and I back up, spinning around to face the balcony. I climb the two steps and look out at the courtyard. The sky is a light blue with just a few gray clouds. The entire palace is blanketed in a lush white, the trees looking bare as they shed their leaves. Winter solstice. It has been nearly five months since I can remember anything. *Five months.* I turn back towards Laris, my feet freezing on the frosted marble, sending an icy chill down my spine.

"Can you send Donovan in here? I'll stay away from him." He smiles and nods before opening the door and speaking to someone outside of it. I step into the dressing room and pull on a thick dressing robe made out of fluffy cotton. It's warm and comforting as I step into the matching slippers. It doesn't take long before a knock on the door sounds. It opens and Donovan walks in, wearing a furry cloak that has snow sprinkled on it. His nose is tinted pink, and his eyes are bright. He looks as if he's just been outside.

"Elaenor!" He exclaims before coming over to me quickly. I smile and open my arms to embrace him as he throws his arms around me. "Do not act suspicious." He whispers in my ear. My face falls but I quickly plaster a smile back on my face.

"Donny!" I return the exclamation and he pushes me back to inspect me.

"How are you feeling?" His back is to Laris, and he raises his eyebrows, asking more than his question reveals.

"Confused, weak." I admit and his lips press into a thin line.

"I brought you some chocolate, I know it's your favorite." He pulls out a brown blob wrapped in parchment, his eyes widening telling me to eat it. I hesitantly grab it and bring it to my mouth. It smells like dirt and grass. I almost hand it back, but something in his look is telling me to trust him.

"You shouldn't be having sweets, Your Grace." Laris stomps over quickly, and I pop it in my mouth before he can take it. I chew into the pressed block and almost gag. I keep a delighted smile on my face as the thick, muddy texture gets stuck in my throat.

"Oh it is so delicious! Is it from that one spot you told me about at the port?" He enthusiastically nods before pulling me to the couch. I force myself to swallow, pushing the thick glob farther down my throat. He reaches for my hands, squeezing the one that holds the parchment that was wrapped around the strange item. I get the hint and tuck the note into my pocket.

"I bet you have all sorts of questions." I nod and he smiles, genuinely. "Well I have been handling the solstice preparations since you have been ill. It is not going as smoothly as if you were doing it, but I think it will turn out okay." He rattles on about random things that he knows mean nothing to me, but it is keeping Laris away from me. I can still feel the thick substance going down my throat. As seconds pass my head feels clearer, more awake. I felt fine before, but it's almost as if a cloud in my mind is blowing away, clearing up any fogginess. The weakness in my legs is dissipating and I feel energized, recharged.

"Oh, Donny, I missed you." I interrupt his prattling. "Can I bother you with a favor?"

"Of course!"

"I would rather like a bath; do you think you can help me to the tub? I would ask Laris, but he seems to think I am contagious." I feign a giggle and Donovan takes my arm, leading me off the couch and to the bathing room.

"Your Grace." Laris warns and I wave him off.

"I am strong enough to bathe by myself, Laris. I'd rather you *not* see me naked." Donovan closes the door behind us and leaves my side to turn on the faucet. The sound of rustling water fills the room as I rip the note out of my pocket.

Don't fall asleep. Don't fight back. - E

"Enzo?" I whisper. I glance up at Donovan and he nods.

"Don't fall asleep. What I gave you should counteract anything he tries to drug you with later."

"I don't understand." I shake my head, reading the note again.

"You have been held captive for months, Elaenor. I don't have time to explain everything to you. You have been drugged so you heal quickly and forget everything the next day. I intercepted the drug that was supposed to come to you this morning, replacing it with nectar. I don't have much time." He looks at the closed door expectantly. "Do not go to sleep tonight. Pretend you are drugged, but do not go to sleep. If you do, you will not wake up. Promise me." I shake my head.

"I don't understand. Why can't I remember anything?" What is going on?

"You will. Just give it time to come back to you, but please listen to me." I nod. "Enzo will come for you. He will get you out of this. Trust him." I nod again. I don't even know him, but I do trust him.

"Theo?"

"He's been in the dungeon since you returned at the beginning of Autumn. They stopped letting me see him." A tear escapes my eye as I fight the urge to vomit. "I'm sorry. I have been trying to get to you for weeks."

"Scarlett, she's gone, isn't she?" I whisper.

"What? No, Scarlett is fine." My legs almost buckle.

"No, she was shot with an arrow." I stammer, reaching out for his arm to steady me.

"Yes, but she recovered fairly well. She's already out. She's with Enzo." He looks behind me. "I'm sorry I couldn't help you sooner."

"Don't. Just explain everything to me when this is over, please." He nods as someone knocks on the door. "Yes?"

"Your Grace, I am coming in." Laris opens the door as I am stepping into the steamy water.

"Laris! My gods, I am *naked*!" I pretend to cover myself as he blushes and looks down.

"Donovan, you need to be leaving now." He nods and touches my shoulder.

"Please let me know if you need assistance in anything else." He bows slightly before following Laris out of the room. I sink into the milky water and rest my head on the back of the tub.

"Enzo?" I reach out, but it feels almost like a haze is bordering the edges of my mind. *"Enzo, can you hear me?"* I get no response.

Chapter Forty-One

I take an obscenely long bath, changing the water twice. My mind is reeling as I try to think about what Donovan said. Scarlett is alive and she's already with Enzo. Theo is in the dungeons. I've been held captive for months? Five months. It's been five months.

Gods. I shake my head, tears slipping free.

When I am finally ready, I step out of the bath onto the cold marble floors. I reach for one of the thick, fluffy towels when I catch my reflection in the mirror.

I can see nearly every bone on my body, any fat I may have had is gone. My eyes are sunken in with dark blue bruises underneath. None of that is what catches my eye. What does is the white scar on my stomach in the shape of a T. I run my fingers across the bumpy surface. The scar looks old, months maybe. It has lost any of the redness that comes with healing and is instead fully formed. A brand.

Tobias *branded* me.

I don't remember any of it.

I tear my eyes away from the mirror and wipe myself off with a towel. I pull on the thick dressing robe again and step into the main room. A tray of food has arrived and is sitting at the table. My stomach grumbles at the sight of pastries and coffee, but my brain is begging me to grab savory items. I don't understand why, but something about the sugar is making me feel ill.

I eagerly shovel eggs and roasted potatoes into my mouth. I eat nearly an entire baguette on the side and drink an entire pitcher of water. When I am finally satiated enough, I push the pastries and coffee aside and climb back onto the couch from my position on the floor. I pull the robe tighter around me as the door opens.

"Ela!" Tobias runs over to me, cupping my face into his hands. "I am so glad you are awake; it's been days. How are you feeling?" He has a hint of stubble along his jaw and his eyes are nearly just as bruised as mine. He looks exhausted and scared. I reach for his face, wanting to feel his skin on mine, but stop myself. *He's been torturing you, Elaenor. Get it together.* "Are you alright, my love?" He looks at me, wrapped around myself in a ball trying to stay as far away from him as possible, and grits his teeth. He releases my face roughly and turns to Laris. "Who has been in here?"

"Donovan, Your Grace." Tobias kicks the table and I flinch.

"I told you no one is to see her!" He picks up the tray of food and throws it against the wall. I burrow deeper into the cushions as he turns to face me.

"Elaenor, everything is okay. Whatever Donovan said, we can fix it. He's been spreading lies, it's treasonous really." I furrow my brows and tilt my head, feigning confusion.

"What are you talking about? What is going on? He just told me about the winter solstice and then helped me to the bathroom to bathe. He wasn't even in here long." He leans down, his eyes frantically going back and forth searching mine. He nods and I offer him a sweet smile.

"Alright, my love." I reach out and cup his cheek as he leans down to kiss me. I let his lips touch mine and I gasp as images flash through my mind.

Blood, chains, hands meeting my skin, daggers slicing through flesh, screams of pain, injection after injection into my thighs, days and nights passing as I lay in this bed. I see images of my coronation gown covered in blood, hands around my neck squeezing until I can't breathe—

"Ela?" I pull his lips back to mine and fight the panic and tears threatening to bubble to the surface. So many memories, moments I have forgotten. Night after night, choking me and stabbing me before having sex with my immobile body. My *drugged* body. I lean back and he looks at me.

"I'm fine, just feel weird." He accepts the answer as he plops down next to me, pulling me into his lap. I let him hold me as my gaze stays fixed on the coffee dripping down the wall onto broken glass and food.

"You've been sick, but I have been taking really good care of you." I nod, my head resting on his chest. My eyes leave the mess on the floor and look towards Laris. He looks alarmed, his hand resting on the hilt of his sword. I let my eyes narrow, and he steps back half a step, his eyes widening.

"Can I go outside, husband?" I say as sweetly as I can. "I see that it is snowing, and I really want to feel it on my skin."

"Do you feel okay enough?"

"I think so, if you come with me?" He stops his fingers that were running through my hair and lifts me off his chest. He smiles at me, his eyes soft and warm.

"Of course, Ela. I would love to." I lean forward and kiss him gently, just a small peck on the lips. His hands tighten around me, and I can feel him harden underneath me. "Maybe we can enjoy ourselves first?" He purrs in my ear, causing a chill to run down my spine.

"I'm rather tired." I whisper.

"Then maybe we shouldn't go outside if you are so tired. I wouldn't want you to overexert yourself." I open my mouth to protest but his lips crash into mine. He forces my lips to part as his tongue reaches for mine.

"Tobias." I sputter as I try to tear my lips from his.

"Just really quick, Ela." He bites my lower lip as he forces me onto my back. It doesn't take him long to get his pants down and softly slip inside me. I gasp at the pressure and clamp my eyes shut. "Look at me. It's just you and me. I love you so much. Tell me you love me." I open my eyes and he is peering down at me. I say nothing. He starts to move, and I instinctually arch my back. I fight against the traitorous warmth spreading between my legs, while simultaneously pretending to be enjoying it. It isn't quick like he predicted; it takes him awhile. It makes me wonder if he truly does prefer it rough.

With every thrust of his hips, a piece of my sanity chips away. A piece of myself. My dignity, my self-worth, all gone as he consumes me. As he steals what is left of my soul and claims it as his own. He wants every part of me, and I have given it to him. I have nothing left to offer. I am nothing but a shell he has molded into the wife he always wanted.

I fake release at the same time he does, and he collapses onto me. When I open my eyes, Laris has his back to us, offering very little privacy.

"Can we go outside now?" I ask as he pulls out of me. He looks down at me and then out to the open balcony.

"No, I don't think so." He stands and I pull my robe down over me.

"Tobias–"

"It's snowing, you'll get even more sick than you already are."

"I feel fine."

"I said *no*, Elaenor!" He snaps and I flinch. I take a deep breath and fight the urge to throw something.

"You said I wouldn't be a captive here! You said I could go where I wanted."

"Yes, when you aren't ill, my love."

"Please–"

"What is wrong with you today? You seem to have awoken with an attitude." He pulls his pants up as Laris turns back to face us, handing him a vial. "You need to relax and it's time for your medicine."

"No, I don't want it." He stalks over to me, and I quickly get off the couch.

"You have to take it, Ela."

"No." I put the couch between us, and he effortlessly walks over it. "Stop!" I yell, running to the balcony. I glance down at the piles of fresh snow before climbing onto the posts. Two hands grab my arms, yanking me off the banister. I slam into the icy marble and look up to Laris holding me down.

"Just take it, Elaenor." He pleads as Tobias shoves his fingers in my mouth. I try to bite him, but he hooks his fingers around my jaw, forcing it open. He dumps the contents down my throat, and I nearly choke. Something oily and sweet glides down and I cough, trying to force it out. Tobias removes his fingers and I shut my mouth. Laris releases my shoulder and Tobias helps me up, my legs shaking.

"See, that wasn't so hard. You'll start to feel better soon." He bends down and scoops up my legs, carrying me to the bed. I try to push against his chest, but I can't.

"Why are you doing this?" I whimper, my arms growing heavy. *Fight it, Elaenor.*

"I am protecting you, Ela. Don't you want to be with me? This is what I have to do to keep you here." I shake my head.

"I want to go home." I cry.

"You are home." I shake my head again as he lays me on the bed.

"This isn't my home." My eyes close and I hear him angrily sigh as he pulls a blanket over me. A cold metal clasp is tightened around my wrist, and I know now that it was the cause of the welts. He's been chaining me to the bed.

Images keep floating through my brain. Screams echoing in my ears. The feeling of blood pooling under me, soaking me. Knives slicing through my skin over and over again while he watches it heal, just so he can repeat the process. Days where I was conscious, and I forgot what happened. Days like this. But I always forget.

Months. I have spent months being drugged by Tobias to forget everything, to heal without evidence. Except for the T. He kept the T.

"Why did you brand me?" I murmur.

"What?"

"My stomach."

"I did it so whenever you fuck another, they know who you belong too. It's a promise to rip every single one of their heads off their bodies." My eyes open slightly.

"Tobias, there has never been anyone but you." I whisper, growing weaker by the second.

"I don't believe you." He kisses my forehead and then it's quiet. A few seconds pass and the door slams. I fight to stay awake, but it's so hard. Everything in my mind is fuzzy, my pulse slowing. Donovan said he gave me something to counteract the drugs, but they must have gotten the dosage wrong.

I fight against the unconsciousness threatening to take me under, but it wins.

Chapter Forty-Two

I don't think I am asleep long, because when I open my eyes, it is barely sunset. The sky is tinted pink and purple, sparkling against the snow. I glance to the doorway, but Laris is gone, and no one has taken his place. I sit up and surprisingly find myself feeling fine. My limbs don't ache, and I can move them easily, my pulse is steady. I pull on my arm, but the chain is tight against the headboard, keeping me within a few inches of it. I look around the room, but no one is in here.

I sigh and rest my head up against the headboard, waiting. There isn't anything I can do but wait. I fell asleep despite what Enzo and Donovan said, but they said to not fall asleep tonight. It is still technically the day and I hope that distinction matters.

But I remembered.

I remembered today and bits and pieces of all of the other days. I *remember*. Which means whatever Donovan gave me had to work somehow.

I watch the sun disappear behind the trees as I hug my legs to my chest. The room grows dark, no fireplace or torches lit as the day bleeds into night. The air is cold, and I keep one of the fur blankets wrapped around me.

I feel like I keep seeing movement out of the corner of my eye, but every time I look it's gone. I have the strange sense that someone is watching me, but I can't make anything out in the darkness.

I see it again, something moving by the couch, and I sit up. My hands fall from my knees as I blindly reach out for anything to protect me, but I come up empty.

"Hello?" I whisper. A dark shadow runs towards me, and I open my mouth to scream before a hand clamps down.

"Shhh, it's me, Nora." Theo's voice is hushed, and I almost break down at the sight of him. His blonde hair is down and wet, flinging icy droplets at me. His clothes are ripped and tattered and I can barely make out dark splotches across his chest where there used to be pale skin. His fingers are ice cold as if he had been stuck in the snow. "We have to go." I nod and he removes his hand from my mouth. He tries to pull me off the bed, but the chain yanks me back with a yelp.

"The chain." I whisper.

"Fuck, okay." He disappears into the darkness, and I can hear him rummaging through drawers. He reappears so quietly I almost scream out, but his cold hands grab my arm. He sticks something into the lock and a loud *click* radiates through the silence. I slide off the bed and grab the dressing robe lying on the floor next to it. I put it on over my nightdress, tying it tightly.

"What's going on?" I whisper into the darkness. I can barely make him out.

"We are getting out of here, Nora. Just stay with me." Theo takes me by the hand, his fingers lacing through mine, before he leads me to the door.

"Theo, wait." I stop abruptly and he nearly staggers back.

"What? What's wrong?" His hands cup my face, searching my eyes in the shadows. I don't allow myself to think before I stand on my tiptoes, pressing my lips firmly against his. He freezes before melting into my kiss. My lips quickly warm his icy flesh as our mouths part and tongues meet. I push, deepening the kiss as much as I can, my arms wrapping around his neck. Theo pulls back, breaking our connection, before leaning back forward and pressing his lips to my forehead.

"I'm sorry I didn't realize it sooner." I whimper. I never let myself realize it. Realize what I felt. Admit that my heart never belonged to my husband.

"We have time, Nora. We can figure this out later, I promise." I nod, his hands still cupping my cheek. I don't believe him. Something is telling me not to step out of this room, but I follow him anyway.

He kisses my lips briefly, before dropping his hands and opening the door. He lets out a small whistle before he freezes and waits. The same two-note whistle is returned seconds later, and he pulls me into the darkened hallway. Not a single torch is lit, making the palace completely black. My bare feet slip on the cold marble as we hurry towards the staircase, and I tighten my grip on Theo's hand.

"We are almost there." He whispers as we turn into the doorway leading to the stairs. We don't pass a single person on our way down, which isn't normal for this time of night. We reach the landing of the first floor and an arm grabs mine. I open my mouth to scream when I hear Donovan telling me to be quiet.

"We have to hurry." He whispers, helping to guide me to the door. The servant's exit is empty as we step into the snow. The sky is a deep purple, and the white, powdery snow brightens the courtyard. My feet instantly burn as the ice burrows into my skin.

My pulse quickens as I see the open gate and not a single guard manning it, my legs uncontrollably pulling us faster forward. I can just barely make out Sybil's black mane in contrast to the white everywhere else. A cry of relief escapes my lips as we cross through the gate. I can feel the tension radiate off of Theo and Donovan, and their hold on me relaxes as we step through.

Everyone stops as a sword is pressed to my neck. The tan arm holding the sword connects to Tobias as he steps around the outside part of the wall. I can feel the blade biting into my skin, and I fight back the urge to swallow against the lump in my throat.

"Did you really think you could just escape, and I wouldn't notice? That I wouldn't notice that all of the guards are suddenly confused on where they should be? Or why Laris was in the dining hall when he was supposed to be watching *her*? That the torches being extinguished in half the palace wouldn't alert anyone? Or how today of all days, Elaenor seems to be lucid? How stupid could you be, brother?" The cold steel presses harder into my skin and I shut my eyes, tears pooling beneath my eyelids.

"Tobias, I don't want to fight you." Theo's voice is loud, stern, but I can tell he's scared. He doesn't want to have to hurt him, but I know he would. He'd do it for me, and that makes my heart hurt.

"You wouldn't win in this fight, brother." He steps closer, his hand snaking around my hips as I open my eyes. I'm turned and pulled against his chest, the sword still threatening to slice my throat. My arms are crossed in front of my chest, still being gripped by my two companions. The icy snow is making my feet numb, causing my breathing to grow ragged. "If you both don't remove your *disgusting* hands from my wife, I will cut them off." Donovan hesitantly removes his fingers from my arm, taking a small step back, but Theo doesn't. He glares at Tobias and opens his mouth to say something, but Tobias speaks first. "I don't give second warnings."

I don't even have a moment to breathe or even think before the sword moves from my neck and comes down onto Theo's hand that's laced through mine. Blood paints the snow crimson as he screams, blood spraying across my stomach and staining my dressing gown a deep red. This is what he tried to do that day outside Chatis. He was going to cut Theo's hand off, and he succeeded.

I stare at the frozen hand lying next to my foot in the snow before I look up at Theo. He's holding his arm, blood pouring out of the hole where his wrist should be. My eyes and mouth are open wide, frozen in disbelief.

"Oh my gods." I whisper as Tobias kicks out at Theo's abdomen, knocking him to the ground. "Theo!"

"Guards!" Tobias yells into the darkness and we are instantly surrounded.

"Don't stop fighting, Nora." Donovan whispers as he closes his eyes. *No.* This can't be happening. Tobias drags me backwards towards the palace as I watch multiple men encircle Donovan and Theo. I push against his arms, clawing my nails through his flesh, but he doesn't loosen.

"Tobias, no." I whisper. I quickly shut my eyes as I hear Donovan begin to scream. *No no no no no.* I cover my ears to try and drown out the despair echoing through the courtyard. This isn't real. This is another nightmare.

Wake up, Nora. Wake up!

Tobias bends down and throws me over my shoulder, stomping through the palace doors. I keep my eyes shut, trying to get rid of the image of Theo's bloody hand and Donovan's face as he closes his eyes. I can see that the lanterns are relit through my eyelids as I squeeze them shut tighter.

"Tobias." I whimper, shaking my head as the tears start to fall. This can't be real; they can't be dead. "Tobias!" I say louder as my fist hits his back. He grunts before he lets out a dark chuckle.

Tobias's hand leaves my back and I ungracefully roll off his shoulder, landing hard on the marble with a yelp. I gasp as the wind is knocked out of me. I open my eyes to the brightly lit throne room, pain shooting from my shoulder. He's pacing, walking back and forth in front of the dais, his hands on his hips, muttering to himself.

"After everything I have done for you–"

"Don't you mean done *to* me you piece of shit." I spit, blood landing on the marble as I pull myself up onto my knees. He turns towards me, his eyes widening. He kicks out, hitting me square in the ribs. I grunt against the pain and grit my teeth as I roll away from him with the force. One deep breath tells me my ribs are broken, or at least badly bruised. I exhale loudly, a small gasp of pain breaking through.

Footsteps come rushing in and something is dropped down next to me. I lift my head to see Donovan's open eyes and mouth, staring at me but unseeing. I let my gaze travel down his face to where his shoulders should be, but there is nothing there. *Oh my gods.* I scream and scramble backwards into someone's legs. I look up at Tobias peering down at me with clenched teeth.

He bends down and grabs my hair, dragging me across the floor until I am sat up against the dais. I kick out, trying to get away from him, but I can't back up anymore. He crouches down in front of me, and I spit blood on his face.

"What the hell is *wrong* with you?" I scream, his eyes flinching as the droplets of blood hit his skin.

"It didn't have to come to this." His voice is even, unwavering as he lifts a hand and wipes the crimson away. Shouting and the dragging of feet sound behind Tobias as Theo is brought into the room. He's kicking, fighting against the guards restraining him. There is blood dripping from his temple, his shirt torn in threads, blood pouring out of his stump. I look back at Tobias, unable to hide the relief I feel from seeing Theo alive. *He's not dead. There is still time to fix this.*

"Why? Why are you doing all of this?"

"You defied me!" He yells as his hands slam down on the ground in front of me. He stands and paces before walking back over to me. "I told you to love me. I told you time and time again to stay away from Theo. You lied."

"You're crazy. You live in a delusion." I shake my head. "I tried to love you. I tried, but you fought me every step of the way." He drops to his knees and slaps me. I shut my eyes against the pain, feeling the skin in my cheek tear against my teeth.

"Stop it!" Theo yells and I hear the sound of flesh hitting bone as he cries out.

"All you had to do was love me." His voice is softer now as he gets closer on the ground in front of me, kneeling so we are face to face and only inches apart. "I just wanted you to love me."

"I did! I did. *You* ruined it, not me." I flinch as his fingers brush my face. "I tried everything to make you love me, make you see me as more than a body to fuck. I tried *everything*. You were the one who constantly hurt me. You were the one who betrayed me. You were the one who *drugged* me, Tobias." My voice softens, pleading. He doesn't understand. He doesn't get it. *He* is the problem here.

"Oh, my love. We can do this again. We can be better." His hand cups my cheek and I hate the instinct to rest my face into his palm. His eyes soften, his head tilting. I shake my head instead, dislodging his hand.

"No. You don't get any more chances." He clamps his mouth shut. "Just kill me and get it over with." I lean as far back against the steps as I can and close my eyes, waiting for the strike. But it doesn't come. Soft hands wipe away my tears and brush against my hips. He pulls me against him, shaking.

"You will never love me while he's alive." He whispers before gripping the back of my neck, forcing me to look at him. "You aren't the problem, Ela. Theo is." He pushes me onto my stomach as he pulls my dressing robe off and my gown up. I wince out as my ribs press against the floor, my breathing ragged and choppy. My eyes frantically search for Theo as his face is also pressed to the ground. My hands try to push against the marble, to lift me up, but he grabs both of my wrists in one of his hands.

"Tobias–" I warn.

"You are going to watch, brother. You are going to watch me fuck *my* wife. She's *mine*." He growls as he lifts my hips and shoves himself inside me. I cry out at the pain and intensity.

Tobias stills inside me, my sobs echoing off the marble walls. Theo is holding my gaze, fury, pure, unrefined fury living in his blue eyes. His eyes are tinted red from straining against the men who hold him in place on his knees, watching Tobias rape me for the millionth time.

"This is what happens when you fuck around, Ela. This is because of you." His hand tangles itself in my hair as he lifts my head off the floor and slams it back down. My hands fall to the floor, but I have no fight left. Blood drips out of my mouth staining the white stone, my breathing erratic. I can tell my nose is broken as the pain burns my eyes.

"Tobias, stop this!" Theo screams, fighting against the men gripping his arms with all their strength.

"Theo." I say, crying out against the sobs in my throat. As Tobias grunts, shoving himself into me with enough force to slide me across the marble.

"How you call for him. How you *plead* for him to save you." Tobias's cruel voice sends shivers down my spine as he moans and stiffens. He's still for a few seconds and then finally pulls out of me. He sits up to right his pants and I try to crawl away, but his nails dig deep into my bare legs as he flips me over and slides me back against him. I reach for any surface to grip, to hurt, to maim, but he restrains me quickly with one hand, the other pressing down on my throat as he leans over me.

"Please, brother, anything. I will do whatever you want."

"I want nothing from you, besides your head on a spike and your heart in my hands." He snarls as he crushes my windpipe. I struggle against his weight, knowing this is the end, this is when he kills me. I can't take a breath, not a single stream of oxygen making its way into my chest. I slice my broken nails through his flesh, drawing blood, but his strength doesn't falter. He'll never falter. I don't struggle anymore; I just stare into his eyes as my arms drop to the floor. His deep blue eyes that are filled with nothing but rage and destruction.

I deserve it.

I did this.

This was all my fault.

If I had just stayed away from Theo, listened to Tobias, none of this would be happening. I just had to keep my mouth shut. I just had to be a dutiful wife and none of this would be happening. Donovan would still be *alive*. Darkness licks at the edges of my vision and I welcome it. I welcome the relief that this will finally be over, but it doesn't end.

Tobias hauls me onto my knees, my back pressed against his chest as he wraps his arm around my shoulders to restrain me. His grip releases from my neck and I inhale loudly, getting as much air into my lungs as possible.

Enzo's voice is still echoing in my head. *Don't fight back. Don't fight back.* But if I do nothing, he's going to kill Theo. If I do fight back, I will die. So I don't. I don't move. I don't breathe. I just stare and I hate myself for it. But I have to think of Scarlett. She's out there. Waiting for me.

No.

How can I stand here and do nothing to save an innocent man? A man that I love?

What am I supposed to do? What am I supposed to do?

"Brother, end this." Theo's voice is weakening and my heart hurts.

"You are *not* my brother." I hear the sharp, unsheathing of a blade as I am thrown towards another man, his arms awaiting. His rough fingers clench onto my upper arms, preventing me from stepping away. I throw myself against him, fighting against his hold.

"No, please!" I scream, kicking and hitting against the metal of his armor. I can't take this. I can't. Tobias takes the outstretched sword and strides closer to Theo. Theo's eyes widen in fear as he fixes on me, refusing to look Tobias in the eye.

"You'll be okay. It's alright." He whispers, attempting to reassure me. *Me.* The person who *doesn't* have a sword to his neck.

"No! No, Theo. We didn't have time. We didn't have enough time." My words are broken, coming out between sobs.

"Don't look, Nora. Look away." Theo's eyes soften, resolved. His skin is paling from the extreme blood loss he is suffering through. He knows what's coming and he isn't afraid, but I am.

I am so afraid of what is going to happen after.

After Theo is dead.

After I mourn him.

Then what? Do I pretend that all along my heart hasn't belonged to him? That he is the one I have loved from afar this entire time? I can't do that. *I can't.*

"Oh how you cry for another man, *wife*. How you beg for more time to love another. I'm curious, Ela, do you know what the punishment is for adultery?" Tobias snickers as he raises a single brow, baiting me.

"Please, Tobias. *Please!*" I scream again as my knees slam into the marble floor, my breathing labored as my ribs stab into my lungs. Tobias's darkened eyes find mine as he lets a sadistic smile creep along his face. "I will give you anything, just please don't kill him." I hate that I am begging, especially begging *him*. I can't just do nothing, even if it means I won't walk away from here. I send a silent message, hoping that wherever he is, he'll hear it.

I'm sorry that we never got the chance to meet.

Tobias comes to kneel before me, the sword out towards my neck, pricking my skin ever so slightly.

"You, my love, have nothing left to give." His voice is nothing more than a snarl.

"*No.*" My eyes widen as he stands. "Tobias, don't do this!" Tobias moves quickly and the sound of blade hitting bone echoes around the room. I scream, louder than I ever have, piercing the ears of everyone within the vicinity. I scream with so much fear, anger, pain, that my throat grows hoarse within seconds. Theo's head drops to the marble floor with a *thud*, rolling away from his limp body. His eyes are open and unseeing, the twins to Donovan's.

Theo is dead, gone. Tobias beheaded his *own* brother. He's gone. No words, feelings, actions could describe the numbness that spreads along my body. Filling every vein with emptiness. I can't breathe. I can't speak. Just tears, emotional wreckage. He's gone.

That numbness quickly fades into fury. Pure, unrelenting fury. I feel my chest rising as my pulse quickens. Electricity flows through my veins, powering through me, fueling the adrenaline. My brows furrow and I bare my teeth ever so slightly, letting my breath flow through clenched teeth. I don't know when or how, but I will kill him. I will kill Tobias, but only *after* he has watched me destroy everything he loves.

The arms restraining me disappear and I collapse onto the bloody floor, sobs no longer wreaking havoc on my body. Short, focused breaths fill the silence instead. Hands wrap around my head, hauling me to my feet with a sharp tug on my hair, ripping strands from my scalp, but I don't whimper. I don't yelp or cry out in pain. I do nothing but stare into his deep eyes that are a bottomless pit of hatred.

"It's time for you to go home, *my love.*"

Chapter Forty-Three

As I stare out across the wasteland. Burning buildings, bodies, trees. I remember everything.

The clouds.

The rain.

The way the humidity spread across the land in a thick blanket, protecting all of those who reside.

My mother's smile as we ran through the grounds, chasing one another. Rolling across the grass. Laughing.

The smell of the flowers when they bloom in the spring and the snow when it would float down from the sky in the winter.

The sound of the birds chirping as they made our hills their home.

But the once green hills are left black and bare. The buildings we would run around, gone. The people I would see every day, whom I used to envy, were reduced to ash. The ones who made it possible for me to be here, today, everyone is gone. My bare feet are pressing into the rubble and bodies of those who died and the buildings that were destroyed. The lives ruined because of *me*.

After years of having the same dream, over and over, I know now it wasn't a dream I was experiencing. It was never just a dream. It was a premonition.

I've finally come home. Where I *begged* Tobias to take me.

But instead of the home I used to know, the home I grew up with, I am left with nothing but glass and bone.

It was *always* glass and bone.

CELAENA CUICO

ABOUT THE AUTHOR

Celaena Cuico *(sell-ay-nuh coo-we-co)* is a 27-year-old bisexual female that was born and raised in Southern California. She was raised with two parents and an older sister, as well as an army of animals. Celaena endured hardships such as an abusive significant other and the unknown that comes with moving across the country twice for a job. She is the author of The Diadem, a series about a young girl thrown into a life of jumping from kingdom to kingdom to survive.

NOTE FROM THE AUTHOR

I have been obsessed with the idea of writing novels since I was a child. As I believed that very few are able to perfect the craft and actually make a living out of it, I took another path. At the age of 26, I graduated with my Masters in Clinical Psychology. Learning the ins and outs of how humans think, feel, and act has become a craft of its own. Being able to take a thought and turn it into action is a function that happens automatically in our brains, we don't have to do anything other than think. However, being able to take those thoughts and pathways to action and put it into words, is another thing.

I will never assume I am perfect or someone who has mastered the art of writing, but what I do have is passion. With that passion, I hope to create a world (or a few worlds) that readers can get lost in. My goal is for you as a reader to take my characters and become them, identify with them. The only way I see that happening is if I put a little bit of myself into each character, which I have done. My own history of sexual/physical assault, psychological abuse, and other horrible things have shaped me into the person I am today. I only hope that I can use my real-life experiences to mold characters you will love and characters you will root for. I only ask that you remember that not all stories have a happy ending.

I want to thank my friends who have supported me on this journey and have provided much needed counsel on this project. I would also like to thank my girlfriend, Maggie, as none of this would have been possible without her love and her continued support of my dreams. I owe everything to you.

Made in the USA
Middletown, DE
10 September 2024

60130301R00222